Praise for SOCKS ARE NOT ENOUGH

WINNER
Calderdale Children's Book of the Year

SHORTLISTED
Roald Dahl Funny Prize
Coventry Inspiration Book Award
Leeds Book Award
Worcestershire Teen Book Award
Warwickshire Schools Library Service Secondary Book Award
Grampian Children's Book Award

NOMINATED
Branford Boase Award

"A rival to Adrian Mole"
GUARDIAN

"A clever, funny, serious book"
Michael Rosen

"Laugh-out-loud funny"
BOOKTRUST

"Quirky and original"
The Guide to Children's Books – CAROUSEL

*"Michael gives us many a chuckle, a true sense of the misery
of a puny teenage boy and cause for admiration at the way he
handles his problems better than the professionals"*
OBSERVER

Mark Lowery is a strange little man with big hair. He lives with his French girlfriend (who is actually English) and their two young children. Mostly he is a teacher but, if he had the necessary skills, he would probably prefer to be:

1) A guitarist
2) A footballer
3) A chimpanzee

Mark's first novel for teenagers, *Socks Are Not Enough*, won the Calderdale Book of the Year Award and was shortlisted for the Roald Dahl Funny Prize and the Coventry Inspiration Book Award. *Pants Are Everything* is his second book.

PANTS ARE EVERYTHING
...when you're definitely NOT a nudist
MARK LOWERY

First published in the UK in 2013 by Scholastic Children's Books
An imprint of Scholastic Ltd
Euston House, 24 Eversholt Street
London, NW1 1DB, UK
Registered office: Westfield Road, Southam, Warwickshire, CV47 0RA
SCHOLASTIC and associated logos are trademarks and/or
registered trademarks of Scholastic Inc.

Text copyright © Mark Lowery, 2013
The right of Mark Lowery to be identified as the author
of this work has been asserted by him.

ISBN 978 1407 13003 3

A CIP catalogue record for this book is available
from the British Library.

Printed and bound by CPI (UK) Ltd, Croydon, CR0 4YY
Papers used by Scholastic Children's Books are made
from wood grown in sustainable forests.

1 3 5 7 9 10 8 6 4 2

This is a work of fiction. Names, characters, places, incidents
and dialogues are products of the author's imagination or are used
fictiously. Any resemblance to actual people, living or dead,
is purely coincidental.

www.scholastic.co.uk/zone

Northamptonshire LRE	
Askews & Holts	

For S, J and S

Working for a Second Chance
Friday

Tasks completed: None.
Things I have learned: Nothing.

My name is Michael Swarbrick and I have two weeks to save my school career. This is because:

1. I was arrested for dancing naked in front of a stolen donkey.
2. I boasted about number 1 on the front pages of a local newspaper.
3. I hacked into a computer network and displayed my buttocks to the entire school.
4. I set fire to myself.
5. Because of 4, I caused an incident of mass streaking.
6. Because of 5, I became an Internet sensation.
7. Because of 1–6, I became a word.
8. I had my first ever snog with the most incredible girl

in the universe. This *should* have been a good thing. However, since she was not actually *awake* at the time, this is considered a very, *very* Bad Thing.

9. I imprisoned an elderly foreign lady and forced her to become a nudist.

10. I destroyed a car in order to send rude messages to someone else's girlfriend. NB: **I did not actually do this.**

My school does not like to expel people. When people in Year 10 or above get in Big Trouble, they are sent on an extended work experience called "Working for a Second Chance".

For the next two weeks I will be working all day, then spending my evenings reflecting on why I am not in lessons and writing about what I have learned. If I work hard and prove I am a decent human, I *may* be allowed back to school.

If not, then I will definitely be kicked out.

Now, many people would look at the above list and say, "You are clearly a bad person. I hope you get run over by a bicycle or bitten by feral children. You deserve it."

The problem is I did not *do* these things. Well. OK. So I *did* do all of them, apart from number 10. But mostly they were not my fault. And the ones that were my fault I did for the right reasons.

Sort of.

There are plenty of people who would love to be expelled

from school. They would have a whale of a time sitting at home all day in their underpants, watching TV and eating crisps. Not me. I *like* school. I *like* learning things. When I am older, I want to work in a nice clean office with a chair that spins round and my own supplies of rubber bands, fountain pens and boiled sweets.

If I do not finish school, I will probably end up doing something I do not enjoy, like hand-washing donated underpants at a second-hand shop.

Therefore, I *must* do well during this placement. I am certain. . . OK, I am *pretty sure*. . . Well, all right, I *think* I am a decent human being. I just need everyone else to realize it. And at the moment, the evidence is stacked against me.

Since the car incident, I have been suspended from school. This morning Mum and I had to go in for a meeting with Mr Whittle (the head teacher) about my work placement. This is the first time I have been in a room with a member of my family since Friday. Indeed, I spent a good portion of the weekend in my room, on my laptop, investigating whether it is possible to divorce them.

For the record, it is not.

Mr Whittle talked about "giving something back to the community" and becoming "more rounded".[1] He said that if

---

1 I presume he meant in the sense of finding out about lots of different things, rather than in terms of my shape, which is already fairly round.

I work hard for two weeks, I will be allowed back in time for the school disco.

Even though I absolutely do not want to go to the school disco, I nodded my head and smiled and tried my hardest to look nice. Mr Whittle took a long look at me and asked if I needed the toilet.

In the meeting, I was given a choice: either the school could find me a placement or I could organize one myself.

I wanted to work at the local library so Mr Whittle allowed me to call them. I was actually quite excited about this – a peaceful fortnight alphabetizing things and making sure the books were perfectly straight sounded like just the ticket. Plus, I would certainly be giving something back to the community. I spoke in my nicest, friendliest voice and explained who I was.

Before I could say anything else, the librarian cut me off and told me I would not be welcome there because they had read all about me in the newspaper. Then she hung up.

Mr Whittle said he was not surprised. He said he would not let me loose anywhere with bookshelves in case I hid behind them in the nude and leapt out at old ladies.

I felt that this was a bit unfair. I *never* took off my clothes in front of that old lady. If anything it was the other way round. This is the problem with people thinking you are a notorious nudist, though. Everyone always expects the worst from you.

Anyway, Mr Whittle said it would be better if the school found me a placement. I will find out what it is on Monday.

By coincidence, my slightly obese best-and-only-friend Paul Beary is being punished in the exact same way. Last week he raided the vending machine storeroom for supplies, then bunked off and attempted to hitch-hike to France. Unfortunately, the only lift he got was from a policeman who drove him straight back to school again.

Paul claims that it took an entire SWAT team to capture him and he was shot by a police sniper. He even showed me the bullet wound.[2]

Paul always tells lies. E.g,

a. His sister's husband owns a rhinoceros farm in Kenya (at which Paul has spent many happy hours *milking* the rhinos).
b. He has a cousin called Silas who got bitten by a radioactive elk in Latvia and now eats grass, has antlers and glows in the dark. And
c. His Uncle Dwayne (who invented the caravan) has "three butt cheeks".

Paul wanted to do his placement in McDonald's so yesterday he went in and told the person on the counter that he won Junior MasterChef last year and wanted to "sprinkle stardust on to their Big Macs".

---

2 His belly button.

5

However, while he was waiting for the manager he "got a little peckish". The manager caught him drinking barbecue sauce directly from the dispenser. Unsurprisingly, he did not get the job and is now banned from every McDonald's in town. He had to organize a placement at his Uncle Dwayne's caravan factory instead.

Working for a Second Chance
Monday

Tasks completed: I "chose" a placement.
What I have learned: That I will not be turning my life around any time soon.

My cretin of a brother says that if you do good things, then good things will happen to you in return. But, if you do bad things. . .

You can probably guess the rest. Ordinarily my brother talks rubbish.[3] However, in this case, I think he may have a point. As previously mentioned, I have been involved in bad things. And now, even though none of them were my fault, I am paying the price.

---

3 Like the time when I was four and he told me that if I licked my finger and put it into the plug socket, I would grow a beard.

Today was my second meeting at school. Mum and I went to Mr Whittle's office. I do not like Mr Whittle's office. It smells of coffee and body odour. A bit like Mr Whittle himself, I suppose. There is a poster on the wall of a crocodile attacking a family of terrified wildebeest. The slogan underneath reads: "Only the Strong Survive". This says a lot about Mr Whittle.

Anyway, when I sat down, Mr Whittle told me he had some good news. He had managed to find me a choice of two last-minute placements. They were:

1) Working for my old counsellor, Chas.
2) Manually removing the guts from dead chickens at a factory called Golden Nuggets.

This was a tough decision to make. Indeed, the only reason I did not opt for Golden Nuggets is because I am allergic to latex gloves. As a result I would have been forced to handle raw chicken intestines with my bare hands for eight hours a day.

I do not wish to sound ungrateful, but working with Chas will be only marginally less unpleasant than this.

Allow me to explain: before the Bad Things happened, Chas used to counsel me for some other problems I was having. E.g, my mother was an insane nudist who disgraced herself in front of the entire city, and I was scared of naked people and donkeys.

7

In fact it is Chas's fault that I was arrested in the first place, which led to all of the other terrible things. Frankly, he is the worst counsellor of all time and he completely ruined my life. This may well stop us from building up a happy working relationship.

As Mr Whittle phoned Chas to arrange a meeting tomorrow, I worried that my school career was being flushed away like an unwanted terrapin.

Following Mr Whittle's phone call I came home. The only other person in the house is my brother, who is laughing and joking next door with his girlfriend. I do not wish to listen to this so I have stuffed cotton wool into my ears.

One of my tasks during this work placement will be to reflect on why I am doing it in the first place. If I explain about my arrest, you may understand why I do not wish to work with Chas.

My Arrest

About two weeks ago, Chas gave me some advice. As a result, Lucy King and I went to Blackpool to solve our problems.

Lucy King is the world's most wonderful person. Sadly, she now hates me. A few months ago, she was number two in *Swimming Times* magazine's "Ten Stars of the Future". It said she is a "hot tip for glory at next summer's European Championships".

I cut this article out and put it into the scrapbook I have assembled for her. This is not a weird thing to do. Lucy *was* my best friend. Best friends are proud of their best friends. They collect pictures and articles of them from newspapers and magazines, along with other important artefacts.[4]

Lucy's dad made her train so hard at swimming that she no longer enjoyed it. She became so desperate that she actually went out with my brother. Luckily she realized how ridiculous this was, and after catching him with another girl, smacked him one in the face. He ran away to Australia straight afterwards.

Unfortunately, he has since returned.

Anyway, to rid me of my fear of donkeys, we hired one on Blackpool beach. After a pleasant trot, we tied it up to one of the piers and hopped into the water so Lucy could see that swimming can be fun.

The perfect plan, right?

Er . . . not *exactly*.

Lucy suggested I should take off my shorts to challenge my phobia of nudity. Despite my shyness, I

---

4 I.e, broken goggle straps, discarded energy bar wrappers, a sticking plaster that dropped off her foot just prior to the Regional Championships butterfly final last year, etc.

did it. By the way, Lucy did not even look or anything. She is not that kind of girl.

For about three seconds, it worked. I felt free and at ease.

Then the problems began.

Things Go Wrong

So, basically, what *should* have happened was:

1. We have a lovely time with the donkey and go for a swim. I remove my shorts and throw them over my head in a joyous celebration of freedom.
2. We return the donkey and happily go home, cured of any problems and issues.

What *actually* happened was:

1. As above.
2. We lose track of time and keep the donkey for longer than we paid for; over an hour longer, as it transpired.
3. Unknown to us, the donkey owner calls the police, and a riot van rushes to the scene. Apparently donkey theft is a serious crime in Blackpool.

4. I learn about 3 when I turn back towards the shore and find an angry-looking policeman is standing at the water's edge staring back at me.
5. I quickly tell Lucy to escape so she does not get into trouble.
6. Lucy whizzes away beneath the murky waves like a beautiful porpoise and emerges on the other side of the pier.

Unfortunately, this was not the end of the story.

The End of the Story
(Which Actually Is Not Even
the Beginning of the Story)

The policeman calmly asked me to come out of the water. I did not want to. I could no longer see my shorts and the sea was protecting my modesty like a giant pair of liquid underpants.

"OK, mister," said the policeman. "Let's not get silly. Hands above your head and on to the beach now."

Very slowly and very reluctantly, I emerged from the waves. Hands in the air. Grey water cascading down my skin. *Everything* on show. It was like a cheap advert for really bad shower gel. Clearly disturbed, the policeman threw the book at me.

When I say "threw the book at me", I do not mean that he arrested me and locked me up in a cell (that happened later). I mean it literally; he reached into his pocket and threw his notebook into the water.

"Urgh. Cover yourself," he ordered. Humiliated, I used the notebook to hide – you know – the *important areas*, and slowly waded on to the shore.

"Whose are these?" he said, lifting up Lucy's clothes.

I did not wish to get Lucy into trouble. "Mine."

The policeman frowned. "What? Even the miniskirt?"

"Yes. I . . . wore it underneath my trousers."

This was a new low.

"Well. A boy who steals donkeys, then flashes at them." He paused to whistle. "When he isn't dressed like a woman. Right. Down the station – we'll see what your parents have to say about this. And you can leave your girly clothes here. I'm not having any of that nonsense in my v—"

He did not get the chance to finish. There was a *CRACK* from above us and something fell from the sky, crashing into the policeman and knocking him to the ground.

How Bad Situations Can Always Get Worse

A lot of things plummet from the sky. For example: rain, meteorites, suicidal kestrels. All of these are relatively acceptable and normal.

However, "acceptable" and "normal" are not words that could be used to describe Paul Beary.

My so-called mate rolled off the policeman, blew the sand out of his mouth and checked his zoom-lens camera. "Still works. Excellent."

Arrest

Thankfully, the policeman survived, despite looking like he had just collided with a planet. "Neither . . . of you . . . move. You're both . . . under arrest," he wheezed. "Just as soon as you help me back to the van."

"Go on, Mike," said Paul.

"No," I hissed, "I am covering my *central zone*."

Paul tutted and led the policeman off the beach. I quickly dressed myself and followed Paul. I guess we could have run away but I did not like the idea of being a wanted criminal and Paul said he could not run, because one of his sister's rhinos had stood on his foot last week.

"Nice one, Paul," I said flatly as the policeman eventually got his breath back, locked us in the back of his wagon and started the engine.

"Hey," said Paul looking hurt. "Blame Lucy. She was the one in a bikini. What am I supposed to do? *Not* take photos of her? Anyway, that pier's a death trap. I was just balancing on a beam up there and it snapped beneath me. I should sue them."

The van bounced across the promenade and joined the main road.

"I should never have told you I was coming here," I said. Stupidly, I had asked Paul for advice on how to act around a beautiful girl. Yes, I know. There was nobody else to turn to, though.

For about the millionth time, I wondered why I was friends with Paul. He latched on to me on the first day of primary school and I have never been able to shake him off since – like a really persistent case of head lice.

Although, if Paul were a head louse, he would be one that you actually felt sorry for. When you brushed him out with a fine-tooth comb, you would probably say, "Aww. Look at that big chubby strange one. He cannot help it, bless him," then put him back so that he could continue to feast on the dead skin of your scalp. This probably does not make sense. Then again, neither does being friends with Paul.

I shook my head. "We are officially criminals. I will probably end up in jail, sharing a cell with someone called Knuckles and getting attacked with sharpened dinner plates and being forced into having home-made tattoos and..."

I started wheezing and took a long gulp on my inhaler.

Paul leaned forward and patted me on the knee. "Don't worry. I'll look after you. It'll be like going on holiday together. What do you think the food'll be like?"

I suppose one of the good things about Paul is that he is far too simple to ever get distressed about things.

"Know what?" he said suddenly. "I can't wait to tell my girlfriend about this."

Paul's Girlfriend

Paul has a girlfriend from France who he met recently when a French swimming team visited Preston. She is amazing because:

1. She is good looking.
2. She is human.
3. She actually exists.
4. She shows no obvious signs of mental illness (apart from being Paul's girlfriend, of course).

"And how is Chantelle?" I asked.

Paul's shoulders dropped. "I miss her so much. She went back to France the other day. I slipped a nice present into her suitcase. After we'd had a massive snog at the bus station, of course."

He demonstrated this with an accurate impersonation of a dog licking syrup off the bottom of a bowl.

"A present?" I asked, trying not to think about Paul slobbering over an innocent girl.

"Oh yeah," said Paul, more brightly. "She's going to be mega-excited. A delicious souvenir of her time in England."

I turned this over in my mind for a few seconds. "*Delicious*? What *exactly* is it?"

Paul smacked his lips. "A doner kebab."

"A kebab. Wow. Nothing like a spot of romance," I said, not bothering to mention that they probably have kebabs in France anyway.

"I know," he grinned. "That's why they call me Doctor Love. Hey, and don't tell Chantelle about me taking photos of Lucy."

I mimed zipping my lips.

Paul stretched out his chubby fingers. "I only do it cos I miss Chantelle. I'm a player, a ladies' man. She knew what she was getting into."

"Nothing strange about spying on girls," I said, raising my eyebrows at him.

"Hey, you can't accuse me of being weird with girls," he said. "You're the one who has a Lucy King scrapbook in your cupboard."

I sat bolt upright. "There is nothing wrong with keeping special artefacts in tribute to a talented athlete."

"Mike, it's got her old verruca sock in it," said Paul.

"So," said the policeman, looking in the mirror as he parked outside the police station. "Been arrested before?"

"Oh yeah, load..." began Paul. I silenced him with a shake of the head.

"All first-time offenders are the same. You did something wrong and now you're at a crossroads. Do you take the right path ... or," he continued, finally turning around to look at us, "do you spend the rest of your lives eating prison food?"

I looked at Paul, expecting him to be as worried as me, but he was licking his lips at the mention of food.

In the Police Station

An hour later, I was sitting in an interview room with the policeman and my parents. In my situation, most young people would get into trouble for getting arrested.

Not me, though. What happened to me was far worse.

I will remind you that my mother was (and unfortunately still is) a disturbingly enthusiastic nudist. She scowled at the policeman as he settled himself opposite us. "Do not say a word to this *evil brute*, Michael," she hissed.

I looked at the ground. "I feel . . . *unclean*."

"Not surprising after the way you've been treated," said Mum. "First they lock you up. Now they interrogate you. What next? Pull off your fingernails and stone you to death. . .?"

The policeman sighed. "Of course not."

"Or will they just electrocute your nipples and be done with it?"

Dad cleared his throat. "Calm down, Joan."

"I'm perfectly calm, Roy," said Mum, taking a deep breath. "I'm just trying to protect our son."

"Michael will be released with a warning," said the policeman. "However, it is perfectly normal for us to have this kind of chat."

Mum tutted loudly. "Here sits a brave young man," she said, grabbing my arm. "He has spent his whole life imprisoned."

"Imprisoned? He's been in trouble with the police before?"

"No, you moron. Imprisoned in society's cotton cells."

"Eh?" said the policeman.

"His clothes, you fool, his clothes. His whole life he's been petrified of revealing his body because *society* has deemed it 'wrong'. And now, finally, he plucks up the courage to do it and you – *you* – lock him up. Michael has obviously embraced nudism..."

"*What?*" I cried.

"...and I want to say well done," said Mum, patting my hand.

The policeman raised a finger. "I'm not sure you should be congra—"

"I am proud of him," she said, putting her arm around me. "And he is proud to be a nudist."

"I really, truly am not," I said.

Dad shifted in his chair. "If the boy says—"

"Whose side are you on here, Roy?" snapped Mum.

The policeman placed both hands on the table. "Look. We're *all* on Michael's side. He just needs to ensure this doesn't happen again."

Mum lowered her voice. "You think you can boss people about because of your uniform. Well, let me tell you – we're all the same underneath. And I can prove it."

She stood up.

"What are you doing?" I said.

She pulled her jumper up over her head.

"This is neither the time nor the place," said the policeman.

"Nonsense!" she said, whipping off her T-shirt.

"Stop! *Please!*" I begged.

The policeman jabbed at a big red panic button on the wall. "Mrs Swarbrick. Do not remove your bra. . ."

It was too late.

Mum pranced around the room. "This feels *wonderful*! Join in, Michael! You're a nudist now!"

As Mum was dragged out by two other officers, she grabbed hold of the door frame: "Freedom and justice for young nudists!"

For a moment, Dad and I sat in total silence. I puffed on my inhaler. Then, even though he is not asthmatic, Dad reached over, took my inhaler off me and had three long drags himself.

Reporter

After Mum was bundled away, Dad signed some forms, and then we sat in the reception area whilst various dangerous-looking people were brought in wearing handcuffs.

Mum finally emerged from a back room with the policeman who had arrested me. Thankfully, she was fully dressed.

As we walked out into the cool evening, she clapped

her hands. "That was so *exciting*. We showed them!"

"Yes," I said. "You showed them *everything*."

Dad smiled sadly.

Suddenly a woman stepped out of the shadows. There was a man standing behind her with a large camera. "Excuse me," she said. "I'm from the *Evening News*."

I did not like the look of this woman. Her mouth was massive and when she spoke she leaned in a bit too close, like her gob was going to hoover you up.

Mum shook her hand. "Joan Swarbrick. How may we help?"

"I'm getting the car," grumbled Dad.

I tried to follow him but the woman stepped out to block my path and smiled at me. I estimated she had about eighty teeth. "Our police sources tell us that you are an *interesting* family."

I did not like the way she said "interesting", like how you might say "freakish" or "monstrous".

Mum grinned. "Well. My husband and I are both nudists. And young Michael here is now a nudist too."

The woman jotted something down on a notebook, muttering, "Ooh, our readers will love this."

"It is *not* true," I said firmly. "Please write that down."

"I think I got that already," smiled the woman, looming over me. The point of her pencil was no longer touching the notebook. "Now, Michael, are you Britain's youngest nudist?"

"Er . . . no."

"So you know others who are younger?"

"I—"

"Aye," she murmured, scribbling in her notebook, "*even younger nudist friends.* Do you love being nude?"

"Oh yes, he's very keen," smiled Mum, ruffling my hair.

I ducked out of the way but Mum tightly gripped my arm. "Not in the slightest bit," I protested.

"Mum knows best. Shall we put that you *do* love it? Our readers just want facts."

"They are not the fac—"

"But you're not saying that it's not *not* true, though, are you?"

"Er . . . yes. . ." I said, struggling to keep up.

"Lovely," said the woman.

"Hang on. I mean . . . *no*?"

The woman was now continuously writing. "*Confused. Excellent.* Could be an angle for the story. So what made you choose *today* to strip off?"

"I did not *choose* today at all."

"Today chose *him*," said Mum, winking.

"What?" I said.

"I *love* it," said the woman, crinkling her nose at Mum. "So, Michael, how did you feel when your mum stripped off during your interview?"

I took a deep breath. "It was utterly horrific."

The woman stopped, pencil poised. "Sorry. Did he say 'horrific' or *'terrific'*?"

"Terrific," nodded Mum.

"Lovely," said the woman. "Now, what's your favourite thing about being nude?"

"But—"

"Your butt?" She nodded in a *whatever-floats-your-boat* kind of way. "*Enjoys flashing his butt.* Interesting."

I slapped my hand against my forehead.

"I love the wind on my bust," added Mum, unhelpfully.

"That sounds *great*," said the woman, stretching her mouth out to its full capacity.

"But—" I said.

"Oh, he loves his butt, doesn't he?" said the reporter. "Never stops going on about it. Butt-butt-butt. *Proud of his body.* Great stuff."

"But—"

"*Butt* again?" The woman frowned. "Hmmm. Don't go overboard, Michael. We want the readers on your side. No one likes a big-head. Do you always strip off in front of donkeys?"

I tried to weigh this question up for a second but my head was pounding. "No."

The pencil danced across the page. "*Strips in front of other animals too.*"

23

"No. Not other animals."

"Sorry. My mistake. *Just donkeys and people.*"

I reached for my inhaler.

The woman studied me intently as I took a puff on it. "*Out of breath.* Interesting."

"I have asthma," I cried, exasperated. Dad pulled up alongside us in the car.

"Course you do," said the woman, giving me an exaggerated wink. "Now, do you mind us using your names in the paper? The police get funny when children are involved."

"Yes, I do," I snapped.

"Be our guest," smiled Mum. "It's S-W-A-R-B-R-I-C-K."

The woman ticked her pad. "*Parental agreement obtained.* One last thing: what is your message to other nudists who might be thinking about taking their clothes off in public?"

Dad hooted the car horn impatiently.

"Join us," said Mum. "Strip off. Live your life. Be nude."

"Man alive!" I said.

"Inspirational," grinned the woman.

I finally freed myself from Mum's grasp and scrambled into the car. As I opened the door, the photographer snapped away.

End

That is all I am going to write today. I have been working for ages and need a snack. My idiot brother and his girlfriend with terrible taste just went out so the coast is clear.

Working for a Second Chance
Tuesday

Tasks completed: Excruciating meeting with Chas.
What I learned: Absence does not make the heart grow fonder.

This morning I returned to school on my own to meet Chas. The school secretary ushered me into the conference room next to Mr Whittle's office. There was a plate of biscuits in there, presumably from another meeting. The selection was rubbish: Bourbons (favoured only by flashy idiots with no taste buds – e.g, my brother Ste), malted milks (poor man's digestive – the kind of biscuit served in hospitals and prisons), and . . . *I shuddered* . . . custard creams.

I tried not to look at my ex-favourite biscuits for ages until, finally, the door was flung open. "Yo yo yo! If it ain't my main dude Mike!" said Chas as he walked in.

Well, I say *walked*. Actually, he more *rolled*. He was wearing those silly trainers with the wheels in the heels. You know, the kind of thing seven-year-old girls wear around supermarkets.

He was also wearing a furry purple tracksuit with the word "HU$$LA" written across it in silver letters. And to top it all off, he had tried to put his hair into dreadlocks. *Dreadlocks*, for crying out loud. Unfortunately, his hair is short and grey so his dreadlocks were more like weird horns. Quite simply, he looked a mess.

Maybe I should explain about Chas. Chas is – *hmm*, how can I put this without sounding mean and cruel?

Er . . . I cannot.

Chas is completely ridiculous. However, he is somehow a professor of psychology at the local university. He is also ancient but honestly believes he is cool.

Now, I will openly admit that I am the *opposite* of cool. For instance:

a. I store important items in a briefcase.
b. Until a few days ago, my mobile phone was about twelve years old and the approximate size of a human baby.
c. At the start of each week I lay out my undies and socks in seven neat piles with Post-it notes on each so that I know which day to wear them.[5]

---

5 Without wishing to be crude, from Monday to Friday I keep things simple – black socks and white briefs. Sometimes at weekends I wear a pair of purple underpants with the word "parp" on the back (a Christmas present from my silliest auntie).

However, the only people less cool than me are those who desperately *try* to be cool.

"I thought you had stopped dressing like this," I said. Back when Chas used to counsel me, I politely told him that he looked like a buffoon. For a time it seemed that he had changed his ways.

"Dressing like what, player?" said Chas.

"Like a chimpanzee who has rampaged through a fancy-dress shop," I said.

Chas nodded. "Oh, yeah, I remember. I turned into Boring Chas for a while. Corduroy trousers and jumpers like a freakin' fifty-year-old."

"You *are* fifty years old."

"Forty-nine," said Chas sharply. "But then after two days, Miss O'Malley's like 'I prefer the old you'. And so I'm like 'Yo! Let's go to Las Vegas and get married.'"

"Married?" I said. "To Miss O'Malley?"

At that moment, Miss Patricia O'Malley came into the room. She used to be my school nurse but she recently and suddenly resigned. She is a nice Irish lady with hands like a polar bear.

"Hello, Michael," she said, enclosing my fingers in her two gigantic palms. "How funny being back here so soon. And how lovely to see you."

"Chas said you married . . . *him*," I said.

"Yes, look." She beamed broadly, holding out a big sausage finger with a diamond ring around it.

"That *is* a large ring," I said. *Large* did not begin to cover it. Seriously, you could have set it on fire and jumped through it on a motorbike.

"Oh yeah," said Chas. "Nothing but the best for P-Dog."

I winced. "P-Dog?"

"The P-Meister. Rice and P. Just pet names for the woman I love. We got married at Big Cliff's Drive-thru Wedding Chapel and Gas Station out in Las Vegas. You can get hitched and fill up your car at the same time."

"Romantic," I said.

Miss O'Malley smiled sweetly at me. "Oh, it was. We got a free bag of barbecue charcoal."

"That's what I'm talking about," said Chas, before rubbing his nose against Miss O'Malley's.

"Please stop," I said. I do not like people who are in love. (NB This does not make me a bad person.)

Miss O'Malley dodged out of the way of him. "Yes. No soppiness in front of Michael. Custard cream?" she asked, pointing to the biscuits on the table. "Your favourites."

"No!" I retorted, slightly too loudly. I took a deep breath. "I am sorry. It is just. . . I do not eat them any more. After . . . *what happened*."

Miss O'Malley put her hand in front of her face, obscuring it like a solar eclipse. "You poor little mite."

"Here's the thing," said Chas. "We know you're a good kid. We don't buy all that stuff people have been saying about you."

"Thank you," I said.

"If you wanna be a nudist, you just let it all hang out, brother. Ain't no business but yours."

There was a long silence. "Maybe we should talk about my work experience?" I said, eventually.

Chas clicked his fingers. "So we get married. And I say, 'Yo, P. You made me feel like the luckiest dude alive. Let's hit the casinos.' So I put one dollar into a gambling machine and – *kerching*!"

Miss O'Malley grinned. "We won five thousand dollars on our first turn."

Chas clicked his fingers. "Right on. So. We hang out in the States for a few more days. Buy ourselves some cool threads. . ." He motioned towards his hideous clothes.

"Oh," I said. "Did you leave them on the plane?"

"Then we decided to check out how they deal with kids' issues over there – gun crime, gang wars, rap beefs. The usual."

I raised my eyebrows. "Rap . . . beefs?"

Miss O'Malley nodded her head solemnly. "That's when two rappers fall out. Ooh, they can be *awfully* mean to each other."

Chas held her hand. "Anyways, so I just say, 'We've got some dough. We can do anything we want.' Now. Mikey. What am I good at?"

I genuinely had no idea.

"Two things. Rapping and helping little dudes like you, right? So straight away, as soon as we get back, we decide to set up a mobile counselling clinic."

My eyes widened. "I hope you are not going to counsel me?"

"Don't worry, dude," said Chas. "Nothing like that. Pick you up early tomorrow. Word."

Then he rolled on out of the room with Miss O'Malley following.

End of meeting. I told you that Chas was a nightmare – after ten minutes of talking to him I still did not have the first clue what my job would actually be.

On my way past the head teacher's office, Mr Whittle came out and told me to work hard and think deeply about why I am doing this placement in the first place. This was a silly thing to say. Of course I think deeply about it. In fact, I think about hardly anything else.

Even so, I will do as he says and continue my tale of woe.

The Journey Home

After escaping from the reporter Dad drove us towards the motorway, muttering about how he wanted to forget this whole sorry episode.

"Oh no, Roy. This is just the beginning," Mum said,

wistfully. "The future's bright. The future's *naked*. How about a family holiday to a nudist camp?"

There was a *thudthudthudthudthud* as Dad momentarily swerved the car on to the hard shoulder.

"Everything all right Roy?" said Mum, before sighing. "Ah, imagine – barbecues in the open air, skinny-dipping, beach volleyball. The whole family swinging free. *Heaven*. We'll book it as soon as Ste comes home."

At the time I did not know which was worse: going to a nudist camp or having my brother back in the country. I was about to mention this when my phone beeped. Eek! A text from Lucy!

Hi, Mike! Hope ur ok. Thanx 4 saving me. Ur a gr8 m8.
IOU 1. Festival tom. Whaddya think? Love LXXXX

The needle on my Lucy-ometer flicked to the very top of the yellow zone.

The Lucy-ometer

Hmm. I did not actually think I would ever mention the Lucy-ometer to anybody. It is an imaginary scale – like the speedometer in a car – that indicates how my friendship with Lucy is going. It is not real – it only exists in my head. There are four coloured sections that the needle could point to (red – *appallingly*, orange – *badly*, yellow – *reasonably well*, green – *outstandingly*).

Many people would say that it is a bit weird but I find it helps me to build a mental picture of where I stand with her. Due to Lucy's punishing training schedule, she does not have time to explain each new development in our friendship in such straightforward terms.

The Text Message

These are the highlights of what Lucy *meant* by this text:

1) XXXX = four *loud* kisses (note the capital letters). At that point in my life, I had only ever been kissed on the cheek once before by a non-family member (Lucy, at the beach earlier that day). That was a lower-case kiss – polite and quick, performed with pursed lips and maximum efficiency. However, a *capital-letter* kiss would be a bit more out of control – lunging and noisy like a camel eating yoghurt. She could easily aim for the cheek but accidentally stray on to my lips.

2) Ur a gr8 m8 = you are my best friend in the whole world. We should go to Boots and have amusing passport photos done together and carry them in our wallets for eternity.

3) IOU 1 = she owes me one. But one what? One *kiss*? Nope – she already gave me four of those. One *treat*? Maybe she could give me a haircut or a signed swimming hat or literally *anything*. One nice *day out*? Like a *date*. But for friends. A *friendship date*!

The only downside of this text – and the reason why it did not carry me into the green zone – was Festival Tom. I did not like the sound of him. People with wacky names like that seem fun the first time you meet them because they wear bright yellow clothes and say things like "Yabadaba-ding-dong" but later on it turns out that they spend all day lying in bed, eating cheese and sobbing. I had to warn her off him.

I composed my reply:

Dearest Lucy. Fear not. The police released me. However, during my interview, Mum committed an atrocity. Perhaps we could discuss this on a friendship date. AMLAT. Michael xxxxx PS: I have heard terrible things about Festival Tom – steer clear. PPS: AMLAT = all my love and tenderness.

For a moment I felt that five kisses and an AMLAT may have been too much.[6] I do not usually use text speak such as AMLAT but I thought it important to try. Also, what if Festival Tom was actually a nice person and he had simply been christened with that name by his zany parents?

I thought about it for a moment, then shrugged. She *was* my best friend after all – I could not allow her to settle for anyone less than perfect. With a triumphant prod, I sent the text.

In the front of the car, Mum was still jabbering on about justice.

My phone beeped. Wow! Lucy was fast!

Disappointment

My heart sank. A text from Paul Beary.

Yo, Mike! Mad day! On way home wiv mum. Not in NE trouble wiv police but no 2nd helpings of dessert for me 2nite. Still – good pics of Lucy in bikini. Well. The 1s that rnt ruined by ur bum anyway. Saw ur

6 Initially these were capital-letter kisses but I reined myself in. There is no point in giving too much away too soon. It would leave nowhere to go in future texts.

> mum @ pol station btw in nowt but a blanket. Wkd!
> Still hot!

Gross. "Hot" and "mum" are not words that should appear anywhere near each other ever. I replied:

> Dear Paul. Delete photos of Lucy immediately and please stop referring to my mother in this way or friendship will be terminated forthwith. PS: I fear you may need psychiatric treatment.

In front, Mum was now slapping her hand against the dashboard to emphasize her points. "We need direct action."

Dad began massaging his neck with one hand whilst steering with the other. "Can't we just forget all about it?"

I shifted uneasily in my seat. "Direct action?"

Mum turned round to face me, her forehead twitching with excitement. "I am going to fight for your right to be naked whenever and wherever you want."

"Oh no."

Lovely News

Just as the car pulled into the driveway, my phone beeped again. This time it was Lucy.

> Haha! AMLAT! LOL! Ur funny. Tom = tomorrow.
> Medieval Festival in Moor Park. Bit sad but might be
> OK. Dad involved. Eek! V embarrassing. Pick u up
> @ 1130am if ur not grounded? Need friend 4 moral
> support. Pls! :)

Green zone, here I come!

There were two obvious awesome things about this text: Festival Tom was not a person *and* I had a friendship date. After the initial excitement generated by these bits of news died down, I tried to analyse this text. Without wishing to sound picky, I did not like the smiley face. It was not as good as four kisses. That said, I had to put it into context. Today we had shared one real-life peck on the cheek and nine text-kisses (including four capital-letter ones). Her lips were probably tired. The smiley face was her way of stretching them out after all the action. I remained formal in my reply so she could rest them.

> Dear Lucy. No. I am not grounded. Indeed, far from it.
> Surprisingly enough, my mum has never been happier
> with me. Consequently I would be delighted to escort
> you to the Medieval Festival. See you then, old chum.

I pushed Send and instantly regretted it.

Old chum?

What was I thinking? It sounded like a dog food. I began to panic, but as I opened the front door I received a reply:

X

Yabba-dabba-ding-dong!

Unfortunately, the happiness did not last for long. I was so busy re reading that single beautiful letter that I did not look where I was going and half tripped over something in the hallway.

I looked down at it and said a very naughty word.

Normally I do not like swearing. It is only acceptable in extreme situations. However, this was *without doubt* an extreme swearing situation.

Unhappy Returns

On the floor was a designer imitation-crocodile-skin sports bag. It belonged to my brother, Ste.

The Dark Lord had returned.

This was not good. I may or may not have mentioned that my brother is the worst person alive, because:

1. **He is seriously vain.** Sometimes he wears girls' make-up to cover his spots, even though he is not a girl. Also, until he went away, he used so much hair gel that, from behind, he resembled a seagull that had been recently rescued from an oil slick.
2. **He is cruel.** When I was about eight years old, my pet hamster gave birth to nine babies. That night, Ste crept into my room whilst I was asleep and put all of them on my face.
3. **He hates me and I was pretty certain that he wanted to kill me.** Earlier I mentioned that Ste used to go out with Lucy King but she dumped him after finding out he was seeing another girl. What I did not mention was that it was my fault she found out about this. In the process of doing so I managed to crush his beloved VW Golf under the wheels of a ten-tonne truck.

I quickly considered my options. I *could* stay still and take my slow, painful death like a man or I could hitch-hike to the nearest docks and stow away on the first boat bound for the West Indies.

The decision was an easy one. *Jamaica, here I come*, I thought, spinning on my heels. Unfortunately, Mum was right behind me, blocking the doorway. There was no way out. I could hear Ste's footsteps on the laminate floor. Closer. Closer. He grabbed me. My whole body tensed. I closed my eyes, waiting for the pain to come. And then...

He hugged me.

Yes.

He *hugged* me.

It was deeply unpleasant, like being crushed by a man-eating plant. For a moment I wondered if this was a better or worse feeling than being brutally murdered by him.

"I've missed you, little buddy," he said, patting my back.

A Changed Man

Five minutes later we were all sitting in the lounge. Ste brought in a pot of tea and a packet of biscuits. In my entire life, I had never known Ste to make anything for anybody else. As he bent down to pour the tea for Mum, Dad and me, I noticed the following changes:

  a. He no longer had a goatee beard.
  b. He was bronzed and healthy looking. This is not how I look after exposure to the sun.[7]

---

7 I have skin like a roughly shaved mole. After an hour on the beach I go the colour of a fire engine and am unable to move for a week.

    c. There was no gel in his hair. He had one of those
       fluffy, scruffy hair dos favoured by surfers and
       members of boy bands. These haircuts annoy me
       because they are messy, yet girls seem to like boys
       who have them. I prefer to keep my hair combed
       and neat but it ends up all shaggy and uneven
       anyway, like the fur of a depressed yak.

"Good to have you home, Steven," said Mum. Predictably, she had whipped off every stitch of clothing when she came inside. Ste still gave her a hug, the big oddball.

"I got you a present, pal," said Ste, handing me the biscuits.

I turned the packet over in my hands. It was covered in squiggly writing that was translated into English on the back. I read it aloud: "Sandwich of the biskits with cream of the custard inside for make taste very nice snack-time."

"Custard creams!" said Ste, enthusiastically. "Your favourites."

This was, of course, back in the days when I still loved custard creams.

As they all stared, I turned them over in my hands, unsure whether or not I trusted them. Serious pressure. I slowly unwrapped the biscuits, took one out, sniffed it and inspected it. It *looked* like a custard cream. And it *smelled* like a custard cream.

"Don't worry, brother. They're hand-made fair trade products. No animals or people were harmed in their production," he said, raising his palm. I noticed that he was wearing about eighteen friendship bands. *Huh!* I thought. *Who would want to be friends with him?*

I narrowed my eyes and nibbled a tiny bit off the corner. It was not inedible. And I did not die straight away. However, it had a slight aftertaste of lemon that I felt was unnecessary. Three out of five. *Nice try, Ste.* I slid them back on to the table.

"Lovely gift," beamed Mum. She leaned forward to take one, yelping as she caught one of her *you-know-whats* on the teapot.

"I got them in Thailand."

"Thailand?" said Dad. "I thought you were in Australia."

"Didn't you get my postcard?" said Ste. When we all shook our heads, he continued, "I was out in Oz for a few weeks, living with Uncle Ian and our cousins. Things got pretty wild – beaches, parties, girls."

Mum giggled. "What are you like?"

Ste clicked his tongue. "Incorrect. What *was* I like? I'm a changed man, and I'll tell you why. So the holiday came to an end and I was on the plane home. Suddenly:

kaboom! Volcano erupts. Ash cloud. Pilot can't see. Emergency stop in Thailand. Disaster. Some people in the country not found, et cetera, but the Stevenator (as I *used* to call myself) thought, *Hey, more days to party.* The airline even gave me some money because I said I'd stick around for a few days while they cleared the backlog of people. So I'm at the airport wondering where the hottest babes are at when suddenly this voice pops into my head with a message."

"What did it say?" said Mum.

You are the most evil man on the planet? I thought.

"It said..." Ste paused dramatically. "'Rainforest bus tour leaving in five minutes.' I'm sure it was ... *the universe* speaking to me."

I felt my face screwing up. "Are you sure? I mean, it sounds like it might have been the person organizing the rainforest bus tour."

Ste pursed his lips. "Well. Yes, of course. But it was like the universe had *told* him to say that. So I got on board and we headed into the rainforest, towards the volcano."

"Was it dangerous?" said Mum.

"Could you have been swept away in a torrent of lava?" I said, gleefully.

"No," said Ste. "Everything had died down by then. Everyone else went off on this guided walking tour but I just felt this *need* to walk off alone. It was like a magnet pulling me through the jungle. After an hour of trekking, I *stumbled* upon this building amongst the trees, miles from civilization. I walked through these huge golden gates and realized it was a monastery!"

"Who was there?" said Mum.

"Monks," said Ste, wisely.

"Were they kung-fu monks?" I said. "Did they beat you up?"

"Nope," said Ste. "What I saw just blew. My. Mind. These monks were known as The Honourable Protectors of the Sacred Primates. They worshipped monkeys."

"Monkey monks?" I said.

Ste nodded. "Yes, Michael. Monkeys are man's best friends."

"I thought that was dogs," I said.

"Incorrect," said Ste. "Give a monkey the chance and he'll do anything for you."

"Inspirational," said Mum.

"Rubbish," I said. I saw a monkey in a zoo once. It did not do *anything* for me and it was not my best friend. In fact it ... well, if you must know ... *went to the toilet* in its hand and threw it at me.

Ste ignored me. "The eruption had driven all of these poor little monkeys out of the rainforest. The monks had been out rescuing them. Monkeys were *everywhere* in the temple. On the floor. On tables. In the monks' beds. Homeless. Confused. Covered in dust. Some of them had all their fur burned off by the heat. They were all pink and wrinkly like miniature shrivelled-up old men. It was . . . *intense*."

He paused to sip his tea. "So I set to work. It was all just so natural. Man. Monk. Monkey. Together at last. I stayed for four days. Feeding milk to the baby monkeys. Treating their wounds. Singing to them. It changed my life. Then, when I woke up on the last day and went to my bag, this baby monkey I'd been looking after – I'd called him *Alan* – was in there, sleeping amongst my dirty pants. He looked so . . . peaceful."

"Next to your pants? He was probably dead," I said.

"Michael," said Mum. "I know you've had a tough day but. . ."

"No sweat, Mum," said Ste. "Until Mike has that kind of an experience, he can't possibly understand. But when I looked at that monkey's face snuggled up to my boxers, everything changed for ever. You know, I believe that the eruption *occurred* just so that my life could be improved."

I looked at him in disbelief. "But you said that some people had not been found yet."

Ste shrugged. "You can't argue with the universe. Have you ever heard of karma?"[8]

"Oh, that sounds fascinating," gushed Mum.

"Well, basically, the monks taught me that if I do something *bad* to someone, *bad* things will happen to me. Either now or in the future, or even after I have been reincarnated."

Reincarnated. *Ha!* I imagined Ste coming back to life as a beetle and me squashing him underfoot. Would *that* be a bad enough thing, Ste?

"But," said Ste, raising a finger, "if I do *good* things, then *good* things will be visited upon me. That's why from now on I'm devoting my life to righting all the wrongs from my past and helping others in my future. So, Michael, I wish to say sorry for everything I've ever done to you."

I nearly choked on my tea.

"You didn't have to do that, Steven," said Mum.

"Hmmm, I think he did," I said.

"But the biggest way I'm going to help the world," said Ste, "is by raising some serious money for these monkeys. I've been emailing Mr Whittle from Thailand and he's really excited."

"Oh super," I said, flatly. I did not wish to be negative,

---

8 At this point, I wish I could have said, "Yes, and I would feel a lot *karma* if you would just get out and never come back." This would have been the best joke I had ever said. Unfortunately, I only thought of it just now and there is nobody here to share it with.

but the teachers at school already thought Ste was the greatest person who had ever lived.[9] This was only going to make things worse.

Ste nodded. "I know. The Stevenator is dead. From now on, I am ... the Steverlizer."

"How inspiring!" said Mum.

"What exactly is the difference?" I said. A stupid new nickname was not enough to make me start trusting him.

"The Stevenator helped himself. The Steverlizer helps others. First on the list: Lucy King."

"Lucy?" I squawked.

"Yeah. The Stevenator treated her badly. Now the Steverlizer has got to make it up to her. Have you been seeing much of her, Mike?"

I shook my head. "Nope." *Apart from our friendship date tomorrow.*

Ste nodded. "OK. Well. If you *do* see her, tell her the Steverlizer wants to apologize."

"I will definitely do that," I said. *Not a chance, Stever-loser.*

"The Steverlizer knows he can count on you," he smiled. "Anyway, I'm so rude. What's new here?"

Mum put her cup down. "Michael's a nudist now."

"Wrong," I said.

---

9 Notice how they allowed him to take three weeks off from his A-levels so he could go to Australia "for personal reasons" (i.e, so that Lucy's dad did not murder him).

"That's great, Mike," said Ste, ruffling my hair. "I always knew you'd do something like that."

"I am going upstairs," I said. "I have things to do." I.e, sticking the receipt from the donkey hire into my Lucy King scrapbook, followed by an early night so I would be fresh for my friendship date.

"Oh, Mikey," said Ste as I left the room. "I forgot."

He dipped his hand into his pocket and tossed something to me. It was a plaited leather band about the width of my finger.

"It's a friendship bracelet," he said. "Hand-made and blessed by the monks at the monastery. They consider it to be a solemn and sacred object."

I squinted at it. "Really? It has plastic beads hanging off it. And it says *chumz 4 eva* on the outside."

Ste waved his hand at me. "To prove there's no hard feelings between us."

I nodded. "Right."

Wrong.

Time for Bed

I have been typing for a long time. My watch says eight-thirty. I think I will stop there and go to bed. If Chas is going to be here nice and early in the morning, I had better make sure I am fully rested.

47

Working for a Second Chance
Wednesday – Day 1 of Actual Work Experience

Tasks completed: Waiting.
What I have learned: If something looks rubbish and sounds rubbish, it probably *is* rubbish.

This morning, Chas was not nice and early.

At eleven-fifteen, just as I was wondering if he would turn up at all, the sound of a loud and unhealthy car engine came roaring down the road.

The source was a Volkswagen camper van. Now, I quite like those colourful old campers with split screens and spare wheels on the front that people spend years restoring. However, the monstrosity that pulled up on my drive was categorically *not* one of those.

1. It was from around 1985 – not cool and compact but bulky and blocky like a Second World War tank.
2. Its colour could only be described as *baby's-nappy-after-a-bumsplosion* brown.
3. I would not sleep in it under any circumstances. It was rusty and grimy, and the high-top plastic roof was covered in moss and filth. In fact, just *seeing* it made me feel dirty.
4. A blue sticker with "Chatricia" written on it ran across

the top of a long, diagonal crack on the windscreen. I am fairly certain that the sticker was holding the glass together.

I went outside. Rap music was booming out from the stereo. Chas hopped out, bouncing to the throbbing beat. "Whaddya think of my sweet ghetto-wagon?"

He slapped the front bumper, which promptly fell off.

I tried not to laugh. "You *bought* this? With actual money?"

Miss O'Malley climbed out of the other door. "Well, it might not be a Ferrari but it's a *start*. We've got big plans."

"Behold, brother," said Chas, fixing the bumper back on. "The Little Dudes' Mobile Counselling Clinic. Let me give you the grand tour."

He led me round the side and threw open the sliding door (which came off its runners and had to be manhandled back on by Miss O'Malley). The back seat had a kind of multicoloured, futuristic space-puke pattern and deep rips into the cushion. The walls were covered in mottled brown stains, like the roof was leaking, and a strong, wet smell was coming from somewhere. I did not dare look in the sink.

Chas patted me on the back. "All of this is thanks to you, dude. If it wasn't for you, Pat and I would never have met. And we wouldn't be doing this."

I swallowed. "I have no idea what to say."

"Say nothing, buddy. Just drink it all in."

There was a short pause.

Miss O'Malley sniffed. "Well, don't *drink in* the water from the tap. A sparrow died in the tank."

"I've been counselling kids for years part-time but now we're going all out," said Chas. "Every day we're gonna hit the road and help any little dude who needs us. You wanna know the best part?"

"You are going to drive me to the library so I can work there instead?"

"Nice one, dude," laughed Chas. "But no. Best thing is we rock it urban-style. Kids love skateboarding, graffiti, rap – all that cool stuff, yeah?"

"Hmm." Personally I think graffiti is appalling, I cannot skateboard because I have no sense of balance (due to my waggly head) and I hate rap music. Indeed, I only own one piece of music – a CD of an Austrian man called Wilhelm Wasserball playing nursery rhymes on a collection of pots and pans.[10]

Miss O'Malley grinned. "There are thousands of youngsters like you who need our help."

"Like *me*?"

Chas held his hands out. "You know – nut jobs, cranks, oddballs."

"Misfits," offered Miss O'Malley, unhelpfully.

---

10 The cover shows him dressed in traditional Alpine clothing, using a spoon to bash the saucepan that is balanced on his head. Thinking about it, he is probably not quite normal.

"Thanks," I said.

Chas clicked his fingers and pointed at me. "We'll talk and drive. Let's get this party started."

The party did not start at all.

Neither did the camper van.

It spluttered a few times, then made a sound like someone slowly drowning in mashed potato. Chas had to call out the RAC, who towed it away. I was told that I could spend the rest of the day completing my journal. Seeing as I did nothing and do not know exactly what I was *meant* to be doing, I cannot write any more about my day of work. I guess I should carry on reflecting on why I am being punished in the first place.

Pre-friendship Date

I was so nervous about my friendship date with Lucy that I barely slept. This nervousness was not because I fancy her. I do not fancy her at all. I was merely concerned that, as her best friend, I had an incredible responsibility. Literally anything could have gone wrong. This was a *medieval* festival after all. She could have caught the Black Death.

I must have drifted off, though, because in the morning I opened my eyes to find a bacon butty and a steaming mug of tea next to my head.

Awesome! Breakfast in bed. This had literally never happened to me before. Mum must have been so proud of me that she had made it as a treat. I guzzled it down, showered and got ready for my big day.

When I came downstairs, Mum and Dad were already sitting at the table.

"Looking smart, son," said Dad.

"Thank you," I said. I was wearing a short-sleeved shirt, a tie and an old pair of Ste's shoes (which were three sizes too big). Unfortunately, the only tie I could find was an elasticated Mickey Mouse one from when I was five years old. I had also *possibly* put on a bit too much of my dad's aftershave.

Mum was, of course, completely naked. "Do you really need all those clothes, Michael?" she said.

"Yes," I replied, staring at the table.

Dad cleared his throat. "Maybe you could just let the lad have his breakfast."

"I have already eaten," I said. "Thank you for my bacon sandwich."

Mum and Dad looked confused for a few moments. Then Mum's nose twitched. "What's that horrible smell? Have you borrowed your dad's disgusting aftershave?"

For the record, if you would like to purchase this aftershave, it is called Scent of a Beast and is available in one-litre bottles. I am not sure they still make it, though. The box features a picture of a man with an Afro and moustache, wearing flares and smoking a pipe. These details tell me it may be quite an old brand.

"Bit harsh," said Dad. "It's a classic."

Mum snorted. "Roy. It smells like toilet cleaner. The only reason I let you keep it is for squirting under the rim of the loo."

"I thought you said it smells manly," said Dad.

"Yes," giggled Mum. "Manly. Like a freshly cleaned gentlemen's lavatory."

Ste came into the room, carrying a huge cardboard box. "Morning, family," he said, before sniffing the air. "Has someone spilled bleach?"

"Michael's started using your father's rancid aftershave," said Mum.

"Ah, Scent of a Beast," said Ste. "I thought they banned it after those people went blind."

Dad noisily ate his toast.

"Mike, if you want aftershave, just borrow mine," Ste said. "I've got forty different types."

"I will," I said ... *if I ever want to smell like the world's worst human being*.

"Oh. And did you enjoy your breakfast?" said Ste, placing the box on the table. "I crisped up the bacon just how you like it."

Incredible. Ste – the man who had once tried to

smooth out my tongue with a sheet of sandpaper – had just made me a bacon butty. I did not know whether to laugh, cry, or regurgitate it. "Thank . . . *you*?" I said.

"Your pleasure is my pleasure," he grinned.

"What's in the box, son?" said Dad.

"Not sure but it stinks," said Ste. "I kept it in my room last night so you guys wouldn't have to suffer."

"So thoughtful," said Mum. "And you're right about the smell. It's like rotten meat . . . slight improvement on Michael's aftershave, though. Waft it over here."

"Yeah," said Ste. "It's from France and it's addressed to a Mr Paul Swarbrick, whoever that is. It got delivered yesterday, just after I got back. I was going to search online for every Paul Swarbrick in the country so I could take it round to its rightful owner."

I rolled my eyes. "No need. It is from France and addressed to someone called Paul. It is almost certainly Paul Beary's."

"Why would he call himself Swarbrick?" said Ste.

"I have no idea but we are talking about a boy who once pretended to have no eyes so he could 'accidentally' stumble into the female changing rooms at the leisure centre," I said. "I will contact him later."

Mum shrugged. "What are we all doing today, then?"

"I'm picking up a car I bought on eBay," said Ste.

"You know, to replace my old one."

I winced. Ste's VW Golf was his absolute pride and joy. Until I destroyed it, that is.

"No hard feelings, Mike," said Ste, patting me on the shoulder. "Let's look to the future, eh?"

"How exciting," said Mum. "And you, Michael? Any more daring nudist raids planned? Let me know if you need a lift. We'll stick it to the police."

"We will not," I said. "I am going to the Medieval Festival in Moor Park."

"Good thinking. Should be packed," said Mum. "Great place to strip off."

"No, Mother," I said. "I am going on a friendship date."

"Wearing aftershave?" said Ste. "Who's the lucky lady?"

I did not like the direction this was taking so I stood up from the table. "I am going outside to wait for my friend. I wish to be early."

Travelling to the Friendship Date

I was exactly forty-three minutes early, to be precise. During this time I texted Paul:

We have a parcel from France addressed to a Paul Swarbrick. Please collect ASAHP (as soon as humanly possible). Judging by the smell it may or may not contain a dead creature. Michael. PS: Why are you having things sent to my house?

Paul replied soon after:

Ace! Soz 4 using ur address – luv Chantelle but dont want a stalker.

Oh, tremendous. She could stalk him at my house instead.

Shortly before Lucy was due to arrive, Ste came out of the house and walked down the road, calling, "Have a brilliant day, brother, and remember to do good things."

I waved back, and before I could stop myself I had wished him a cheery "You too."

I was surprised at my own friendliness towards him. I mean, a bacon butty was not enough to earn my forgiveness for all the misery he had caused me throughout my life. However, it *was* a tasty sandwich, and given the choice between an evil Ste who made me breakfast and an evil Ste who did not, it was an easy decision to make.

A few minutes later, Lucy's parents' old camouflage-print Land Rover swung into our road. Lucy wound down her window and greeted me with a beautiful smile. By this I mean the smile of a person who is beautiful *on the inside*. Although she happens to be beautiful on the outside as well.

"Ooh, you look smart," said Lucy's mum, who was driving. Lucy's mum looks a bit like Lucy, only older and a deep shade of orange. "Did I just see your Steven walking down the road?"

I ground my teeth together. "Yes. He has returned from his exile in Australia."

Lucy's mum grinned mischievously. "Ooh, Lucy. You can get together with him again."

"Awful idea," I said.

Lucy rolled her eyes. "I don't think so."

"We'll see," said Lucy's mum. "You hop in the back, Michael."

The Kings' Land Rover is one of those old-fashioned ones with the canvas covering the rear half of it, bench seats in the boot and no rear windows. I was about to pull myself up on the step at the back when I froze in surprise.

Lucy's Dad

Lucy's dad Dave (my ex-swimming coach) glared out from the back of the Land Rover. He is the most petrifying person ever because:

    a. He is six foot five and has biceps like unruly

watermelons.

b. People talk about looks that could kill. When Dave stares at you, it is more a look that slices you open and rips out your lungs.

c. He is violent. A car once clipped his Land Rover in the swimming pool car park so he beat it up. Yes, he did not beat up the *owner* of the car. He beat up the *car itself*.

d. Dave was in the SAS, until he lost three fingers during hand-to-hand combat training.

Now, all of this stuff was not a shock to me. The shocking thing was his outfit. He wore leather sandals with criss-cross straps up his bulging calves; a brown tunic and chain mail vest; and an iron helmet with a nose guard. Wrapped around his hand was a chain with a spiky metal ball attached to the end of it, and a long sword was propped between his legs.

"Mario," he said, getting my name wrong as usual. "You've got fatter since we kicked you out of the swimming club."

I tried to smile as I climbed inside.[11]

"See, Lucy," he said. "First the fat goes to your

---

11 He was referring to the international swimming gala when I offended the mayor of a small French town by sporting a large and detailed picture of a man's *thingy* on my back. The picture was, of course, drawn by my brother whilst I was asleep.

backside. Then your head. . . That's what'll happen to *you* now you've quit swimming."

"Quit swimming?" I cried. There was a strange empty feeling in my stomach. I mean, do not get me wrong. Lucy was my best friend and I would support her decision, but she was the second-most-promising swimmer in the UK. Would swimming even be able to exist without her? "But you are . . . excellent."

"See. Even old flabby-arse here agrees with me," said Dave, jabbing his sword into the wooden floor.

Lucy leaned back over her seat. "I decided last night. After we . . . I mean *I* had that swim in the sea." (I realized here that she was protecting me, which was sweet of her. If Dave thought I was to blame for her giving up, he would have pulled out my pancreas.) "I just think I should be having fun instead of training all the time. And I *thought* we agreed we wouldn't talk about it, Dad. I'm sorry for destroying your dreams of Olympic glory but please can we just leave it?"

"Sure thing," said Dave. "Just like you left your swimming career behind."

"Well, *I'm* glad you've stopped all that swimming nonsense," chipped in Lucy's mum. "You can concentrate on important things, love, like boyfriends."

I winced.

"Mum!" said Lucy.

"Here we go again," growled Dave.

"I was engaged to your father by the time I was your age," said Lucy's mum. "You need to start young; get in first before the good ones get snapped up."

"I'm still at school," said Lucy.

Her mum swung the Land Rover over a mini-roundabout. "Of course. You shouldn't settle down with Mr Right till after your GCSEs . . . but there's no harm in getting him off the market early."

Dave King emitted a rumbling sound from deep within his body. "I didn't give up half my life so she could chuck her future away for some flaming boy."

"I'm thinking of our daughter's future happiness," said Mrs King. "Me and all my sisters got married early. And look at the perfect men *we* found."

I looked at Dave King and took a long drag on my inhaler.

I know, I thought, *how about a joke to lighten the mood.* "That is a very good costume, Dave," I said. "But I think it might be out of fashion."

Response: uncomfortable, painful silence.

To be fair, this was all it deserved.

Lucy's mum pulled up at a red light. "David's re-enacting the Battle of Hastings. It's his first ever one. He's an Anglo-Saxon."

Dave cracked his knuckles. "Yeah, and we're gonna

rip them Normans to shreds. Try an' invade us? Well, let's see how they like a bit o' this."

Without warning, he swung the metal ball right in front of my face, like he was caving in someone's skull.

"We've been through this three times now," said Lucy. "It's not a *real* battle. It's a *re-en-act-ment*. The Normans are *supposed* to win. You have to do a few before they'll let you go on the winning team."

Dave's shoulders slumped and he began picking at his leather wrist protectors with his thumbnail.

"Can anyone smell Toilet Duck?" said Lucy's mum.

A Wonderful Moment

On arrival at the car park for the Medieval Festival, I hopped out of the back of the Land Rover and rushed round to open Lucy's door for her.

Lucy climbed out. "Aw. You're so sweet," she said, in the same voice you might use when speaking to a baby with yoghurt all over its face.

Then, guess what? She linked arms with me.

Honestly.

Linked!

Things that link:

1. Chains.
2. The beaks of two romantic parrots.
3. The arms of two very good friends.

I nearly had an asthma attack.

"Oh, I see," said Dave, gathering his weapons together. "*This* is why you've quit swimming. You're going out with Marek here."

"*What?*" cried Lucy, way *too* horrified for my liking.

"I think you can do much better, love," said Lucy's mum.

"Thanks a lot," I said.

"Michael is my friend," said Lucy. "He's the last person on Earth I would go out with."

"Thanks again," I said.

Lucy turned to me. "Oh, I don't mean it like that. I meant you're such a good friend I could *never* spoil our friendship. . ."

"Me neither," I said, swallowing hard.

"But, if I do go out with Michael – or anyone else – then that's my business."[12]

"Huh. What do I care?" said Dave, looking away. The whiteness of his knuckles around the chain and the

---

12 This would have been the greatest sentence in history if it had been three words shorter.

throbbing veins in his forehead indicated that, actually, he cared a lot.

"Calm down, love," said Lucy's mum. "Remember what the doctor said about avoiding stress."

"Oh, I'm calm all right," said Dave, not sounding very calm at all. "She can do whatever she wants. Now, if you don't mind, I've got some Normans to crush."

He stalked off angrily, with Lucy's mum following.

Happy Moments

Lucy and I walked towards the park. "Sorry about my parents," she said. "Dad's not taken me quitting swimming well, and as for Mum..."

"Getting married young is a very bad idea," I said, before adding quickly, "unless you find someone really good."

"You know, Mike," she said, after a long pause, "you *do* smell a bit like Toilet Duck. Mind if I spray you with perfume?"

Obviously I *did* mind smelling like a girl but I could not say no to Lucy.

She pulled a tiny bottle out of her bag and squirted me in a big cloud. At first it made me wheeze but then

I got used to it. It smelled lovely, like the scent of fresh pillowcases mixed with bubble gum. But, best of all, it smelled of Lucy.[13]

"Thank you," I said, remembering something in my pocket from the day before. "Oh. I got you a friendship band."

I did not mention that Ste had given it to me.

"I thought we could make our friendship official," I said.

She tied it around her wrist. "Aw. Chumz 4 eva."

"That is us," I said.

"I got something for you too. To say thanks for saving me yesterday."

She pulled a chocolate cupcake out of her bag. "I made them with Mum. Now I'm not swimming I don't have to follow Dad's *Olympian diet*."

"Wow!" I said. "I can keep the wrapper in my scrapbook."

"Scrapbook?" she said.

"Not important," I replied, eating the cake and carefully folding the wrapper into my pocket. I mean, *I* know that there is nothing weird about my Lucy King scrapbook but you can never tell what other people might think, especially when their name is on

---

13 Not that I go around *sniffing* Lucy. It is just that over the years I have got used to her lovely scent.

the front of it.

Lucy smiled and hooked arms with me again. Everything in the world felt good.

For now.

The Medieval Festival

We walked through the park together, past stalls selling various medieval food and knick-knacks, and even a falconry display. I have to say that it was a nice event. There were hog roasts and jesters and places where you could have your photograph taken whilst being stretched in a rack.

"So your brother's back then?" she said suddenly as we stopped at a stand selling "100% genuine medieval mobile phone accessories".

"Yes," I sighed.

"Huh," she said. "He's such an idiot."

"Total idiot. He even got a free holiday to Thailand on his way home. What an idiotic thing to do."

I did not mention the bacon sandwich. That would have made him sound unnecessarily kind. Lucy absent-mindedly began picking up the old-fashioned silver tags and cloth phone covers with scenes from the Bayeux tapestry on them.

"I bet he spent all his time on the beach," she said.

"Yeah. Being an idiot, probably."

"I imagine he's all tanned. . ." Her voice was filled with contempt.

"Er. . ."

Another long pause. She picked up a castle-shaped phone charger. "Has his hair gone blond from the sun?"

"I am not really sure. . ."

"He'd look stupid if it has," she said quickly.

"Like a big stupid blond-haired loser."

"He's probably had a thousand girlfriends," she said, then suddenly looked up at me. "He hasn't, has he?"

"No. He is more interested in monkeys now."

Lucy pursed her lips. "They're welcome to him. I'm over him and over the moon because of it."

"'Scuse me," said the woman behind the stall. "You gonna pay for that?"

Lucy and I both looked down at the silver mobile phone charm she was holding. It had a single word dangling from it, written in old-fashioned calligraphy.

The word was "love".

Text Message

I am going to stop typing now. Chas just texted me the

66

following: "Yo, homeboy. The old girl's fixed and ready to roll.[14] See you tomz. Peace."

I have spent several hours on the computer so I am going out for some fresh air and perhaps a packet of Rich Teas (newly installed as my number-one biscuit since I cut all ties with custard creams). They are an excellent temporary favourite – unspectacular yet dependable until I commit to something permanently.

Working for a Second Chance
Day 2 – Thursday

Tasks completed: Sitting.
What I have learned: Nobody wants to spend time in a poo-brown camper van.

Whilst I was at the corner shop buying Hobnobs[15] last night, I saw Paul Beary, mauling the chocolate bars. He looked absolutely shattered. Apparently he is working like mad on his placement because his uncle is paying him (which I think is kind of against the rules).

Anyway, I could not help but think about how, in

---

14 I presume by "old girl" he meant the camper van and not Miss O'Malley.

15 There were no Rich Teas. For this reason I have relegated them to number four on my list – if I cannot trust them to be in a shop then they will have to face the consequences.

comparison, I am doing nothing. Unless I work hard I am scared I will not be allowed back into school.

Today when Chas and Miss O'Malley turned up, Chas kept the engine running. I guess this was so it did not break down again.

"Am I meant to be able to see the road through the floor?" I said, looking down through a rusty hole as we drove along. This made me feel queasy so I looked up at the sticker on the windscreen instead.

"Chatricia. . ." said Chas, noticing what I was looking at. "A mash-up of our names. A sign of our love. And here's another one. You like my ink? I got it in Vegas."

He rolled up the sleeve of his "Born to Rap" hoody as we stopped at the lights. Tattooed to his puny bicep was a picture of Miss O'Malley's face. Seriously – her *face*, with the words "Our love is for ever, our hearts beat as one" underneath.[16]

I gulped. "Oh, that is. . ." – *Do not say revolting* – ". . .*unique*. Is it . . . *permanent*?"

"Sure is, buddy," said Chas. "Just like my love for the P-Machine." He tensed his arm and her tattooed face moved up and down as though she was swallowing something unpleasant.

I knew how she felt.

---

16 Unfortunately, the tattooist must not have been very good. Although the hair was fairly accurate, her eyes had no pupils and there was a fair amount of shading under her chin that made her look like she had a beard.

From the back, Miss O'Malley patted my shoulder with her huge paw. "Chas wanted me to get his face done on my buttock but I said no."

There was a very awkward pause.

"So," I said, "I was wondering what my job will be."

Today's Work

"OK," said Chas, "we're gonna find some little dudes with issues. And you're here to show 'em that no matter how bad their problems are, they can come through the other side, just like you did."

"Did I?" I said. "Because it was only after you finished counselling me that all my *real* problems started."

"Nah," said Chas. "You're way better than you used to be. You'll be freaking awesome."

Miss O'Malley clapped. "Right you are, husband. The Moorfields Estate won't know what's hit it."

My stomach lurched. "The Moorfields Estate? Why are we going there? It's the roughest place in Preston."

Chas looked confused. "But that's where the gangs and the crime and the kids with issues are."

"But what if one of the gangs . . . *gangs up* on me?" I said.

"Chillax, bro," said Chas. "You're with MC Rhyme Ninja. I

grew up on the streets."

"You were homeless?"

"Figure of speech, man. I mean I dig these people. You're safe with me."

We pulled up outside a row of shops, one of which was boarded up. The bus stop over the road had been smashed in.

Chas shook his head. "Welcome to Moorfields – Preston's forgotten ghetto. The homeys round here need help but no one cares – 'cept us."

"What are we going to do?" I said, looking around at the deserted streets.

Chas said mysteriously, "If you drive it, they will come."

They did not come.

We sat there for three hours. Every time anyone came along, Chas bounced excitedly in his seat and said, "Get ready. . ." but they always just walked straight past.

Miss O'Malley was in the back watching *Pimp My Crib* (an American show where they do up people's houses when they are out) on her laptop.[17]

The only person who we got close to speaking to was a weird-looking kid who was trying to set fire to the timetable in the smashed-in bus stop. He was short and skinny and had a head shaped like a light bulb. When Chas opened the door to

_____

17 Miss O'Malley's laptop keys are massive, by the way – it is more like a garden patio than a keyboard.

call to him, he ran off.

Eventually, we gave up and drove home in silence.

Even if I cannot learn anything from working with Chas, it is important that I work hard in other areas. I have to show that I am taking this seriously and trying to figure out where I went wrong. I must continue my story.

The Medieval Festival Continued

I did not like the way Lucy was holding the "love" pendant whilst talking about my brother. She was not still in love with him, was she?

Bacon sandwich or not, the guy is an ape. When he goes out to nightclubs (underage, of course) he smothers his face in a special moisturizer called Skin Shimmer, which has thousands of tiny flakes of silver in it.

As Lucy's best friend I had to say something. "Erm. I know this is a *historical* festival but . . . maybe you should be thinking about the *future*, not the *past.*"

Like how we are going to spend the next twenty years going on friendship dates and talking about what a swine my brother is.

Lucy hurriedly dropped the charm. "Of course. What came over me?"

Suddenly there was an announcement over the tannoy,

saying the battle re-enactment was about to start.

We followed a stream of people who were walking towards the battle arena. Actually, "battle arena" makes it seem grander than it was. Really it was just a roped-off area of grass with a hump on one side. A group of men were gathered at either end. In my opinion, it would have been a far more convincing ancient battle site if it had not been right next to a public toilet.

Because we were at the halfway point, we had a good view of both armies. On top of the hump, about thirty men in medieval warrior garb were standing around chatting. One, who I guessed was William the Conqueror himself, was sitting on a white horse and wearing a gold crown. At the other end of the arena was a similar group. One of them emerged from behind a tree wiping his hands on his tights. He had clearly been enjoying a medieval toilet break.

Pre-battle Entertainment

A jester was entertaining the crowd. He bounced past us on a pogo stick whilst juggling fire clubs. "Oooh, he's good," said Lucy.

"He looks like a crusty punk to me," I said.

I am not a big fan of crusty punks. You know the

type: all piercings and green hair and mangy dogs on strings, usually found sitting about on benches or arguing with the police.

As he bounced past us, he caught all three of his fire clubs with a flourish, put them out on his (pierced) tongue, flipped off the pogo stick and caught it. Then he bowed in front of us and flicked out his hand. A small bunch of flowers appeared from up his sleeve. He handed them to Lucy, winked and bounced off again.

Lucy's face turned red and she clutched the flowers to her chest.

"I have got wet wipes," I said. "If you want to give the flowers a clean. He looked a bit . . . *scummy*."

"Well, I think he's good-looking," said Lucy, suddenly sounding offended. "He looks . . . *dangerous*."

"Lucy! He probably has not had a bath since about 2003. The most dangerous thing about him would be the risk of catching fleas."

Let Battle Commence!

"The year is 1066," came a voice over the speakers, and the soldiers picked up their weapons. "The place is Hastings in southern England. The Norman army, led by King William, have sailed from France and found high ground from which to attack the Anglo-Saxons, who have been marching for several days."

Both armies cheered and waved their swords and shields in the air.

Lucy squeezed my arm tightly and pointed towards the Anglo-Saxons. "Oh no, what's Dad doing?"

Whilst the other Anglo-Saxon soldiers shook their weapons and shouted "Hooray", Dave was stalking up and down in front of them, looking menacing. One of his fellow soldiers patted him on the arm to calm him down. Dave shook him off and he backed away.

"Let battle commence!" said the voice on the tannoy.

The three hundred or so spectators cheered as the Anglo-Saxons charged towards the Normans. When the Anglo-Saxons got close, the Normans broke out of their wall of shields and engaged them in very slow, deliberate sword fights, some of which were right in front of us. After a few clinks and chinks, one of the soldiers would pretend to thrust his sword into the other one's chest or neck. The loser would then drop to the ground with an agonized, over dramatic howl. Occasionally an arrow with a sponge tip would hit someone, who would then stagger around before collapsing. It was altogether fairly entertaining.

Until it started to go wrong.

Lucy's Dad Goes Nuts

After five minutes of delightful violence, the majority of Anglo-Saxons had been killed. Well, I say killed. Of course they were still alive. Most were rolling around on the grass moaning preposterously. A couple were having a nap.

Lucy's dad and King Harold were the only two who remained alive. They were about ten yards from us. Dave was kneeling over the king, who was lying on the grass holding an arrow to his eye and yelling unconvincingly, "Ow! They got me right in me peeper!"

"Don't go, Your Majesty," cried Dave King, his voice cracking as he clasped Harold's hand. "We can still win this!"

Seemingly disagreeing with Dave on this point, King Harold promptly died.

Dave's head dropped.

"Uh-oh," said Lucy, nervously biting her fingernails. "This doesn't look good."

"And so," said the announcer, "the Normans were victorious. The surviving Anglo-Saxon soldiers surrendered to their new king: William the Conqueror."

All across the battleground, the Normans cheered. One of them joyfully held Dave's arms behind his back to take him prisoner.

"He won't like that," mumbled Lucy.

She was correct. He *really* did not like it.

Dave suddenly leapt up like a salmon, flinging the Norman over on to his backside. "I will never be your slave!"

The crowd said, "Ooh!" A couple of them even chuckled. They must have thought it was part of the show.

"Steady on," hissed the Norman, just loud enough for us to hear, as he climbed to his feet. "Did you read the plan? Any Anglo-Saxons left alive must surrender."

"Never!" roared Dave. He pulled his sword from his belt and swiped it through the air, barely missing the top of his opponent's head.

The Norman dived on to the ground. "Stop! Stop, you maniac!" he cried, rolling desperately out of the way as Dave King thrust his sword down into the earth. He scrambled away, with Dave in hot pursuit, then dived into the public toilets and slammed the door behind him. Uncertain chatter spread through the crowd. Next to us, a child hid his face in his mother's skirt.

Dave, now empty-handed, spun round to face the other Normans. "Who else wants some then?"

The soldiers closest to him started to edge backwards, including some of the corpses from the battle.

I looked at Lucy. She had turned white.

The announcer's voice sounded nervous. "Er ... although there was some resistance ... this was ... swiftly crushed by the conquering forces."

One of the archers standing next to William the Conqueror shot an arrow, which clunked as it hit Dave on the shoulder.

I breathed a sigh of relief. "Well, at least that is over."

You see, even as a casual observer of this battle re-enactment, I knew that when hit by an arrow, it was the done thing to lie down on the floor and play dead.

But not Dave.

He slowly turned towards the archer, his eyes burning. Then, still staring, he reached down, picked up the arrow and snapped it in half. "Your arrows cannot hurt me."

"But you're meant to lie down," whined the archer.

"I lie down for no man," snarled Dave.

The archer became exasperated. "But you're *dead*."

"No," growled Dave. "*You're* dead."

Another "Ooh!" came from the crowd.

Changing History

I learned about the Battle of Hastings at primary school. From what I can recall, none of these things happened:

1. A crazed Anglo-Saxon soldier did not produce a smoke bomb from his undies and hurl it at William the Conqueror and two of his archers. I do not think that smoke bombs existed in 1066. In fact, I am not sure that undies did either.
2. The same lone soldier did not make a kamikaze charge up the hill, before performing what wrestlers refer to as a "double clothes line" on the king's two bodyguards, simultaneously knocking both of them to the floor.
3. William the Conqueror's horse did not gallop away from the battle site in mortal fear, crashing through a hot-dog stand.
4. King William was not knocked off said horse when it ran underneath a set of football posts and his chest smacked into the crossbar.
5. His horse did not then hurtle off in the general direction of Sainsbury's.
6. The lone Anglo-Saxon soldier did not stand on top of the hill, yelling: "Crawl off back to France, you wimps!"
7. A commentator did not say a very rude word over a tannoy system.

Aftermath

The crowd were silent. Lucy's arm felt limp, like the tentacle of a wounded octopus.

Then something extraordinary happened.

Someone behind me began to clap. There was a short pause before another person joined in. Then another and another. Gradually the applause spread, building in speed and volume until a great wave of noise surged through the spectators and they began chanting "Eng-er-land!"

Up on the hill, Dave King slowly turned to the crowd as they swept on to the battlefield towards him. In moments, they had hoisted him on to their shoulders and were parading him around like a hero.

But he did not look triumphant. His eyes searched the crowd until they met Lucy's. What was that look on his face? Was he . . . lost? Confused? Perhaps even *scared*?

I turned to Lucy but she had disappeared.

Even Worse

I unsuccessfully searched everywhere for Lucy and she did not answer any of my eighteen calls. At the missing-children's tent I told the man I was looking for a beautiful sixteen-year-old girl. He said, "Aren't we all," and turned away.

I decided to wait by her dad's Land Rover.

But then the situation deteriorated.

A small knot of people was gathered by the gates, surrounding somebody who was talking to them from on top of a wooden box. Some of them were filming on their mobile phones. One or two of them were turning away, seemingly in disgust.

The speaker had her back to me, but as I got closer I recognized her. And then, just as I was about to flee, she turned round and saw me.

"Oh no," I said.

My mother grinned and waved. The group of people in front of her parted slightly so they could turn to face me. Unfortunately, this meant that I could see exactly what she was wearing.

Or, more precisely, what she was *not* wearing.

My mother had no top on and had painted her body bright blue. Fortunately, she had covered her *things*. *Un*fortunately, she had covered them with two rosettes, each with a picture of my face on.

"Here he is!" she exclaimed. "Preston's proudest nudist!"

Twenty mobile phones were pointed at me. I forced my way past them. "What on Earth are you doing?" I said, pulling her down.

"Protesting for your right to be naked, of course."

I put my head in my hands.

"This is a family event," said one of the stewards from the Medieval Festival, pushing her way towards Mum. "Get dressed and go home."

Mum was holding a T-shirt. I shoved it over her head to cover her and dragged her away.

The steward escorted us right to the bus stop so I was unable to wait for Lucy in the car park. It was only when we got there that I noticed what was on Mum's T-shirt. It was a picture of my face behind bars with the words "Jailed because I love to be nude" on it.

"Do you have to wear that?"

"Not at all," said Mum, pulling it up over her head. A couple of lads in the bus queue made some crude comments that I would rather not repeat.

I yanked the T-shirt down again. "That is not what I meant. Where did you get it?"

"Your brother made it for me on the computer last night, after you'd gone to bed."

"Ste? Why?"

"Because he *cares* for you, Michael."

I snorted.

"Don't be like that, Michael. He's always been a lovely boy. And now he's become even better. We both see what a terrible injustice you suffered on the beach. It's not fair that you should get arrested for doing what you want to do."

"But I do not want to do it. Please understand that."

Mum took a deep breath. "Very well. I respect your wishes. You are not a nudist..."

"Thank you."

"...on the outside at least," she continued. "But I won't give up your fight."

I was about to ask her how it was possible to be a nudist *on the inside* when the bus arrived. As I walked to a seat, leaving Mum to pay, I got a text message from Lucy:

Sorry I went. Hope u get home ok. L.

And that was that. No kiss or anything. Well, at least she had not been cooked on the hog roast or attacked by one of the peregrine falcons. I felt terrible for her – she must have been mortified after her dad's performance. As Mum tried to convince the bus driver to have a "Justice for Nudists" poster in his window, I replied:

Lucy. As your best friend I can offer the following services: a. holding hands, b. shoulder to cry on, c. friendship hugs. Please text the letter you would like me to provide. AMLAT. Michael.

I received no reply. The Lucy-ometer was now teetering at the very bottom of the green zone.

Home

When we arrived home, there was a white BMW 3 Series parked on the driveway. It had blacked-out windows, a soft top and alloys you could see your face in.

"Steven's new car looks nice," said Mum. "He must have bought it with the insurance cheque from the one you crushed."

Inside the kitchen, Ste was sitting with Paul Beary, who had his back to me and was hunched over Ste's iPad. The huge box was on the floor.

"How did your date go?" said Ste.

"Fine," I said. I was still fairly sure I did not like him. "Nice car."

"Thanks," he said. "I went on eBay and the person selling it had accidentally listed it as a BWM. Not a BMW but a *B-W-M*! They'd made a spelling mistake. Nobody else had even looked at it cos it didn't come up on their searches. Totally incredible. I got it for a thousand quid. It's worth fifteen times that at least. I mean, I'd prefer it in black but you can't have everything, right?"

Typical Ste. Always coming up smelling of roses.

He smiled. "You know what I think. This is karma. The universe is saying, 'Well done, Ste, for helping those monkeys. Here. Have an awesome car. Now go and do some more good stuff and maybe we'll give you some money for a respray.' And that's why I'm helping Paul here."

The Woes of Paul Beary

At the sound of his name, Paul turned round. His eyes were swollen, like two great big red onions, and there was snot pouring out of his nose.

"Are you ... OK?" I said. I had not seen him this depressed since they cancelled his favourite TV show.[18]

Paul motioned to the enormous box on the floor so I opened it. Inside was a pink suitcase. He nodded for me to open that as well. As soon as I undid the clasps I gagged. The suitcase contained a mouldy, shrivelled kebab that looked and smelled at least a week old.

I remembered our conversation in the police van. "Is this from Chantelle?"

Paul's chins wobbled. "She dumped me!" He took a crumpled piece of paper out of his pocket. On it were written three words, the ink smudged with tears: "*La Fin*. Chantelle."

---

18 This was a late-night show called *Bikini Trampoline* and it was all about. . . Well, I think the title pretty much sums it up.

"It's from Chantelle," blubbed Paul. "It means 'the end' in French."

I could not have guessed that on my own.

"She must think I'm disgusting," he said, farting sadly.

"I do not wish to be unsympathetic here," I said, "but you *did* put a flipping kebab in her suitcase."

Paul looked at Ste with his big soppy eyes. "Do you think the universe is punishing me for all the bad things I've done? Taking photos of Lucy? Being such a ladies' man? Maybe I deserve this."

"Possibly," said Ste, tapping his iPad, "but we'll win her back."

"How?" I said. "I do not know many girls who like finding mouldy fast food in their luggage."

"I knew it!" said Paul angrily to himself. "I should've bought her those earrings. I just wanted her to remember me..."

Being a good friend, I did not mention that she would be very unlikely to forget him – not with all her clothes stinking like a greasy takeaway.

Ste had opened Chantelle's Facebook page. "The Steverlizer knows a thing or two about the ladies from when he was a bad person. May I say, Paul, she *is* very beautiful."

"Thank you."

"She's rejected Paul as a friend. . ." said Ste, clicking back to his own home page.

Ste's Facebook ID was simply "The Steverlizer". His profile picture was him on a white sandy beach with a green drink in his hand and a black-and-white monkey on his shoulder. He appeared to be reaching up to feed the monkey.

Hang on! I thought. Something was not quite right about the photo.

I squinted at it, but before I could get a better look, Ste scrolled down away from it. "I'm sending her a friend request to see if I can sweet-talk her into taking him back. There. Done." He logged out. "Let's see if she takes the bait."

"You're the best," said Paul, wiping his eyes. "What should I do next? Bombard her house with flowers and call her mobile every ten minutes, twenty-four hours a day?"

Ste shook his head wisely. "We need to show her what she's missing out on. Have fun. Meet some chicks. I'll tell her all about it."

"Will she not get mad and never want to see him again?" I said.

"Nope," said Ste. "She'll get jealous and go crazy for him. Oldest trick in the book."

"But I don't want any other girls," said Paul.

"You're not going to *do* anything. You're just going to *look* like you are."

"If you're sure. . ." said Paul.

"Mike can help," said Ste. "Couple of handsome chaps like you should have no problems."

I half smiled. The last time any girls paid me attention was that time when I got my head stuck in the railings at school. And that was only to cover my face in make-up, then take photos.

"I'll start right away," said Paul, logging on to his account.

"This all sounds interesting," said Mum, suddenly appearing at my shoulder. "I think I'd like one of these Facebooks."

"I can set you up if you like," Ste said

"Hey!" said Paul. "Look at this link someone just sent me."

My eyes opened wide and I felt the blood drain away from my face.

Reflecting

I am going to stop right there. I do not feel like I could continue just now – I am way too tired to face up to what happened in the kitchen when I looked at the iPad.

However, at least I am getting somewhere with my story, which is more than I can say about my time with Chas. Perhaps tomorrow we will do something worthwhile, but I am not holding my breath.

Working for a Second Chance
Day 3 – Friday

Tasks completed: Doing nothing again.
What I learned: Whenever you try to help people, they always think you want to sell them something.

This morning we parked in the same place as yesterday and waited for about an hour. In this time Miss O'Malley watched two and a half episodes of *Pimp My Crib* on her laptop.

"Y'see, Michael," she said, "I'm trying to get decorating ideas for the clinic so we can make it more attractive."

The only way to make this heap of junk more attractive would be to smash it to pieces with a large sledgehammer, I thought.

"Check," said Chas. "We need an urban vibe so . . . HEY! HEY! YO!"

He shoved his arm across me to slap the passenger-side window.[19] On the other side of the road, the weird-looking kid from yesterday was setting fire to a bin.

"Yo," called Chas. "Wanna talk about your issues?"

The boy stayed put, eyeing Chas up and nervously flicking his cigarette lighter. His hair was blond and straggly, like cress grown in a dark room. Chas hopped out to talk

---

19 Unfortunately, he was wearing a basketball vest so I got a faceful of the most incredibly hairy armpit I have ever seen (or, for that matter, smelled). It was gross – like he had a wet dog in a headlock.

to him. We could hear their conversation through the open window:

Boy: My right foot's a six but my left's a seven.
Chas: Say what?
Boy: Are they real or fake?
Chas: Er. . .
Boy: The shoes.
Chas: [*Opens and closes mouth repeatedly.*] Shoes. Which shoes?
Boy: Dunno. You're the one selling them.
[*Three-second pause.*]
Chas: No. Not *shoes. I*ssues.
Boy: You're *not* selling shoes?
Chas: Why would I—
Boy: There's a bloke who comes round in a van selling jeans. Just thought—
Chas: No. *I*-ssues. Like how comes you ain't in school?
Boy: Waste of time.
[*Boy walks off flicking cigarette lighter.*]

Chas returned to the camper and rubbed his eyes. "I could tell he . . . *needed help.* It was written all over his soul."

I decided not to make a lame joke about the soles of his shoes.

"I don't get it," said Chas. "I thought they'd be queuing up round the block for help."

I took a deep breath. "Without wishing to be negative, are you surprised? I mean, nobody knows why we are here. We look like a family having a really bad holiday."

"That's it!" said Chas. "You're right. Let's roll."

After we had shot away down the street (well, after Miss O'Malley and I had given the motorhome a push-start), Chas dropped me at my house and said he had things to do.

I feel better for having said what I did to Chas. I could tell he really wanted to help that strange boy. Even if the boy did not wish to be helped, I guess he deserved the chance to try.

Awful Publicity

Back in the kitchen, the link had taken Paul to the Evening News website.

"You're famous, bro," grinned Ste.

I had forgotten all about the reporter outside the police station the day before. My hands trembled as I took the iPad off Paul and began to read.

I have just searched online for the article, which is sadly still in the archive section of the newspaper's website:

The Law's an Ass!

Preston lad flashes at bobby and donkey
By Imelda Snook

Police today appealed for calm after arresting a teenager for stripping naked on Blackpool beach. The young naturist, Michael Swarbrick from Preston, stole a donkey before frolicking naked in front of it, in what one onlooker described as "a bizarre satanic ritual".

Police released the young exhibitionist with a formal warning. But only after his forty-seven-year-old mother, herself an infamous nudist, stripped off during his police interview – an act that young Michael gleefully described as "the most terrific thing I have ever seen".

"This is not behaviour we encourage in Blackpool," said the arresting officer. "All other local nudists must remember that this is a family resort and that they should remain clothed at all times."

Remorseless

Outside the police station, Michael was unrepentant about his crime. "I'm proud of my peachy bottom and

I love people looking at it," declared the teenager, breathlessly fumbling for his inhaler.

Describing himself as "the chosen one", Swarbrick was only unsure of one aspect of his behaviour, exclaiming: "I don't know who I enjoy flashing at most – donkeys or people."

Shadowy

The fourteen-year-old is rumoured to be the ringleader of an underground network of even younger nudists. One police source described him as a "potentially dangerous figure" in the shadowy world of teenage naturism.

Indeed, even on the steps of the police station, he and his mother – who confessed to "loving the wind on her bust" – brazenly demanded that others should follow them in their twisted enterprise. "Join us. Strip off. Live your life. Be nude" is the slogan that the Swarbricks have adopted for their campaign of terror.

Sales of thick curtains and window shutters are expected to soar across Lancashire as petrified residents attempt to shield themselves from a predicted wave of copycat offences. Donkey owners in Blackpool may request panic alarms to link them directly to the town's police stations.

The story was accompanied by a picture of me from behind as I climbed into Dad's car. My jeans had slipped down at the back to reveal what some people call a "builder's bottom".

There was a caption underneath that read: "Full-moon loon: Swarbrick defiantly flashes his generous buttocks as he is released from custody".[20]

"It is all lies," I said, my eyes throbbing.

"You're right," said Mum.

"What?" I said. Was she actually on my side?

"Yes," said Mum. "It says I'm forty-seven. The cheek of it. I'm only forty-three."

I shoved the iPad across the table.

"Hey, Mike," said Paul. "This'll be in tonight's paper. Do you think you'll make page three?"

"The page-three nude," said Dad, wearily, as he came into the room.

"For the millionth time," I said, "I am not a nudist."

"I understand. . ." said Mum, crossing her arms.

"Thank you."

". . .you've been brainwashed into thinking it's wrong."

"No."

---

20 I swear my bottom is not as big as the photo makes out. Something must have been done to the picture. They have made it look like I am smuggling a pair of beach balls down the back of my trousers.

"...but you can still help others. People will see this and think, *Yes! Anything is possible!* They'll be stripping off in your honour left, right and centre."

I groaned.

Ste placed his hand on mine. "Just think of all of the people you'll be helping."

"I am going upstairs now," I said, leaving the table. Mum and Ste both tried to call me back but I needed to be on my own.

I was becoming famous.

School

At school the next day I was expecting a barrage of abuse and humiliation. As a result, I took emergency action. I deliberately made myself five minutes late so as to avoid everyone in the playground. This might not seem like a big deal but I do not like to be late at all. In three and a half years, I have only ever had one late mark.[21]

When I arrived for school, Ste's BMW was parked in the staff car park. Yes, the *staff car park*. He had said

---

21 Year 7 – when my idiot brother and his mates gave me such a vicious wedgie that my undies were reduced to rags. Paul Beary lent me his PE shorts but they were about eighteen sizes too big and full of Monster Munch crumbs, which itched like crazy.

that he was coming into school to re-enrol in sixth form (of course they had kept his place open for him, even though he had been off for ages) and to "organize some monkey stuff".

Amazingly, he had actually offered me a lift (after bringing me another bacon butty for breakfast). The old Ste would never have let me inside his car. Last year Mum insisted that he should start giving me a lift to school every day in his Golf. She backed down when he bought a roof rack to tie me on to.

I was sorely tempted by the opportunity but I had to turn him down. People would be bound to stare at a car like that and I could not risk more publicity.

Although I was late into registration, my form tutor Miss Skinner's wonky eyes were pointing off in two different directions so I was able to sneak in unseen.

"Has anyone mentioned the newspaper article, Paul?" I whispered, slipping into my seat.

Paul shoved two Toffos into his mouth at once. "Nope. Most people don't even read the papers, and anyway. . . *Holy crud!*"

His mouth fell open and a string of brown drool from the toffee dribbled down on to the desk. He did not notice because he was staring straight ahead.

I very slowly turned to follow his eyes.

More Awful Publicity

On the interactive whiteboard screen was a photograph of me, naked at the beach, my bare bottom on show. Underneath it was written: "'Join me! Be nude! Feel alive!' – *Michael Swarbrick*."

Paul's face was frozen into a pained smile. "I didn't know what Ste was going to use the photo for, honest. If I had—"

Paul was interrupted as the rest of my form noticed the photo.

Have you ever seen penguin feeding time at a zoo? They start insanely honking and squawking and flapping about. That is pretty much exactly what happened next.

People screeched uncontrollably. Hands ruffled my hair. Laughing faces were shoved in front of mine.

Miss Skinner desperately hammered at the keyboard, her crazy eyes spinning around all over the place, but the screen was frozen.

I scrambled out into the corridor but things just got worse. As I staggered along I saw that the whiteboard in the next room was showing the same picture. And the next. And the next. The whole network had been overridden. In each room I could see pupils going crazy and teachers frantically attempting to get rid of the photo.

I ran.

What had Ste done?

The Aftermath

The next few minutes are a haze. I had two main concerns:

    a. I was desperate to escape. However:
    b. I do not agree with playing truant so did not wish
       to leave school grounds under any circumstances.

As a result, I ended up running in confused circles round the playground, trying to find a hiding place but not wishing to break school rules.

In the end the office staff felt sorry for me and brought me inside. I was all light-headed and dizzy, like that time when my brother sat on my head throughout the film *The Wind in the Willows*, savagely and repeatedly guffing.

My face was so pale that the school called Mum, who arrived almost straight away. She swooped in and hugged me tightly. "Well done," she whispered into my ear before turning to Mr Whittle, the head teacher. "And as for *you!*"

Mr Whittle had just come out of his office and had not yet had the chance to tell me off. He opened his mouth to speak but Mum interrupted him. "I hope you are happy with yourself. *This* is what happens when you force children to wear a uniform, when you shove them into their neat little straitjackets against their will."

My throat felt dry. "But Mum..."

"Quiet, dumpling. You're in shock," said Mum. She narrowed her eyes at Mr Whittle. "This poor, delicate boy is torn apart inside. He wants to be nude but *your rules* tell him he's wrong..."

"I really do not," I said, muffled by her jumper.

"See. He's in denial," said Mum.

"Only because it is not true," I said.

Mr Whittle cleared his throat. "All evidence points to—"

Mum clutched me into her chest. "But he will be a symbol for people like him who want to be nude. And *that's* why I'm proud of him."

Mum made a *see-what-you've-done-now* face to Mr Whittle and bundled me back towards the car.

That Evening

As soon as I got home, I went straight to my bedroom and thought about Ste. Of course he would pull a stunt like this one with the whiteboards. Ever since he stepped off the plane, he had been waiting for his chance to humiliate me. And I had been stupid enough to think that he might have changed.

Later on, I heard the expensive roar of a finely tuned car engine outside. A few moments later, Ste came into my room. "How's it going, buddy?"

I glared at his smarmy, arrogant face. "How do you think? I now have the most famous buttocks in Preston."

Ste nodded. "I live to give."

"Why did you do it?"

"To get your message out there," he said, confused. "I had to pull in serious favours from the chicks on the IT desk and Paul had to give me one of his photos but—"

"You have ruined my life."

Ste's mouth fell open. "But . . . I thought you wanted people to know you're a nudist, and to help others become nudists and—"

"Why on Earth would I want that?"

"That's what Mum told me," Ste said, his bottom lip beginning to wobble. "I just . . . wanted to help you. It breaks my heart that I've upset in the past. All I want is – *sniff* – to make you – *sniff* – happy again."

He took several rasping breaths and wiped his eyes. Was he . . . *weeping*?[22] "Mike. I was a bad person."

---

22 The only previous time I had seen him cry was when I accidentally spilled tomato soup down his favourite white jeans just before a date with one of his many girlfriends. As punishment, he poured two pints of milk on to my bed so that, for six months afterwards, my mattress stank like an old yoghurt.

"*Was. . .?*"

"I thought this would . . . make you like me," he said, his voice faltering. "I don't want us to be brothers."

"Me neither," I said.

"I want us to be best friends."

"Oh."

He composed himself. "I'm sorry for the whiteboards. I should have asked you first."

He hugged me again. Before this week, the closest he had ever come to hugging me was demonstrating illegal wrestling moves.

I kept my body rigid until he released me. "I love you, buddy," he said.

I did not know how to respond to this. I mean, there was no way I could forgive him so easily for everything he had ever done to me, but still, he seemed very convincing. And over the next few days, he would become more and more helpful.

Isolation

The next morning, Ste brought me scrambled eggs on toast in bed. Whilst I was still asleep he had ironed my shirt and polished my shoes. Then he drove me to school in his car *and* let me choose the radio station. At school, he even went to Mr Whittle's office to convince him that the whiteboards had been his fault. Unfortunately, Mr Whittle did not believe him and just thought he was trying to stick up for me. Like all of the staff at school, Mr Whittle believes Ste is incapable of wrongdoing.

I thanked him anyway. OK, he was not successful, but still – I had to accept that this was a *very* nice thing to do. Maybe Ste *had* changed. Before going off to get ready for some "monkey stuff", he gave me five quid so I could buy something nice for dinner.

In fact, for the first time ever, my day went rapidly downhill *after* I stopped spending time with Ste. As soon as I got to registration, Miss Skinner gave me a message from Mr Whittle sending me to the Isolation Suite.[23] This is where people are sent when they are too disruptive to stay in class. It is a classroom with about ten single desks around the outside, facing the wall. As soon as you walk in you can smell the sour stench of villainy and failure. I was told to wait there for Mr Whittle.

The only other pupil in there was a girl in my year called Kelly, who is missing a front tooth and has her hair pulled back so far she is barely able to blink. At this particular moment, she was squirting spit on to the

---

23 She said she could not bear to look at me after what I "had done". Ironically, because of her wonky eyes, this meant that she actually *did* look straight at me.

carpet through the gap in her teeth.

"All right, nudist?" she said.

Greeted by a girl who spits indoors. Another new low.

A few minutes later, Mr Whittle walked briskly into the room. At this point, I did not know him very well, except that he is a sweaty, bald man who speaks quickly and abruptly, like someone who has a lot to say and no time to say it. He seemed angry that Mum had got the better of him the day before. Our conversation went like this:

Mr Whittle: Right. Interactive whiteboard. Tell me.

Me: I . . . I . . .

Mr Whittle: Wrong answer. Next.

Me: Honestly, sir. It was not me.

Mr Whittle: Nonsense. Mummy not here to protect you now. IT desk unattended. You late. School system overridden. All evidence points at you, Swarbrick. We know about Saturday.

Me: I can explain. That was an acci—

Mr Whittle: I had a dog once. Wall fell on it.

Me: Oh.

Mr Whittle: Died instantly.

Me: Ah.

Mr Whittle: Crushed.

Me: That is. . .

Mr Whittle: Had to scrape it up with a shovel.

Me: . . .

Mr Whittle: Made a bad decision. Stood under an unsafe wall. Woke up dead. You made a bad decision yesterday.

Me: But sir. If I could just exp—

Mr Whittle: Don't try to turn this school nude. Can't have. My students. Stripping off. Willy-nilly. Got me?

Me: But sir. . . Yes, sir.

Mr Whittle: Isolation. Rest of week. Right. Special upper-school assembly. Now. Sports Hall. Follow me. Kelly. No spitting on carpets.

Special Assembly

One whole week in Isolation! This was not fair.

I followed Mr Whittle to the hall. He walks almost as fast as I run, with tiny rapid steps. All the way he kept pointing at people. "You. Mobile away." "You. No gum." "You. Stop laughing at the nudist."

As I struggled to keep up with him, I was thinking that we only have special assemblies at the end of the year or when there is Big Trouble. Was it going to be all about me and how we should not strip off in public?

All the students from Years 10 to 13 were jammed into the Sports Hall. I was made to sit right on the edge of my row, next to one of the PE teachers, presumably so he could rugby-tackle me if I decided to streak. From the Year 11 benches, Lucy gave me a little wave as I sat down.[24]

Eventually Mr Whittle came on to the stage and everyone stopped talking. "Quick notice," he snapped. "Just seen caretaker. Graffiti. Boys' toilets. Drawing of scampering nudist. Underneath, written: 'I love...'" He paused for a moment, looking like he had smelled something disgusting. "'...*Swarbricking.*' We *will* test handwriting. You *will* be caught."

He glared directly at me.

The announcement sparked a wave of sniggering and whispering. A thousand heads all turned towards me, one by one, as the word "Swarbricking" was passed around the room. I wanted to sink through the soles of my shoes.

Swarbricking.

Unbelievable. I had become a word. I imagined the new addition to the dictionary:

---

24 To some people this may have looked like she was swatting a fly but I am convinced it was a wave.

swarbrick:

1. *v.* to cavort naked in public: *He liked to <u>swarbrick</u> merrily through a meadow.* Also: **swarbricked:** *Yesterday I <u>swarbricked</u> all the way home and now I have a rash under my armpits;* **swarbricking:** *She was <u>swarbricking</u> so much that she neglected her cat.*
2. *adj.* naked: *Ooh, he's completely <u>swarbrick</u>. He'll freeze unless he puts some pants on.*
3. *n.* an act of *swarbricking: Let's go for a <u>swarbrick</u>. I'll bring a flask of tea.*

And, presumably:

swarbricker:

n. one who *swarbricks.*

Worse News

Mr Whittle silenced the room with a loud "Right!" Everyone faced the front instantly. "Now. Reason for assembly. Year 13 student. Been away. Steven Swarbrick."

The Steverlizer!

As Ste swaggered out on to the stage everyone whooped and clapped. Some of the girls squealed and wriggled as though they were being electrocuted. Kelly fired out a deafening wolf whistle through the gap in her teeth right into my ear.

Some people might be surprised at this reaction but, basically, there are two kinds of people in our school:

a. The ones who want to *go out* with Ste (i.e, the girls).
b. The ones who want to *be* Ste (i.e, the boys).

Only two people were not cheering. They were me (I may have been sort of ready to accept that Ste had improved a bit, but I was not going to go all *twelve-year-old-girl-at-a-pop-concert* over him) and Lucy, who was pursing her lips and looking up to the ceiling.

Ste raised his arm in the air and everyone fell silent. "Thanks, Brian," he said, clicking his fingers and pointing towards Mr Whittle. Mr Whittle clicked and pointed right back at him. If I had called him Brian he probably would have kicked me.

Ste was holding a remote control in his other hand. With the flick of a switch, the projector screen at the back of the stage turned on. "Don't worry, I'm not going to do what my brother did with the whiteboards yesterday."

I have no idea why anyone would find this funny but everyone in the room creased up. Even Mr Whittle turned red, trying not to laugh.

"I wish you would, Ste!" cried out Kelly as the noise died down. This sparked a whole load of shouts of "Me too! Me too!" from the girls.

Ste gave an *I-know-I'm-beautiful* smile, then he said, "I want to talk to you about something very close to my heart. A couple of weeks ago, I was trekking through the jungle in Thailand..."

The room fell quiet as he told his monkey-nursing story, flicking the remote control to show pictures.

He told us that the monkeys were Spectacled Langurs – small, sinewy black monkeys with white mohicans and white rings like goggles around their eyes. Now, I will accept that the pictures were *very* cute. However, I think that it was a bit OTT how all the girls went "Awwwww" each time he showed one. And as for the response when he showed the picture of Alan sleeping in his underpants... It was like being stuck in a room with five hundred asthmatic geese.

"So anyway," he said, "here's the score. We're gonna raise some serious money and we're gonna get those monkeys back on their feet. Now, who wants to help?"

There was a massive cheer.

"I can't hear you!"

An even louder roar followed.

"So. Boys, get your James Bond tuxedos ready. Girls,

put on your slinkiest dresses."

He paused, the room silent, then his voice slowly built to a crescendo: "Because in a few weeks' time we're gonna rock out at the Funky Monkey Ball: Woodplumpton Village College's first ever super-smart, glitzy-glamorous black-tie party!"

I put my fingers in my ears as the room reached fever pitch. Even Lucy was chatting excitedly to the girl next to her.

Personally I do not understand the excitement about school discos. All that happens is the boys hang around in the toilets all night, eating sweets and having burping competitions, whilst the girls stand in a big circle on the dance floor, shuffling about and pretending to know the words to "Macarena".

Or at least that is what happened at the last disco I went to.[25]

Ste grabbed hold of a rope at the side of the stage that led up to the ceiling. "We're gonna have DJs, arcade games, funfair rides. It's gonna go off! And I'm going to send every penny over there to help monkeys like Alan."

Then, with one almighty yank on the rope, a net opened up above us, sending hundreds of balloons tumbling down. People were patting them around and

---

25 Admittedly that *was* when I was in Year 2 at primary school.

whooping and popping them, and all the time a great chant grew louder and louder until almost everyone (including Mr Whittle) was joining in: "*Ste! Ste! Ste!*"

Huh, I thought. *Trust him to make everything worse with his charity and his balloons and his monkey balls.*

Reasons *Why* This Makes Things Worse

Surely I should have been *happy* that Ste was finally doing something for others. Surely raising money for homeless monkeys is a *good* thing. Surely the world is a better place with a *nice* Ste in it rather than his usual awful self.

Well, of course it is. And yes, I *was* impressed with him for organizing the ball (seriously – how bitter and nasty would I have to be to think otherwise?).

However, as the teachers struggled to gain control over the balloon-bouncing bedlam, I could not help thinking that he was making things worse for me:

1. First of all it made *me* look even more terrible. OK, so maybe that makes me sound selfish. But I have spent my entire life looking pathetic next to Ste. And now, just as everyone thought I was a creepy donkey-flasher, Ste had managed to

become more wonderful.

2. Despite knowing that what he was doing was really kind, I could not stop myself from thinking about all the terrible things he had done to me. Could he possibly have changed overnight?

After Ste's speech, everyone pushed excitedly out of the hall. As the crowd died down, I felt a tap on my shoulder.

Lucy.

She smiled at me like I was a seal pup wearing a neck brace. "I saw you on the whiteboard."

"That was not me," I lied.

"It looked like your bottom."

Lucy King recognized my bottom. Was this good or bad?[26]

"I was worried when you disappeared at the festival," I said.

Lucy bit her lip. "Sorry. Rubbish friend. I was … making the most of my new freedom. How about you?"

"I have been unjustly sent to Isolation," I said.

"Poor you," said Lucy, wrinkling up her nose. A shaft

---

26 **Bad** – I have always thought I have quite a large bottom – for a human anyway. **Good** – maybe she thought it was memorable and perfectly formed, like two satsumas on a plate (although hopefully not bright orange, covered in tiny dents and with a little green growth under each buttock).

of sunlight shone down through the skylight in the roof, straight on to her. Her teeth glistened and her brown hair glowed with a thousand different dancing colours.

"So are you going to the ball?" she said.

The sun went behind a cloud.

"No way!" I said. "I do not like discos. Plus this is Ste – there must be a catch."

I was not ready to tell Lucy about the bacon sandwiches or the lift to school he had given me.

Lucy tutted. "Of course I know *that*! Still, the ball will be *amazing*. I never went to stuff like that when I was swimming. I'll wear my new dress! It's all short and strappy and... Mike... are you OK?"

I shivered. "Yes, I am perfectly short and strappy ... I mean *happy*." I took a deep breath. "You know, I *will* probably go to the disco ... for a couple of minutes at least."

"But you just said you hated discos."

"Did I? Oh..."

"You're not just going not because I'll be wearing a short dress, are you?"

"What? That is nuts!" I laughed like I was completely demented for at least ten seconds longer than was strictly necessary.

Lucy gave me a funny look.

Time to change the subject. "So ... er ... *ahem* ...

what actually happened at the festival?"

Lucy ran her fingers through her hair. I was delighted to notice that she was still wearing the friendship band I had given her. "Oh, Dad was *so* embarrassing. I just *had* to get out of there. I was crying and upset and then –" she suddenly looked happy and secretive at the same time "– I ended up having a *really good time*."

The way she said the last bit made me feel uneasy.

"I checked the bins in case you had been chopped up into minuscule pieces and disposed of like an old cucumber," I said.

"Aww," she said. "We should hang out again."

"Friendship date?" I grinned.

"Hmmmm. . ." Lucy patted my hand. "Let's not call it a *date*, eh?"

I was about to ask why not when a voice called across the Sports Hall. "Hey, Mike!"

Lucy's face dropped.

Unwanted Guest

Ste sauntered over and shook my hand. "Michael. How are you?"

I withdrew my hand and said nothing. Even if he *was* being nice, I could not let Lucy know this. The

112

last thing I wanted was for him to muscle in on our friendship.

"And Lucy," he said, licking his lips. "It's been a while."

The last time Ste had seen her she had just smacked him one in the face.

"I'd better go," said Lucy but, strangely enough, made no effort to leave.

"I know you're still mad at me but. . ."

Ste put his hand on Lucy's shoulder but she shook him off. "Leave me alone, you repulsive toad."

Excellent!

Ste nodded sympathetically. "I deserve that for what the old me did. Can I make it up to you?"

"I'm not going to the ball with you, if that's what you mean," said Lucy.

"That is karma," I grinned.

Ste held his palms up. "I wasn't going to ask. I think that would've been very rude of me. I was just going to say sorry for what I did."

"Well. . ." said Lucy, looking flustered. "Thanks, but I'll probably go with someone else anyway."

"Who?" said Ste and I at the same time.

Lucy looked Ste in the eye and smiled. "My new boyfriend, of course."

No Time Off

As I was typing earlier, I heard the phone ring. Mum called up to me but I wanted to finish the section (plus I am still not speaking to her) so I decided not to answer. However, just after I finished typing that last bit, a note was slid under my bedroom door, which read:

"Mr Whittle rang. Wants you to have a target – thinks you should aim to complete your ten-day placement by next Sat (1 wk tom). Chas is 'well stoked' – you'll have to work this weekend tho. I guessed you'd like to be finished a few days earlier so I said this is fine."

So, bang goes my weekend. Not that I had any plans, but still. . .

I cannot figure out why Mr Whittle is so obsessed about me finishing a week tomorrow. There is no way I am going to ask Mum to explain – that would involve a conversation.

Working for a Second Chance
Day 4 – Saturday

Tasks completed: Witnessing a robbery.

What I learned: Forty-nine-year-olds should not skateboard.

As has been the case every day this week, I ate breakfast in my bedroom today – dry cereal from a variety pack – in order to avoid the rest of my family. Unfortunately, the only box left in my pack was Sugar Puffs. I do not really like Sugar Puffs. They have the same texture as polystyrene and they make your wee smell funny.

Anyway, I was barely halfway through it when the camper van crawled down the road. Early for once! I rushed out to meet it and . . . oh my word. It looked like it had been graffiti-tagged by a three-year-old holding a spray can between his feet. Here is a summary:

1. Picture on the sliding door, which I presume was meant to be Chas but looked more like a cross between Prince Charles and a goat.
2. Speech bubbles coming from Prince Goat's mouth saying: "Being bullied?", "Problems at home?", "Still wet the bed?", etc.
3. On the other side, large green stencilling that read: "Little Dudes' Mobile Counselling Clinic – bust ur issues here."

"What d'you reckon?" said Chas as we drove off.

"It is . . . very colourful," I said. I could have followed this up with "like cat vomit". However, this would not have been fair. At least he was trying.

"Totally rad to see you on a Saturday, dude. And what a freaking awesome idea of your head teacher – work *this* weekend so you can celebrate the end of your placement at the school rave *next* weekend."

Of course!

Although it seems like ages since Ste made his speech about it in the Sports Hall, the Funky Monkey Ball has not actually happened yet; in fact it is next Saturday. Mr Whittle must think that by having it as a target, I will be more likely to work hard on my placement.

How wrong could he be? After everything that has occurred recently, I would honestly rather spend next Saturday night getting paper cuts on my eyeballs. Chas has agreed to work through the weekend just to help me, though, so I decided not to be negative. "Oh . . . great!"

Chas had another surprise in store. Miss O'Malley (who was not with us because there was a *Pimp My Crib* omnibus on Channel 4) had built a small skateboard ramp with her bare hands.[27] It looked really professional. Chas told me that before she became a nurse, Miss O'Malley had trained as a carpenter. I had literally no response to this.

---

27 I know what you are thinking but, no, this is not a spelling mistake. I did not mean to write "bear hands".

When we parked (this time near an adventure playground on the estate), Chas slid the ramp out and pushed it right up to the side of the camper so that "little dudes can skate in, get counselled and skate out again".

He then got his skateboard out. I will repeat here that he is forty-nine years old. "I gotta show 'em I'm cool so they'll trust me," he said.

As today was Saturday, there were a few more people around than during the week. When Chas started pumping rap music out of his stereo, small groups of kids gathered around the adventure playground, watching. Off to the side, the funny-looking boy from the day before was sitting on a bench on his own, watching us intently.

"Well," sniffed Chas, rotating his neck. "Let's give 'em a show."

The Show

What happened next probably lasted about half a second but I will cherish it for ever:

1. Chas took three deep breaths and dropped the skateboard on to the ramp.
2. He jumped up with both feet.
3. Unfortunately, he forgot about the door frame of the camper van, which he smashed his head into.

117

4. This caused him to land right on the corner of the skateboard, which shot out from under him. . .
5. Which launched him seven or eight feet in the air, where. . .
6. He did a full backflip, then landed on the tarmac with a resounding crunch.

Apart from the whirring wheels of his upside-down skateboard, the world seemed frozen in silence. Chas lay crumpled on the ground, his limbs twisted like a broken TV aerial.

I rushed over and helped him to his feet. "Too much freakin' varnish, dude," he said.

I tried not to laugh. I really did.

But this line was just way too much for me and I just began to giggle and then Chas caught my eye and he started laughing too and within moments we were both leaning against the camper van and each other, howling so much that we were crying.

We did not notice the kids from the adventure playground coming over, but soon they were surrounding us, good-naturedly telling Chas that he was the greatest skater of all time and asking if he could do it again so that they could get a film up on YouTube?

Meanwhile, a few of them were showing Chas how it was done, flying down the ramp on BMXs and mini scooters and skateboards, then grinding along the pavement or hopping up on to a bench next to the van.

Chas was delighted that the kids were having fun – offering them skating tips (which I am glad to say they ignored) and very delicately asking them what life on the estate was like.

I was actually impressed with him. I mean, OK, of course he still used words like "mac daddy" and "groovalicious" way too often, but he did not mind the kids making fun of him for it, and somehow he just seemed to click with them. Before long he was giving them casual advice about homework or parents or part-time jobs.

After a while he came over to me. "You were right, broseph – the graffiti and the ramp really pulled the kids in."

"Your lack of co ordination was a bigger draw," I said.

Chas laughed again and said, "You're busting my buns." At this point I realized something – I was happy. For the first time in ages I was just grinning like an idiot for no reason. Life felt good.

Then I noticed a swift movement out of the corner of my eye. It was that strange-looking kid. He ran over, grabbed Chas's skateboard and shot off on it down the street. Chas went to chase him but, being ancient, he was nowhere near fast enough.

Chas came back shaking his head. "That's a kid I'd like to get to know."

"He's a freak," said one of the lads on the ramp. "Got expelled for setting fire to the school."

Chas said nothing. We went off soon after, leaving the ramp there for the kids to mess about on. I am back at home now, finishing off my Sugar Puffs from this morning and carrying on with my work.

Lucy's New Boyfriend

"Boyfriend?!" I squeaked, like a mole being poked with a stick.

The needle on the Lucy-ometer swung down to orange.

Ste smiled. "Great. I'm delighted you've found someone special."

What? The old Ste would have gone nuts.

Lucy seemed surprised by his reaction too. "Oh. Well. Thanks. I guess."

"Who is he?" I said, taking a drag on my inhaler.

"His name's Spyder," said Lucy, still looking at Ste.

"Like the creepy-crawly?" I said.

Lucy pursed her lips. "No. With a 'y', actually."

"And when did you meet this ... *Spyder*?" I said. I felt totally let down. Best friends should tell their best friends when they have a new boyfriend so that their best friend can tell them never to see him again.

Lucy nibbled her fingernail. "At the Medieval

Festival. Just after I ran off. I was really upset and he … cheered me up. He's so *cool* and *different*. Just what I need after all that hassle with swimming and everything…"

Her eyes flicked to Ste as she said this.

"Who or *what* is he?" I said bitterly.

"He's a skateboarder. And a bungee-jump instructor," she continued, counting on her fingers. "Oh, and a juggler."

"The *juggler*?" I cried. She was going out with that fire-swallowing clown from the festival.

"He sounds great," said Ste, putting his hand on Lucy's arm. This time she only half-heartedly nudged him off.

OK, so maybe I should have been a bit happier for her. But come on! Lucy had a *crusty punk boyfriend*, for heaven's sake. She would spend so much time with him at music festivals she would forget about me. Then they would probably get married by a Druid priest and live in a tepee and own scabby dogs and have equally scabby children with rat-tail hairstyles and stupid made-up names like Zebra-Kong or Lemon-Rabbit, and Lucy would end up getting dreadlocks and busking with a tin whistle in town and eating from bins, and frankly the whole thing was so horrible I wanted to cry.

"Well," said Lucy, "the pierced tongue makes kissing fun."

"Urgh. . ." I said, my insides churning, "you do not know where he has been."

"He's been at university since September."

My brain felt like the lid of a pan of potatoes, about to boil over. "Student, eh? What's he studying? How to avoid soap?"

Lucy tutted. "Biochemistry with Genetics."

I had absolutely no idea what that was. "And . . . how old does he think you are?"

Lucy scowled. "Spyder's really cool, *actually*. He says age is just a number."

Or in your case, a number plus about two years, I thought. On this particular day Lucy was exactly sixteen years, two weeks and one day old.[28] This *Spyder* had to be at least eighteen. I found it very unlikely that he would be interested in a sixteen-year-old girl (even Lucy). I therefore concluded that she *must* have lied about her age.

"Well, I hope you will be very happy together," said Ste calmly. Way *too* calmly in fact. Someone should have been talking sense into her. Even if this was Ste.

"He won't be able to come to the ball, though," I said, "School pupils only."

"That's not fair," said Lucy.

---

28 Worked out from information on the Preston Piranhas Swimming Club notice board (Register of Members). On the same document, Dave King had recorded my name as Miguel Swadbridge and my date of birth as 9 September 1925.

Not fair? Not fair is when your best friend ditches you for some lice-ridden hippy.

"Of course he's welcome," smiled Ste. "I just want to help those poor monkeys."

"I hope you have a lot of fun," I said, trying not to sound totally jealous. "Well, I had better go – I have got things to do."

Such as weeping.

Isolation

So I spent the rest of the day in the Isolation Suite, along with mono-toothed Kelly and a procession of the school's most dangerous pupils. Despite the constant blizzard of chewed-up bits of paper being blown at me through Biro tubes and my sadness about Lucy, being in there was not all bad, for the following reasons:

1. Soggy paper excepted, it saved me from any real bullying. For the time being at least.
2. I got to miss cross-country. Through my window I could see Paul Beary staggering along. His weekly sick note must have been rejected by the PE teacher again. This is no surprise because, instead of a normal illness, he always says he

has bubonic plague or a burst intestine (from trying to milk a rhino), etc. Also he cannot resist signing the notes with a "comedy" name – e.g, Dr Hugh Jarse or Dr Mustafa Weewee or Dr Masif Floppy-Boobies.

At home time, I had to stay for an extra ten minutes so I "would not encourage people to strip off in the bus queues". By the time I left, the whole campus was empty apart from the caretaker, who was aggressively scrubbing the front gate.

To my horror I realized he was cleaning a picture of a naked man leaping in the air, drawn in permanent marker. Written around it were the words "Swarbricking is Really Fun!"

I hurried away before the caretaker saw me. Why would someone abuse my name in such a manner? Again.

Little did I know that this was merely the start of an evil global movement.

The Long Way Home

I was so wrapped up in my thoughts, I barely noticed Lucy standing on the pavement. "Hi, Mike. I just wanted to say sorry about before."

"Why?" I said.

"I should've told you about Spyder earlier. Everything's been mad since I quit swimming, though. Do you want to come round to mine?"

"Yes, please," I said, a bit too quickly.

We started walking and I offered my arm to her in the hopes of a link-up. Lucy looked at it as though I had a terrible skin complaint. "Probably best not to link. What with me having a boyfriend."

I pulled my arm away.

"I saw the graffiti," said Lucy. "Poor you."

"Another disaster," I said. "I am sure to get the blame, even though it was n*whaaaarrrrgh*!"

I did not mean to say the last bit. This was an involuntary reaction as Ste's white BMW sped past, swerved off the road and screeched to a halt on the pavement in front of us.

"Fancy a lift?" Ste said, cheerfully removing his sunglasses. Although it was late October, it was sunny enough to have the soft top down.

"You almost killed us," said Lucy, whilst looking admiringly at the car's leather interior.

"Did you do that graffiti?" I said.

Ste put his hand over his mouth. "Michael, I saw it and I am *appalled* that you could think that. You told me you don't want to be a nudist and I respect you for it. In fact, I even refused to help Mum with her latest scheme."

I was about to ask him what this scheme was but Ste caught Lucy looking at him. She blushed and looked away.

Ste brushed his hand through his shaggy hair. "I'm off to the printers to order the ball posters but I would *love* to give you both a lift."

Lucy frowned. "I doubt my boyfriend would be happy."

Ste held up his hands. "He's got nothing to be worried about. Just ... trying to be nice. Well. Enjoy your walk."

He drove off at high speed whilst Lucy watched him disappear round the corner.

After a couple of minutes of silent walking, we came to Lucy's house. Her mum must have been waiting because she rushed out to meet us.

Her face was flushed with excitement. "There's a dishy young man waiting for you in the back garden, Lucy."

"Spyder?" said Lucy. "In the garden? Why didn't you let him in the house?"

"Your father said he looked like a tramp. Thought the cat might catch worms off him."

Lucy rolled her eyes. "How embarrassing."

"Oooh," said Mrs King, "d'you think he could be *the one*?"

Lucy smiled and hurried through the side gate, followed by her mum. No one told me what to do so I tagged along.

Spyder

In the back garden, Lucy and her mum were watching Spyder, who was in the middle of the lawn. Dave's sword from the battle re-enactment was balanced on his chin and he was juggling a garden gnome, a chainsaw (switched on, its sharp teeth spinning round rapidly) and a replica (I hope) hand grenade. I guessed he had got these from the garden shed, which was open.

Dave King looked on angrily through the kitchen window of the house.

Spyder threw everything into the air, sat down and caught them one by one with his bare feet. He then rolled backwards into a headstand and, with a sudden spring of his arms, did a backflip. Bowing low, he produced some flowers from his sleeve and handed them to Mrs King. She giggled and fanned herself with them.

Not bad. Six out of ten. Could have been more but: a. I had seen the trick with the flowers before; and b. I am not impressed by show-offs.

Inside the house, Dave was tearing a dishcloth into strips.

"I'll leave you two lovebirds to it," said Mrs King, skipping back into the house with her flowers.

Without warning, Spyder lunged at Lucy open-mouthed, his tongue piercing flashing in the sun. They engaged in a sloppy kiss that went on way too long.

The needle on the Lucy-ometer plummeted into the red zone.

"A-*hem*," I said.

Spyder and Lucy turned to face me. She wiped her lips. "Sorry, Mike. I thought you'd gone."

"Who's this?" said Spyder. He was wearing a pair of bright green pantaloons that he may well have stolen from backstage at a pantomime, and a long, multicoloured woollen coat.

"He's my ... er ... younger brother," said Lucy quickly. *Younger brother.*

Spyder walked over, reached up to my ear and produced a two-pound coin from it, which he held out in front of me. I was not impressed by this because:

1. The coin was clearly not in my ear.
2. I am not three years old.
3. Judging by his filthy fingernails and *old-rug* smell, the coin was a breeding ground for germs.

"You in sixth form too?" he said.

"Sixth form?" I said, looking over to Lucy, who was suddenly very interested in something on the lawn. So I was right: she *had* lied about her age. I coughed. "Yes. I am in Year 12, whilst *my sister* here is in Year 13."

Lucy mouthed "thanks" to me.

"Cool," said Spyder. "We're having a Halloween party on Friday at my student house. Wanna come? It's gonna be extreme."

"No," said Lucy. "Mike's way too young."

Spyder shrugged. "He's, what, seventeen? Only two years younger than me. Age is just a number, right?"

"I would love to come," I said, not taking my eyes off Lucy.

I do not know why I said this. I am fourteen years old, for heaven's sake. What on Earth would I do at an extreme student house party? Who knows what they would get up to? There would be drinking and loud music and probably towards the end of the night they would sacrifice a goat. In any case, I had not been to a party at someone's house since I was five years old.[29]

However, I knew I *had* to go. Who else would look after Lucy? She was not old enough to be there. Spyder

---

29 Complete disaster – pass the parcel was fixed so the birthday girl won (OK, it was a lame gift – a porcelain ornament of a frolicking kitten. But still – IT WAS IN MY HANDS WHEN THE MUSIC STOPPED!).

suddenly leapt on her again. He looked like he was trying to suck out the entire contents of her body.

"I will let myself out then," I said, not quite loud enough for Lucy to hear me over the slurping.

Lucy's back door is down the side of her house, next to the garden gate. As I walked past, it opened quickly. A hand shot out and roughly dragged me inside.

"OK, Maurice," growled Dave, closing the door silently. "We're safe to talk."

I was reasonably convinced I was about to die.

We were inside the utility room. There were a lot of wet clothes hanging up on an airer next to me. I did not dare to look in case some of Lucy's – you know – *smalls* were dangling there.

"Right," he said, "Lucy's been acting very strangely since she quit swimming: moody, new boyfriend, hanging around with weirdos. No offence."

"None taken," I said. I have noticed that people only ever say "no offence" after they have just said something highly offensive. Also, people only say "none taken" when in fact plenty has been taken.

"I've been down about Lucy quitting on me. I lost it a bit at the Medieval Festival."

"I had not noticed," I said, my eyes firmly pointed towards the floor.

Dave took a deep breath. "But I've calmed down now.

I reckon Lucy's just having a blip. We need to get her swimming again."

"Right," I said. If this meant getting rid of Spyder (and getting out alive), then I was all for it.

"I'm giving you a top-secret mission – keep your eye on Lucy."

"You mean . . . *spy* on her."

Dave looked disgusted. "No! What do you take me for?"

Hmm . . . I am not sure. . . A complete maniac?

He sighed. "No. I just want what's best for Lucy. I want her to swim. I want to be her coach again. It's important to . . . to *her*. Understand?"

I nodded.

"Good. What d'you know about this Sponger?"

My mouth was dry. "Erm. He is a student. And a juggler. Oh. And he has dirty fingernails."

"Dirty fingernails," Dave said, as though I had just mentioned that Spyder kept the head of a murdered dolphin in his rucksack. "Typical. When you lose three fingers like I did, you value the fingernails you've got. Dirty fingernails equals laziness. Laziness gets men killed in a war. I *hate* a man with dirty fingernails."

I subtly checked my own.

"So will you do it?" he said.

"I . . . suppose. . ."

Now, I would like to make something clear. I was not agreeing to spy on Lucy. And I *was* aware that Dave wanted Lucy to go back to swimming, even though she did not like it. However, Dave was sort of right – someone needed to make sure she was safe. In this sense, *keeping my eye on her* was not a bad thing. Plus I wanted very much for him not to kill me.

At that point we heard Spyder and Lucy coming down the path. Dave pretty much carried me through the house, then shoved me out of the front door and told me to leg it.

Home

When I got home, Paul and Ste were chatting in the porch. They both nodded vaguely as I approached but did not stop their conversation.

"But did she *say* anything in her email about *me*?" said Paul.

Ste held up his palms. "Not yet, buddy. Chantelle's only sent one message so far. Just keep the faith. Why don't you and Mikey bag some babes this weekend? Chantelle will be totally jealous when I tell her."

"Huh," said Paul. "Fat chance of meeting any babes when I'm with *him*."

"Fat chance of you meeting any babes full stop," I said.

Paul grinned. "I get loads of female attention. They can't get enough of my sweet booty. Remember when that hot older woman chatted me up in town?"

"*Older?*" I laughed. "Older than the sun you mean – she was about a hundred and twelve."

"Not true! She was super-fit."

"She was on a mobility scooter. And she only came over to tell you that your trousers had split down the back."

"Still counts," smiled Paul. "But back to the point: you."

"Me?"

"Yeah, it was bad enough when girls thought you looked like something out of *Lord of the Rings*. Now you're a nudist as well, my reputation's in tatters. No offence."

"None taken," I said. This time I meant this – it is impossible to be *actually* offended by Paul. In the nicest possible way, he is just a big simple idiot. "Anyway, I cannot see you at the weekend. I am going to a student party."

"Ace – I'll come with you," said Paul, brightening up. "Student girls love me."

"Which student girls are these?" I said.

"Medical students," he said, trying to sound

mysterious. "They find me . . . *interesting*."

"Probably because they think you belong in a jar," I replied.

Ste raised an eyebrow. "Is Lucy going to this party?"

"Yes, as a matter of fact she is," I said, before adding, "With her boyfriend."

"Good for her," said Ste.

I went inside.

Inside the House

In the house, Mum was sitting in front of the computer, working frantically. As soon as she saw me, she minimized her window and bounced over.[30]

"Oh, Michael!" she beamed, flinging her arms around me.

"Getoffgetoff!" I yelled. "Put some clothes on, for pity's sake."

Mum sighed. "Oh, my angel. The police and the school have brainwashed you. But you mark my words, I'll have you *Swarbricking* about in no time."

"Swarbricking?"

---

30 Yes, literally "bounced". She was completely naked, her skin still tinged blue from the day before.

Mum patted me on the head. "Oh, you're so clever, turning your name into a word. The school told me. I've used it on your Facebook page."

A chill descended over my body. "My ... *what*, sorry?"

I do not do social-networking websites because:

a. I have very few friends. I do not need a website to stay in touch with them. A piece of string and a few plastic cups would be sufficient.
b. People post pictures of themselves on these sites. My brother says that when I smile in photos I look like a serial killer, and when I do not smile I look like I am swallowing some sick.

Mum rubbed her hands together. "Steven refused to help me so it took ages but here it is. . ."

She maximized the window on the computer and – *oh my life* – it was horrible. The page was entitled: "Swarbricking: Join us. Be nude. Feel alive, man." There was a picture of me in the nude on the beach and three posts that read:

1. Being nude in public is great fun.
2. Break the law. Strip off now.
3. Don't be shy, Swarbrick yourself silly.

"What is the meaning of this?" I cried. The only positive

was that, as yet, the page had zero friends.

Mum sighed. "I see your torment and I think – *How many poor souls are out there, suffering like this?* It's our responsibility to help them to free themselves. Then maybe you'll be freed as well."

End of the Day

Well, I feel like I have typed enough for now. Despite the fact that I have just been typing about some pretty awful things that happened to me, I guess that today has been pretty successful. In fact, this is the most cheerful I have felt in absolutely ages. I think I may celebrate by putting on my novelty slippers, grabbing a chocolate mousse from the fridge and playing some online Scrabble. Woo-hoo! Saturday night! Let the good times roll.

Working for a Second Chance
Day 5 – Sunday

Tasks completed: Humiliation.
What I learned: People are never grateful.

This morning, Chas swung the camper into the car park by the adventure playground.

"Oh my!" said Miss O'Malley.

"You're busting my coconuts," said Chas.

The skateboard ramp had been completely burned to a crisp. Smoke was rising from it and it was surrounded by a big scorched patch of tarmac.

We went over, Chas's rap music still pumping out. Miss O'Malley nudged the ramp with her foot and a lump of charred wood fell off. "Twenty hours of work up in smoke."

"Chillax," said Chas. "What's done's done. Hey yo! You see anythin'?"

Chas was calling over towards the adventure playground, where the weird-looking kid was leaning against the fence. He screwed up his face. "Nope."

Then, very deliberately, he pulled a lighter out of his pocket and began flicking it and putting his hand through the flame.

I swallowed hard. I really do not like fire at all.

Miss O'Malley said, "Ach, the cheek of him!"

"Cool your beans, momma," said Chas, then told the boy, "Burning stuff ain't cool, bro. I'd left it for your community."

"Didn't do nothing," said the kid. "Anyway, it were rubbish. Too much varnish. Went up like a chip pan."

Chas spoke before Miss O'Malley had the chance. "Dude. I know life must be tough for you to act like this."

The kid ran his hand through his scraggy hair. "Ain't acting like nothing, granddad."

Chas sniffed. "But I got a dude here who's had problems and come out the other side."

I realized he was talking about me.

The kid tossed his head back.

"Uh-huh," said Chas. "This kid's mom was a nudist."

"No need to mention that," I said.

"And so was he."

"Not strictly true."

"And he wets the bed."

"Where did that come from?"

The kid smiled for the first time. I noticed his teeth were all blackened, like overcooked parsnips. "Bed-wetter. Gutted."

"I must categorically state that I *never* did that," I said.

"Shh," whispered Chas. "Roll with it. Sorry, but we gotta make him think other people have worse problems than him."

I suppose I could see the logic of this but it really did not seem fair.

"Michael once wet himself in Year 7," said Miss O'Malley, unhelpfully.

"Nice one, Wetty," said the kid.

Miss O'Malley raised her massive hand to her mouth. "Oops. Sorry. I've just remembered. The *wet* one was that *rotund* boy. Beary."

Lovely – mixed up with Paul Beary.

"Ah yes, Paul Beary," said Miss O'Malley. "I remember. Said

he was half man, half wolf and he was marking his territory." She paused for a moment. "Strange he should choose to mark his territory in his trousers."

"Shame you weren't here earlier," said the kid. "You could've put the fire out with your soggy pants."

"You wanna chat about anything?" said Chas. "S'what we're here for."

"What music have you got on?" he replied.

Chas glanced behind him. The music was still playing – some nonsensical idiot rhyming about "stomping down the ghetto" and wanting to know "where my dogs is at".[31] "Oh that? That's some sick beats I picked up in the States. MC Slap Dat and DJ Crunk Time."

"Rubbish," said the kid, walking off.

"Definite progress," said Chas.

"He burned me ramp," said Miss O'Malley.

"He thinks I wet the bed," I said.

Chas smiled and, despite myself, I smiled too. Looking back now, this was an interesting reaction; I mean, if this had happened a week ago I probably would not have smiled at all. However, seeing how good Chas was with the other kids yesterday kind of makes me trust him more. And I never thought I would say that.

---

31 I would suggest that, if he does not know, he is probably not a responsible dog owner and should only let his dogs off the lead in enclosed spaces.

The rest of the day passed without incident. A couple of the kids from yesterday popped over in the afternoon, and Miss O'Malley promised she would order some wood and come back in a few weeks to help them build a replacement ramp. They were mad about what the weird kid had done but said that they were not surprised – apparently he is "a total psycho".

Things Get Serious

I remained in Isolation for the rest of the week. On Wednesday, Paul was sent there after refusing to do French because it made him "feel sad". He told me that the Halloween party at the weekend (and the possibility of making Chantelle jealous) was the only thing keeping him going. I felt bad for not really wanting him there, even though he disgraces himself at all social functions. (E.g, the Christmas fair back in primary school. Someone – not me – had told him that the statues of Jesus and Mary in the crib were made of chocolate. You can probably guess the rest.)

Meanwhile, two things became school-wide obsessions:

1. **The Funky Monkey Ball** – There were posters

all over the place advertising the fact that tickets would be on sale the next day, and you could not go anywhere without listening to conversations about limos and new dresses and who was snogging who.

2. **The Facebook Page** – I blame Paul for this. He got caught looking at it in ICT. Apparently the whole class was on the same page within seconds. As they were doing a film-making module, many of them subsequently left links to "amusing" animations that they had made of me scampering about in the nude. Of course, this directed more traffic to the site. Within hours it had over two hundred friends.

This was not the end of my problems, though. When I left school on Wednesday, the building was empty, apart from one of the music practice rooms. Walking past the door, I heard some musicians and singers in there. They were playing this old song called "Hey Jude". But, as I stood there and listened, I realized that they had changed the words. Here it is in all its "glory":

Hey Nude, you've lost your pants,
Go do a dance
In front of a donkey-ey-ey,

Remember, to keep your hands to the front,
Or it will cru—unch
Your little willy.[32]

They must have been filming it because within hours a video of their performance was up on the Facebook page, and the number of friends had doubled. I begged Mum to delete the page but she told me she had forgotten the password.

The monster was no longer under her control.

Rescued from Isolation

The next morning, Mr Whittle and Ste came into the Isolation Suite together. Mr Whittle told me that Ste had an idea to help cure me of my "illness". The conversation went as follows:

Mr Whittle: I used to own a dog.
Ste: Was it crushed under a wall, sir?
Mr Whittle: No. Different one. Nightmare. Reminds

---

32 A couple of the kids whose voices have not broken yet sang a very high-pitched harmony over the top, which would have actually sounded quite moving, had it not been a humiliating song about me.

me of young Michael here.

Me: Oh.

Mr Whittle: Used my house as a toilet. Cocked its leg on my wife. Did its business on my pillow.

Me: Yikes.

Mr Whittle: Whilst I was sleeping on it. Imagine waking up face-to-face with *that*.

Ste: Must've been terrible for you, Brian.

Mr Whittle: It was, Steven. Anyway. Got an expert in to toilet-train it. You know. One last chance. Prove it wasn't a complete degenerate. But it failed. I'll spare details. Let's just say I found out the hard way. Had to throw away a perfectly good pair of shoes. Socks as well.

Ste: Poor you.

Mr Whittle: Wife had to scrape out my toenails with a toothpick.

Me: Urgh.

Mr Whittle: Point is. Gave the dog a chance. It didn't take it. So. Straight to the vet. Lethal injection. Back of the neck. Dead. Instantly.

Ste: That's karma. It did bad things. . .

Me: It was a *dog*.

Mr Whittle: Quiet, Swarbrick. Anyway. Steven here's come to toilet-train you.

Me: But sir, I am perfectly able to . . . do *that*.

Mr Whittle: Figure of speech. You help Steven. Do something good for once. Maybe avoid the lethal injection.

Me: The *what*?

Ste: I'm selling tickets to the Funky Monkey Ball today. Thought you could help.

Me: You mean . . . instead of being in Isolation?

Mr Whittle: I'll leave him in your capable hands. And remember. Sometimes the kindest thing for a dog is to put it down.

He spun round and scuttled out.

"Thought I'd get you out," said Ste. "Can't be nice in here."

Kelly the one-toothed wonder gave him a leering grin. "I'll help you any day, Ste."

"Maybe another time," said Ste, giving me a look of theatrical horror. I have to say that this made me laugh. What was happening? Did I . . . *like* him now?

"Erm . . . thanks for helping me."

The words sounded strange coming from my lips towards the person who had spent most of his life tormenting me, but he had changed so much. He had *never* helped me like that before.

Ste patted my shoulder. "No problem. Just trying to be the brother I always should have been."

"I thought the ball was not for a while," I said, as we walked down the corridor. "Why are you selling tickets today?"

"Well," said Ste, "first we need to have the money before we can book the entertainment. Plus homeless monkeys can't wait around. We're going to send all the profits straight out to Thailand so the school can adopt Alan."

Ticket Sales

I followed Ste into the Sports Hall, where he had set up the following:

1. A table and two chairs in front of the stage. On the table was a huge stack of tickets with gold holograms of monkeys on them.
2. Five or six inflatable palm trees on the stage, along with lots of real tropical plants in pots.
3. Professional-looking posters advertising "the greatest night in school history".
4. Chantelle's suitcase for collecting the money.[33]
5. An MP3 docking station, which was playing the

---

33 Ste had got rid of the smell of kebab by spraying it with Dad's Scent of a Beast aftershave. I have to admit that, yes, it did smell like Toilet Duck after all.

soundtrack to *The Jungle Book*.

6. A giant cuddly-toy monkey dangling above the stage. It was in a harness and attached to the same rope Ste had used for the balloons during his assembly.

At that moment the bell rang and Ste led me to the chairs. "Action stations" he said.

Within a few minutes, a queue snaked all the way round the Sports Hall. Mr Whittle trotted up and down it, keeping an eye on me the whole time..

My job was to collect the money and write people's names down on a list, whilst Ste handed out the tickets. The tickets sold fast, even at thirty pounds a pop.

It seemed awfully expensive to me, but the rest of the upper-school seemed to disagree and the suitcase was soon filling up with money. After a while, Paul waddled up, carrying a bowl of fudge tart and custard from the canteen. "Hey guys," he said, shovelling pudding into his mouth. "I'll take two tickets."

"*Two* tickets?" I said.

Paul dropped the spoon into his bowl and sucked some spilled custard off his jumper. "In case Chantelle goes back out with me."

I spoke in my kindest voice. "Is that a good idea? a. She is currently not your girlfriend; and b. Even if she was, she lives in France. How is she going to get here? You cannot exactly give her a backy on your bike."

"Give love a chance," said Ste, ripping out the tickets.

Paul handed me three sweaty ten-pound notes.

"I am sorry, Paul," I said, "tickets are thirty pounds *each*."

"Incorrect." Paul expertly scooped up every last droplet of custard from the bottom of the bowl with his finger, then licked it clean. "You owe me thirty quid for the Halloween party tomorrow night."

"Do I?" I said, trying not to think about the fact that it was only a day away. "What for?"

"You'll find out," grinned Paul, squeezing the tickets under the waistband of his trousers (where he hides a lot of important things to keep them "safe *and* warm"). "Any news on Chantelle?"

"Not yet," said Ste. "But you have a great time at that Halloween party and watch this space."

The people kept on coming. There were loads of them. All of the girls would giggle like morons and twiddle their hair when they spoke to Ste, completely ignoring me, of course. Ste would tell them how he would definitely think about maybe dancing with them at the ball, and as they left in a state of absolute delirium he would say things like, "The universe knows I'm doing good things, brother."

Towards the end of lunch time the crowds died down. Ste hoisted the suitcase on to the stage and began counting the money. After a short break without serving anyone, I looked up to see Lucy standing in front of me.

My eyes almost popped out. "Wow. You look ... different."

"Hey hey hey, Lucy!" said Ste, turning round from his money counting. "How's it going? I *love* your new look."

"Er. Thanks," she said.

I must say that I did *not* like her new look at all. The front of her hair was dyed bright red and she was wearing a nose stud. OK, it was only tiny, but people get addicted to these things. They start off with one simple piercing and end up looking like the inside of an old lady's sewing bag.

She was also wearing dark lipstick and had bags under her eyes. Without wishing to sound cruel, she looked like she might have been trying out her fancy-dress costume for the Halloween party a day early.

She yawned.

"Are you OK?" I said.

"Oh, it's nothing," she said, rubbing her eyes. "I was out with Spyder last night. I didn't get back till half-ten."

"And what were you doing until that ungodly hour?" I said, sounding like someone's grandpa.

"It was really cool. We went to an

abandoned warehouse to watch this band called Hedgehog Bloodbath."

"They sound like one of those heavy-metal groups who just shout and scream and puke up on each other."[34]

Lucy tutted and smiled at the same time. "Actually, they were excellent. You'll probably hear some of the tunes at the Halloween party. Still looking forward to it?"

"You could say that." *But of course you would be completely wrong.* "Was it not dangerous at this gig you went to?"

"Well ... a bit, but I mainly stayed at the back, away from the people who were headbanging and smashing into each other."

Thinking about a room full of moshing Spyder lookalikes made me feel quite polluted. "I just want you to be safe."

"I was fine," she said. "Spyder and his mates were with me ... until they went off to a nightclub. But I got a bus home ... eventually."

I looked at her with horror. "They left you stranded? At a bus stop? On your own?"

"You should've called me for a lift," said Ste, coming

---

34 I googled them later that night. They are a sweaty bunch of greasy-haired, topless idiots whose songs include "Exploded Eyeball", "Animal Toilet" and "There's a Fluffy Kitten in My Freezer and I've Eaten Its Head". They sound like *lovely* people.

over to the table.

"Well . . . I suppose, but. . ." She suddenly seemed to wake up. "No. No way. You cheated on me, remember."

Ste put his hands up. "Guilty and very sorry. Anyway – Mike, have you told Lucy the good news?"

I squinted. "The what?"

Ste grinned. "She's our five-hundredth customer."

Lucy looked a little embarrassed.

"No," I said, checking the list. "I think that is an error. I am up to ticket number four hundred and ninety-f—"

"You win a prize," said Ste, over the top of me.

I looked at him. "You did not say anyth—"

"Oh really? *Wow!* Thanks," said Lucy. Then she narrowed her eyes. "Hang on. I don't have to go with *you*, do I?"

Nice.

Ste coughed. "No. Of course not. What? Thought never crossed my mind. Ha ha. But you get to keep the cuddly monkey."

Lucy looked up above the stage and her eyes opened wide. "Wow. It's *really* cute. But it's a bit *big*. I'm walking home today and. . ."

Ste clicked both fingers and pointed at her. "I'll bring it round in my car sometime."

As I collected her money and ripped a ticket off for

her, Lucy bit her lip and said, "OK, cool."

But Ste had already resumed his money-counting. Lucy stood there for a moment, looking at the back of his head like she was waiting for something. Then, when whatever she was waiting for did not happen, she turned and meekly walked away, her shoes clicking against the floor.

"She still likes you," I said, the words slipping out before I had a chance to think them over.

Ste smiled humbly. "Nah. I don't think so."

Then he went back to counting the money, humming as he worked.

Preparing for Spyder's Halloween Party

On Friday evening, I was delighted to be out of school but completely terrified of what Spyder's Halloween party was going to be like. In fact, I toyed with the idea of not going but decided that looking out for Lucy was way more important than whether I was happy or not. My plan was straightforward: go inside, find Lucy, check she is OK, then exit before anything gets out of hand.

However, there was no way my parents would allow me to go to an extreme student party so I told Mum I was going trick-or-treating with Paul. Mum was not too keen because she did not want the police to have another excuse to pick on me. However, Ste (who was still being the perfect brother) told her he was going to drive me round and look after me so she said yes.

I had no idea what to wear so I plumped for my smart clothes from Sunday. I figured that if Mum asked me why I was going trick-or-treating dressed like that, I could say I was a haunted accountant.

Anyway, I was in the bathroom, brushing my teeth, when the front doorbell rang. I went downstairs to open it and was struck completely dumb.

A Truly Scary Halloween Nightmare

Paul Beary was standing on my front porch, holding his camera and wearing *the* scariest outfit I have ever seen:

    a. Flashing red devil horns with matching pitchfork.
    b. Painted red face with drawn-on moustache and beard (a combination that made him look like a space hopper).

And worst of all:

c. A bright red all-in-one Lycra leotard, which covered his entire body apart from his face. It was so tight it was like a second skin and almost completely see-through. I could see *everything*, from his leopard-print underpants to his great big, dinner-plate-sized – you know – *raspberry ripples*. And, without wanting to be cruel, *nobody* looks good in a leotard. Even a supermodel would struggle to pull it off. Paul looked like a novelty balloon.

"Scary or what?" said Paul, doing a pirouette.

"Honestly, Paul? The most petrifying thing I have ever witnessed."

Paul gave one of his big grins. "Perfect. I've had it since I was nine. I can't believe I can still fit into it."

"Neither can I," I said, taking deep breaths. "What possessed you to wear it?"

"The beard makes me look older. It'll help me with the chicks. Plus they can see my undies. Thought I'd give 'em a treat."

At that moment, Ste came up behind me. "Hey hey hey, Paul. Looking good, man. The girls at the party won't know what's hit 'em. And," he lowered his voice, "if you score with any babes, I'll give them free tickets to the Funky Monkey Ball."

"What a guy," said Paul, pushing his way into the house. "Any word from Chantelle?"

"We're in contact," said Ste, mysteriously. "Make sure you get loads of photos tonight."

As I was about to close the front door, I noticed a large carrier bag on the step. "What is this?"

"Your costume, of course," said Paul. "I knew you'd forget so I chose this one for you from the fancy-dress shop. This is why you owe me thirty quid. Took me hours to choose."

"But I hate fancy dress," I said.

I do not like to be stared at so fancy dress is an absolute nightmare for me. I wonder why anybody would *choose* to go out dressed as a nun or a pirate or a cow. Unless that was their job, of course.[35]

Paul put his arm around me. "Mike. It's a Halloween party. Everyone'll be wearing fancy dress. You'll look like a complete idiot in normal clothes."

"You don't want Lucy being all embarrassed about you in front of her boyfriend, do you?" said Ste.

I picked up the bag. They were both right. The last thing I wanted to do was stand out. And anyway, there was no way I could look any more stupid than Paul.

Oh, how wrong could I be?

---

35 OK, so I have just realized that being a cow is not really a *job* as such. It is more a *species*. Still, you get my point.

The Party

Fifteen minutes after Paul handed me the plastic bag, I was sitting miserably in the back seat of Ste's car. The roof was down because my costume was so massive that it would not fit inside otherwise.

I was dressed as a giant custard cream.

It was the worst costume ever. For a start, it had nothing to do with Halloween. It was about seven feet high and four feet wide, made entirely of thickly stuffed nylon. As a result, I was overheating, even in the cold evening air. There was a hole in the front of the biscuit for my face. I was barely able to bend my arms and legs, which stuck out from the custard in a kind of cat-diarrhoea-coloured leotard.

When we arrived, Ste and Paul had to pretty much crowbar me out of the car. Then Ste drove off and we walked to the front door. Well, I sort of shuffled like . . . er . . . a giant custard cream with legs.

Paul knocked proudly. From inside, we could hear laughter and thumping music. Suddenly I got the jitters. "We do not belong here. This party is not for kids like us. I look ridiculous and I am scared and—"

"Relax," said Paul, his devil horns flashing. "Anyway. You said it yourself: this is an *extreme* Halloween party. Everyone'll be in fancy dress. I guarantee it."

Guarantees are meant to be one hundred per cent,

rock-solid promises. Well, except when the person doing the guaranteeing is Paul, of course.

Therefore when Paul made this *guarantee*, I should probably have gone straight home.

Stupidly I trusted him.

End of the Day

Well, that is all I am going to write today. I have this funny feeling in my belly – a bit like the night before a holiday or when I am opening a packet of biscuits: I am actually looking forward to working tomorrow. Wow! I never ever thought I would type that! I have just had a real laugh for the last few days and, compared with everything else that has happened recently, my job is a lot of fun.

Working for a Second Chance
Day 6 – Monday

Tasks completed: Rap therapy.
What I learned: Camper-van roofs are not stages.

Today, Chas turned up wearing a baby-blue onesie with a large gold chain hanging around his neck. A man in dark glasses was squashed between a pile of speakers and sound equipment in the back of the camper. "S'my main man, Rahim," said Chas, driving towards Moorfields.

"Hello," I said.

Rahim said nothing.

"Rahim lays down the tracks for me to bust my rhymes," said Chas.

"I have no idea what that meant," I said.

"For sure, baby. I forgot you ain't down with the urban ting," said Chas. "Rahim's my DJ. He plays records and I rap. Says I'm the best rapper in the UK right now. Ain't that right, Rahim?"

Rahim said nothing.

Despite doubting Rahim's judgement somewhat, I felt like I should seem interested. "How long have you been DJing?" I said.

Rahim said nothing.

"By the way," said Miss O'Malley from the front seat, "Rahim here's deaf as a post."

"Don't stop him DJing," said Chas. "He *feels* the vibration. Gets the rhythms of the beats through his boots, like roots. Of a tree. See?"

I allowed Chas to finish his – *ahem* – "rap". He raised his eyes in a *hey-what-do-you-think* way.

I did not reply because I did not wish to upset him; not now we were getting along. However, it *was* rubbish and made no sense. On top of that, he rapped in a horrible nasal American accent, which sounded more like a Welsh person freeing a lump of cheese from up the back of his nose.

I chose my words as carefully as I could. "So, and I do not wish to be cruel here, a *deaf* person says you are the best rapper in the country?"

Chas nodded.

"Right," I said. "And why is he here today?"

"We gonna do us some rap therapy."

Rap Therapy

Chas parked up by the back fence of Moorfields Academy (the local secondary school), and Rahim set up the DJ decks and speakers next to the sliding door of the camper. The school is all concrete buildings and razor-wire fencing – more like a high-security prison for violent offenders than a place of learning.

"I went round to see the head teacher at her house last night," said Chas. "I know her through my youth work. Said I've got an idea for stopping kids from cutting class."

For about half an hour, Rahim played music out of the sound system. A few groups of kids, who were clearly nicking off, came over. Rahim mimed a five-minute lesson on how to mix records, before Chas had a quick chat to them outside the van. I stayed inside with Miss O'Malley, making them hot chocolates on the stove.

All six of the kids who came over to the van slipped back into school pretty much straight afterwards. "See – s'working," said Chas.

Something about this bothered me, though. "By giving them DJ lessons and hot chocolate, are you not just encouraging them to stay away from school tomorrow, though?"

Chas sucked his teeth. "This school's got the highest truancy rates in the county – nearly ten per cent of little dudes cut class every day."

"Well, why are you giving them a reward for nicking off?"

"Ach, Michael, it's not always that straightforward," said Miss O'Malley.

"Damn right," said Chas. "Sometimes there ain't no one at home to listen to 'em, or *tell* 'em they need to be in school. The kids who nick off are often the ones with the biggest problems."

"The clever thing is, we'll be back tonight," said Miss O'Malley.

"This was just a taster session – get 'em interested," said Chas. "I told the kids that if they spend the rest of the day in school they can come back later for a full lesson."

"So you get them to go back to school now. . ."

". . .then keep 'em off the streets and out of trouble tonight as well. And tomorrow night and every night after. That's when I can find out why they're missing school in the first place."

This seemed like a clever idea. I had always seen Chas as a bit of a simpleton but maybe there was more to him than that.

"Don't worry," said Miss O'Malley. "It's illegal for you to work after eight in the evening so you won't have to come."

I felt surprisingly disappointed about this and was about to say something when we noticed the strange-looking kid peering over at us from on top of a brick wall.

"Time to engage this little dude. Yo, Mike. Hand me the mic," said Chas, pointing to where it lay on the table. "I'm in the zone like a man on a phone."

"That makes no sense."

"I'm squeezing out rap, like a dog doin' a cr—"

"Have the microphone," I said.

"Cool. Give me a leg up," said Chas.

Miss O'Malley and I hoisted Chas up on to the roof. He was surprisingly light, like he was made of twigs. This might have been because Miss O'Malley was taking all the weight on her enormous platform of a hand. "Drop a beat, Rahim!" he shouted.

Rahim said nothing.

Then Chas did a really silly thing. He tried to send vibrations to Rahim through the roof of the camper. He did this by *stamping* on the roof. Unfortunately, the roof is made of thin plastic. His foot went straight through it like a hole punch.

Luckily he was not badly injured (unlike the roof, which had a massive hole in it). Even so, by the time Miss O'Malley had shoved his leg back through, the kid had run off.

Chas brought me straight back home whilst he, Rahim and Miss O'Malley went to try and find something that would fix the hole.

The Party

An angry girl with green hair opened Spyder's front door. "Get lost, urchins. We don't *do* trick or treat."

She tried to shut the door but Paul pushed past her. "We're here. Party's started. Woo!"

The music in the room stopped.

Silence.

From the front doorstep I could see about twenty people in the lounge. All of them possessed at least three of the following things:

1. Ripped clothes
2. Massive, clumpy boots
3. Multiple facial piercings
4. Tattoos covering most of their visible skin
5. Shaved head or Mohican

Oh and, for the record, not one of them was in fancy dress.

I could not bear to look but, unfortunately, I had no

choice.[36] The partygoers just stood there in shock as Paul grabbed a slice of pizza off a table and wandered straight up to a bunch of girls, saying, "I'm Paul. Perhaps you've heard of me?"

Did he have no shame?

The angry girl shouted, "Spyder. Gatecrashers."

Spyder appeared with Lucy clinging on to his arm. Since yesterday, Lucy had added two piercings to her ears and one to her lip. She looked relieved to see me and gave a nervous wave.

"What's going on, man?" said Spyder to Paul.

The "music" (some kind of weird drumming thing) had started again, and Paul was now dancing in a style that can only be described as "aggressive grinding".

The girl pointed at him and me. "These *infants* broke into your house. Now, I know you enjoy hanging around with children –" she glared at Lucy, who burrowed behind Spyder's arm "– but they're ruining the mood."

Spyder looked at me and grinned. "Well, Mike's Lucy's brother. And this guy –" he turned to Paul, who was now attempting to spin around on his head "– well, he's . . . different. I like that. Let 'em stay."

"Spyder. A word in the kitchen," said the girl, pulling

---

36 a. Due to the tightness of the head hole I was unable to turn away, b. The size of the costume meant I could not reach round to cover my eyes, and c. I was so tall that I was stuck underneath the porch of the house.

him away. When Lucy tried to follow, the girl added, "Alone."

Spyder prised Lucy's fingers off his multicoloured jacket and gave her a peck on the cheek. "Come in, Mike. Don't be shy," he said, before following the girl through a door at the far end of the front room.

I made a *help* face to Lucy. With a lot of yanking and grunting, she managed to drag me inside. Unfortunately, as I tried to walk sideways into the house, my enormous costume knocked a row of drinks off a table, which resulted in a whole load of swearing and abuse.

Lucy apologized on my behalf and pulled me to the bottom of the stairs, where my costume was no longer touching the ceiling. A quick scan around confirmed that this definitely was not the kind of place I could feel comfortable in. Firstly, the room was a mess – all brightly painted swirly patterns on the wall and a sticky carpet. It smelled damp and smoky, and there were old dirty plates with cigarette ends stubbed out on them everywhere.

As if that were not enough, these were the activities taking place:

a. A competition between three men for who could drink a bottle of beer quickest through a straw . . . *up their noses*.

b. A girl showing off the tattoo of a tiger's face covering her entire back. She accidentally revealed a tiny corner of her bra strap. This was too much for Paul, who lost control of his break-dancing and put his foot through one of the speakers.

c. A man with a broken arm impressing a load of people with a story that ended: "...upside down, slamming back towards the ramp and I just thought, *Why am I using a shopping trolley as a skateboard?* Crunch – hospital – plaster cast!" This was apparently hilarious and was greeted with cries of "You're off your head."

"I'm so glad you're here," said Lucy. "This is *awful*. I don't know anyone and that *horrible girl* is Spyder's ex-girlfriend Tasha and she's being mean and I don't even know if Spyder's right for me."

"Really?" I said, not smiling, even though I felt pleased about Spyder.

Lucy ran her fingers through her hair. "I just wanted to have some fun but..."

Her face sort of folded up. A tear ran down her cheek and through the ring that had pierced her lovely lip.

I was about to tell her that I would help her to get home when there was a loud cry from above us. "Stair grind!"

I looked up and just had time to bundle Lucy out of the way. A total lunatic was trying to surf all the way down the banister rail whilst standing on a kitchen tray. Balancing awkwardly, he shot down the rail, smacked his head on the ceiling and flew head first into the front door, where he lay completely still in a crumpled heap.

The room fell into nervous silence.

"Is he OK?" I said.

The man slowly stood up and shakily raised the tray into the air. Finally, he broke into a massive bloody-toothed grin. Everyone went wild, patting him on the back and telling him how extreme he was.

"Awesome!" cried Paul, forcing his way into the circle of people who were congratulating this maniac for almost killing himself.

"Can anyone get more extreme than that?" said the banister buffoon.

"Me!" said Paul, putting his hand up like a six-year-old. "I can!"

"Cool. Let's see what you've got."

Paul sat down on the sofa and demanded a cigarette lighter from the unconvinced-looking people gathering around him.

"What's he going to do?" said Lucy.

I knew but decided I would rather not say.

How To Make Friends and Disgust People

<u>Warning</u>: If you have a weak stomach, or if you are a pregnant woman, then please do not read this section.

Paul leaned back on the sofa, his legs high up in the air. Then he placed the cigarette lighter next to his bum and flicked up a flame.[37]

He frowned and puffed out his cheeks (the ones on his face that is). Nothing happened for a few moments. His face went pink, then red, then purple. The spectators moved closer. Someone said, "Is this it?" Then, suddenly, Paul broke wind ferociously, sending a jet of yellow flame three feet into the air.

At first, this was met with silence.

Then someone said, "Awesome."

The punks piled around him, giving him friendly punches on the arm and saying, "Do it again!" and "This kid rocks!" The imbecile who had grinded down the banister called out, "Dude, you singed off my eyebrows. Cool!"

"How is that cool?" I said to Lucy.

"No idea," she replied, shaking her head.

---

37 It is not too late to stop reading this section now. And I will just add that there was a thirty-second gap in proceedings here, when Paul realized that the lighter had a picture of a woman in a bikini on it and when you turned it upside down her clothes disappeared.

As Paul repeated his revolting trick, two heavily tattooed girls bent down either side of him and kissed him on the cheek whilst he took a photo on his camera.

Finally, the cheering died down. "What else have you got?" said one of the punks.

Paul, who now had two lipstick stains on his face, said, "I bet I can put more M&M's in my mouth that anyone here!"

"Extreme!" someone cried, grabbing a large bowl of sweets off the table.

Unbelievable. Paul had become the most popular guy at the party.

I turned away from his human dustbin impression but the edge of my costume smacked Lucy in the side of the head. "Sorry," I said, and tried to change the topic. "I like your piercings."

I did not, actually – I thought they were abominations, like graffiti on the side of Buckingham Palace – but I did not want to make her feel bad. As her best friend I had a responsibility to cheer her up.

Looking at the floor, she slowly pulled on her lip ring. It came off in her hand. "It's a fake," she said, before putting it back on. "They all are. I'm just … trying to fit in."

"Phew," I said. "I am really glad."

Lucy looked up at me. "Why's that?"

I took a deep breath. "Because I think you are beauti—"

"Shots! Who wants shots!" cried Spyder, rocking through the crowd towards us with a bottle of clear liquid and some small glasses. Tasha was right by his shoulder.

"Not for me," said Lucy.

"Ha!" said Tasha. "Told you she wouldn't be able to take it, Spyder."

Lucy scowled. "Fine," she said defiantly. She snatched the bottle, poured herself a glass and threw it down her throat in one go.

"I think that might have alcohol in it," I said, but by this point Lucy was bent double, her face screwed up in pain.

Tasha sniffed. "Pathetic."

Lucy brought her face up level with Tasha's, her jaw clenched with the same determination that I had seen her demonstrate before hundreds of swimming races. "Again."

Tasha pursed her lips.

"Is that a good idea?" I said, but Lucy did not seem to hear.

Spyder poured her another. And another. And another. Each time, Lucy swallowed the whole lot in one gulp. By the fifth, she barely even registered it.

"S'nothing," she said, kissing Spyder full on the lips. Tasha stormed off.

I turned away. Paul was now in the centre of the room, surrounded by about twenty people. His cheeks were swollen like a really greedy squirrel. A girl held up a single M&M to the enthralled crowd. She forced it in between Paul's stretched lips. "Fifty!" she screamed. Paul raised his fists in the air and everyone went crazy, shouting stuff like "Legend!" and "I want to marry him!"[38]

Amazing. Finally, Paul had found people who thought that being a dirty beast was a positive character trait. In a way I felt pleased for him – I did not think that people like this existed. As he went through the lengthy process of chewing and swallowing, someone shouted out, "More entertainment!"

"Get your fire clubs out, Spyder!"

"Fire clubs?" I said. "But I think he may have been drinking."

This sounded dangerous.

Spyder looked up from Lucy. I noticed that after he had moved his face away, Lucy carried on snogging fresh air for a few seconds, as though she had not realized he was no longer there. She opened her eyes

---

[38] This last comment was shouted by the banister grinder. Therefore I do not think it counts.

and looked around nervously to check no one had seen. I politely looked away.

"OK," said Spyder. "They're out in the garden."

Everyone trailed outside, discussing Spyder's extreme juggling skills. I was left alone with Lucy, who was suddenly giggling like a maniac. "Come on, Mike! Let's go wash the fire clubs!" She dragged me through the house by my arm, my huge costume smashing into everything along the way. As she passed the kitchen table, she picked up a glass and downed the contents.

I frowned. "I think you have had en—"

"You know what's great about you?" she said as we reached the back door. Her face was a little too close to mine, her breath smelled like disinfectant and she was wagging her finger under my nose. "You're *you*. You might be a giant custard cream. But you're still *you*. And that's the thing, y'see?"

She looked at me sideways and nodded solemnly, as though she had just imparted some great wisdom.

"Are you . . . *drunk*?" I said. I had not really spoken to a drunk person before. One Christmas my dad had three glasses of wine and told a rude joke about Rudolph the Red-Nosed Reindeer but that was about it.[39]

Lucy gave a lopsided smile and put her finger to her

_____
39 In actual fact he did not even reach the punchline because Mum sent him to bed.

lips. "Shhhh. Who knows, Mike-ay? Lettuce getchou outside."

She shoved me forward into the back-door frame and I became completely stuck.

"Don't panic! I'vad special training in thissortathing," slurred Lucy, her voice muffled by my costume.

I was about to ask her *at what point in her life* had she been trained in shoving seven-foot-tall custard creams through doorways when she slammed into my back, flinging me out like a cork from a bottle.

We lay tangled up on the cold patio. I was on my back, unable to move, like a biscuit-themed tortoise. "S'nice and cosy," Lucy said, snuggling her face into the costume.

"Please help me up," I said.

Lucy pushed herself up on to her feet and looked around as though she had no idea where she was. Then, with a huge effort, she dragged me to my feet. "Less go wash Spyder now. He's verrry, verrry good but I dunno if I even like 'im."

She hiccupped loudly and made off towards a small patch of grass at the back where everyone was standing in a circle. I had to keep her from walking into a bush.

By the time we reached the wall by the edge of the overgrown lawn, four flaming clubs were spinning through the darkness, leaving white trails behind them.

I tried to get Lucy to sit down on the wall but she insisted on standing up, her head moving back and forth like a charmed snake. Spyder caught the clubs and took a bow.

Then, everything began to go wrong.

As the applause died down, Paul walked out into the circle. "I'll have a go," he said. "We do this at the dojo. It's part of my kung-fu training. Here, Mike. Film it for me." He leaned in close to me as he handed me his camera and its case. "It's already recording on night vision. If any chicks leap on me at the end, make sure you zoom in."

He went to the middle of the lawn and began stretching.

"Come 'ere," said Lucy, even though she was already leaning her full weight on to my shoulder. "Can 'e juggle?"

She shouted the last bit so loudly that I had to move my head away. This slight movement caused her to almost topple over. I put Paul's camera on to the wall so that I could steady her with both hands. Her personal safety was way more important than Paul Beary's love life.

Paul weighed up the clubs in his hands. On the other side of the circle, Tasha nudged Spyder and pointed towards Lucy, who was now swaying from side to side.

A low chant began of "Paul! Paul! Paul!"

At this exact moment, Lucy let go of my arms. "Wassissname?" she said loudly. "Paul. Can 'e juggle?"

We would never find out the answer.

Paul's Juggling Career

In reality, I would estimate that Paul's juggling career lasted for slightly under five seconds but, at the time, it seemed to go on for an eternity. This is a summary:

- 0   seconds: Paul releases his fire club precisely as Lucy says the word "juggle".
- 0.5 seconds: Lucy totters dangerously from side to side.
- 2.0 seconds: The fire club approaches its highest point, just as Lucy suddenly lurches to the right.
- 2.5 seconds: I flick my eyes nervously from Lucy to the juggling club (which is now beginning to descend) and back again.
- 3.0 seconds: Lucy loses her balance, staggering backwards into Paul and knocking him out of the way. She remains in the middle of the garden, gormlessly looking around.
- 3.5 seconds: I look up. The fire club is returning to Earth and is about to land on Lucy's lovely head.

4 seconds: I leap forward like a desperate frog, barging her out of the way.

4.5 seconds: The juggling club lands on my back. Three different noises come in quick succession: "Thump!" then "Woof!" then "Aaarrrghh!"

Thump! Woof! Aaarrrghh!

"Thump" was the fire club landing on my back. "Woof" was my nylon custard cream costume going up in flames. And "Aaarrrgh!" was me realizing I was on fire.

Straight away I leapt to my feet, screaming and panicking. Someone shouted, "Stop, Drop, Roll!" at me.[40] A drink was thrown on to my back but made the flames worse and I was now a giant blazing custard cream with flames licking up into the sky and I fumbled for the poppers and ripped them off and I was on the ground and people dragged the costume off my back and hurled it to the ground and stamped out the flames.

And then there was silence. I slowly pulled myself to my feet. "I am OK," I said, breathlessly.

So there I was, standing in the middle of the garden wheezing, surrounded by a whole host of crusty punks,

---

40 Clearly someone who had been on fire many times before.

all of whom were at least five years older than me. My body was cooling down but there was a stinging pain in my right shoulder.

I picked up my inhaler (which had been tucked inside my costume) from the grass and took a gulp on it. As I recovered my breath, I noticed something strange about the silence in the garden. Very slowly, I looked around me. Twenty mouths hung open. Forty eyes bulged out of people's heads. I looked down at myself. At that moment I realized that, in their haste, the people who had rescued me had ripped off my undies as well.

I was completely naked.

Unexpected Reaction

As I desperately covered myself with my hands, the banister buffoon said three simple words:

"What. A. Legend."

Everyone cheered.

As I scrabbled around the lawn for my underpants, people were patting me on the back and saying stuff like, "*The* best party trick of all time!" and "Extreme!"

"You know what?" said someone. "We should *all* get naked."

This was met with a rousing chorus of "Yeah!"

I picked up my undies, which were now just a blackened rag. "Does anybody have any spare briefs?"

Nobody seemed to hear.

"Come on!" cried someone else. "Let's strip off!"

Within moments, they had all whipped off their clothes, even Paul Beary,[41] who cried out, "Let's all do a Swarbrick!" As they leapt around the garden like shaved lambs, they joined in his evil chant: "Swarbrick – Swarbrick – Swarbrick". Good grief it was horrible.

"Hey! Let's go into town!" cried Tasha.

In their crazed state, the party guests formed a disgusting pink conga line and followed her through the gate. As the last person disappeared, I realized Lucy was still sitting on the lawn, her head lolling round in circles. Spyder was standing over her (nude, of course), looking nervously from Lucy to the gate and back again.

I bent down to see if she was OK. She made a noise that sounded like "Rashamashalash."

"She all right?" said Spyder.

I stood up quickly. "Clearly not, you big crusty idiot. You got her *drunked-up* on your . . . *firewater*."

"Hey, take a chill pill, man."

---

41 The only thing more off-putting than his body was the fact that he had kept on his underpants, devil horns and face paint. He looked like a sinister face drawn on to a butternut squash.

"Hurry up, Spyder!" called Tasha, standing impatiently by the gate. "They're halfway down the street."

"Gotta go," said Spyder. "Look after Lucy, eh? Tell her it's been . . . fun while it lasted. And usually we have a rule at parties – last people tidy up. See ya."

With that, he patted me on the back and sprinted naked out of the garden. I was left alone on the lawn with a drunken Lucy and a load of discarded clothes.

Leaving the Party

After putting on the only clothes I could find that did not smell like old wet ropes (for some reason, *all* the crusty punks had a strange musty odour), I sat Lucy on the wall. She stared into space and began happily singing a song (presumably by Hedgehog Bloodbath) about shaving her legs with a chainsaw.

I needed help fast but I could not call my parents after lying to them, and I *definitely* did not want to call Lucy's. Therefore I had only one option: I phoned The Steverlizer.

Luckily he was "cruising around" and said he would be five minutes. "Everything's going to be fine," I said, propping Lucy up as she nearly fell off the wall. "Ste's on his way."

Lucy took a deep breath and a strange smile spread

across her face. "Thass nice."

Then, suddenly and without any warning, she lunged forward.

The Most Amazing Thing That Has Ever Happened to Anyone

Her face bashed into me. Her lips mashed up against mine. And I realized: she was kissing me.

Seriously.

I am not lying. This is not a Paul Beary story. Lucy King kissed me. *On the lips*. I very nearly exploded. Obviously I had never once in my life considered what it might be like to kiss Lucy but I must say it was … well … *awesome*, like slurping a warm peach.

For the first few seconds anyway.

Then it went wrong.

My first mistake was to try to kiss *her* in return.

You see, as this was my first official on-mouth kiss, I had no previous experience. *I should be doing something*, I thought.

Unfortunately, all I could remember was some advice that Paul Beary once gave me, which was "when you're snogging a bird [*his word*] just imagine you're sucking the scales off a fish. Chicks [*his word again*] go crazy for it".

Foolishly I tried this. Two bad things happened:

1. The power of my suction caused a terrible tooth-clash, like plates colliding in a bowl of dishwater.
2. Lucy gagged so I pulled my lips away quickly. Even I know that during a kiss the girl is not meant to chuck up into your mouth.

"Naughty," she said, trying to tap my nose but poking me in the eye.

I looked at her glassy expression and realized that this was wrong. Lucy did not *really* want to kiss me. She was blind drunk. She did not know what she was doing or maybe even who I was. I tried to say something. Genuinely I did. But she grabbed the back of my head, yanked me towards her and began snogging at me wildly.

This second phase of kissing was not exactly lovely. It was all teeth and tongue and sloppy lips, like snogging a llama. I wanted her to stop. But then again I did not wish to be impolite. And everybody knows you should not shock a drunk person. So, I allowed her to continue for a couple of seconds.

Oh, OK, three minutes.

As her initial excitement tailed off, she settled into a fairly slow, sloppy pace.

Then her ROLM[42] slowed down.

Then it ground to a halt.

Then I felt the weight of her entire body pressing against my lips.

Finally, she began to snore.

Wonderful.

She had fallen asleep.

Chas

I have just had a text from Chas. It read: "Roof fixed & lookin superfly. Pick u up 8am tomz. Peace out."

Eight o'clock? That seems very early for Chas. I am going to have to go to bed now.

Working for a Second Chance
Day 7 – Tuesday

Tasks completed: Unsuccessful graffiti prevention.

What I learned: It is easy to get the wrong impression.

---

42 Rate of Lip Movement.

"Hey. . ." I said as I came round the corner. The weird kid with the yellow-cress hair was spray-painting something on to the side of the camper van. Chas and Miss O'Malley were nowhere to be seen.

I would love to say that I strode up to him purposefully and confronted him. However, even though up close I realized that his body is all skinny and droopy like an old daffodil, I just stood there petrified. I do not like confrontation and those other kids said he was a psycho.

I had been gone half an hour. Chas had sent me to buy cups of tea in a nearby café (the stove in the camper had blown up last night apparently). Unfortunately, the café was actually not that nearby at all and I had to walk really slowly on the way back so as not to drop the three magma-hot polystyrene cups.

The kid stopped spraying, turned round towards me and gave a brown-toothed sneer. "What?"

"I. . . Chas! Help!" I cried.

Slowly, the kid walked over and raised the spray can in front of my chest. Then he proceeded to spray . . . well . . . two large circles next to each other on to the front of my jacket, and a smaller circle inside each one.

"This is an outrage," I spluttered, unable to protect myself because of the hot drinks. "You have given me a . . . *lady-chest.*"

At that point, Chas and Miss O'Malley turned up. "Yo, Mikey. Just nipped over to the schoo—"

"This person was defacing the clinic. And now he has defaced me."

"Woah! Nice jugs!" said Chas. "Yo, P-Meister. Get the camera."

"It is not funny," I said, grinding my teeth together.

"Ooh, Michael," said Miss O'Malley. "Shall I go home and find you a bikini?"

They all began giggling at this. At first I was angry, but as Miss O'Malley dabbed my chest with a tea towel I shook my head and let out an exasperated half-laugh.

"That's what I'm talking about," said Chas. "Go with the flow."

The kid had a mischievous grin on his face. Chas slurped his tea and squinted at what he had painted on to the van. "Perfect."

I looked at the graffiti. And even though it was not really my style (it was all *urban* and *gangster*), I had to concede that he had created a very, very good picture of a dog. Underneath he had written "Flip Flop" in bubble letters.

"So this is what's been going down?" nodded Chas.

The kid shrugged.

"How very brave," said Miss O'Malley.

"What is going on?" I said.

"Graffiti therapy," said Chas. "Part of the urban counselling experience."

He then told me the whole story:

1. Yesterday, they had fixed[43] the roof of the van and

---

43 Well, I say "fixed". Actually, they had nailed a bit of plastic sheeting on to the hole in the roof, which was already sagging from last night's rain.

come back to the estate in the evening.

2. After a wickedly successful (his words) evening of reaching out to the estate through the medium of rap music, he was just packing away when old Cress-hair (*my* words) came over and said that Chas was "the world's worst rapper".

3. With Rahim DJing, they carried out a "hyper-rad" rap-off in front of all the local kids.

4. The kid comprehensively "whooped Chas's sorry butt", after which Rahim uttered his only two words of the day: "Kid wins."

5. Afterwards, Chas finally chatted to the kid (whose name is Jamie) for a while. Jamie had been suspended from school a few weeks ago after he set fire to a notice board. He was only meant to be away for a day but had not gone back since.

6. Jamie told Chas that the only two lessons he misses are art and music. As a result Chas invited him to drop by today to "express himself".

"So where is Rahim?" I said.

"I'm going solo with my rap career," said Chas. "We broke off our collaboration for musical differences."

"Chas didn't like it when he said Jamie here was the winner," whispered Miss O'Malley, loud enough for Chas to hear.

Chas grunted then nodded towards the picture on the van.

"Flip Flop? This your dog, player?"

Jamie stared at the ground.

"Is there something *about* this dog we should know?" said Miss O'Malley gently.

The frown on Jamie's face got deeper.

"So," said Chas. "The head teacher's letting me work with you to get you back to school."

Jamie pulled a cigarette lighter out of his pocket. He lit the flame in front of the spray can and pressed down the button to make a flame-thrower, which he aimed at the picture of the dog, leaving a bubbling, scorched mess on the side of the van. Then he legged it as fast as he could.

Chas inspected the damage. "Wow," he said. "He *does* need help."

I could not have agreed more.

We sat in the van for the rest of the morning but we had no other visitors. Rain was dripping in through the patched-up hole in the roof so I stayed as far away as possible, desperately trying to wash the *boobs* off my jacket with water from the sink (after the initial shock and secondary mild amusement had worn off, I was left feeling very concerned about the damage to my third-favourite jacket).

I am now home. And, for the record, the jacket is ruined.

Not Exactly Part of the Plan

Lucy falling asleep was not really a glowing review of my kissing technique. It is a bit like if you went on *Come Dine with Me*, but instead of giving a mark out of ten at the end, you just spewed up all over the camera.

However, the *worst* part was when she moved her lips away from mine, nuzzled into my shoulder and broke off her snoring to say, "I love you..." in a sleepy, dreamy voice.

My bottom lip wobbled. "Well, I lo—"

"...Ste," she finished, cuddling me really tight.

I felt like a sharpened chopstick had been shoved under my ribs.

About two seconds later, the Steverlizer himself strolled into the garden. Perfect timing. "Hey hey hey, Mikey," he said. "Sorry I'm late. Half the roads in town are blocked. Something's going on down by the uni."

I was so worried about Lucy (not to mention happy, sad, embarrassed and confused about my first proper snog) that the importance of this last comment completely passed me by. I did not realize at the time but things had become very serious.

Ste eased Lucy up over his shoulder like a fireman and carried her back to his car. After scooping up Paul's camera from the garden wall, I followed.

"Sniceancomfy," she mumbled as Ste placed her down on the back seat. "Think I'll have a snoozysnooze."

"Thank you for coming," I said.

There was no doubt – he had done me (and Lucy) a massive favour.

"No problem," said Ste, speeding off down the road. "Do good things and good things will come to you, right?"

His eyes flicked towards the rear-view mirror as he said this.

Lucy's House

At Lucy's, Ste carried her to the front door and I knocked. She was just about awake enough to cling to his neck.

Lucy's parents opened the door. Dave was wearing camouflage-print pyjamas and Mrs King's face was covered in what looked like hardened meringue. When she saw Lucy she rushed over. "Oh, darling!"

"What've you done to her?" snarled Dave at my brother. "I'll wring your flippin' neck."

"Whoa, easy!" said Ste, stepping backwards. "She got drunk at a party. Mike phoned me and I brought her home."

Dave fixed me with his laser-like gaze. "Your fault, eh, Milton? You were meant to keep your eye on her."

Lucy's mum looked horrified. "You asked him to spy on her?"

"Not *spy*. Just *look out* for her," Dave said. He held his arms out to Ste. "We'll take care of her from here."

"No," said Lucy, her eyes still closed and her voice a distant moan. "Lerrim stay. I want Ste."

Ste gave a *what-can-I-do* shrug.

Dave King's face turned red. "She doesn't know what she's talkin' about. She needs me."

"I wanna be Ste's lil' monkey," wailed Lucy.

I gulped.

"Bring her in, Steven," said Mrs King, standing aside.

"Over my dead body," said Dave, blocking the doorway with his considerable bulk.

"She wants Steven," Mrs King snapped. She turned back to Ste and her face lit up. "Come on. We'll settle her down and then you can get home and rest."

"No. I'll stay out on the driveway in my car tonight," said Ste. "You can come and get me if anything happens."

Dave leaned forward. "If *anything* happens to my precious daughter, son, I will *definitely* come and get you."

Lucy's mum rolled her eyes. "Oh, go to bed, David."

She ushered Ste and Lucy inside. Before I could ask what I should do, the door had slammed shut in my face.

The perfect ending to an abominable night.

Not Actually the End of the Night at All

By now it was almost ten o'clock. I ran all the way home. Well, OK, so I ran about a hundred metres before getting out of breath and walking the rest of the way.

In the distance I could hear police sirens wailing. A helicopter flew overhead, towards the city centre, its bright beam scanning the streets. Was there a murderer on the loose? Had a rampaging hippo escaped from a zoo? Had the police finally caught up with Paul?

When I opened the front door, Mum and Dad were waiting for me in the living room. Mum was completely nude and dancing from one foot to the other. Dad was in his armchair looking very grave.

"You've done it, darling!" she cried, not even saying hello. "Go on, Roy, show him."

Dad nervously spun the TV control round in his hand. "Are you sure this can't wait until tomorrow?"

Mum grinned. "Nope. He should celebrate his

achievements now. And, may I say, well done for stealing those clothes. Did you have to escape from the police?"

"Now you have *really* lost me," I said. "Please may I go to bed?"

"Oh, you'll sleep a lot better once you've seen *this*." Mum snatched the remote and fast-forwarded through the local news. "Aha!" she said, after whizzing through two stories (a pork-pie-eating competition and an OAP fitness class).[44]

Local News

Below I have summarized the news clip as accurately as possible. You can probably watch it online if you prefer but, from personal experience, I would recommend that you do not.

[*Newsreader in studio speaking directly to camera.*]

Newsreader: . . .just in: Chaos in Preston as a "bunch of naked louts" run wild. Our Current Affairs

---

44 Both of which were definitely more amusing at 8x the normal speed. You should have seen those old people move!

Correspondent, Belinda Broom, is at the scene. Belinda, what's happening right now?

[*Cut to smartly dressed woman standing outside, next to a "University of Preston" sign. Lots of blurry pink figures are wildly leaping about in the background.*]

Reporter: Well, tonight we could call this programme the "Nine O'Clock *Nudes*".

Newsreader: Very good, Linda.

Reporter: Thank you, Jeremy, but I can confirm that my name is *Be*linda. And this is no laughing matter. Hundreds of naked people are rioting on the streets of Preston tonight. It is believed to have started when a small conga line of nudists danced towards the city centre. Eyewitnesses say that other people – mainly students – began joining them; coming out of Halloween parties and pubs, stripping off, and swelling the numbers until the conga line was well over fifty metres long. Soon they had taken over the roundabout here behind me and . . . well . . . they were giving passers-by a real eyeful.

Newsreader: Do we know the reasons behind this?

Reporter: Hard to say at this stage, Jeremy. I spoke to one very young man who said that they were, and I quote, "Swarbrickers" who just wanted to "Swarbrick". Now, I *have* found a Facebook page for them. It is very much an underground movement, but tonight it's thrust itself into the mainstream.

Newsreader: What are they doing now?

Reporter: Here outside the university, we have an uneasy stand-off between the unruly revellers and police. You can see the nudists in the distance behind me. They charged around for an hour or so, dancing and cartwheeling and leaping on to the bonnets of cars, gradually growing in numbers the whole time before being chased off by police. This scattered them about but they were able to regroup quite quickly and... *Oh goodness,* Jeremy. They're coming towards me. I can confirm, the nudes are coming.

[*Camera pans round to reveal charging mass of nudists.*]

Reporter: Quick. Back in the van.

[*Reporter escapes. Nudes surround camera, dancing and chanting, "Swar-brick-ing! Swar-brick-ing!" The unmistakable face of Paul Beary appears in front of the camera and screams, "Swarbricking for ever!" Screen goes blank. Picture returns to newsreader.*]

Newsreader: [*Shuffles papers and clears throat.*] Ahem. Well. In other news, a farmer in Garstang has been teaching one of his chickens to roller-skate...

Uneasy Feeling

Mum pressed Stop. "Now, come and have a look at this."

I followed her over to the computer and she opened the Swarbricking Facebook page. *Unbelievable.* The site had three thousand, seven hundred and twenty-nine friends... I blinked. Three thousand, seven hundred and *thirty ... thirty-four ... forty-two...* People had even started advertising on there.[45]

"You've gone viral," grinned Mum. "People out there are desperate to meet you. *This* is the power of the internet. Imagine it – we could invite them all here in a big jamboree of nakedness. You could give inspirational talks, show them how you've battled your own demons to become the nudist you are today."

"Make it stop," I said, turning to Dad in desperation. "You've *got to do something.*"

Shoulders hunched, Dad stared at his slippers.

The Following Morning

The day after the Halloween party was Saturday. I had not slept well at all because I was so worried about:

45 The post read: "Stay warm *and* Swarbrick this winter – wear cling-film underpants. Available now from my eBay store."

1. Lucy being drunk.
2. Lucy being in love with my brother.
3. The most disastrous kiss of all time.
4. Global Swarbricking. And, to top it all off:
5. I had a nasty burn on my shoulder.

When I awoke I had two texts. One from Paul ("Wkd nite. Nude girls everywhere! Wish I'd had my camera! Did U get it? All those chicks made me miss Chntl even more. PS: UO me £30 for the costume"). The other was from Ste, sent ten minutes previously ("RU OK? The Steverlizer needs spare pants and socks pls! Bring them round Lucy's asap if u can").

For the first time in my life, I did not really want to see Lucy. What on Earth would she think about someone who had bored her to sleep with his kissing technique? It felt like someone had snapped the needle off the Lucy-ometer, then stamped on it repeatedly. Even so, I owed it to Ste to do as he asked.

I went into his room and opened his underpants drawer. It was full of crisp, white designer-labelled undies – kind of how you would imagine David Beckham's underwear drawer.

In spite of this, I did not wish to *touch* them. Touching another person's underpants is just something you do not do – like chewing their toenails or picking their nose. In the absence of a glove, I needed something else to protect my hands. Poking out from the back of the drawer I could see a small plastic bag.

Perfect.

I emptied the contents of the bag into the drawer so I could slip it over my hand when . . . *yikes!*

Inside the bag was a set of baby clothes. *Clothes. FOR A BABY!* You know – like a person but smaller.

I held each item up one by one. They all had "aged 6–9 months" on the label. There was a T-shirt with "Daddy's Little Helper" on it, a tiny bobble hat, a pair of trousers, which had a big hole in the backside and were therefore completely useless, and a jumper with "Babe Magnet in Training" across the front.

Bit weird, I thought, racking my brains. There are no babies in my family. Ste has no friends with babies (as far as I know). There are not even any babies in our street. So who were they for? Did Ste have a secret child that I did not know about?

A cold mist seemed to creep around my feet. *Of course* Ste had a secret child. He was probably *married* and leading a double life. *No* – even worse – he had probably *stolen* the baby on the plane and he was hiding it in the boot of his car and feeding it nothing but doughnuts and Dr Pepper and all this *niceness* was just a big front for the evil person he really was.

I made up my mind – straight away I would stomp over to Lucy's and tell her about this baby and that would be the end of his chances with her and then . . . and then. . .

"Good morning, my Swarbricking sensation," said Mum, appearing at the doorway. "You found Ste's monkey clothes then? Gorgeous, aren't they?"

"His what?" I said.

"His clothes. For the monkeys. Funny, isn't it – he's buying human clothes for wild animals and we're trying to get humans to take their clothes off!"

"Of course," I said. "The monkeys."

I suddenly felt very, very silly. A monkey is probably not much bigger than a human baby; and the hole in the trousers was obviously for a tail, which humans do not usually have. Ste did not have a secret baby. He was nice now. He spent his time helping primates. He *had* changed. Maybe it was about time I changed too.

I took a deep puff on my inhaler. My initial reaction had surprised me a lot. Did I *want* Ste to be evil? Did it help me to have someone to dislike? Or was it just that I did not want anybody going anywhere near Lucy?

Using the bag as a glove, I picked up his pants. "I said I would take these round to Lucy's for him. I . . . owe him one."

"Great to see you getting on better with him," said Mum. "The Swarbricking's really *loosened you up*:

inspiring others, helping your brother. Now, don't forget to not wear your coat."

Lucy's House

Ste's BMW was still on Lucy's driveway, a blanket spread across the back seat and Paul's camera on the dashboard, but Ste was not inside it. I knocked on the front door. After a few moments, Dave King opened it.

"You!" he growled, grabbing me by the collar, shoving me up against the wall of the house and slamming the door behind him all in one. "Why didn't you stop her?"

I swallowed hard. "I . . . I am sorry." I could barely breathe and my feet were dangling off the floor.

Flecks of foamy spit gathered in the corners of his mouth. "*You* were there when she quit swimming. *You* were there when she met that juggling punk. *You* were there when she got drunk, and now, surprise surprise, *you* were there when she met up with that flamin' brother of yours again. If she gets back in with him, she'll never go in another swimming pool in her life."

I tried to speak but my throat seemed to be completely closed.

"In the army, people get hurt cos of idiots like you. How do you think I lost these? Eh?"

He let go of my collar to shove his three finger stumps in front of my face. The veins in his neck stuck out like pipes.

I leaned against the wall, breathing deeply. It was clear by the way he glared at me that he expected an answer. "SAS combat training. . .?"

The words had a peculiar effect. His arm flopped. He opened and closed his mouth a few times. Then he let out a long sigh and his shoulders sort of crumpled like a cheap tent.

How odd. I was about to ask if he was OK when the front door opened.

"Hiya," said Lucy's mum. "Steven said you'd be popping round with his stuff. He's upstairs having a well-earned shower."

I smiled weakly.

"What are you doing?" she said to Dave, who was now squatting down with his back to the wall, shaking his head. She rolled her eyes at Dave and led me inside. "He's been up and down for days."

Another Day Ticked Off

I am going to stop typing now. My brother and his girlfriend are making a load of racket next door. As far as I am aware,

197

they were meant to be preparing things for the ball on Saturday. However, they seem to be having a pillow fight or something equally noisy. I am going to actually go downstairs to watch TV.

I have just thought: the ball is now only four days away. *Four days.* That means I have three days of my placement left. After that I will be allowed back to school. I did not think I would ever say this but I will probably miss going to work with Chas.

Working for a Second Chance
Day 8 – Wednesday

Tasks completed: Counselling.
What I learned: Sometimes you can surprise yourself.

"So," said Chas, driving me towards the estate this morning, "the head-freaking-teacher of Moorfields Academy drops round to the van last night when I'm doing my rhyme school. Says truancy's right down and enthusiasm's up. Plus she's loving how we reward the little dudes for turning up at school. Says that if we can smarten the camper up a bit, she'll even think about giving us some funding."

"That is brilliant,". I said. And I meant it too.

"Bust me, brother," he said, pulling up at the lights and holding his fist out to me. I stared at it for a few moment then, with a big smile, touched my fist against it.

"We had better sort this place out then," I said, looking around at the brown stains on the walls and the grimy floor.

"We're way ahead of you, brother," said Chas. "They're filming a series of *Pimp My Crib UK*. Pat's on the net at home right now, applying for us to get on. Imagine – velvet wallpaper, palm trees, freaking awesome sound system, the works."

"Right," I said. "But, up until then, maybe we could just *clean* it a bit? I have got wet wipes."

"Let's do it."

About two hours later, I was walking to the bin by the shops with a bagful of rubbish, thinking about how *satisfying* cleaning was, when something whacked me on the back of the head. I turned round and looked up. Jamie was sitting on the roof of the chip shop, his legs dangling over the edge. A stone was lying by my feet.

"All right, nudist?" he said.

I waved and carried on towards the bin.

"Soz about painting them boobs on you," he called.

I faced him again, my hand blocking the sun. "It is fine," I lied. "I put the coat in the wash."

"Are you really a nudist?" he said.

I swallowed hard. "No, but some people think I am. It all got a bit out of hand. . ."

"Sounds like me," said Jamie. "Everyone thinks I'm bad but I'm not. I just don't trust people, cos of what happened to Flip Flop."

He hunched his legs up to his chin and sucked on the zip of his jacket. I looked around me. There was nobody else here. Then something really weird happened. It was like a blindfold being lifted. I just saw him differently. He stopped being the little fire-starting skateboard thief and suddenly became, well, *vulnerable*.

What did those other kids call him? A psycho? A freak? He did not seem to be either of those things. Sitting up there on the chip-shop roof, he just seemed like a quiet, slightly different lad who everyone got the wrong impression about.

He was right – he *did* sound a bit like me.

Then I realized something else. He was talking to me about his problems. He *wanted* to talk to me. Now, what was it that Chas just said? *"All these kids need is some dude to listen to them."*

"How is your dog?" I said, struggling to think of anything else to say.

Jamie took a deep breath. "Some guy nicked him."

"As in . . . *stole*?"

"Left him tied up outside the shop and he just walked off with him."

"Did you ask for him back?"

Jamie sighed. "This guy's massive. Dangerous. He just laughed at me."

"I can tell Chas if you want?" I said. "He might be able to help."

Jamie thought for a moment, then disappeared over the other side of the chip shop without answering.

"Great counselling," said Chas, back at the van, when I told him all about it. "Respect to your bad self. You got some serious skills. He opened right up."

"But I did not do anything."

"He trusts you. He sees someone who's even worse off than him. He wants help and, when he lets us, we'll give it to him."

Chas drove me home soon after. He wanted to go back to his place and check on how Miss O'Malley was getting along with her application before heading back to the estate with her later on for the evening workshop.

I wonder if Jamie will turn up?

Lucy's Room

The walls of the hallway, stairs and landing were all plastered with photos of Lucy finishing races or kissing gold medals. A huge trophy cabinet stood at the top of the stairs, bursting with medals and cups.

When I reached the landing, Ste poked his head round the bathroom door and I handed him the *Baby Market* bag with his underpants and socks inside.

"You're the best," he said. "Lucy's still asleep. I won't be long."

The door closed. Alone on Lucy's landing, I felt awkward, like a burglar. A door with her name on it was right next to the bathroom. Although petrified of her seeing me, I had an overwhelming urge to check she was OK. I peeped round her door and tiptoed in. The room was very girly. Well, I *say* the room was girly. I cannot say this for certain as it was the first time I had ever officially been in a girl's bedroom.[46]

Lucy was curled up, half under the bed covers, still wearing her clothes from the night before. By the bed there was a (thankfully empty) bucket. She looked so peaceful and still and... Hang on ... was her back *actually* rising and falling at all? I had heard about people drinking too much and terrible things happening and...

I went straight to the bed to check on her. *No movement*. I whispered her name into her ear. *Nothing*. Panicking, I bent down and lightly pressed my fingers to her neck to check for a pulse but she was suddenly woken by a loud click as the bathroom door was unlocked.

Her eyes snapped open to be greeted by my face two inches in front of hers and my fingers reaching

---

46 When I was younger my cousin used to make me go in her bedroom, where she would dress me as a girl and call me Princess Michaela. I have always tried to block it out, though, so I do not think it counts.

for her throat.

She screamed.

I screamed.

"Mike! What are you doing here?!" she yelled, pulling the covers over herself.

"I . . . thought you might be dead. I am not spying on you whilst you are asleep."

What a stupid thing to say.

Lucy flopped back on to her pillow. "My head hurts."

At that moment, Ste strode into the room topless and with a towel wrapped around his waist. His stomach muscles were bulging out in what some people refer to as a "six-pack".[47]

"Ste?" said Lucy, sitting up again and blushing. "How. . .?"

Ste placed his hand on her shoulder, making sure he tensed every muscle in his body as he did so. "You got drunk. But don't worry, The Steverlizer brought you home. Then he stayed outside all night to make sure you were OK."

A funny look spread across Lucy's face at this point. It was similar to the one Paul Beary has when he finds a loose Rolo at the bottom of his school bag. "You did

---

47 I think that these things look silly, like the surface of a badly made apple pie. This has nothing to do with the fact that my stomach looks like a large, pale bag of custard in comparison.

all that . . . for *me*?"

Ste actually looked embarrassed. "The Steverlizer just wants to make the world a better place."

"I saved you from a fire," I whined.

Unfortunately, this was drowned out by Lucy letting out a loud moan. "Oh . . . I bet I look a total mess."

"Not at all," said Ste. "You've never looked more beautiful."

I practically reached for the sick bucket myself. However – and despite the make-up smudged across her face and the ring that was half-hanging off her lip – I quickly said, "Yes. I agree."

Lucy rubbed her eyes with the wet flannel. "I can't remember anything."

My ears pricked up. "*Anything* at all?"

"Well," she said, "one minute Paul was juggling and . . . something caught fire. . ." Her hand went to her mouth. "Did I do something stupid?"

"No," I said, shaking my head and trying not to grin. This was ace! I felt like dancing the hokey-cokey. She did not remember our calamitous kiss! Obviously it would have been better if she had remembered the good part (i.e, the bit when she was actually not drooling and snoring) but beggars cannot be choosers. I was in the clear!

Now some people might say that a *good friend* would have told her what had happened so that she knew the truth. But what would that have achieved? Nothing. And in any case, what could I have said? "Yeah – moments after I set myself on fire you snogged me and it was so much fun that you fell asleep, then admitted that you love my brother." I decided to keep quiet.

"Course not," said Ste. "You were out like a light. You didn't even wake up when your phone was going off in your ear."

Lucy reached for her phone and tapped the screen a few times. "Text from Spyder. . . 'Hey, Lucy. Going back out with Tasha. Hope u got home ok. X.' Huh. What an idiot."

She did not seem too bothered, which was nice. The corners of Ste's lips twitched into a tiny smile.

"Oh, you're awake, love," said Lucy's mum, striding into the room. "Last time you'll be drinking alcohol, I hope. Lucky you had this fine young man to help you."

"It was nothing," I said, before realizing she was talking to Ste.

She opened the curtains, bathing the room in light. "I can't be too mad with you, though, Lucy. I had a few glasses of champagne the night me and your father got engaged, and I was only your age."

I was a bit disturbed by the way she looked at Ste when she said this.

"Right then, Steven," said Mrs King, holding his hand in both of hers. "Please stay for some breakfast. It's the least I can do. Bacon and sausage OK?"

"Oh, yummy," said Ste. "I'll get dressed and give you a hand."

As soon as he had slipped off to get changed, Mrs King turned back to Lucy and rubbed her hands together excitedly. "Oooh! Cut me a slice of beefcake, Lucy! Momma's hungry!"

"Moth-*er*! He's half your age," cried Lucy in pretend anger. "What are you like?"

Orange, over the top and completely terrifying, I thought.

"Anyway, he cheated on me, *remember*," said Lucy.

"Young boys make mistakes," said Mrs King. "It's up to us women to turn them into men."

It is worth noting that Mrs King did not offer me any breakfast before she left the room, even though it was *me* who had saved Lucy from being burned alive in the first place.

Lucy squinted at me. "Is something wrong?"

"No."

"Are you sure I didn't do anything silly last night?"

She looked like she was about to cry. A sudden feeling came over me, like a huge wave breaking over a sea wall. *I* wanted to make Lucy feel better. *I* wanted to be the one who put flannels on her forehead. *I* wanted to be the one who got a cooked breakfast off her mum.

This was it.

This was my moment.

I would tell her. I *had* to tell her now, before it was too late. I would tell her how *I* almost burned to death saving her life and how *I* looked after her and how *we* shared a romantic kiss.

But most of all, I would tell her that she was the most brilliant girl ever.

I cleared my throat. "Lucy. I want to tell y—"

Suddenly the colour drained from Lucy's face. "Get out."

"I am sorry. . ."

"I'm going to be s—" She slapped her hand over her mouth, her cheeks swelled up and she lurched towards the bucket.

I escaped on to the landing just as she made a noise I would rather not have associated with her.

"Everything OK?" said Ste, who was now dressed.

"Do not go in there," I said, my back against the door. "She is not well."

"Oh, the poor thing," said Ste, "I must help. You go downstairs – I know you get a bit squeamish about stuff like this."

A splashing sound from inside the room caused

me to wince.

As Ste went inside the bedroom and closed the door behind him, I could hear her retching whilst he said, "There, there," and, "I'll hold your hair out of the way."

Feeling like the last Rich Tea in the biscuit tin, I dragged my feet down the stairs, bumping into Lucy's mum at the bottom. She was holding a plate. On it, she had arranged Ste's cooked breakfast into a giant heart with six (yes, *six*!) long, thin sausages for the outline, and the eggs, bacon, tomato and beans in the middle.

Waiting

Back at home, I spent the afternoon in my bedroom, worrying about Lucy.

Ste finally returned at about half past five, carrying his iPad under his arm. "How is she?" I said, as soon as he came through the door.

"Much better, thanks. I bought her some Maltesers and we watched *Finding Nemo* on the iPad. It's her favourite film."

"I know," I said.[48]

---

[48] I also happen to know that her favourite flower is a daisy, she learned to ride a bike aged three, and if she could have any superhuman power it would be mechanical flippers. Source: various.

"What can I say? I dare to care. Oh ... and she wanted me to thank you for popping round."

"Really?" I said in a bit too much of a shrieky voice.

"Oh yeah. She thinks the world of you. In fact, I noticed she was wearing that friendship band I gave you."

Rumbled. "Ah. Yes. About that. . ."

Ste held up his hands. "No worries. To me, friendship is a gift. I gave that gift to you and you passed it on to Lucy. And now she's giving it back to me. Full circle. In fact, without you, Lucy and I would not be friends again. And who knows what the future holds. . ."

Despite everything he had done for her, this did not fill me with joy.

". . .which is why," continued Ste, "it's such a shame about what happened to the friendship band."

I narrowed my eyes. "What do you mean?"

"It fell in the sick bucket."

Lovely. Our friendship – drowned in chunder. Was it just me or was this a very bad sign?

"Anyway, I dropped Paul's camera off on the way home," said Ste. "He's still really down about Chantelle."

I felt awful about this. Then I remembered how Paul had encouraged everyone to Swarbrick the night before and the feeling passed.

"Well. I've saved his photos on to my iPad and I won't rest until I've made Chantelle jealous."

"Are you sure that is a nice thing to do?" I said.

"Of course. Paul's a lovely young man who'll enhance her life. She just doesn't realize it yet. I've told him to do as many good things as he can – you know, get the universe on his side."

"Right."

"And, by the way, it looks like it was an *awesome* party last night," he said, raising his eyebrows and giving me a friendly jab in the arm. Even though I was not sure what he meant, I jabbed him back and, for only about the third time ever, we both laughed at the same time. Then he ruffled my hair and skipped upstairs.

Paul Beary "Helps Out"

The following morning, Ste left the house early. Although it was Sunday, he was going into school to start making preparations for the Funky Monkey Ball. Mr Whittle was opening up the school specially to help him.

At about nine o'clock, I received a strange phone call from someone claiming to be from the *Evening News*. I hung up immediately, not realizing the significance of this at the time.

At about three o'clock, the doorbell rang and no one else answered it. Paul Beary was standing on the doorstep, grinning excitedly.

"You seem very happy," I said.

Paul put his hand inside his jacket. "Ste told me I should do good things and he's right – helping other people *does* make you feel happier. I sent the video into the paper and ... *ta-dah*!"

He pulled out a newspaper and thrust it in front of me. It took me a moment to pick up on what I was meant to be looking at.

More Fame

The headline read: "Supernude! Naked Riots Were a Tribute to Flaming Hero!" Basically, the "world exclusive" told how the naked riots were sparked by "the heroic actions of the king of the Swarbrickers" (me). Pages two and three were taken up by a series of stills from a video, which I recognized from the events at Spyder's party. I had obviously recorded them accidentally when I put the camera down on the wall. They were:

1. Paul (face pixellated out) throwing the flaming club in the air with the caption: "Fat chance of catching this: Obese clown tosses flaming torch into night sky."

2. Lucy underneath the torch (face also pixellated out). Caption: "Juggling jeopardy: Mystery hottie unaware she is about to be struck with blazing killer club."

3. Me charging into Lucy. Caption: "Custard dream: Dressed as a biscuit, heroic Swarbrick leaps to the rescue."

4. Me lying on top of Lucy, on fire. Caption: "Blazing biccy: Swarbrick is engulfed in flames."

5. Me taking off my costume. Caption: "Just in the (Swar)*brick* of time:[49] Magnificent Michael whips off melting costume."

6. The crusty punks all stripping off as well. Caption: "Strip of a lifetime: Punky partygoers get a piece of the action."

Essentially, the story focused on the idea that the rioters were inspired by me saving Lucy's life. And, although *they* were a "bunch of degenerates" who "brought shame on this great city", I was actually quite a nice person. My only crime was "to associate with such desperate morons" when, clearly, I was "an example that not all nudists are numpties". It also described me as a "shy and humble hero who did not wish to boast about his

---

49 I have to say that, of all of the dreadful puns, this one is by far the lamest.

actions when we rang him this morning".

There were four ways I could feel about this:

a. Outraged at Paul. I mean, I *definitely* did not want any more publicity.
b. Kind of relieved that the article did not criticize me and there were no pictures of my – you know – *parts*.[50]
c. Grateful that Paul at least *tried* to do the right thing.
d. Happy that, for the first time in my life, I was a hero.

On balance then, the article was slightly more good than bad. I mean, if everybody is convinced you are a nudist anyway, it is better to be a brave one than an evil one. I tried to cling to the positives. "Mostly this is not terrible."

"Great," Paul beamed. "Now I just have to wait for good stuff to happen to me."

Text From Chas

I have just received the following text from Chas:

---

50 One photo showed a blurred *portion* of my body but, frankly, it could have been anyone's bottom.

Radical newz bro. Jamie came 2 rap therapy 2nite.
Wants us 2 help him. All thanks 2U. CU tomz. Word.

OK, so I am trying not to look too pleased with myself right now but it is difficult. It sounds to me like I might have just done something good for a change!
I am going to try not to think about the fact that I only have two more days left.

Working for a Second Chance
Day 9 – Thursday

Tasks completed: Dog recovery.
What I learned: Sometimes big hands have big advantages.

Today I witnessed something incredible.
    "We're going to war today, bro," Chas said as I climbed into the camper. He was wearing a bandanna, which he said was a gift from a retired gang leader he had met in the USA.[51]

---

51 From what I could see, the "bandanna" showed a map of the USA made up of a collage of kitchen items (bowls, spoons, dishes, etc.) along with the title "The United *Plates* of America". This led me to believe it was actually a tea towel.

"You are going to have a *fight*?" I said.

"Oh, good lord, no," said Miss O'Malley. "We're going to war against Jamie's issues. We're going to get his dog back."

"Amen," said Chas. "Once we do that we can work on his other problems. Then we'll turn his life around."

"It's all thanks to you, Michael," said Miss O'Malley. "Last night Jamie said that seeing how bad your life is made him realize he can overcome anything."

I did not say anything but I could not stop myself from grinning. In fact, I even whistled along as Chas rapped to the rattling beat of the engine. Here is a sample of his "phat rhymes":

> Yo, I'm MC Chas,
> King of razzmatazz.
> Suckers and fools
> Better follow my rules.
> I got a wife called Pat,
> I bust it out like a cat
> Sayin' meow.
> I ain't a cow
> Cos a cow goes moo
> But I say, "Flip you!"

This was followed by statements like: "Word to your mother, homes" and "Bust out my grapes, momma. Don't crust up my energies" and "Hit me with a beat sandwich, P-Dog".[52]

OK, so his rapping skills *were* horrendous but I was so elated that I did not mind. When he had run out of things to rap about, I asked, "Did you get anywhere with *Pimp My Crib UK*?"

Miss O'Malley made a *who-knows* face. "We'll see. I've got a good feeling about it."

A makeover for the camper van would be brilliant. My cleaning yesterday had improved things slightly but the fact is that you cannot make a diamond ring out of an old potato.

We met Jamie near the secondary school. Although he clearly wanted help, he seemed extremely nervous about confronting the dog thief and did not wish to get into the camper at first. It took Chas twenty minutes of sitting on the kerb with him, gently chatting, before he finally climbed in and directed us to a house in a cul-de-sac. One of the front windows had been boarded up. The messy garden was home to a washing machine, which lay on its side. There was a sign on the gate warning about a dog. It did not say "Beware of the chihuahua" or "Watch out, poodle about" or anything like that. No. It read: "Stay out or dog will rip off UR throat".

"So this is the place?" said Chas, pulling on a pair of aviator shades.

---

52 Chas has now hired Miss O'Malley as his official DJ. He claims that this has nothing to do with the fact that Rahim thought Jamie was a better rapper than him.

Jamie nodded. "His name's Dan Steel. He's nuts – be careful."

Chas chewed on a toothpick. "No one said it'd be easy but I'm sure this dude'll listen to reason. Now, what's your pooch called?"

"Flip Flop," said Jamie.

Chas strode up to the front door and whacked on it. There was a long pause, and then he stepped back as the scariest person I have ever seen opened the door. Even more scary than Dan Steel, however, was the enormous, vicious-looking dog that he was dragging back by the collar.

"Flip Flop!" cried Jamie.

"*That is* Flip Flop?" I said. With a name like that I was expecting something fluffy and cute.

"Yep. I gave him that name cos he lost half an ear in a fight. He's a cross between a wolf and an Argentinian bear-hunting dog," said Jamie. "He's sweet when you get to know him, though."

Wow! I thought. I knew this estate was rough but come on! How hard would you have to be to steal one of those things?

After a short conversation at the door, Chas came back up the path and sat down in the camper van. The man continued to stare at us whilst the dog savaged the door frame.

"How did it go?" said Miss O'Malley.

"Will he give me my dog back?" said Jamie.

Chas drummed his fingers on the steering wheel. "Jamie.

217

Have you ever considered owning a *different* dog?"

Jamie looked horrified.

"What could I do?" said Chas to Miss O'Malley. "The guy said he'd fight me for it."

"Ach," said Miss O'Malley. "Let's sort this out."

What happened next was pretty much too amazing to put into words. Basically:

1. Miss O'Malley got out of the van, strode into his garden, flipped the washing machine the right way up and rolled up her sleeve. She told Dan Steel she would arm-wrestle him for the dog.
2. Laughing his head off, Dan chained the dog to a stake in the middle of the garden. Then he knelt down opposite her, his elbow on the washing machine.
3. They assumed the arm-wrestle position. Dan Steel looked at her gigantic hand as it enveloped his and instantly stopped laughing.
4. There was a short arm wrestle, followed by a loud clang (as a hand was rammed down on to the washing machine), then a whimpering noise.
5. Miss O'Malley apologized profusely. Then she used her nurse's training *and* her carpentry training to make the man a splint from one of his rickety fence panels and advised him to go to A & E to have his arm checked out.
6. A very thankful Jamie got his dog back and it

dragged him home.
7. Chas and Miss O'Malley took me to the café for a celebratory cup of tea.

Although I am safely home, I am still shaking with excitement. I have this incredible *need* to continue my story. It seems like the more I enjoy the placement, the more I want to carry on explaining why I am doing it in the first place.

Unexpected Guest

The taxi had a sign on the side saying "Manchester Airport Cabs". This clue led me to believe that it had come from Manchester Airport. The driver helped an ancient woman out of the back. She was pointing at a piece of paper.

"I told you. This is the place," the driver said, dumping her case on to the pavement. "Is this old bag yours?" he called over. I was not sure if he meant the suitcase or the woman.

"I do not think so," I said.

The driver sniffed. "She owes me sixty quid but I can't get a word of English out of her."

The old woman's face lit up when she saw me. She was only about four and a half feet tall from the soles of her Velcro shoes to the top of her fluffy white hair. The skin of her face was wrinkled but her eyes flickered with mischievous energy.

"Purl-ur. Swarbrick," she said, shuffling towards me like a Dalek, her arms outstretched.

I stepped behind Paul, using him as a human shield.

"Swarbrick?" said the driver. "Where have I heard that before?"

"Nowhere," I said. "Nowhere at all."

"She sounds French; maybe I can translate," said Paul.

I was just about to tell him that his French skills would not be of any use in this situation (I mean, why would we need to order six Big Macs from her or ask her where the nearest topless beach is?) when Dad came outside.

"Everything OK?" he said.

"Purl-ur. Swarbrick," grinned the old woman, inanely. Her accent was so strong that it was hard to pick out what she was saying.

"Look. I don't care who pays me but if someone could just—"

"Roy," said Mum, stepping out of the house. "Get your wallet out. We'll pay the fare."

"Are you mad?" cried Dad.

"This is a momentous occasion, Roy," said Mum as she helped the old woman through the front door. "The first Swarbricker has arrived."

A Startling Revelation

Mum sat the old lady down in the kitchen with a cup of tea. "It's obvious," she smiled. "She's here to see you, Michael. I only put our address online yesterday."

"You did what?" shrieked Dad.

"Are you mad?" I cried. "*Any* nutter could turn up here."

Mum put her hand in front of her mouth. "Oh. I hadn't thought of that."

"This has gone too far now, love," said Dad.

"Roy, I realize I *may* have made a teeny little error. . ."

"Telling the world where we live is a pretty massive error, actually," I said.

". . .but Swarbrickers are gentle souls," she continued, nodding towards the old lady. "And if we can help just one person to free themselves then it'll all be worth it. Our house could be a centre – no, an academy – for nervous nudists. One day we'll look out of the window and the garden will be jam-packed with naked bodies. I can see it now: *The Michael Swarbrick Foundation for Struggling Swarbrickers.*"

"Awful," I said.

"Eh?" said the old woman, leaning forward.

Mum sighed. "Poor thing. She's confused. Her whole life she's been trapped inside her clothes and now, in the winter of her years, she sets out on a pilgrimage to find the inspirational young man who will finally help her to become a naturist. What a beautiful story."

"How could she have read about me?" I said. "She does not understand English."

The old woman removed her false teeth and placed them on the side of the table. "Purl-ur. Ssshhwarbrick."

"Any luck translating this word, Paul?" said Mum. Since arriving, the old lady had said nothing else.

"Purl-ur?" said the old woman, taking a sudden interest.

"Well," said Paul, chewing the end of his pencil. My French dictionary was open on the table in front of him. "*Swarbrick* we know. This other word could be lots of things. It's hard cos of her accent. Let's see: there's *pulper*, which means 'to pulp'."

"Nice one, Mum," I said. "You've invited her into the house and she wants to *pulp* me."

Mum tutted.

"Then," said Paul, "we've got *pelle* – a shovel or a scoop. Or *pâlir*, which means 'to turn pale'."

I took a blast on my inhaler. "Of course I have turned pale. There is a mad old woman in the house who wants to batter me to death with a garden tool."

"Nothing else makes sense, apart from one," said Paul, "*peler*, which means 'to skin' or . . . '*to peel off*'."

"She is going to *skin* me like a rabbit," I said. "That seals it. I. AM. CALLING. THE. POLICE."

Mum clapped her hands. "Of course! I told you! She wants to peel off her clothes and go Swarbricking!"

At that moment the front doorbell rang. The last thing I saw as I left the room was the old woman's happy yet confused face as Mum mimed how to unzip her coat.

Front Door

I paused and peered out through the spyhole. *Lucy!* Yikes.

I quickly looked at myself in the hall mirror.[53]

"Hi, Mike," she said as I opened up.

"You look amazing ... *ly* well," I said, stepping outside and closing the door behind me.

She blushed, which was nice. "Aw – you're sweet. I saw the paper today. Why didn't you tell me you'd saved me from that fire? I'd forgotten all about it and I just

---

53 Waggly head – *check*. Weird face – *check*. The strange embarrassed smile of a person who is trying to conceal the fact that his ancient French stalker is hiding in the kitchen getting a nudity lesson off his mum – *check again*.

wanted to thank you properly for being brave."

Now it was my turn to blush. "Well. . ."

"Maybe I could take you out on another friendship date to show my gratitude?"

Fantastic! It was like the shattered remains of the Lucy-ometer had been lovingly fixed back together with an extra section – blue for "beyond the realms of human happiness".

"I would love that."

"Great," said Lucy. "Maybe it'd be fun to invite . . . *other people* too."

I shook my head. "Nah. Best with just the two of us."

"Sure there's nobody you'd like to bring along?"

I mentally flicked through the address book of my friends and considered each one in turn:

1. Paul Beary – under no circumstances whatsoever, and not just because of the photos he took of Lucy in her bikini either. Whenever he is around girls, he does something creepy.
2. Er, actually that is it. Just Paul.

"Nope," I said. "Us two it is then."

"Sure there's nobody else. . .?" she said, puffing out her cheeks. "Such as a *friend* or . . . ooh – I don't know – *a relative*?"

I felt like I had been headbutted in the stomach. "You mean . . . *Ste*?"

On second glance at the Lucy-ometer, I noticed that there was also a new section at the other end of the scale – purple for "unmatched horrendousness". And this was the direction in which the needle was rapidly swinging.

Lucy tried hard to look surprised. "Ste? Wow! I hadn't even thought abou—"

"Oh good, we can take someone else," I said quickly.

"But, since you mention it. . ." she went on. "I suppose we *could* let him tag along."

At that moment, Ste pulled up in his car. Impeccable timing.

Now, I know what you might be thinking – why was I being so negative about him? At this point I was actually beginning to *like* Ste. Surely I should have been happy for him to come out with us?

And, yes, you are probably right. In fact, afterwards I felt embarrassed because of my reaction. However, I could not help but think that, eventually, Lucy was going to have to choose between the two of us – and who was she going to pick? The good-looking charity worker with the six-pack and the BMW, or the stumpy nudist with the pot belly and the bicycle?

Ste was speaking on his mobile phone as he stepped

out on to the drive. "Why *English* cigarettes? Surely he'll smoke oth. . . Well . . . I *can* buy them but. . . Look, something's come up. Bye."

He hung up and came over smiling. "Hi, Mike. And Lucy. You're looking better. Hey. I almost forgot. I still owe you that cuddly monkey. I'll bring it over later."

Lucy giggled maniacally.

"Who are you buying fags for?" I said.

Ste pretended to swat a fly. "Ah . . . you know."

I did not know, as it happened.

"How are the ball preparations going?" said Lucy before giggling again.

"Really well, thanks. It's gonna be a great night. I can't wait to get out to Thailand afterwards and help those monkeys."

Lucy looked suddenly disappointed. "You're going away?"

"Straight after the ball, to make sure the monkey money gets to the right place. School's letting me do distance learning. I'll be back in a month, though."

"Phew!" said Lucy. "I mean, good for you. Anyway. Mike and I are going out tonight. *As friends.*"

I was not particularly keen on how firmly she added the last bit.

"Great," said Ste. "Have fun."

He winked at Lucy, lightly squeezed my shoulder

and walked straight through the front door. This was awesome – he had completely missed her hint.

"Please come with us!" yelped Lucy, before putting her hand to her mouth. Oh, how degrading. She was begging like a hungry orphan.

Ste slowly turned round. "I'd love to but I've got to fill in a load of forms for the school's adoption of Alan."

Lucy laughed crazily again. "Well. Take a few hours off. I was . . . I mean, *we were* just saying how much we'd like you to be there too."

"Oh, cheers," said Ste. "Well, in that case, yeah. I'll come for a few hours. What are you doing?"

"Anything you want..." said Lucy, before hastily adding, "I mean. Whatever we decide together."

Ste shrugged. "Bowling?"

"Definitely," said Lucy.

"Cosmic," I said flatly. There are crippled pigeons with better average bowling scores than me.

"Pick you up at seven," he said.

Lucy flapped her arms around frantically. "Eeek. I'd better go and get ready."

"It is only four o'clock," I said. The needle on the Lucy-ometer was snatched from my hands, tied to a brick and thrown into the sea.

Final Scores

So bowling that night was *amazing*. Against all the odds, I *actually* won. Ste cried his eyes out and stormed off and Lucy was so impressed she bought me a blue Slush Puppie. Then we arranged a date for the following week at a "paint-your-own-plate" café, where we would spend a whole happy afternoon decorating pottery with romantic messages for each other and eating scones.

Well, not quite.

In actual fact, at the end of the game, the scores were:

Lucy: 134 points
Ste: 186
Me: 7

Yes. Seven. Things did not *really* go to plan. I think I had a faulty ball. It was like trying to bowl a banana. Indeed I achieved my best score (four) when I dropped the ball whilst carrying it to the line. It dribbled along and glanced the end pin before three other pins sort of keeled over in embarrassment. It turns out I am better at bowling when I am not actually bowling at all. Even worse was the way Ste and Lucy high-fived each other whenever they got a good score, and the way he went up when she was about to bowl and physically showed her how to improve her technique.

The only good thing was when Lucy pecked me on the cheek afterwards and said, "Never mind". Obviously, now that I was a veteran of actually snogging her, my reaction to this was totally cool and sophisticated. Well, OK, so maybe I wriggled about and let out a squeal of joy.

Unfortunately, this feeling evaporated when she immediately put her hand to her mouth and made the kind of noise you might make after finding someone else's tooth in your rice pudding.

Not exactly the response I was looking for. From there to the car she kept her distance from me.

Ste started the engine. "Ice cream back at ours?"

Lucy nodded but said nothing more the whole way home.

When we got back, I went straight to my room. I did not want ice cream. If my bowling was anything to go by, I would probably miss my mouth with the spoon. I had suffered enough humiliation for one night.

Or so I thought. Unfortunately, my humiliation had not even begun.

Room with a (Horrifying) View

When I got to my room, I took the Lucy King

scrapbook out of my walk-in cupboard so that I could stick the bowling scoresheet into it (obviously I planned to swap mine and Ste's names over). Flicking through it as I crossed the room, I did not check my bed before plonking myself down on it. This was a mistake. I instantly shot up back up in the air, as if electrocuted.

The old French woman was lying in my bed. *In my bed.* And, judging by the bare, wrinkled shoulders that were poking out from above my Spider-Man duvet, she was not wearing any clothes.

Unfortunately, this was confirmed for me when she sat up, causing the covers to fall away. She looked like a great big shrivelled sultana. And her ... *parts* were touching my *sheets*.

"Peler, Shhwarbrick," she grinned, toothlessly.

"Get out!" I cried, pointing to the door.

Saying this was a mistake. Despite her lack of English, she understood the command perfectly. Calmly, she threw back the covers and shuffled across the carpet like a wet paper bag in the breeze. Trust me – this is not something you can ever *un*-see.

Just as she reached the door, someone knocked on it from the other side. "Michael, are you in there?"

Lucy! Oh no!

"Do not come in!" I said, leaping in front of the old woman and accidentally brushing against her skin.

Gross – it felt like a long-forgotten peach.

"Can we chat?" Lucy said. "Whilst Ste's in the bathroom."

I ushered the old woman away. "Can you not say it *through* the door? I am engaging in my pre-bedtime rituals."

Rituals? It sounded like I was dancing about with a goat's skull on my head.

I could hear Lucy's hair rustling against the door. "It's *private*. I remembered something . . . *from the party*."

Eeek! She had remembered our kiss. Of course – that was why she had suddenly gone weird after bowling. But how much had she remembered?

The handle turned from the other side but I flung myself against the door. "One moment."

Firstly, I had to get rid of the old woman.

But *where*? I scanned the room. My options were:

Through the window. Verdict – way too cruel.[54]
Into my walk-in cupboard. Verdict – the only
    possible solution.

I shoved her inside it and shut the door. Just as I was about to invite Lucy in, I noticed the Lucy King

---

54 Plus, I am literally the softest person on Earth and there is no guarantee that I would be able to overpower her.

scrapbook lying in the middle of the room. I dived over and grabbed it. Then, in the absence of anywhere better to put it, I opened the cupboard, shoved it into the old woman's hands and slammed the door again.

"Come in," I said, leaning against the cupboard door and failing to sound calm.

Up until that moment, if anybody had told me that my best friend and the loveliest person on Earth, Lucy King, would one day be standing in my bedroom, I would never have considered that the experience would leave me feeling disgusted, disturbed and wanting to cry.

"Were you talking to someone?" said Lucy.

"Who, me? No. The very thought..." I said, smiling unconvincingly.

Lucy closed the door behind her. "Look, I don't know how to say this but earlier I sort of got this ... blurred memory and..." She held her head to the side like a glorious owl. "What was that?"

A cold sweat spread across my back. "What was what?"

There was a muffled knocking on the door behind me. "Er ... that."

"Just me. Vertical tap-dancing against doors is one of my hobbies." I back-heeled it several times.

"O-*kaayy*," said Lucy. "Well ... *anyway*, so I got this picture and I need to know..."

By now I was really stamping on the door to drown

232

out the ever louder knocking from the old woman. I nodded encouragingly for Lucy to continue.

"I need to kn… Hang on," said Lucy, moving me aside and opening the cupboard. "It's coming from in here."

Double Disaster

Lucy screamed.

The old woman grinned out at us, as naked as a newt, the duvet on the floor by her feet and the book in her hands.

"Michael," said Lucy, her voice shaking. "Why is there a nude old lady in your cupboard?"

I tried to act surprised. "How did she get in there?" I said.

"Have you been … keeping her prisoner?"

"I can explain…" I said, racking my brain. Was she:

1. A pet?
2. A cleaner whose clothes had been sucked up into the Hoover?
3. A dummy who had come to life?

"… actually I do not think I can."

Lucy backed away. "I'm scared."

"Peler Swarbrick?" said the old woman.

"Everything OK?" said Ste, appearing at the bedroom door.

"Could not be better," I said.

Lucy flung her arms around him and buried her head in his chest. "Your brother's got this old woman under lock and key and she's nude and..."

After patting Lucy on the arm, he picked up the duvet and gently wrapped it around the old lady's shoulders. "Don't worry – she's covered up."

The old woman gazed at him dreamily.

"Thank you," said Lucy, regaining her composure. "And ... hang on. Why's she holding a book with my name on it?"

"You do not want to look in that," I said.

It was too late. Lucy had already removed it from the old lady's hands. "The Big Book of Lucy," she said, flicking through the pages. "A scrapbook. All about me. Pictures ... of me ... newspaper clippings ... of me ... how ... *sweet*."

She said "sweet" like she actually meant "really, really weird".

"And ... what is this, Mike?" she said, holding one page open, a worried expression on her face.

I looked glumly at the floor. "It is a plaster that fell

off your foot before the Regional Championships."

"A what?"

"I thought it was a nice thing to keep," I said, hopefully.

"It has my blood on it, Michael. My *blood*."

Lucy stared at me, bewildered and disappointed and scared all at the same time. Like if someone had just come round and sewn chicken's legs on to her dog or something. "This is *not* normal, Mike."

"Come on, Lucy, I'll take you home," said Ste. "And Michael, I won't rest till I've found you the best doctors money can buy."

I stood stock-still in my bedroom, listening to Ste's car roaring off down the road. Lucy had taken the scrapbook with her, probably in order to have it destroyed. In just one short minute I had gone from being Lucy's best friend to being a kidnapper *and* a stalker. Having sunk to the very bottom of the ocean, the Lucy-ometer was promptly swallowed by a squid.

"Peler Swarbrick?" said the old woman.

I dropped to my knees.

End of the Day

I do not wish to write any more. The end of my friendship with Lucy is the saddest thing that has happened to me. There really is no way back. It is not like I did something that could easily be forgiven, like borrowing her roller skates and forgetting to return them or accidentally eating her last Fruit Pastille. As far as she is concerned, I am like a faulty toaster – not worth keeping and potentially dangerous.

Working for a Second Chance
Day 10 – Friday

Tasks completed: Watching everything go up in smoke.
What I learned: Wherever I go, problems follow.

Today was an absolute disaster. It was meant to be the last day of my placement. After today I should have been able to resume my school career. Unfortunately, that is no longer the case.

I should be in the camper van, helping Chas, but I am not. I am currently sitting in the Isolation Suite back at school, waiting to see Mr Whittle. He is in his office, trying to figure out what he can possibly to do with me now.

The day started well enough.

When we parked in our usual place on the estate, Jamie was waiting for us. We spent most of the morning sitting around in the camper with him, just talking about Flip Flop. Jamie was pretty upbeat but he did tell us a lot of other reasons why he was not at school. Chas told him that he would do everything he could to help. Once again, he really impressed me with how he got Jamie to talk without putting any pressure on him at all.

However, there were two different events that spoiled the day. The first was when Miss O'Malley's phone rang. "Ooh – it's the people from *Pimp My Crib UK*," she said, answering it excitedly. However, as she listened to the person on the other end, her face slowly became more and more disappointed. "Rubbish," she said, hanging up. "Just cos it's not a home doesn't mean it doesn't deserve a makeover."

"Can you not just pay someone to do the work for you?" I said.

Chas looked pretty gutted. "No dice, dude. We spent all our dollars on the camper. My wallet's bare, you dig? That was our last chance."

"And we've got that head teacher coming over this morning," said Miss O'Malley. "She won't be keen to fund us if she doesn't think we can improve the place."

"And if you cannot get any funding?" I said, but the look on Miss O'Malley and Chas's faces kind of answered for me.

The second terrible event came soon after, when the head teacher of Moorfields Academy dropped by.[55] A bird like woman who moved quickly and jerkily, she did not seem too impressed with the patched-up roof, stained walls, disgusting upholstery and damp smell.

"So," said Chas, "we did our best to tidy the place up like you asked. The one with ... *personal problems*. D'you think we're worth a bit of investment?"

"Professor Swaffham-Bunstable, your results speak for themselves . . . but this is not what I meant when I asked you to improve your camper van. You cannot really expect me to pay you to entertain my students in here, can you?"

"Just give us some time," begged Chas. "We'll sort this."

The head teacher took a deep breath. "Very well. I will delay my decision for another two weeks. But that is it. The vehicle must be completely renovated by then."

Miss O'Malley ran her huge hands through her hair. "But where can we get the mon—"

"We can work with that," said Chas, attempting to give the head teacher one of those ghetto-handshake-hug things.

Her whole body stiffened and at that moment she appeared to notice me for the first time. "And who is this?"

"Ach," said Miss O'Malley. "This is Michael."

---

55 Before she got there, Jamie left – he did not wish to speak to her but promised to return later on.

"Should he not be at school?"

"I'm on an extended work placement," I said. "I was having . . . problems."

The head teacher's eyes widened. "I knew I recognized you. You're that boy from the newspapers. You go to Mr Whittle's school, don't you? He mentioned you at our local head teachers' conference." By the look on her face, nothing that he had told her had been particularly nice. She turned to Chas. "Are you counselling this boy as well?"

"Nah, he's helping us out. Chatting with the kids and stuff."

"Mr Swaffham-Bunstable," she said, "he is – *ahem* – a notorious nudist. I do not wish my most vulnerable students to be associating with . . . *people like him*."

"He's only got one more day left," said Chas.

"That is irrelevant," said the head teacher. "I really must question your judgement in allowing him to be here at all. What if my students get counselled by you and come back to school completely stark naked?"

"That won't. . ." began Chas.

The head teacher silenced him with an aggressive eyebrow. "Will it not? Because, as far as I am aware, he has inspired a lot of people in the past. He leaves this instant or I will not even consider your funding request for one second longer."

"No way!" said Chas. "I made a promise to my main man, Mikey. He's gotta stay till the end of today."

She pursed her lips.

"That is not fair on you," I said quietly. "I will not be the person to stop you from helping people. Please take me back to school."

"Quit your jibber-jabber, Mike. That's crazy talk."

"No," I said. "It is better that you help lots of people rather than just me. Please. I want you to."

It took a lot of persuading but eventually I got my own way. Obviously this was the right thing to do and I am glad I did it, so why has it made me feel a million times worse? It just seems that trouble follows me around like toilet roll stuck to my shoe.

I do not wish to think about this any more so I will continue my story.

Terrible Night

After Ste and Lucy left, Mum came and helped the old lady into my bed. "Well done for getting her to Swarbrick around, Michael," she said, "but it's been an exhausting day. Let's not overdo it."

Unwilling and unable to argue, I was led to the camp bed that had been set up for me in the front room. It was uncomfortable and small but I cocooned myself in my sleeping bag, buried my head in the pillow and tried to ignore the cruel world beyond.

I was almost asleep when the front door opened and Ste came into the lounge, causing me to sit up. "Hey, Mike – glad you're awake. I wanted to say thank you."

"For what exactly?"

"Well, if it wasn't for you, Lucy and I wouldn't be officially back together."

I was not surprised by this; it was pretty much inevitable from the moment he got off the plane. However, even though I knew Ste had changed into a much better person, I still felt like my stomach had been shoved up into my throat. I did not want Lucy to be with Ste. I did not want her to be with anyone.

"Good for you."

"Thanks. So The Steverlizer takes her home and she's like 'Ooh, that brother of yours is a bit odd. . .'"

"She said that?"

"Well, no."

"*Phew.* What did she say?"

He shook his head. "I'd rather not upset you. Anyway. I comfort her. She tells me how she feels. We're an item again. Mission accomplished."

I looked up. "You planned this all along?"

"Course. I've been playing it cool, pretending not to care about that Spyder character, letting her do the running, being kind but not seeming interested. All the classics."

"Is that not . . . *wrong*?"

Ste looked completely puzzled. "Er . . . no. When it comes to ladies, you can't blunder in and hope for the best. You need a strategy. Like in a war. And – well – I knew that in your own spectacular way, you'd help me to get back in with her. You are the best."

"You mean . . . you *planned* for Lucy to hate me as well?"

Ste laughed. "How could I possibly *plan* to put an old woman in your cupboard? And, as for the scrapbook, a *used plaster*, Michael? Yikes."

I put my head in my hands. "My life is ruined."

"Don't be down," said Ste. "These things balance themselves out."

"You think so?" I said, trying not to sound too hopeful.

"Definitely. Yes, *your* life is ruined, but *mine* is perfect. So, you know, chin up. Every cloud has a silver lining."

I should have picked up on this comment at the time – I mean, it is not exactly what a nice person would say, is it? And after he spoke, he kind of put his hand over his mouth like he had not wanted the words to slip out. However, I was so desperate about what had happened with Lucy that I barely even noticed. "Please can you speak to her for me?"

Ste recovered himself and smiled kindly. "Leave it

with me, eh? Now get some sleep. You look terrible."

Shocking Wake-up Call

That night I had a nightmare. I was trapped in that picture from Ste's Facebook page – the one on the beach. Except, in my dream, I was the monkey, sitting on *Lucy's* shoulder, and she was feeding me Twiglets. Ste (also a monkey – what can I say? I have weird dreams...) was on her other shoulder, and just as I was about to eat the Twiglets he snatched them off me and held them above my head, taunting me...

I suddenly woke up. The Twiglets were still there, either side of my face, all skinny and brown, with something drooping off them like half-set treacle.

I blinked, realized what I was looking at and scrambled away, tipping the camp bed on top of me. They were not Twiglets – they were the mad old French woman's bare legs. And the droopy treacle stuff was the saggy skin around her ankles. And, even worse, the bare legs were connected to the rest of her bare body. She was just sitting there, snoozing in front of the TV news, with her feet either side of my pillow.

I wriggled out of my sleeping bag and laid it over her, shuddering.

At that moment Dad came into the room.

"Please can you do something about . . . *this*," I said, gesturing towards the old lady.

Dad took a deep breath. "You're right, son. This has gone too far and we need to. . ."

His voice trailed off as soon as Mum entered the room. "Ah, there she is," she said, noticing the old lady "She wasn't in her bed – she's got a real habit of walking off. Now, what were you saying, Roy?"

I looked at Dad hopefully. Was he about to tell Mum to kick Madame Bare Cheeks out of the house and back to France?

Er . . . no.

He did not make a noise but, if he had, it would have been *hissssssssssss*, like a tyre being deflated. "Nothing, dear," he said eventually, before scuttling out of the room.

Rebellion crushed.

Mum fussed around the old lady, straightening the cushion behind her head. "Ah, look at her, Michael – so peaceful now. See the difference that Swarbricking is making to her life? She reached out to us and we've helped her – and I'm sure she'll just be the first of many."

"All I want is to be left alone. *Dad!*" I cried. "Please talk some sense into Mum."

Dad was now on the phone in the hall. He put his hand over the receiver. "I'm a bit busy, son. Sorry."

And with that he went back to his phone call. *Excellent* – Mum wanted to turn the house into a naked therapy centre and he was enjoying a nice little chat.

The only good thing about that morning was that Mum allowed me to have the day off school. Apparently I did not look good after my night on the camp bed and she said I would need my strength if Swarbrickers were going to start flooding into the house from around the world.

The downside of this was that, although I did not have to face anyone at school, I had a lot of time on my hands. I spent the day in Ste's room, avoiding the old lady. Meanwhile, my thoughts rattled along in the following manner:

The world is unfair.

↓

No matter how nice you are to someone,
and how much you care for them, you put one
blood-soaked plaster in a scrapbook and one naked
old lady finds her way into your cupboard,
and you are a nutter for life.

↓

And as for her going out with Ste.

Well, this was worst of all. I mean, he was . . .
he was . . . he was. . .

↓

OK, so he was *nice* but what had that got to
do with anything? Why did I need a reason for not
wanting her to go out with him? Nobody asks me why
I do not like coloured toilet rolls or giant fruit.[56] I did
not like her going out with him and that was that.

↓

She should have been going out with
someone *better*. Someone dependable and sweet
with hidden qualities. Someone like. . .

↓

Me? Who said that? How did *that* thought
get into my brain? Ha! The very idea. Well, since you
mention it, I suppose I *could* fit the bill of being
Lucy's escort. I daresay I would do a reasonable job,
not that I have considered it before. . .

↓

I should send Lucy a short text; nothing too weird
or pushy – just a quick hello. Yes, that would be an
excellent idea. Any objections from anyone? Nope.
Thought not. Good.

---

56 Although, if anyone did ask, the reasons would be: flaky texture and the fact that it
makes me feel like I've been shrunk. It should be obvious which one is which.

On reflection, my text to Lucy was not short (four messages long). And it probably *was* slightly weird and pushy. I am not proud of it. In my defence, though, I was not thinking straight. It makes me cringe to see it again but here it is:

Dearest Lucy. I apologize wholeheartedly for the shock you suffered when finding the old lady and also the book I keep as a tribute to you. I only have this book because I think you are a brilliant and special person. With this is mind, maybe you should think carefully about who you go out with. I mean, I know Ste is really nice and everything, but there are other options and it would be a good idea to try some of them out before you commit to someone who might not be perfect for you. Thank you for reading this. FYBFAMM. Michael x PS: FYBFAMM = forever your best friend and maybe more

She did not reply.

Ste

When Ste came home at five, he found me lying on his bed feeling very nervous. My mobile was by my side, as it had been since I sent the text six hours earlier.

"All right, mate?" he said.

I sat up. With every minute of silence from my phone, I had become increasingly nervous about what I had sent, rereading it again and again. What would Lucy think of me now? And Ste had been nothing but brilliant to me recently – how could I try and prise her away from him like that? I had become a terrible, selfish person. The only good thing was that Ste seemed happy – Lucy would never have told him about the text, no matter how creepy it was. From now on, I would be a good brother and a good person.

"This your phone?" he said, picking it up.

"Yes, but I do not use it for bad things," I said quickly.

Ste laughed. "No offence, Mike, but it's rubbish. Look, I've just bought a new one, why don't you have my old BlackBerry?" Before I could give an answer, he had put my SIM card into his old phone and handed it over.

This kindness only made me feel more guilty about the text I had sent. "Thank you," I said glumly.

"No probs. I needed an upgrade for the charity work and my new girlfriend. You know how it is," he said.

I did not, as it happens.

Ste pulled an envelope out of his school bag. "Check this out. Arrived today."

Inside the envelope was a piece of paper with a load

of squiggly writing translated underneath into English. It read:

Ho Hin Animal Training Centre
Purchase Certificate

This certificate is the official ownership record of: ALAN (Nine-month-old Spectacled Langur – *Trachypithecus obscurus*)

Purchased by: Steven J. Swarbrick (UK citizen), who is a licensed owner of primates in Thailand.

Followed by a load of information about Ste's responsibilities as a monkey owner.

"The school's officially adopted Alan," he said.

Although I was impressed by the certificate, a few things seemed strange about it. "I thought you found the monkey in a monastery, not an animal training centre."

Ste answered immediately. "Correct, but the monkeys have to be *trained* how to live in the wild again. The monks run their own facility."

"Of course," I said. That was not the only odd thing, though. Whilst we were on the subject, I thought I should just clear up my confusion. "How come your name is on the certificate, not the school's?"

"You need a licence to adopt a monkey," said Ste, very quickly this time. "And you have to be an individual person to own a licence. I'm afraid I had to *pull in a few favours* to get the paperwork through quickly."

"Ah?" I said. "*That* is why you had to buy those cigarettes?"

Ste frowned. "Cigarettes...?"

"I heard you on the phone, talking about how English cigarettes were all someone would smoke."

A broad smile slowly spread across Ste's face. "Ah. Yes. Of course. The cigarettes. Yes. That's exactly what they were for. A bribe to get the licence done quickly. Guilty – sometimes you've got to bend the law a little bit but, if it's for the good of something else..."

There was something in his smile – *relief?* – that suddenly made me feel suspicious. I had nothing to be suspicious about, of course, nor did Ste have any reason to feel guilty. Or did he?

"Well, sorry to disappoint you, Mike," he said. "But, as you can see, I've done nothing wrong. The monks are training Alan up as we speak. As his owner, I'll be allowed to help release him back into the wild when I go out there."

I squinted. *Sorry to disappoint me?* What a strange thing to say. I had not accused him of doing anything wrong. Why was he being so defensive? Then something else crossed my mind. "Why do you need to adopt him then?"

Ste's eye twitched irritably. "What are you talking about now . . . *buddy*?" He tried to sound all jolly at the end, but he did not quite pull it off.

"If Alan is going to be released into the wild, why do you have to adopt him?"

"Well," said Ste. Was his face turning blotchy? "The monks train the monkeys to live back in the wild. Someone has to pay for this, right?"

I nodded slowly.

The blotches got darker. "And then, when they've been released, the monkeys still come back to the monastery sometimes. The monks feed them, and someone has to pay for this, right? So nice people like me adopt the monkeys and this helps the monks to pay for their good work. So if you've finished with the interrogation, I've got a date to prepare for."

Ste began noisily looking through his shirts whilst singing to himself (which he never usually does). There was a really heavy tension in the room, which was only broken when the doorbell rang.

Time Up

I will have to continue later. Mr Whittle's secretary just came in to the Isolation Suite and told me to get down to his office straight away. I feel really nervous. I just wish I could still work with Chas. And I did not think I would ever say that. However, it is obvious that if he ever manages to sort out the camper (which I very much doubt he will), it would be way too late to save my school career. Whatever happens, I am going to have to finish my placement somewhere else. Who knows what Mr Whittle will have in store for me?

Working for a Second Chance
Day 10 – Friday Continued – 2 Hours Later

Tasks completed: Being given a new placement.
What I learned: Newer is not necessarily better.

Beforehand, I thought my meeting with Mr Whittle would be pretty unpleasant. I was wrong. In actual fact, it was *very* unpleasant. It was like going to the dentist for a filling and coming out carrying all of your teeth in a plastic bag.

When I got there, Paul Beary was sitting outside, next to a man who looked exactly how you would expect Paul to look in twenty years. They were both wearing matching "Dwayne Beary Caravans" T-shirts.

"This is my uncle," said Paul.

"The one who invented the caravan?" I said.

The uncle raised his eyebrow at me. "No, son. I *re*-invent caravans. Classic ones. Buy 'em cheap. Do 'em up. Make 'em smart. Sell 'em on."

"Like I always said," grinned Paul, "my uncle who *re*-invents caravans."

"But you always. . . Oh, never mind," I said.

"Have you come to get your placement signed off so you can go back to school?" said Paul. "Mine's been brilliant."

"I would rather not discuss mine," I said.

Paul has lost weight from all of his hard work – I do not think I have ever seen him looking so healthy. "Uncle Dwayne's been paying me to work for him," he said. "I'm using the money to make my night at the Funky Monkey Ball super-special by fl—"

"Michael Swarbrick," the secretary interrupted, as she poked her head round Mr Whittle's door. "The head teacher will see you now."

As I stood up and shuffled into Mr Whittle's office, a disturbing thought came to me: the Funky Monkey Ball is tomorrow. *How wonderful* – another chance for Ste to be crowned as the world's greatest living human.

Inside his office, Mr Whittle did not stand up to greet me. He told me today definitely could not count as a full day of work but the school had not been able to find me an alternative placement for my remaining day. For some reason, nobody wanted a notorious nudist to come and work for them.

"Not even Golden Nuggets'd have you," Mr Whittle said. "Too toxic for a job gutting chickens. New low for this school. You remind me of my son. He's an idiot too."

The phone rang.

"Yes?" he barked. "Who? You're joking. After what Swarbrick did? Well. Send him in then. Hurry up." He slammed the phone down. "Your lucky day, Swarbrick. Looks like you've been given a final chance. Meet your new boss."

At that moment, the door opened. Standing in the doorway was the absolute worst person in the universe.

"You are kidding me," I said. "It was *his* fault I got suspended in the first place."

Now, I do not think I can explain who I will be working for tomorrow, or what is so wrong with them, without first finishing my story. So before I explain what happened next in Mr Whittle's office, I will do just that.

An Unexpected Guest II

So I was in Ste's room when the doorbell rang. "Maybe you should get that," said Ste, clearly wanting to get rid of me.

Downstairs, I opened the front door and before I knew what was happening, a thick finger had been jabbed into my chest. "Where is she, pig-dog?" growled the finger's owner in a thick French accent. A complete stranger to me, he was short, round and dangerous-looking, like a barrel of boxing gloves. Over his shoulder I could see a rental car parked on our driveway.

"I do not know what you mean?" I said, trying to close the door.

The man jammed it open with his foot. "First you put the kebab that is – *'ow you say* – rotten in my daughter's suitcase. And now you steal my *maman*. 'Ow dare you insult my family in this way?"

Kebab? Suitcase? Hang on.

At that moment, a girl climbed out of the car. "It is not 'im, Papa. 'Ow could I ever be attracted to *this*?"

I recognized her straight away, despite the look of disgust on her face. *Chantelle.* But what was she doing here?

"No offence," she smiled.

"None taken," I replied, flatly.

"Ah, *bonjour* Jean-Pierre, *bonjour* Chantelle," said the old woman, nonchalantly, from behind me. She was stark naked.

"What is this?" screeched Chantelle's dad, turning purple. "She is without 'er clothes. You English monster!"

"*Grand-maman!*" Chantelle cried joyfully, embracing the old woman (and seemingly not bothered about touching her leathery old skin).

"Grandma?" I said.

Chantelle's dad pounced towards me. "I kill you Pearl-eh Swarbrick."

"No, Papa!" screamed Chantelle, leaping in front of him.

"Stop!" cried the old woman.

They all froze.

"What on Earth is going on here?" demanded Mum, storming down the hall.

"Ah! You made it," said Dad as he cheerfully followed her.

Squeaking, rusty cogs began to turn in my brain.

Peler Swarbrick.

Purl-ur Swarbrick.

Paul Swarbrick.

That was the name on the parcel containing the doner kebab. That was the name Paul had given to Chantelle.

Inside the House

In the kitchen, the old woman was jabbering away in French. Chantelle held her hand whilst her dad stared murderously at Paul, who had raced round to my house as soon as I had phoned him. My dad looked happier than he had done for weeks. Mum sat opposite him, glaring at him stonily.

This is the basic gist of what Chantelle translated for us:

1. Upon finding the doner kebab in his daughter's luggage, Chantelle's dad had gone ape and forced her to cut all ties with Paul. This is because "you cannot trust a boy who thinks mouldy meat is romantic".

2. Forbidden from contacting her "little cabbage" (*her words*), Chantelle had spent several days moping around, depressed. Her father (who is maybe a *tiny* bit controlling) was constantly checking her Facebook page, emails *and* mobile phone to make sure she did not get in touch with him.

3. The old woman did not like to see her granddaughter upset. Finding the address for "Paul Swarbrick" (or, as she pronounced it: *Purl-ur Swarbrick*) in Chantelle's diary, she had sneaked off to find him. Apparently, she had a habit of wandering off on her own but had never gone this far before.

4. Upon arriving at the house, she had tried to find out whether Paul or me or even Ste was the boy she was looking for, but every time she had said the name, a strange woman (Mum) had insisted on her taking off her clothes. She did not mind

257

this, though, as it reminded her of her younger days on the nudist beaches of southern France.

Chantelle's dad shook his head. "But why you do this, Maman? And why should I not rip this fat boy to pieces like the baguette that is stale?"

Paul grimaced. The old woman began speaking rapid French again and, frowning with concentration, Chantelle translated for us at every pause.

"She says when she was a young girl in France ... she 'ad a boyfriend who she love ... but 'er father said she could not see 'im ... because she was too young ... and they wrote the secret letters to each other ... then she ran away one night ... and they were married ... and that is 'ow she came to 'ave a son and a granddaughter who she love very much ... and she want for me ... to not lose my English muffin 'ere ... because ... one day ... we could be as 'appy as she was ... and we should do anything for love ... whether it be me ... or Paul ... or the unusual boy with the wobbly 'ead who is in love with the girlfriend of 'is brother."

Who, me?

Chantelle hugged the old woman. "Oh, *Grand-mère*. Is beautiful."

Then the old lady pushed Chantelle's arms towards

Paul, who was crying.[57] They had a long, tight hug. Chantelle's dad ground his teeth together.

Dad grinned. "Then yesterday, I thought, *Hang on, this is all a bit fishy. She isn't here to be a nudist.*"

Mum became very interested in the tablecloth.

He continued. "So I rang the French Embassy in London and left my details and . . . well . . . I guess they tracked down the family in France who'd lost their grandma."

Ah – so *that* is what he had been doing on the phone.

"We live near the airport and we catch the flight almost straight away. You are a fine, clever man, Monsieur Swarbrick," said Chantelle's dad.

I genuinely thought Dad's head would float off his neck he looked so pleased with himself.

"Well," said Mum. "Thank you for going behind my back."

"I was trying to do the right thing, love. . ." said Dad, holding out his hand.

Mum shook him off.

"Papa, can we stay?" begged Chantelle.

"No," replied Chantelle's dad abruptly.

There was a rapid, angry exchange in French between Chantelle's dad and Grandma. Finally the dad sighed. "Ah, Chantelle. I am sorry. I only want to protect you."

---

57 Although afterwards he told me that this was caused by "rust in his bionic eye".

"You can all stay here tonight if you like," said Dad.

"Thank you but no," said Chantelle's dad. "You 'ave, 'ow you say, the peculiar wife, Monsieur Swarbrick. We wish to keep our clothes on."

At that point, Ste came into the room. "Hey guys, just going off to see Lucy and – *whoa...*" He suddenly looked like a toddler who has been caught holding a pair of scissors in one hand and a bald family cat in the other. "Oh... Ah... Gotta go."

As he shot out of the house, Chantelle angrily said something in French. From the way her grandma and dad both said "Chantelle!" afterwards, I am guessing it might have been pretty rude.

"What's wrong?" said Paul.

"Nothing," replied Chantelle stiffly. "Let us make the most of the short time we 'ave."

I did not have time to ask Chantelle about her behaviour towards Ste because her family left for their flight almost immediately. There was a tearful farewell at the door. Paul tried to run alongside the car as it drove away, but he lasted about three steps before collapsing into a wheezing heap. I went to see if he was all right but he staggered off alone.

"Well, *that* was a happy ending," said Dad gleefully. "Apart from Paul, of course."

Breakfast in Bed

Having brought the camp bed up to my room (my bed was still off-limits, due to the old-lady germs), I did not sleep well that night. Mainly I was thinking about Ste. Chantelle's reaction to him (and his to her) was really unusual. I also spent a long time trying to figure out my new phone, just in case Lucy had replied to my text and it had got lost in all the apps and other stuff I did not understand.

In case you are interested, she had not.

The following morning, Ste came in with a steaming cup of tea (sixty per cent milk, with four sugars – perfect) and two slices of toast (lightly toasted, heavily buttered and cut into triangles – my favourite). "Morning, Michael. And how's my brilliant brother this morning?"

I sat up and nibbled at the toast. Part of me wanted to quiz him about Chantelle but this seemed rude after he had just fed me.

Ste opened my curtains and said, very casually, "Lucy mentioned you last night."

I nearly spat out my tea. "Really?"

He waved his hand. "Something about maybe she'd been a bit harsh on you . . . perhaps the scrapbook wasn't *that* bad. . ."

Holy moly – a glimmer of hope. The squid that had eaten the Lucy-ometer gave a joyful burp – was it about to *bring it up again*?

I reached for my new phone. "Should I text her?" I stopped myself from saying "again".

Ste shook his head. "No, no. Give it time. Oh, and, speaking of which, let me give you my new phone number." He tapped the keys of my phone quickly, then tutted and mumbled something about a silly mistake. Then he typed again and handed it back.

At the time this did not strike me as particularly suspicious but, looking back, it was a moment that would change my life for ever.

"Lift to school in five minutes?"

Lift to School

I had almost sat down in the passenger seat of Ste's car when he yelled, "No!"

I froze, my buttocks hovering in mid-air.

"Sorry, mate," he said. "Don't want you to be uncomfortable."

Three different-coloured marker pens were on the seat, on top of a sheet of paper.

"I was adding information to the ball posters with

them. Just toss them in the back seat," he said.

I did this, but it left my hands a smudged mess of blue, green and red ink.

"Oh, *nightmare*, they must have leaked," said Ste.

"Maybe I should go inside and wash my hands," I said.

"Nah. You can hardly tell. Plus I've got to meet Brian at ten to nine."

And with that, we set off with the top down. I probably should mention that what Ste said was not entirely true. I mean, yes, we were nearly late. However, this was purely because he had spent about three years in front of the mirror, trying to make his hair look like he had not spent any time on it at all. No, I mean the other bit was not true. You could easily notice the ink – I was covered in it.

When we arrived at school, I scuttled off towards the Isolation Suite. At the bottom of the stairs, I bumped into Paul, who was looking shifty.

"Hey, Paul, how are you feeling?"

"Depressed about Chantelle, of course. It feels like when I got kicked out of that band just before they went to number one in Moldova.[58] But I'm gonna do

---

58 The band he was referring to was apparently called "Six Pack". He was allegedly thrown out after they realized there were seven of them, and the others were jealous that he "got all the honeys".

something about it. Look."

He checked over both shoulders, then motioned for me to peek inside the enormous rucksack he was carrying.

"Crikey!" I said. It was completely stuffed with chocolate bars, bags of crisps and fizzy drinks.

"I sneaked them out of the vending machine storeroom," he whispered. Paul is a vending machine monitor – he has the job of assisting the dinner ladies in tidying the stock cupboard and filling the machine. I have always thought this is like putting an owl in charge of cleaning your hamster's cage.

"Why?" I said.

"Supplies. I'm hitch-hiking to France to start a new life with Chantelle."

"Are you mental? You are fourteen!" I said. And anyway – he only had a rucksack-full of snacks. I doubted they would last him to the school gates.

"I can't live without her. By the time they realize I'm gone, I'll be on the ferry."

I took a blast on my inhaler. "Paul. This is ridiculous. You will be marked absent. They will wonder where you are."

"Love is not ridiculous, Michael. Cover for me. Tell them I had to rush home because my mum was trapped in the washing machine . . . or my dad's foot had exploded *again*. Anything. Farewell, old friend."

With that, he shook my hand, afterwards checking his palm to make sure the ink had not rubbed off from me.

Now, at the time I was not aware that Paul would manage to get a grand total of one mile towards France before being picked up by a policeman and brought straight back to school in time for morning break. Nor did I know that he would be suspended, just like me, and spend two weeks working for his uncle.

Therefore, as I watched him sneaking towards the back entrance of school, I just thought, *Good on you! Go for it!* Do not get me wrong – I *knew* how stupid this whole idea was. I *knew* exactly how little possibility there was of success. Also I would never normally condone nicking off school. However, I *loved* the way he was doing whatever it took to make his life better.

Suddenly my new phone beeped. *Lucy.* Hands quivering, I read the text:

Feel bad. Meet me by staff car park in 2 mins – quiet place 2 chat. Really need to speak to u. xxx

I checked the time. One minute to nine. I was due up in Isolation immediately but I could not pass up this opportunity. Buoyed by Paul's bravery, I decided to act first and think about the consequences later.

This would be a terrible mistake.

I sped down to the staff car park. Lucy was standing there, all alone. It felt like someone was dancing around inside my belly.

"Mike," she said, in the same way you might say "sludge" or "worms". There was a long pause.

"I got your text," I said.

She looked at me blankly, but before I could say anything a huge grin spread across her face. "Ste!"

Ste was walking across the car park with Mr Whittle, sharing a joke. When they reached us, Mr Whittle stopped smiling. "You. Isolation. Five minutes ago."

Meanwhile, Ste gave Lucy a kiss. "Hey, thanks for waiting, gorgeous."

I was completely confused about Lucy. "But I was..." I looked to Lucy for help but she was too busy kissing Ste. Shoulders slumped, I gave up and turned back towards the school.

I had gone about three steps before I heard a blood-curdling scream. "My car!"

Ste was sprinting across the car park, with Mr Whittle and Lucy following.

I could just about see his car from where I was standing.

In big green and blue and red letters, right across the bonnet, someone had scrawled: "LUCY KING! WILL YOU SWARBRICK WITH ME?" along with a rather detailed picture of a boy and a girl, holding hands in the nude.

Mr Whittle clenched his fist. "What kind of depraved lunatic would do such a thing?"

Strangely enough, all three of them turned to stare at me.

"It was not me," I said, holding my hands up in defence. And it was that exact moment when I realized that the ink on my hands exactly matched the ink on the picture. "Ah. I can explain. Ste. Remember. The markers."

"He used them. Then chucked them on your back seat. Horrendous," said Mr Whittle, able to see inside because the top was still down.

Ste looked like he was about to cry. "Please tell me it wasn't you, Mike. I only wanted to be your friend."

"It honestly was not me," I said.

Mr Whittle looked like he was about to erupt. "Nudist graffiti on car. You a nudist. Caught red-handed. And green-and-blue-handed, for that matter."

"I came to meet Lucy. She texted me. Look." I held up my phone but Lucy looked completely astonished.

"I have no idea what he's on about," she said. "I was meeting Ste."

Ste took the phone out of my hand. "Please say he's telling the truth. I couldn't handle it if my brilliant brother had done this to me." He jabbed a few buttons.

"Messages. Inbox. Nothing. Oh Michael! Why?"

He held it up for Mr Whittle.

"But it must have deleted itself," I said.

"How could that possibly happen?" said Mr Whittle.

Exactly, I thought. But this thought only lasted a moment because my eyes met Lucy's and everything seemed to stop dead. She looked completely and utterly disgusted with me. The squid that was digesting the Lucy-ometer suddenly bumped into a sea mine and exploded into a billion tiny pieces.

"Lucy, please. . ." I said but she turned away.

"Steven. Escort this delinquent to my office," growled Mr Whittle. "I'll follow once we've got this covered up."

Things Suddenly Change

As soon as he had frogmarched me out of earshot, Ste hissed, "Sometimes plans just work to perfection, eh, Michael?"

I stopped dead. "You mean, *you* did all this?" I said. Looking back, it seems silly that it was only at this moment that I realized that Ste had set me up. Call me gullible or stupid but it had not even crossed my mind, even when I saw that the ink on my hands matched the picture on the car. I thought it was just a coincidence.

I mean, I knew that the markers were his, but anyone could have taken them off the seat and done the graffiti – the top was down, after all. The last person I would expect to draw on Ste's car would be Ste himself. And, more to the point, was he not supposed to be nice these days?

Ste dragged me on, his thin lips twisted into a demonic smile. "That's what you get for trying to get Lucy to split up with me. I was sitting with her yesterday lunchtime. She nipped to the bogs and her phone went off in her bag. I read her text, of course." He said this bit like it was perfectly normal and acceptable. "And who should it be from but you – begging her to dump me."

"But..."

"No buts, Mike. This was not a nice thing to do after I've been so kind to you recently. So I deleted the text and decided to have my revenge this morning. I mean, ever since you crushed my Golf, I've been waiting to crush you but, since I needed you in order to get closer to Lucy, I had to pretend to like you."

I felt cold. "You are evil."

Ste sniffed. "Not evil. Just not to be messed with, that's all. It didn't take much to change Lucy's number to mine on your new phone and get you to turn up just where I wanted you. By the way, I can't believe you fell for the trick with the marker pens. And as for the car, well, I want to have it resprayed anyway, so it's a small price to pay. Now I'll leave you here for Mr Whittle, so, if you'll excuse me, there's a hot babe in the car park who needs a snog."

With that, he tightly pinched my cheek and left me to wait outside Mr Whittle's office alone.

To this day, Ste has continued to go out with Lucy – she is, of course, the girlfriend to whom I have referred several times.

The only thing was, I could not imagine that the text message I sent was the only reason *why* he went to all that trouble. I mean, Ste did not exactly have anything to worry about, did he? It was not as though Lucy was going to dump him for the kid who kept her stolen verruca sock in a scrapbook, was it? There must have been something else, but the only other reasons I could think of were something to do with:

a. Chantelle – their reactions when they saw each other in the kitchen were totally bizarre.
b. The monkeys. He got so prickly over nothing when I asked him questions in his room. Had I scratched the surface of something he was trying to keep hidden? Did it work in his favour to make me look as bad as possible?

Frankly, this was completely unimportant. I was about to get suspended from school.

Present Day

So, fast-forward two weeks to today and I can reveal that, of course, the person who has just offered to allow me to work for them is . . . none other than The Steverlizer himself. He wants me to help out at the ball tomorrow night.

That is why I had to explain what happened with the car before I revealed this. Had I not just explained how he got me into trouble, you would probably consider his offer of work to be an act of charitable kindness – he was helping from the goodness of his heart. Hmm . . . yes, and maybe Santa Claus will turn up at the ball and give me a life-sized model of Lucy made entirely out of chocolate Hobnobs.

I begged Mr Whittle to allow me to work for someone else. Mr Whittle became very impatient. He told me he was fed up with wasting time on me. I had a stark choice – say yes to finishing my placement with Ste and I return to school on Monday. Say no and I do not.

Extremely reluctantly I said yes. I mean, it is only for one day. It cannot be that bad, can it?

Well, OK, I think we all know the answer to that.

Working for a Second Chance
Second Attempt at Day 10 – Saturday

Tasks completed: None.
What I learned: Even when you reach rock bottom there is
always somewhere lower you can plunge to.

Working for Ste

This morning when I went downstairs, Ste had already gone
out. He had left me the following note on the dining table,
which read:

> *Mike,*
> *Be ready later.*
> *Ste*

Charming.

As a result, I spent the morning alone in my room. At about
eleven, he returned.

"Everyone! I've got an announcement!" he shouted.

At first I ignored him, but after the fifth time of asking, I
dragged myself downstairs. This was the first time I had been
in a room with my whole family since the incident with the

272

grafitti on Ste's car. Doing my best not to look at anyone, I stayed by the door.

"Everything OK, Steven?" Mum said.

Ste was pretty much jumping up and down with excitement. "Just pumped up, that's all. The Steverlizer couldn't sleep last night, thinking about how he's gonna miss Lucy when he goes to Thailand tonight. And he thought, *What would make me happy?*"

I knew what would make *me* happy.

He did a drum roll on the table with his fingers. "Lucy's hand in marriage."

"What?!" I shrieked.

"Tonight at the ball, on stage in front of everyone, I'm going to ask her to marry me. And I want all of you there."

Mum held her hands over her mouth and made a sound like a rusty tricycle.

Dad leaned in towards him. "Think very carefully before you get married, son." He motioned his head towards Mum, and lowered his voice. "*Very* carefully indeed."

Ste laughed. "This is the ultimate prize for all of The Steverlizer's hard work. I know you're worried that I'm young. I'm a ladies' man. I'm too good-looking to tie myself down."

"Not really my main concerns," I said, feeling like I was on top of a rickety fence in a gale-force wind.

Ste ignored me. "But I'm almost eighteen. Lucy's sixteen."

"That is *very* young, love," said Mum. "But, if

you're happy. . ."

Ste put his arm around her. "We won't get married straight away, but I'm desperate to make this commitment before I fly out. I love her. She's the girl I want to spend fifty per cent of the rest of my life with."

"Fifty per cent?" said Dad, frowning. "Is that . . . *possible?* How could I. . . I mean, how could *someone* get away with that?"

Mum tutted loudly. She and Dad have not been getting along well since he called the French Embassy. Mum thinks he is a spoilsport who sabotaged her dreams of a naked training centre in the back garden. Meanwhile, Dad has finally realized he can stand up to her. The thorny tension between them has been yet another good reason to stay in my room for the last few weeks.

"Easy," said Ste. "I'll spend half my time here, fundraising for homeless monkeys, and the other half in Thailand, helping them. I want Lucy to know that, even though I'll be on the other side of the planet, I'm committed to her."

This was horrible. Ste would probably train one of the monkeys to carry the ring for him at their wedding and afterwards it would leap on my face and gouge my eyes out, and the last thing I would ever see before being blinded would be Lucy in her wedding dress, newly married to the worst person who has ever lived.

"But you have only been going out with her for a few weeks," I said.

"Love does not wear a watch, Michael," smiled Ste, arrogantly. "This is what I want, and of course it's what she wants. Her mum's delighted. She got married when she was seventeen *and* she thinks I'm ace. She even gave me this."

He pulled a small box out of his pocket and flipped open the lid to reveal a sparkling diamond ring. "It's Lucy's grandma's."

I slapped my hand across my eyes.

"Wouldn't miss it for the world, love," said Mum.

"Cool. Be there at seven-thirty. Brian says you can watch from the balcony," he said, before kissing Mum and shaking Dad's hand. Then he rushed off back to school.

I felt like someone had flicked a switch inside me. OK, Lucy hated me, and she loved Ste, and she would never listen to me. But still, I could not let this happen – not without *trying* to do something about it, anyway. Someone had to save her. And there was only one person I could speak to.

The Only Person Who Could Help

I cycled straight round to Lucy's house. Her mum answered the door. "Oh hello, Michael," she grinned. "Have you come to congratulate Lucy?"

"Not exactly," I said.

"Good. Keep it as a surprise. In any case, she's in town buying a dress for tonight, courtesy of that lovely brother of yours. He gave her three hundred pounds. Now *that's* what I call husband material."

"I was hoping to speak to Dave."

Mrs King stepped outside and pulled the door shut behind her. "He's not taken the engagement news well. In fact, he's gone all strange. I wouldn't disturb him."

I puffed up my chest. "This is a matter of life and death."

"He's in his shed, but don't say I didn't warn you. And if he asks, I've gone to *Tan-Fastic* to top up my tan."[59]

After letting me in through the side gate, she scurried off to get spray-painted like a garden fence. I walked round the back and knocked on the shed door.

"Go away," growled Dave.

After a deep puff on my inhaler, I went inside.

Dave was sitting at a table. He was wearing his camouflage-print pyjamas and had warpaint on his face. Weirdest of all, though, he was playing with two Action Man toys, making various gun and explosion noises.

"I'm going to rip your brains out!" he roared. I backed away, until I realized he was actually pretending to be one of the Action Men talking to the other one.

"Don't do it!" he replied, in a strange foreign accent.

"Time to die," he said, before smashing the Action Men

---

59 I was quite amazed by this. I mean, she was already bright orange. In fact, judging by her colour, a better name for the shop would have been *Tan-gerine*.

against each other, with all manner of grotesque gurgles. Then he took a deep breath, placed them solemnly on the table and turned to face me. His eyes were red and sunken, and he seemed somehow smaller.

"You've heard the news then," he said, quietly.

"I was hoping you could stop it," I said.

Dave laughed bitterly. "Nothing I can do now."

"You can do something. . ." I said. "You were in the SAS."

There was a pause. Finally, Dave sniffed and held up the three stumps of his missing fingers. "You know how I lost these, Marvin?"

"You said an idiot caused you to lose them. During hand-to-hand combat training."

"Huh," said Dave, rubbing his eyes. "I never said anything about combat training."

"Oh. . ."

After a lengthy silence, he raised his head and stared directly at me. "It was a potato-chopping injury."

"A what?" I said.

"I lost my fingers chopping flaming potatoes!" he shouted, slapping the table so hard the Action Men flew up in the air.

I did not dare to look at him.

Dave's voice dropped to a hoarse whisper. "I wasn't in the SAS. I wasn't even a real soldier. All I ever wanted was to be a hero."

Then he did something I was definitely not expecting. His weather-beaten face screwed up tightly, his shoulders shook

277

and he started making this weird squeaking noise, like a rabbit being sawn in half.

He was *sobbing*. Dave King, the most frightening person I have ever met, was sobbing like a little girl.

Talk about awkward!

I patted him on the shoulder. "Of course you were a real soldier," I said, using the same tone you might use when telling a two-year-old something like, "Of course you know how to use a big boy's toilet."

Dave did not seem to mind. "Thanks, Melvyn [it did not feel right to correct my name at this point]. But I wasn't. I've wanted to be one ever since I was a nipper. Soon as I left school I did all the interviews, the fitness tests, the assault courses. Everything. Passed with flying colours. Only one problem. . ."

"What was that?"

He shook his head. "I kept getting people's names wrong."

"Really?" I said, chewing my fingernails. "I had not noticed."

"No. Honestly, I do. It's a thing of mine. Something up with my brain. I can't help it, Moses."

I let this one go as well.

"They said I'd put lives at risk. You know – I'd shout 'Oi, Jim! I've got you covered!' but really I'd mean John. Then Jim would stand up and get hit with a bullet. And that was that. On the scrap heap. So I got a job in the kitchens at the army barracks."

"Important job," I offered.

"Huh. Not when you want be a hero it ain't. Did it for

seven long, boring years. I used to get so frustrated in there, chopping the veg and washing the pots when I should've been training to fight. I was hacking away at a spud one day, dreaming it was an enemy soldier's head. . ."

My hand slid towards the door handle.

". . .took me eye off the knife and *thunk*! Fingers gone." He made a violent chopping motion with his hand, then started making squelching noises and miming blood spurting everywhere. "I lost my job. My home. Everything. All I'd ever wanted was to be a hero. And now I was an unemployed vegetable chopper carrying three of his fingers in an ice-cream tub."

My mouth formed a perfect "O" shape.

"So when I said an idiot caused me to lose my fingers. . ." he sniffed. "I meant me."

"Lucy is proud of you," I said, desperately trying to cheer him up.

"Huh," said Dave, "Lucy still thinks I was a soldier."

"You mean. . ."

He sighed. "Well, she was still young. I always told her that Daddy worked for the army. Which was true. Then, when she grew up, the time never seemed right to tell her. Especially straight after the accident. I went a bit nuts, see."

"What did you . . . do?"

"Silly things. Became a nudist. Just like you are now."

"Well . . . not *really* like me at all," I said.

Dave smiled weakly. "We had a naturist holiday to get away from it all. I saw Lucy swimming in the sea and I decided right then I'd train her up and get her to the Olympics."

This story was familiar to me. It coincided with my first ever meeting with Lucy (aged three), when I was thrown off a donkey into a group of naked people (including Dave King himself).

"I did it so she'd think I was her hero." I could see his normal levels of anger pouring back into his face as he whacked the table again and again to emphasize his points. "*That's* why I pushed her so hard. *That's* why I always let her think I'd been in the army, even if I hadn't. *That's* why I kept her away from boys. *That's* why I made a fool out of myself at that Medieval Festival. Because I wanted my daughter to be proud of me. And then maybe she'd be able to live up to her dreams like I never did. All this swimming training was never about her. Never. It was all about me."

He sagged down in his chair again. "Why should she listen to an old failure like me? It's time I let her do what she wants."

"She might go back to swimming?" I offered.

Dave gave a half-laugh. "Not now your brother's back on the scene. If my wife has her way, Lucy'll be married within a year."

I gulped.

"Now go away and let me get back to my game."

Early Evening

After leaving the shed, I rode home, my legs so wobbly I could barely feel them. Ste was going to snatch Lucy away for ever and there was nothing anybody could do. And then, just as I was putting my bike away in the garage, I realized: this is the whole reason why he wants me to help him tonight. He could have asked her to marry him somewhere private but he did not – he wants to do it in public so I am forced to watch. He knows exactly how much this will destroy me. I am helping him at the ball purely so he can rub my nose in it.

What a swine.

There is no getting out of it, either. If I do not go, he will see to it that I am kicked out of school.

I guess I should stop here. I need to go and get ready for the worst night of my life.

Working for a Second Chance
Day 14 – Saturday (Continued)
(Or is it Day 15? I mean, it has turned midnight, after all, so technically it is now tomorrow. Well, OK, I know it is *today* but. . . Oh forget it, I have more important things to think about.)

A lot of things happened this evening. I am not really sure whether my situation has improved or not. What I do know is that things have changed. Completely.

Preparation

At about six o'clock, Ste rang my mobile.[60] We did not have a conversation, more just a series of orders: "Be here at seven-thirty sharp. Bring my holdall with you. There's a plastic bag with a costume in it on my bed. Put that in the holdall with my iPad. Got it?"

In Ste's room, I shoved the plastic bag into his imitation-crocodile-skin sports bag without even looking inside it (a mistake, as I was to find out later). The holdall contained baby clothes for the monkey, a load of Ste's stuff, a big pile of Thai currency bundled up with rubber bands and his first-class boarding card. *First class!* That must have cost a fortune.

Then it hit me – he was paying for this with money from the ball tickets. He could have bought the cheapest seat possible but he did not – he ripped off those poor monkeys for every penny he could. On top of that, I bet that he took the three hundred pounds for Lucy's dress out of the ball money as well.

---

60 And, yes, his number came up as "Lucy King" on the screen. I changed his name to "Worst Person Alive" straight afterwards.

If people only knew what a slime bucket he was. . .

However, I thought, *what is the point of knowing this information*? I had no proof, and if I tried to tell anyone about it, they would either not believe me or not care.

Wearily, I picked up Ste's iPad from on top of his pillow. It must have been hibernating because the screen came on to reveal his Facebook page. He had changed his profile picture from the photo of him feeding the monkey on the beach to one of him and Lucy sharing a single strand of spaghetti.

I shoved it roughly inside his bag and trudged downstairs.

The Ball

Dad drove Mum and me to the ball. The atmosphere in the car was pretty frosty – when Dad moaned about a cyclist cutting him up, Mum said, "Oh. Why don't you call the French Embassy to complain about him?" The rest of the journey was completed in silence.

When we arrived at school, I hauled Ste's bag out of the car and dragged it round to the back playground, which was crammed with people. There was a set of dodgems and one of those things where you wear a Velcro suit and jump up off a trampoline and stick to a furry wall, and a gladiator joust and a hot-dog stand and a candyfloss machine. The boys were all wearing suits and the girls were in dresses and everyone looked like they were having a great time.

There was a huge sign up outside the Sports Hall – about twenty feet high. In small letters at the top, it read: "Welcome to the Funky Monkey Ball". The other ninety per cent of it was taken up by a picture of Ste's grinning face.

Someone shouted, "Hey, nudist! Glad you're dressed," at me. Mum nudged my arm and said, "See. Still famous." I suggested we go inside where it might be dark.

Inside, the corners of the hall were fairly shadowy, although disco lights were spinning and flashing across the dance floor. The walls were covered with giant sheets and there were fake jungle plants and inflatable monkeys dotted all around the place. In one corner, some of the prettier Year 12 girls were serving tropical drinks from behind a bar in bikinis and grass skirts.

The teachers were all in a roped-off section at the back, pretending that their plastic cups did not contain wine. There was a DJ on the stage, next to a screen with a scrolling message that invited you to text your messages and photos and have them displayed to the room (cost: 50p plus standard message rate, terms and conditions apply).[61]

Down one side of the room, the girls were shuffling awkwardly from foot to foot in time to some awful pop tune that was pumping out of the sound system. The boys stood

---

61 Most of the texts on there at this moment were things like: "Let's all dance completely Swarbrick" and "Paul Beary is smoking hot!" (I am fairly certain that Paul sent this one himself).

opposite them – a huge gangway in between – crushing Coke cans against their foreheads and punching each other in the arms.

Lucy's mum strode towards us, dragging Dave behind her. She was now pretty much the colour of a tomato. "Ooh, this is so exciting," she said to Mum. "Lucy doesn't suspect a thing but that son of yours is *so* lovely. I can't wait for the wedding. I'll buy a new frock and a hat and—"

"Do you not think they're a bit . . . *young*?" said Dad.

"Nonsense," said Lucy's mum, "who wants to see a wrinkly has-been in a wedding dress, eh? Ooh, Dave and I know all about young love. You'd never guess, to look at him now, though."

"Eh?" said Dave, turning slowly to face us. I have to say, he looked *terrible,* like a sad face drawn on an old apricot.

Mrs King rolled her eyes.

I felt an arm around my shoulder. "Yo, family!" said Ste. "How's it going?"

"Perfect," I said.

"Hello, *future son-in-law*," grinned Mrs King.

Dave stared blankly at him.

"Go into the teachers' area. Have a glass of wine," said Ste to Mum and Dad. He was wearing a perfectly cut tuxedo (*no doubt paid for at the expense of the monkeys he was meant to be helping*, I thought).

"Lovely," said Dad.

"Not for you, Roy," said Mum. "You'll only get giddy."

"Hopefully," said Dad. Mum made to answer him but he cut her off. "It's about time I had some fun, after all this Swarbricking nonsense you put us through."

With that, he wandered off. Mrs King linked arms with Mum and began yabbering about weddings as they followed him. Dave stayed where he was, eyes glazed, looking off into space.

At that point, Ste put his hand on my shoulder. "Right, Mike. Time for you to go and get changed. You're the entertainment."

Before I could ask what he meant, he was shoving me through the crowds, leaving Dave King on his own in the middle of the room.

Backstage

"I definitely do not wish to do this," I said. We were standing behind the curtain at the side of the stage, the disco lights flashing against our faces. Ste's holdall was by my feet.

Ste patted my bare shoulder. "I told you – the other guy pulled out. Someone has to do it. What's your problem?"

I took a blast on my inhaler. "It is a. dangerous, b. completely embarrassing, c. pointless, and d. I am virtually naked."

Time for an explanation: I had just got changed into my costume. It comprised:

1. A pair of leopard-skin underpants with strands of flappy material hanging off them and. . .
2. Er . . . that was it.

The pants were tiny – at least three sizes too small – and were so tight around the middle that I looked like an egg timer. Luckily, however, the world was spared an even more disturbing view by the climbing harness that I was wearing around my waist.

Ste tutted. "It's a *monkey*-themed ball. You're Tarzan."

"I could have dressed as a monkey."

"Mike," he said, tightening my harness. "You don't have a choice. Think of all the good things I've done for you. I forgave you for ruining two cars. I rescued you and Lucy from that party, and now I'm saving your school career."

"But it only *needs* saving because you ruined it in the first place."

Ste slapped me lightly on the face three times. "Well, you shouldn't go around telling girls to split up with their boyfriends, just so you can steal them yourself."

"I—"

"You see, Mike, you're no different to me. You just want Lucy for yourself. Difference is, I've got her and you haven't. And, well, I'm in a position to teach you a lesson."

"But why?"

"Because, my dear brother, I enjoy it," he said, tugging the

287

harness so tight that it pinched the flabby flesh on my inner thighs. "And because you keep trying to mess things up for me."

The harness was attached to two wires, one on either side of my waist. These wires led high above the stage, to the same pulley system that Ste had had used to hang the balloons during his speech, and the giant cuddly monkey when he was selling tickets. There was also a rope dangling down with fake leaves and vines twisted around it, which I was supposed to look like I was swinging from.

"Has this thing been fixed since *Peter Pan* last year?"

"Almost probably."

"What?!" I wailed. "That kid swung around all over the place. He headbutted Tinker Bell in the face."

"Just hold your rope and don't make any sudden movements," he said, yanking down hard on a second rope, which also led up into the pulley system. The harness got even tighter around my waist. Another pull lifted my feet off the ground. One more and I was floating.

"All right, Mike?" said Ste, hauling me even higher.

"I think it is pressing against my lungs," I croaked, gripping the rope. By now I was dangling fifteen feet off the ground, looking down at the floor and slowly spinning round.

He tied that rope to a hook on the wall, then went to the backstage area. There was a third rope back there – hidden behind the stage curtain – with a long metal rod at the bottom of it. Craning my head upwards, I could see that the pulley system I was attached to could be moved along a set of runners on the ceiling.

"Ready, DJ?" said Ste, grabbing the metal rod with both hands and bracing himself like a sprinter at the start line.

The DJ gave the thumbs up.

"Now!" said Ste.

The DJ pushed a button. The music was replaced by a deafening Tarzan cry.[62] Ste ran behind the curtain, pulling the metal rod with him. I lurched forward and violently swung from one side of the stage to the other. A flash of blurred faces turned towards me. Then the cry came again and he dragged me back. This time I swung so far up at the end that I nearly crashed into the wall.

"Again!" cried Ste, flinging me back and forth twice more. On the final one (shortly before I slammed shoulder first into the stage rigging), I noticed that loads more people had poured into the Sports Hall and were packing out the dance floor. The DJ pressed a button and the music restarted, twice as loud as before.

Back Down to Earth

After lowering me to the floor, Ste unclipped the wires from

---

62 You know the one. It sounds like a yodeller being stabbed with a fork. It is hard to spell it but I would hazard a guess at: "Aaaarrrgghhh-aa-aa-aa-aaaargh-aa-aa-aa-aaaarrrgh!"

my harness. "You got them dancing, Mike. Well done."

"I am going to get dressed and go home," I said, loosening the harness so I could reach my inhaler.

Ste raised his hand. "Not so fast. You're going to do a couple more swings later. Plus, you've got to stick around to watch me pop the question."

"No, thank you."

His face relaxed. "Well, I'm afraid you have to. If you want me to sign off your work experience anyway. Have a dance. I'll call you when you're needed."

With that, he pushed me through the door, down the stairs and on to the dance floor. In public, and dressed in only a tiny pair of pants and a harness, I felt just a teeny bit embarrassed so I hid behind a large plastic palm tree.

"Yo, Mike! Nice panties," said Paul, dancing over to me. To my absolute amazement, he was with Chantelle. She smiled sweetly and waved at me.

"How did you. . .?" I said.

Paul grinned. "Told you I'd need two tickets. Like I was saying yesterday, Uncle Dwayne's been paying me every week – I flew Chantelle and her grandma over with the money I'd saved."

I shuddered. "Her grandma is back in the country?"

"Yeah, and guess what!" said Paul. "She keeps stripping off in my house! I've seen the lot!"

"I can imagine," I said, trying not to imagine at all.

"It's all thanks to your brother as well," said Paul.

"How do you work that out?"

"Well, if it wasn't for him helping me to make Chantelle jealous, or getting me to do good things to help people, I'd never have won her back."

I gave this comment the response it deserved – silence.

"Great party, no?" said Chantelle.

"Correct," I said. "No."

"Lucy King was asking where you were," said Paul. "Wanted me to dance with her as well, but I had to let her down gently – I'm taken."

Lucy was asking after me? But why? There was no way I could see her dressed like this. Plus, was there any point? She probably just wanted to tell me what a freak I was and within an hour she was going to be engaged to Ste anyway.

"I'll get us some drinks, my petite French fry," said Paul, waddling off.

Chantelle did not reply. Her jaw was jutting out towards the front of the room.

I followed her gaze. She was staring at Ste, who was onstage, chatting to the DJ.

The Steverlizer

"I 'ate that boy," she snarled.

"There could be literally a billion reasons why," I said. "I

291

have been meaning to ask you what your reason might be?"

"'E 'as been 'arrassing me on the internet."

"Sorry?" I said. It was hard to pick out her voice over the music.

"'Arrassing me with 'orrible messages," she said. "Saying 'e wants to 'ug me and kiss me and other things I won't say because I am a girl who is nice."

"But he helped Paul to win you back," I said.

Chantelle gave a fake laugh. "Not this boy. 'E sent me fake photos of my beautiful Paul being kissed by these girls with tattoos and silly 'air and told me I should never go near 'imself again. I told 'im leave me alone but 'e started sending pictures of 'imself on the beach with a monkey who is, how you say, *fumeur*."

"Fume-*what*?" I said.

"You know. The thing with the cigarettes and . . . *aha!* That word!"

She was pointing up at the whiteboard with the text messages on it. There were a few new ones (e.g. "Hey, Swarbrick – next time, swing without your kecks on!" etc.). "Which word?"

"The one that is written about my beautiful Paul by some girl who like him."

I found the one she was referring to (and did not bother to mention that Paul had definitely sent it himself): "Paul Beary is smoking hot!"

"Yes! Smoking! Imagine making a monkey smoke a cigarette.

Oh, I cannot stand looking at that boy. Not on my special night with Paul. I do not wish to upset my 'andsome man."

With that, she followed Paul to the bar.

Smoking. A smoking monkey?

At that moment jigsaw pieces began to fit together in my head. The pictures of Ste on Facebook. I had seen those pictures myself. I had seen the photo of him on the beach with a monkey and *oh my word. . .*

Backstage II

Avoiding Ste, I ran backstage. His holdall was still on the floor. I pulled open the zip and flicked on his iPad, which was still on his Facebook page. Unfortunately, there was no sign of the picture. Of course – as soon as he started raising money for the monkeys, he would have removed it.

I closed the internet and browsed his files. *Yes!* There it was, saved in a folder called "Thailand pics". Without enlarging it was difficult to see exactly what was happening – I mean, unless you were really looking you would probably miss it – but at 400% zoom you could see it clearly. He was not *feeding* the monkey at all. He was *lighting a cigarette for it*.

What kind of a twisted individual would do such a thing?

And there was something else dodgy about the picture. He was *on a beach*. I realized that this was what made

293

me suspicious when I first saw it. In his story he had been somewhere off in the rainforest. He had never mentioned a beach. What else had he been lying about?

My eyes flicked towards the door. He could come in at any time.

Now what was the centre called again? Quickly, I took his adoption certificate for Alan out of the bag, went back online and searched: "Volcanic eruptions Ho Hin Thailand".

The search seemed to take for ever – the school's wireless signal must have been really weak. My heart was thumping.

Finally the results came up. Mainly there were a load of sites about bars and beaches in Ho Hin, but eventually I stumbled on an extract from a site about Thailand's geography – seven simple words that made my blood run cold:

"There are no active volcanoes in Thailand."

My mouth dropped open. He had made the whole thing up. Every single word of it. Of course nobody would check. Why would anyone question The Steverlizer? If there were no volcanoes, then there was no volcanic eruption, then there were no homeless monkeys, then—

"Find anything interesting?" said Ste behind me.

I shot to my feet. "You are evil. The whole time you said you were helping Paul you were actually trying it on with Chantelle, behind his back. I know you are lying about everything else too. There is not even a flipping volcano in Thailand."

Ste opened his mouth but I carried on speaking. It was like

jumbled-up bits of Lego were being rapidly stacked together to make a house. "And – *hang on a second* – why does this monkey need *clothes*? You said you were flying to Thailand to release it into the wild. Wild monkeys do *not* wear T-shirts with 'When it comes to girls, I *drool*' written on them."

A cruel smile spread across Ste's lips. He pulled the iPad out of my hands and calmly jabbed at it a few times. "Well, Mike. I guess you deserve an explanation."

"Yes, I do," I said. The bass from the DJ speakers was thumping hard in the background. "And so does everyone else."

"As far as Chantelle goes, I mean, come on. Why would I sit back and let her go out with the human doughnut? That is not going to improve her life."

"Not fair," I said, "Paul may be obese but at least he is not nasty. And what about all of your other lies? Your plane was not grounded by an ash cloud."

Ste took a long, weary breath. "There *was* an ash cloud, just not from a volcano in Thailand. We had to land there, though, and I agreed to stay a few days. So that part's true. Anyway, I'm sitting on the beach having a drink. . ."

"You mean you did not go to the monastery?" I said.

"Well . . . not exactly," said Ste. "Anyway, these hot babes are walking past in bikinis and so *obviously* I'm checking them out when *wham!* Suddenly this monkey *drops* from a tree in front of them. And I mean *drops* – like a coconut – right at their feet. It's not moving and the girls are freaking out and screaming that it's dead and this guy comes out of nowhere – pale, short, pot-bellied . . . bit like you, actually."

"Thanks a bunch."

"And he starts *resuscitating* this monkey, pumping its little chest, blowing into its mouth. And after a few moments the monkey comes back to life, leaps up on his shoulder, gives him a kiss and scampers back off into the trees. And these girls are all over this dumpy guy like *We love you* and *We'll see you tonight* and *Please be our boyfriend* – literally almost fighting over him. The guy gets their numbers and walks off up the beach into the trees. So I follow him to say well done and guess what!"

"I have no idea," I said.

"He's sitting on the floor with the monkey on his lap and he's *lighting a cigarette for the freaking monkey*."

I felt a cold sweat building on my bare back. "Wha. . . *Why?*"

"Exactly. The guy's all spooked at first but he calms down and explains that he's Canadian but he's been there for three years and the monkey is his *pet*. And he does this pretty much every day on different beaches around Thailand – cruising about, getting his monkey to fake its own death, then bringing it back to life so he can pull girls. The perfect crime.

"Anyway, so I'm like *Get me one of these monkeys, dude*. And he says that they cost top dollar. I mean, yeah, you can buy a monkey at a market for twenty quid out there, but these ones are specially trained by these monks."

296

"The ones who worship monkeys," I said.

Ste shrugged. "More like *used* to worship monkeys but got kicked out of the monastery for selling them on the black market. They train monkeys up for TV or films or just for people who want an awesome pet – they charge thousands for them. Anyway, I visited the training centre and put a deposit down on this one called Alan and that's when I got the idea for the fund-raising."

"So let me get this straight," I said. "You organized this ball so you could buy a highly trained monkey which you are going to use to pull girls. Is that not . . . dishonest and cruel?"

Ste looked like I had just accused him of eating live bunny rabbits. "How dare you? Alan will be well fed, loved, cared for. He'll have all the cigarettes he can smoke."

"*Cigarettes?*" I said. "It is not natural for a monkey to smoke."

"It's normal at the training centre – how else do you think they get them so obedient? And I'm not a monster, Mike. I'll get him some nicotine patches and gum. He'll be smoke-free in no time."

"But what about all those people who think they are raising money to save homeless monkeys, eh?" I pointed towards the dance floor.

"Alan *was* an orphan. He was made homeless by people chopping down his forest. I didn't lie about that. What's wrong with giving him the chance of a new life?"

I could not believe I was hearing this. "*Everything*, when you are lying to people like that. And what about Lucy? Need I remind you that you are about to ask her to marry you?"

Ste sighed. "I told you before. I'm gonna spend six months a year out in Thailand – having fun with girls, saving more monkeys, maybe even training them myself and renting them out to guys who need help with the ladies – and six months here raising more money to support myself. I can't be a ladies' man all year round. I need stability. I need to tie someone down here so she'll wait around for me. Someone hot who loves me completely."

"I am going out there to tell everyone," I snarled.

"Don't think so," said Ste, tapping at his iPad. "You see, I've told you my secrets, and I need to be sure you won't tell anyone else. . ."

Blackmail

"Since Lucy quit swimming she's been all over the place, struggling to make her mind up about things," he said, opening a password-protected folder. "I've tried to frighten her away from you but she keeps on saying that maybe she *should* be friends with you after all because maybe this scrapbook of yours was not *that* terrifying and was actually quite sweet and made her think about things."

"Really?" I said, a warm glow spreading through my whole body. I remembered Paul saying that Lucy had been asking after me. "What things?"

"Swimming or some old tosh like that. I wasn't really listening. Anyway, I'm perfectly happy for you to be friends with her. . ."

"Good. Because best friends tell their best friends when someone is being evil and—"

Ste put his finger over my mouth. "That's what I thought, which is why I need to make sure you don't."

He opened a folder and a film came up on the screen. The angle was funny, like the camera was lying on the ground on its side. Even so, I could clearly see where it was.

"That is Spyder's back garden," I said. "At the Halloween party."

"Correct," replied Ste. "It's from the same video Paul took to the newspaper the other week. Only I cut this bit before I gave the camera back to him."

He pressed Play. On the video, Lucy was snogging me. Then, very clearly, she fell asleep on my shoulder.

"You must be an *awesome* kisser, Mike," said Ste.

"Delete that straight away," I said. "Lucy does not know about it."

"She remembers *something* about kissing you," said Ste. "But she can't recall *exactly* what happened."

"Well, then," I said, "I think it would be better if we just got rid of it."

"My pleasure," said Ste, instantly deleting the file.

"There," I said. "Well, now I have nothing to worry about so, if you don't mind, I am going to speak to Lucy."

Just as I reached the door, Ste cleared his throat. "There is *another* film, though." I froze and slowly turned round. Ste had pulled a second video up on the screen. "Check this out."

This clip started at the exact moment the other one finished. Lucy was slumped against my shoulder, clearly unconscious as I supported her. And then something unexpected happened. I grabbed her and began snogging her.

"This did not happen," I said.

"Oh it did, Michael," said Ste. In the shadows of the backstage area, the glow of the screen gave his face a demonic look. "It's right here."

"No," I said, my face heating up. "She snogged me, *then* she fell asleep. You could see it on the other video."

"But the other video does not exist any more," said Ste. "You made me delete it, remember? Right here we have proof that you waited until Lucy fell asleep before pouncing on her."

"How did you. . .?"

"Oh, come on, Mike, it's not hard to play a film in reverse. Insane how realistic it looks though, eh? She'll be completely freaked out if she sees this."

"But why?"

"Like I said. I need to be sure that my secrets stay secret. You love Lucy; you're like a dog with your tongue hanging out when she's around. You're only nice to her because you fancy her and the thought of her never speaking to you again is way more important than her 'feelings'[63]."

I started gabbling about how it was not true, but Ste spoke over me. "Now if you'll excuse me, I've got a job to do."

With a flick of his wrist, he clipped the metal wires back on to my harness. Before I knew what was happening, he had hoisted me up six feet into the air. I was face-to-face with him now, the straps digging into my belly.

"I can still speak to her from up here," I said.

"We both know that's not going to happen," he said, waggling my cheek. "But just in case. . ."

He reached into his bag and pulled out a thick rubber band from one of the money piles. Then he forced my hands behind my back and tied them together. Finally, he stuffed a pair of his underpants into my mouth. *Disgusting*. OK, I know they were clean but come on! They had touched his bum, for heaven's sake.

With three or four good yanks on the rope, he hoisted me higher until I was twenty feet above the stage. Then he took hold of the steel pole and disappeared behind the back curtain, dragging me across until I was right over the middle of the stage, where he left me silently and slowly spinning. As he went back into the hall through the side door, he gave me a wave and a wink.

---

63 He did that annoying quotation-mark thing that people do with their fingers to show that something is a load of rubbish.

The Worst Few Minutes of My Life

Although I was obscured from everyone's view by the top curtain above the stage, I could crane my head downwards and look out on to the room. By now the party was in full swing. I could make out Mum and Dad, still in the teachers' area. Dad was having a great laugh with some of the PE staff. Mum was scowling off to the side. By the stage, Paul and Chantelle were having an animated discussion. Paul seemed shocked by something she was saying and kept shaking his head in disbelief.

Soon, the music cut out and Mr Whittle came on stage with a microphone. "Ladies. Gentlemen. Steven Swarbrick."

The audience cheered wildly as Ste walked on to the stage. I tried to wriggle my hands out of the elastic band but they were held tight.

"Cheers, Brian," said Ste, raising his hands to the audience. "I thought you should all know that so far we've raised eleven thousand pounds for the homeless monkeys of Thailand."

Cue another massive round of applause.

"But before I let you carry on partying, I've got a special announcement to make. Can I get Lucy King up on stage here, please?"

A murmur spread through the crowd. Lucy was pushed forward reluctantly by her friends. She was wearing a short black dress and she looked absolutely gorgeous. And as I looked at her, shyly biting her lip as she shuffled on to the stage, I thought, *Am I as bad as him? Would I keep quiet and let her ruin her life just so I could stay close to her? Or would I risk losing her for ever just to protect her from him?*

I carried on spinning.

"Babe. . ." said Ste. The crowd fell silent. Jealous girls on the front row nudged each other. Lucy looked self-consciously around her.

". . .I know we're young but I've got something to ask you. . ."

Then something clicked inside me.

A Moment of Realization

It is hard to explain what happened next, or even what caused it. It was like a door opened inside my brain, and I stepped into a room where everything was completely clear and made sense. Ste was wrong. I was *nothing* at all like him. My feelings were not important. Lucy was about to get engaged to a guy who wanted a smoking monkey slave to help him pull other girls. And I had to stop it. Not for me. No. I did not care if he showed her the video. My life was already a total mess but hers did not have to be. At least I could save her from his misery and lies. Here was my chance.

Below me, Ste dropped to one knee, pulling the ring out of his pocket. I swear one of the girls in the crowd screamed, "Nooooo!" Lucy's mum was leaning right over the edge of the

303

stage, clapping excitedly. ". . .Lucy King. Will you m—"

I spat the underpants out of my mouth and they floated downwards, landing on Lucy's face. She whipped them off and stared up at me in surprise.

"Stop!" I screamed.

Unfortunately, this caused several problems:

1. The violence of my yell caused me to lurch forward so I was upside down.
2. Unfortunately, I had loosened my harness earlier. I slid through it, dragging my Tarzan trunks off.
3. Luckily, or unluckily, depending on how you look at things, my feet became caught up in tangle of harness and trunks and I remained there, hanging by my feet like a big naked bat.

The crowd made a noise like a thousand hedgehogs being sucked up into a vacuum cleaner.

"Do not do it, Lucy!" I yelled, unable to cover myself as my hands were still behind my back.

"He wants to turn you into nudists!" shouted Ste, drowning me out over the microphone. "I tried to help him but he's deranged!"

The crowd booed. Drinks were hurled up at me. Suddenly Mr Whittle was underneath me, jabbing me with a long stick. "Get down from there, you revolting boy!"

Lucy face was twisted in horror. "What are you doing?"

"Do not listen to him!" I cried. "He is not helping the monkeys. He wants to buy one to help him pull girls and he just wants to string you along and he has got a video of me snogging you when you are asleep but I do not care if you see it. I just want to save you!"

"Ignore him, babe," said Ste. "He's mental."

"Where's your evidence, Swarbrick?" growled Mr Whittle, poking me again.

"Check his iPad!" I yelled. "There is a picture of him lighting a fag for his monkey slave."

Ste turned to the crowd. "Be my guest. There's no such photo."

"You repugnant oaf," said Mr Whittle to me. "How dare. You ruin. This event."

But the crowd were all pointing at the screen on the stage because it had suddenly been filled by a photo of Ste on the beach with the monkey. It had been cropped and blown up so that no one could be in any doubt that Ste was lighting a cigarette for it.

"Ah," said Ste, "I can explain."

People were muttering now and Ste was looking for an escape route and over to the side of the stage I could see Chantelle happily putting her mobile phone back into her bag and the last thing I thought before I fell was how lovely Paul's girlfriend actually was.

The Fall

It should not have taken me, or anybody else, by surprise but I guess there were so many other things going on that I had kind of forgotten that I was naked and upside down, dangling precariously by my ankle. And so, when I *did* fall, I barely had time to prepare myself.

It was like slow motion. Head first. Ste ducking behind Lucy, who was suddenly getting closer and closer. Her arms covering her face. Shutting my eyes against the inevitable. . .

SLAM! We collided heavily.

I slowly opened my eyes, petrified of seeing how badly I had damaged her. But very quickly I realized I was not on top of Lucy. She was off to the side, on the floor beneath her dad. He must have somehow dived on to the stage and swooped in to save her.

I had landed on Ste! He was groaning in agony and his arm was going off at a wonky angle and he tried to stagger away but Dave King was on his feet, blocking his path, and Ste skidded to a halt and I thought for a moment that Dave was going to beat his brains out and prove himself a hero but. . .

No!

A blood-curdling yell silenced the whole hall and Paul Beary came flying through the air, kung-fu-kicking Ste right in the buttocks and sending him flying across the stage. "That's what you get for harassing my Chantelle and ripping off the whole school!" he yelled. Dazed and confused, Ste tried to crawl off, but he had only gone about three feet when Paul did a wrestling move on him that could only be described as *The Big Belly Slam-down*.

The crowd erupted like someone had just scored a last-minute goal. As Ste lay there groaning, Paul totally milked it and began moonwalking up and down the stage. I guess he deserved this moment of triumph, though, and no one was clapping more than Chantelle, who looked completely and utterly besotted.

"You'd better be able to explain yourself," said Mr Whittle, peeling Ste's crumpled body off the floor.

Meanwhile, next to me, Lucy was moaning softly, and suddenly Dave King was crouching over her and cuddling her and saying very, very gently, "Daddy's here, love, daddy's here."

And in between her sobs, she whispered, "He made me sad again, Dad. Make it all right."

"I will, love," said Dave, showing that there is more than one way to be a hero.

Then I stood up and realized that since Paul had stage-dived into the crowd (crushing about six people in the process), everyone else in the room was now staring at my completely naked body, but I could not cover myself because my hands were still tied together with the rubber band.

Suddenly from behind me, I felt a coat being wrapped around my shoulders. I looked around and Mum was there, covering me up. "I'm sorry, darling," she said, "for everything."

My knees gave way and I fainted.

The End

When I woke up, the hall was empty and strewn with rubbish, and I was still onstage. Ste was being questioned by the police somewhere. Mr Whittle was standing over me. He told me that he supposed I did a good thing but, technically, I still had not finished my work placement because this day could not possibly count, seeing as how I was working for a fraudulent criminal. I asked about Lucy but Mum said she had already left.

Mum and Dad took me home. As she drove, Dad placed his hand on top of hers and she allowed it to stay there. "It was good of you to cover him up," he said.

So that is that. I have been typing now for four hours and, even though there is no way I will be able to sleep, I guess I should think about stopping for the night.

Earlier on I said that I was not sure if tonight has improved my situation or not – I *am* sore all over, I still have not finished my placement, and everyone in school has once again seen my most private areas, after all. However, I have just realized that this does not matter. I stopped Ste from stealing from those monkeys *and* I saved Lucy from his evil clutches. Whatever happened to me is not important.

Text

My phone has just beeped.

Holy moly. It was a text message.[64] I have read it about thirty times in the last few minutes. It is really long and is just . . . well . . . I will type it out so you can see for yourselves:

> Hi, Mike. Thank u so so much. U made me see what a bad
> person ur bro is (not that I wudve said yes – I'm only 16! –
> but sweet of u anyway!!!) so thank u. I miss u as my friend.
> Been thinking about u and your scrapbook 4 a while. Ur a
> lovely person & u do lots of nice things. Wish everyone else
> knew how good u r. Love Lucyxxxxxxxxxxxxxxxxxxxxxxxxxxxxx
> xxxxxxxxxxxxxxxxxxxxxxxxxxxxxxxxxxxxxxxxxxxxxx

Oh my word. I mean, I could barely count how many kisses there were! OK, so I did count. And re-count. There were sixty-eight. This is probably a world record. She thinks I am good! She is right though: nobody else knows this and if only there was another way of. . .

HANG ON!

I have had an idea. Maybe there *is* a way I can help someone else *and* make the school realize that I am not so bad after all. Time for bed now and I will try to organize it in the morning.

---

64 Well, two actually, but I was not so interested in the one from Paul telling me about how on the way home he had seen Chantelle's bra strap by accident.

Epilogue

Pimp My Clinic

We have just finished packing away the tools and the paints and the empty boxes when we hear the taxi pull up. Chas is back! We finished with minutes to spare. The car door closes. Footsteps on the path. Then they stop. A few of us giggle nervously but the others say shhhh.

By now, Chas must have found the end of the ribbon, which was tied to his front door. I can imagine his puzzled face as he begins to follow it towards his garage, where the camper van is parked.

I look at the people squashed into the camper van: paint-splattered, dusty, relieved, but most of all happy. Paul Beary and his Uncle Dwayne (who luckily enough had a load of spare furniture and fittings kicking around his workshop) are sharing a king-size Yorkie bar. Mum is playfully wiping the paint off Dad's nose. He puts his arm around her, barely keeping the smile from his face, as she clasps a tight hold of his hand and gives it a kiss. I am delighted to say that she is fully dressed. Miss O'Malley is rubbing her enormous hands together.

The morning after the ball – one week ago today – I asked all of them if they would come and help me. They all said yes. Because this is the thing – most people will do good things if they get the chance. Mr Whittle agreed that since Ste had raised the charity money under false pretences, maybe this would be a worthwhile way for us to spend it.

The garage door handle turns. Knuckles are bitten. Eyes are clamped shut. Laughter is silenced. Tears are wiped from eyes.

We have all spent the entire day here. Paul came very early this morning with his Uncle Dwayne. Dwayne said he had seen much worse and, apart from the rust, which he could patch up in no time, all it needed was a bit of TLC. So whilst he welded, Paul, Miss O'Malley and I stripped out the dated units and old chairs with a set of crowbars. This was a lot of fun.

A streak of light appears at the bottom of the garage door as it begins to open.

Then Mum and Dad came. They helped Miss O'Malley with her amazing carpentry skills to put together the fitted cabinets from the kits Dwayne had brought. Meanwhile, Paul and I laid a new floor whilst his uncle worked around us, putting in the new seats and table and fold-out bed.

Then the door is flung open and everybody cheers.

Chas stands there, completely frozen, the other end of the piece of ribbon in his hand. He is surprised, amazed and delighted all at once. But he does not have a moment to figure out what is happening because Miss O'Malley leaps forward, her massive hands up in the air like some kind of dinosaur, and pounces on him. And suddenly they are rubbing noses and kissing and even I am cheering because it does not make me feel sick any more.

Within seconds, we are all outside so Miss O'Malley can show him the improvements – the cream leather seats with the red stripe down the middle; the shiny new sink and oven that are fitted into the glossy cupboard units; the cool curtains; the black-and-white chessboard lino floor.

I mean, it is not finished but Paul's Uncle Dwayne says he will take it into his workshop and give it a respray and fix the roof and get a mechanic to look at the engine and hey – it's what's inside that counts, right? Everyone smiles at this because we all know what he means.

I have to say that finishing the job makes me feel good about myself but there is still one person missing. As everyone else sits in the camper and drinks lemonade, I wander around on the driveway kicking bits of gravel about.

And then I see an old camouflage-print Land Rover parking on the road. Within seconds I am sprinting down the drive and I get there just as she opens the door.

Lucy.

She is beaming widely. I notice her hair is wet and there are red marks around her eyes.

"Sorry, Mike," she says, "I've been training at the pool."

"I thought you quit."

"Can't waste time," says Lucy, grinning mischievously.

I look confusedly at her dad.

"Nowt to do with me, Michael," he says, finally getting my name right.

"It's down to you," she says.

"Me?" I say.

"Yes. I wanted to tell you at the ball, before everything

happened. It was your scrapbook that made me realize. I mean, I know it's a bit weird and a little bit disturbing but when I read all the old newspaper clippings again it made me remember what I loved about swimming – the competition, the winning. I mean, it wasn't all about Dad pushing me. I pushed myself too. And I did love it – it all just got a bit too intense for a while, that's all. But I've had a break and I'm ready to go again. Anyway – it's got to be more fun than going out with your brother, right? And even though I'm going to work just as hard, I'm going to make more time for myself too. And my friends. . ."

I smile.

"One rule is – I'm taking a back seat from now on," says Dave. "I'm only there to support."

"But you're the best coach ever," says Lucy, kissing him on the cheek. "I want you to help me. The European Championship trials are in six months."

"Steady on," says Dave. "Let's not push it, eh?"

And we all smile at the same time because we know how much things have changed. Then I notice something wrapped around her wrist.

"The friendship band," I say. "You are wearing my friendship band."

"I fished it out of the bucket straight after it fell in," she says. "It took ages to get the sick off but I could never throw it away."

And so, with my smile almost wider than my big waggly head, we link arms and walk down the driveway together.

Acknowledgements

Writing this book has been a lot of fun but it's also been pretty tough. There have been a lot of times when I've been in such a muddle that all I could do was scratch my head, eat biscuits and break wind angrily.

The following people helped to cheer me up, push me on and get the book finished:

Right at the top of the green zone of the Lowery-ometer is the incredible Alice Swan, who prevented the book from being longer than The Bible, and gave me loads of encouragement and great ideas when it threatened to be rubbish.

An invite to my extreme Halloween party goes to Gillie Russell, my amazing and lovely agent. Thank you for absolutely everything!

Free tickets to the Funky Monkey Ball to everyone else at Scholastic and Aitken Alexander Associates for being so supportive, talented and generally nice.

Friendship bands (hand-crafted by the monkey-worshipping monks of Thailand) to all three of my friends for asking how I'm getting on with the book and putting up with my lame answers for the last two years.

Family holiday to a nudist camp for all the Lowerys for *still* not turning into the family from the book.

Sixty eight capital letter kisses and an AMLAT to Sar, Jasmine and Sam for making me so happy.

A MARRIAGE
FIT FOR A SINNER

BY
MAYA BLAKE

Published in Great Britain 2015
by Mills & Boon, an imprint of Harlequin (UK) Limited,
Eton House, 18-24 Paradise Road, Richmond, Surrey, TW9 1SR

© 2015 Maya Blake

ISBN: 978-0-263-24930-9

Printed and bound in Spain
by CPI, Barcelona

Maya Blake's hopes of becoming a writer were born when she picked up her first romance aged thirteen. Little did she know her dream would come true! Does she still pinch herself every now and then, to make sure it's not a dream? Yes, she does!

Feel free to pinch her too, via Twitter, Facebook or Goodreads! Happy reading!

Books by Maya Blake

Mills & Boon Modern Romance

Married for the Prince's Convenience
Innocent in His Diamonds
His Ultimate Prize
Marriage Made of Secrets
The Sinful Art of Revenge
The Price of Success

The Untameable Greeks

What the Greek's Money Can't Buy
What the Greek Can't Resist
What the Greek Wants Most

The 21st Century Gentleman's Club

The Ultimate Playboy

In December 2015 look out for *Brunetti's Secret Son* featuring Romeo from *A Marriage Fit for a Sinner*

Visit the Author Profile page
at millsandboon.co.uk for more titles.

CHAPTER ONE

'ONE PLATINUM CHRONOGRAPH WATCH. A pair of diamond-studded cufflinks. Gold signet ring. Six hundred and twenty-five pounds cash, and…Obsidian Privilege Card. Right, I think that's everything, sir. Sign here to confirm return of your property.'

Zaccheo Giordano didn't react to the warden's sneer as he scrawled on the barely legible form. Nor did he react to the resentful envy in the man's eyes when his gaze drifted to where the sleek silver limousine waited beyond three sets of barbed wire.

Romeo Brunetti, Zaccheo's second-in-command and the only person he would consider draping the term *friend* upon, stood beside the car, brooding and unsmiling, totally unruffled by the armed guard at the gate or the bleak South East England surroundings.

Had Zaccheo been in an accommodating mood, he'd have cracked a smile.

But he wasn't in an accommodating mood. He hadn't been for a very long time. Fourteen months, two weeks, four days and nine hours to be exact. Zaccheo was positive he could count down to the last second if required.

No one would require it of him, of course. He'd served his time. With three and a half months knocked off his eighteen-month sentence *for good behaviour*.

The rage fused into his DNA bubbled beneath his skin. He showed no outward sign of it as he pocketed his belongings. The three-piece Savile Row suit he'd entered prison in stank of decay and misery, but Zaccheo didn't care.

He'd never been a slave to material comforts. His need for validation went far deeper. The need to elevate himself into a better place had been a soul-deep pursuit from the moment he was old enough to recognise the reality of the life he'd been born into. A life that had been a never-ending whirlpool of humiliation, violence and greed. A life that had seen his father debased and dead at thirty-five.

Memories tumbled like dominoes as he walked down the harshly lit corridor to freedom. He willed the overwhelming sense of injustice that had festered for long, harrowing months not to explode from his pores.

The doors clanged shut behind him.

Zaccheo froze, then took his first lungful of free air with fists clenched and eyes shut. He absorbed the sound of birds chirping in the late-winter morning sun, listened to the distant rumble of the motorway as he'd done many nights from his prison cell.

Opening his eyes, he headed towards the fifteen-foot gate. A minute later, he was outside.

'Zaccheo, it's good to see you again,' Romeo said gravely, his eyes narrowing as he took him in.

Zaccheo knew he looked a sight. He hadn't bothered with a razor blade or a barber's clippers in the last three months and he'd barely eaten once he'd unearthed the truth behind his incarceration. But he'd spent a lot of time in the prison gym. It'd been that or go mad with the clawing hunger for retribution.

He shrugged off his friend's concern and moved to the open door.

'Did you bring what I asked for?' he asked.

Romeo nodded. '*Sì.* All three files are on the laptop.'

Zaccheo slid onto the plush leather seat. Romeo slid in next to him and poured them two glasses of Italian-made cognac.

'*Salute,*' Romeo muttered.

Zaccheo took the drink without responding, threw back the amber liquid and allowed the scent of power and affluence—the tools he'd need for his plan to succeed—to wash over him.

As the low hum of the luxury engine whisked him away from the place he'd been forced to call home for over a year, Zaccheo reached for the laptop.

Icy rage trembled through his fingers as the Giordano Worldwide Inc. logo flickered to life. His life's work, almost decimated through another's greed and lust for power. It was only with Romeo's help that GWI hadn't gone under in the months after Zaccheo had been sent to prison for a crime he didn't commit. He drew quiet satisfaction that not only had GWI survived—thanks to Romeo—it had thrived.

But his personal reputation had not.

He was out now. Free to bring those culpable to justice. He didn't plan on resting until every last person responsible for attempting to destroy his life paid with the destruction of theirs.

Shaking out his hand to rid it of its tremble, he hit the Open key.

The information was thorough although Zaccheo knew most of its contents. For three months he'd checked and double-checked his sources, made sure every detail was nailed down tight.

He exhaled at the first picture that filled his screen.

Oscar Pennington III. Distant relative to the royal family. Etonian. Old, if spent, money. Very much part of the establishment. Greedy. Indiscriminate. His waning property portfolio had received a much-needed injection of capital exactly fourteen months and two weeks ago when he'd become sole owner of London's most talked about building—The Spire.

Zaccheo swallowed the savage growl that rumbled from his soul. Icily calm, he flicked through pages of Pennington celebrating his revived success with galas, lavish dinner parties and polo tournaments thrown about like confetti. One picture showed him laughing with one of his two children.

Sophie Pennington. Private education all the way to finishing school. Classically beautiful. Ball-breaker. She'd proven beyond a doubt that she had every intention of becoming Oscar's carbon copy.

Grimly, he closed her file and moved to the last one.

Eva Pennington.

This time the growl couldn't be contained. Nor could he stem the renewed shaking in his hand as he clicked her file.

Caramel-blonde hair tumbled down her shoulders in thick, wild waves. Dark eyebrows and lashes framed moss-green eyes, accentuated dramatically with black eyeliner. Those eyes had gripped his attention with more force than he'd been comfortable with the first time he'd looked into them. As had the full, bow-shaped lips currently curved in a smouldering smile. His screen displayed a head-and-shoulders shot, but the rest of Eva Pennington's body was imprinted indelibly on Zaccheo's mind. He didn't struggle to recall the petite, curvy shape, or that she forced herself to wear heels even though she hated them, in order to make herself taller.

He certainly didn't struggle to recall her individual atrocity. He'd lain in his prison bed condemning himself for being astounded by her singular betrayal, when the failings of both his parents and his dealings with the *establishment* should've taught him better. He'd prided himself on reading between the lines to spot schemers and gold-diggers ten miles away. Yet he'd been fooled.

The time he'd wasted on useless bitterness was the most excruciating of all; time he would gladly claw back if he could.

Firming his lips, he clicked through the pages, running through her life for the past year and a half. At the final page, he froze.

'How new is this last information?'

'I added that to the file yesterday. I thought you'd want to know,' Romeo replied.

Zaccheo stared at the newspaper clipping, shock waves rolling through him. *'Sì, grazie...'*

'Do you wish to return to the Esher estate or the penthouse?' Romeo asked.

Zaccheo read the announcement again, taking in pertinent details. Pennington Manor. Eight o'clock. Three hundred guests. Followed by an intimate family dinner on Sunday at The Spire.

The Spire...the building that should've been Zaccheo's greatest achievement.

'The estate,' he replied. It was closer.

He closed the file as Romeo instructed the driver.

Relaxing against the headrest, Zaccheo tried to let the hum of the engine soothe him. But it was no use. He was far from calm.

He'd have to alter his plan. Not that it mattered too much in the long run.

A chain is only as strong as its weakest link. While all three Penningtons had colluded in his incarceration, this new information demanded he use a different tactic, one he'd first contemplated and abandoned. Either way, Zaccheo didn't plan to rest until all of them were stripped of what they cherished most—their wealth and affluence.

He'd intended to wait a day or two to ensure he had Oscar Pennington where he wanted him before he struck. That plan was no longer viable.

Bringing down the family who'd framed him for criminal negligence couldn't wait till Monday.

His first order of business would be tackled *tonight*.

Starting with the youngest member of the family—Eva Pennington.

His ex-fiancée.

Eva Pennington stared at the dress in her sister's hand. 'Seriously? There's no way I'm wearing that. Why didn't you tell me the clothes I left behind had been given away?'

'Because you said you didn't want them when you moved out. Besides, they were old and out of fashion. I had *this* couriered from New York this morning. It's the latest couture and on loan to us for twenty-four hours,' Sophie replied.

Eva pursed her lips. 'I don't care if it was woven by ten thousand silk worms. I'm not wearing a dress that makes me look like a gold-digger *and* a slut. And considering the state of our finances, I'd have thought you'd be more careful what you splashed money on.' She couldn't stem her bewilderment as to why Sophie and her father blithely ignored the fact that money was extremely tight.

Sophie huffed. 'This is a one-of-a-kind dress, and, unless I'm mistaken, it's the kind of dress your future husband likes his women to wear. Anyway, you'll be out of it in less than four hours, once the right photographs have been taken, and the party's over.'

Eva gritted her teeth. 'Stop trying to manage me, Sophie. You're forgetting who pulled this bailout together. If I hadn't come to an agreement with Harry, we'd have been sunk come next week. As to what he likes his women to wear, if you'd bothered to speak to me first I'd have saved you the trouble of going to unnecessary expense. I dress for myself and no one else.'

'Speak to you first? When you and Father neglected to afford me the same courtesy before you hatched this plan behind my back?' Sophie griped.

Eva's heart twisted at the blatant jealousy in her sister's voice.

As if it weren't enough that the decision she'd spent the past two weeks agonising over still made her insides clench in horror. It didn't matter that the man she'd agreed to marry was her friend and she was helping him as much as he was helping her. Marriage was a step she'd rather not have taken.

It was clear, however, her sister didn't see it that way. Sophie's escalating discontentment at any relationship Eva tried to forge with their father was part of the reason Eva had moved out of Pennington Manor. Not that their father was an easy man to live with.

For as long as she could remember, Sophie had been possessive of their father's attention. While their mother had been alive, it'd been bearable and easier to accept that Sophie was their father's preferred child, while Eva was her mother's, despite wanting to be loved equally by both parents.

After their mother's death, every interaction Eva had tried to have with their father had been met with bristling confrontation from Sophie, and indifference from their father.

But, irrational as it was, it didn't stop Eva from trying to reason with the sister she'd once looked up to.

'We didn't go behind your back. You were away on a business trip—'

'Trying to use the business degree that doesn't seem to mean anything any more. Not when *you* can swoop in after three years of performing tired ballads in seedy pubs to save the day,' Sophie interjected harshly.

Eva hung on to her temper by a thread, but pain stung deep at the blithe dismissal of her passion. 'You know I resigned from Penningtons because Father only hired me so I could attract a suitable husband. And just because my dreams don't coincide with yours—'

'That's just it. You're twenty-four and still *dreaming*. The rest of us don't have that luxury. And we certainly don't land on our feet by clicking our fingers and having a millionaire solve all our problems.'

'Harry is saving *all of us*. And you really think I've *landed on my feet* by getting engaged for the second time in two years?' Eva asked.

Sophie dropped the offensive dress on Eva's bed. 'To everyone who matters, this is your first engagement. The other one barely lasted five minutes. Hardly anyone knows it happened.'

Hurt-laced anger swirled through her veins. '*I* know it happened.'

'If my opinion matters around here any more, then I suggest you don't broadcast it. It's a subject best left in the past, just like the man it involved.'

Pain stung deeper. 'I can't pretend it didn't happen because of what occurred afterwards.'

'The last thing we need right now is any hint of scandal. And I don't know why you're blaming Father for what happened when you should be thanking him for extricating you from that man before it was too late,' Sophie defended heatedly.

That man.

Zaccheo Giordano.

Eva wasn't sure whether the ache lodged beneath her ribs came from thinking about him or from the reminder of how gullible she'd been to think he was any different from every other man who'd crossed her path.

She relaxed her fists when they balled again.

This was why she preferred her life away from their family home deep in the heart of Surrey.

It was why her waitress colleagues knew her as Eva Penn, a hostess at Siren, the London nightclub where she also sang part-time, instead of Lady Eva Pennington, daughter of Lord Pennington.

Her relationship with her father had always been difficult, but she'd never thought she'd lose her sister so completely, too.

She cleared her throat. 'Sophie, this agreement with Harry wasn't supposed to undermine anything you were doing with Father to save Penningtons. There's no need to be upset or jealous. I'm not trying to take your place—'

'Jealous! Don't be ridiculous,' Sophie sneered, although the trace of panic in her voice made Eva's heart break. 'And you could never take my place. I'm Father's right hand, whereas you...you're nothing but—' She stopped herself and, after a few seconds, stuck her nose in the air. 'Our guests are arriving shortly. Please don't be late to your own engagement party.'

Eva swallowed down her sorrow. 'I've no intention of being late. But neither do I have any intention of wearing a dress that has less material than thread holding it together.'

She strode to the giant George III armoire opposite the bed, even though her earlier inspection had shown less than a fraction of the items she'd left behind when she'd moved out on her twenty-first birthday.

These days she was content with her hostess's uniform when she was working or lounging in jeans and sweaters while she wrote her music on her days off. Haute couture, spa days and primping herself beautiful in order to please anyone were part of a past she'd happily left behind.

Unfortunately this time there'd been no escaping. Not when she alone had been able to find the solution to saving her family.

She tried in vain to squash the rising memories being back at Pennington Manor threatened to resurrect.

Zaccheo was in her past, a mistake that should never have happened. A reminder that ignoring a lesson learned only led to further heartache.

She sighed in relief when her hand closed on a silk wrap. The red dress would be far too revealing, a true spectacle for the three hundred guests her father had invited to gawp at. But at least the wrap would provide a little much-needed cover.

Glancing at the dress again, she shuddered.

She'd rather be anywhere but here, participating in this sham. But then hadn't her whole life been a sham? From parents who'd been publicly hailed as the couple to envy, but who'd fought bitterly in private until tragedy had struck in the form of her mother's cancer, to the lavish parties and expensive holidays that her father had secretly been borrowing money for, the Penningtons had been one giant sham for as long as Eva could remember.

Zaccheo's entry into their lives had only escalated her father's behaviour.

No, she refused to think about Zaccheo. He belonged to a chapter of her life that was firmly sealed. Tonight was about Harry Fairfield, her family's saviour, and her soon-to-be fiancé.

It was also about her father's health.

For that reason alone, she tried again with Sophie.

'For Father's sake, I want tonight to go smoothly, so can we try to get along?'

Sophie stiffened. 'If you're talking about Father's hospitalisation two weeks ago, I haven't forgotten.'

Watching her father struggle to breathe with what the doctors had termed a cardiac event had terrified Eva. It'd been the catalyst that had forced her to accept Harry's proposition.

'He's okay today, isn't he?' Despite her bitterness at her family's treatment of her, she couldn't help her concern for her remaining parent. Nor could she erase the secret yearning that the different version of the father she'd connected with very briefly after her mother's death, the one who wasn't an excess-loving megalomaniac who treated her as if she was an irritating inconvenience, hadn't been a figment of her imagination.

'He will be, once we get rid of the creditors threatening us with bankruptcy.'

Eva exhaled. There was no backing out; no secretly hoping that some other solution would present itself and save her from the sacrifice she was making.

All avenues had been thoroughly explored—Eva had demanded to see the Pennington books herself and spent a day with the company's accountants to verify that they were indeed in dire straits. Her father's rash acquisition of The Spire had stretched the company to breaking point. Harry Fairfield was their last hope.

She unzipped the red dress, resisting the urge to crush it into a wrinkled pulp.

'Do you need help?' Sophie asked, although Eva sensed the offer wasn't altruistic.

'No, I can manage.'

The same way she'd managed after her mother's death; through her father's rejection and Sophie's increasingly unreasonable behaviour; through the heartbreak of finding out about Zaccheo's betrayal.

Sophie nodded briskly. 'I'll see you downstairs, then.'

Eva slipped on the dress, avoiding another look in the mirror when the first glimpse showed what she'd feared most. Her every curve was accentuated, with large swathes of flesh exposed. With shaky fingers she applied her lipstick and slipped her feet into matching platform heels.

Slipping the gold and red wrap around her shoulders, she finally glanced at her image.

Chin up, girl. It's show time.

Eva wished the manageress of Siren were uttering the words, as she did every time before Eva stepped onto the stage.

Unfortunately, she wasn't at Siren. She'd promised to marry a man she didn't love, for the sake of saving her precious family name.

No amount of pep talk could stem the roaring agitation flooding her veins.

CHAPTER TWO

THE EVENT PLANNERS had outdone themselves. Potted palms, decorative screens and subdued lighting had been strategically placed around the main halls of Pennington Manor to hide the peeling plaster, chipped wood panelling and torn Aubusson rugs that funds could no longer stretch to rectify.

Eva sipped the champagne she'd been nursing for the last two hours and willed time to move faster. Technically she couldn't throw any guest out, but *Eight to Midnight* was the time the costly invitations had stated the party would last. She needed something to focus on or risk sliding into madness.

Gritting her teeth, she smiled as yet another guest demanded to see her engagement ring. The monstrous pink diamond's sole purpose was to demonstrate the Fairfields' wealth. Its alien weight dragged her hand down, hammering home the irrefutable point that she'd sold herself for her pedigree.

Her father's booming voice interrupted her maudlin thoughts. Surrounded by a group of influential politicians who hung onto his every word, Oscar Pennington was in his element.

Thickset but tall enough to hide the excess weight he carried, her father cut a commanding figure despite his recent spell in hospital. His stint in the army three decades ago had lent him a ruthless edge, cleverly counteracted by his natural charm. The combination made him enigmatic enough to attract attention when he walked into a room.

But not even that charisma had saved him from economic devastation four years ago.

With that coming close on the heels of her mother's ill-

ness, their social and economic circles had dwindled to nothing almost overnight, with her father desperately scrambling
to hold things together.

End result—his association with Zaccheo Giordano.

Eva frowned, bewildered that her thoughts had circled
back to the man she'd pushed to the dark recesses of her
mind. A man she'd last seen being led away in handcuffs—

'There you are. I've been looking for you everywhere.'

Eva started, then berated herself for feeling guilty. Guilt
belonged to those who'd committed crimes, who lied about
their true motives.

Enough!

She smiled at Harry.

Her old university friend—a brilliant tech genius—
had gone off the rails when he'd achieved fame and wealth
straight out of university. Now a multimillionaire with
enough money to bail out Penningtons, he represented her
family's last hope.

'Well, you found me,' she said.

He was a few inches taller than her five feet four; she
didn't have to look up too far to meet his twinkling soft
brown eyes.

'Indeed. Are you okay?' he asked, his gaze reflecting
concern.

'I'm fine,' she responded breezily.

He looked unconvinced. Harry was one of the few people
who knew about her broken engagement to Zaccheo. He'd
seen beneath her false smiles and assurances that she could
handle a marriage of convenience and asked her point-blank
if her past with Zaccheo Giordano would be a problem. Her
swift *no* seemed to have satisfied him.

Now he looked unsure.

'Harry, don't fret. I can do this,' she insisted, despite the
hollowness in her stomach.

He studied her solemnly, then called over a waiter and exchanged his empty champagne glass for a full one. 'If you

say so, but I need advanced warning if this gets too weird for you, okay? My parents will have a fit if they read about me in the papers this side of Christmas.'

She nodded gratefully, then frowned. 'I thought you were going to take it easy tonight?' She indicated his glass.

'Gosh, you already sound like a wife.' He sniggered. 'Leave off, sweetness, the parents have already given me an earful.'

Having met his parents a week ago, Eva could imagine the exchange.

'Remember why *you're* doing this. Do you want to derail the PR campaign to clean up your image before it's even begun?'

While Harry couldn't care less about his social standing, his parents were voracious in their hunger for prestige and a pedigree to hang their name on. Only the threat to Harry's business dealings had finally forced him to address his reckless playboy image.

He took her arm and tilted his sand-coloured head affably towards hers. 'I promise to be on my best behaviour. Now that the tedious toasts have been made and we're officially engaged, it's time for the best part of the evening. The fireworks!'

Eva set her champagne glass down and stepped out of the dining-room alcove that had been her sanctuary throughout her childhood. 'Isn't that supposed to be a surprise?'

Harry winked. 'It is, but, since we've fooled everyone into thinking we're *madly* in love, faking our surprise should be easy.'

She smiled. 'I won't tell if you don't.'

Harry laid a hand across his heart. 'Thank you, my fair Lady Pennington.'

The reminder of why this whole sham engagement was happening slid like a knife between her ribs. Numbing herself to the pain, she walked out onto the terrace that overlooked the manor's multi-acre garden.

The gardens had once held large koi ponds, a giant summer house and an elaborate maze, but the prohibitive cost of the grounds' upkeep had led to the landscape being levelled and replaced with rolling carpet grass.

A smattering of applause greeted their arrival and Eva's gaze drifted over the guests to where Sophie, her father and Harry's parents stood watching them.

She caught her father's eye, and her stomach knotted.

While part of her was pleased that she'd found a solution to their family problems, she couldn't help but feel that nothing she did would ever bring her closer to her sister or father.

Her father might have accepted her help with the bailout from Harry, but his displeasure at her chosen profession was yet another bone of contention between them. One she'd made clear she wouldn't back down on.

Turning away, she fixed her smile in place and exclaimed appropriately when the first elaborate firework display burst into the sky.

'So…my parents want us to live together,' Harry whispered in her ear.

'What?'

He laughed. 'Don't worry, I convinced them you hate my bachelor pad so we need to find a place that's *ours* rather than mine.'

Relief poured through her. 'Thank you.'

He brushed a hand down her cheek. 'You're welcome. But I deserve a reward for my sacrifice,' he said with a smile. 'How about dinner on Monday?'

'As long as it's not a paparazzi-stalked spectacle of a restaurant, you're on.'

'Great. It's a date.' He kissed her knuckles, much to the delight of the guests, who thought they were witnessing a true love match.

Eva allowed herself to relax. She might find what they were doing distasteful, but she was grateful that Harry's visit to Siren three weeks ago had ended up with him bailing her out, and not a calculating stranger.

'That dress is a knockout on you, by the way.'

She grimaced. 'It wasn't my first choice, but thank you.'

The next series of firework displays should've quieted the guests, yet murmurs around her grew.

'*Omigod*, whoever it is must have a death wish!' someone exclaimed.

Harry's eyes narrowed. 'I think we may have a last-minute guest.'

Eva looked around and saw puzzled gazes fixed at a point in the sky as the faint *thwopping* sound grew louder. Another set of fireworks went off, illuminating the looming object.

She frowned. 'Is that…?'

'A helicopter heading straight for the middle of the fireworks display? Yep. I guess the organisers decided to add another surprise to the party.'

'I don't think that's part of the entertainment,' Eva shouted to be heard over the descending aircraft.

Her heart slammed into her throat as a particularly elaborate firework erupted precariously close to the black-and-red chopper.

'Hell, if this is a stunt, I take my hat off to the pilot. It takes iron balls to fly into danger like that.' Harry chuckled.

The helicopter drew closer. Mesmerised, Eva watched it settle in the middle of the garden, her attention riveted to its single occupant.

The garden lights had been turned off to showcase the fireworks to maximum effect so she couldn't see who their unexpected guest was. Nevertheless, an ominous shiver chased up her spine.

She heard urgent shouts for the pyrotechnician to halt the display, but another rocket fizzed past the rotating blades.

A hush fell over the crowd as the helicopter door opened. A figure stepped out, clad from head to toe in black. As another blaze of colour filled the sky his body was thrown into relief.

Eva tensed as if she'd been shot with a stun gun.

It couldn't be...

He was behind bars, atoning for his ruthless greed. Eva squashed the sting of guilt that accompanied the thought.

Zaccheo Giordano and men of his ilk arrogantly believed they were above the law. They didn't deserve her sympathy, or the disloyal thought that he alone had paid the price when, by association, her father should've borne some of the blame. Justice ensured they went to jail and stayed there for the duration of their term. They weren't released early.

They certainly didn't land in the middle of a firework display at a private party as if they owned the land they walked on.

The spectacle unfolding before her stated differently.

Lights flickered on. Eva tracked the figure striding imperiously across the grass and up the wide steps.

Reaching the terrace, he paused and buttoned his single-breasted tuxedo.

'Oh, God,' she whispered.

'Wait...you know this bloke?' Harry asked, his tone for once serious.

Eva wanted to deny the man who now stood, easily head and shoulders above the nearest guests, his fierce, unwavering gaze pinned on her.

She didn't know whether to attribute the crackling electricity to his appearance or the look in his eyes. Both were viscerally menacing to the point of brutality.

The Zaccheo Giordano she'd had the misfortune of briefly tangling with before his incarceration had kept his hair trimmed short and his face clean-shaven.

This man had a full beard and his hair flowed over his shoulders in an unruly sea of thick jet waves. Eva swallowed at the pronounced difference in him. The sleek, almost gaunt man she'd known was gone. In his place breathed a Neanderthal with broader shoulders, thicker arms and a denser chest moulded by his black silk shirt. Equally dark trousers hugged lean hips and sturdy thighs to fall in a precise inch above expensive handmade shoes. But nothing of his attire disguised the aura he emanated.

Uncivilised. Explosively masculine. Lethal.

Danger vibrated from him like striations on baking asphalt. It flowed over the guests, who jostled each other for a better look at the impromptu visitor.

'Eva?' Harry's puzzled query echoed through her dazed consciousness.

Zaccheo released her from his deadly stare. His eyes flicked to the arm tucked into Harry's before he turned away. The breath exploded from her lungs. Sensing Harry about to ask another question, she nodded.

'Yes. That's Zaccheo.'

Her eyes followed Zaccheo as he turned towards her family.

Oscar's look of anger was laced with a heavy dose of apprehension. Sophie looked plain stunned.

Eva watched the man she'd hoped to never see again cup his hands behind his back and stroll towards her father. Anyone would've been foolish to think that stance indicated supplication. If anything, its severe mockery made Eva want to do the unthinkable and burst out laughing.

She would've, had she not been mired in deep dread at what Zaccheo's presence meant.

'Your ex?' Harry pressed.

She nodded numbly.

'Then we should say hello.'

Harry tugged on her arm and she realised too late what he meant.

'No. Wait!' she whispered fiercely.

But he was either too drunk or genuinely oblivious to the vortex of danger he was headed for to pay attention. The tension surrounding the group swallowed Eva as they approached. Heart pounding, she watched her father's and Zaccheo's gazes lock.

'I don't know what the hell you think you're doing here, Giordano, but I suggest you get back in that monstrosity and leave before I have you arrested for trespass.'

A shock wave went through the crowd.

Zaccheo didn't bat an eyelid.

'By all means do that if you wish, but you know exactly why I'm here, Pennington. We can play coy if you prefer. You'll be made painfully aware when I tire of it.' The words were barely above a murmur, but their venom raised the hairs on Eva's arms, triggering a gasp when she saw Sophie's face.

Her usually unflappable sister was severely agitated, her face distressingly pale.

'*Ciao*, Eva,' Zaccheo drawled without turning around. That deep, resonant voice, reminiscent of a tenor in a soulful opera, washed over her, its powerfully mesmerising quality reminding her how she'd once longed to hear him speak just for the hell of it. 'It's good of you to join us.'

'This is my engagement party. It's my duty to interact with my guests, even unwelcome ones who will be asked to leave immediately.'

'Don't worry, *cara*, I won't be staying long.'

The relief that surged up her spine disappeared when his gaze finally swung her way, then dropped to her left hand. With almost cavalier laziness, he caught her wrist and raised it to the light. He examined the ring for exactly three seconds. 'How predictable.'

He released her with the same carelessness he'd captured her.

Eva clenched her fist to stop the sizzling electricity firing up her arm at the brief contact.

'What's that supposed to mean?' Harry demanded.

Zaccheo levelled steely grey eyes on him, then his parents. 'This is a private discussion. Leave us.'

Peter Fairfield's laugh held incredulity, the last inch of

champagne in his glass sloshing wildly as he raised his arm. 'I think you've got the wrong end of the stick there, mate. You're the one who needs to take a walk.'

Eva caught Harry's pained look at his father's response, but could do nothing but watch, heart in her throat, as Zaccheo faced Peter Fairfield.

Again she was struck by how much his body had changed; how the sleek, layered muscle lent a deeper sense of danger. Whereas before it'd been like walking close to the edge of a cliff, looking into his eyes now was like staring into a deep, bottomless abyss.

'Would you care to repeat that, *il mio amico*?' The almost conversational tone belied the savage tension beneath the words.

'Oscar, who *is* this?' Peter Fairfield demanded of her father, who seemed to have lost the ability to speak after Zaccheo's succinct taunt.

Eva inserted herself between the two men before the situation got out of hand. Behind her, heat from Zaccheo's body burned every exposed inch of skin. Ignoring the sensation, she cleared her throat.

'Mr and Mrs Fairfield, Harry, we'll only be a few minutes. We're just catching up with Mr Giordano.' She glanced at her father. A vein throbbed in his temple and he'd gone a worrying shade of puce. Fear climbed into her heart. 'Father?'

He roused himself and glanced around. A charming smile slid into place, but it was off by a light year. The trickle of ice that had drifted down her spine at Zaccheo's unexpected arrival turned into a steady drip.

'We'll take this in my study. Don't hesitate to let the staff know if you need anything.' He strode away, followed by a disturbingly quiet Sophie.

Zaccheo's gaze swung to Harry, who defiantly withstood the laser gaze for a few seconds before he glanced at her.

'Are you sure?' Harry asked, that touching concern again in his eyes.

Her instinct screamed a terrible foreboding, but she nodded. 'Yes.'

'Okay. Hurry back, sweetness.' Before she could move, he dropped a kiss on her mouth.

A barely audible lethal growl charged through the air.

Eva flinched.

She wanted to face Zaccheo. Demand that he crawl back behind the bars that should've been holding him. But that glimpse of fear in her father's eyes stopped her. She tugged the wrap closer around her.

Something wasn't right here. She was willing to bet the dilapidated ancestral pile beneath her feet that something was seriously, *dangerously* wrong—

'Move, Eva.'

The cool command spoken against her ear sent shivers coursing through her.

She moved, only because the quicker she got to the bottom of why he was here, the quicker he would leave. But with each step his dark gaze probed her back, making the walk to her father's study on the other side of the manor the longest in her life.

Zaccheo shut the door behind him. Her father turned from where he'd been gazing into the unlit fireplace. Again Eva spotted apprehension in his eyes before he masked it.

'Whatever grievance you think you have the right to air, I suggest you rethink it, son. Even if this were the right time or place—'

'I am *not* your son, Pennington.' Zaccheo's response held lethal bite, the first sign of his fury breaking through. 'As for why I'm here, I have five thousand three hundred and twenty-two pieces of documentation that proves you colluded with various other individuals to pin a crime on me that I didn't commit.'

'What?' Eva gasped, then the absurdity of the statement made her shake her head. 'We don't believe you.'

Zaccheo's eyes remained on her father. 'You may not, but your father does.'

Oscar Pennington laughed, but the sound lacked its usual boom and zest. When sweat broke out over his forehead, fear gripped Eva's insides.

She steeled her spine. 'Our lawyers will rip whatever evidence you think you have to shreds, I'm sure. If you're here to seek some sort of closure, you picked the wrong time to do it. Perhaps we can arrange to meet you at some other time?'

Zaccheo didn't move. Didn't blink. Hands once again tucked behind his back, he simply watched her father, his body a coiled predator waiting to strike a fatal blow.

Silence stretched, throbbed with unbearable menace. Eva looked from her father to Sophie and back again, her dread escalating. 'What's going on?' she demanded.

Her father gripped the mantel until his knuckles shone white. 'You chose the wrong enemy. You're sorely mistaken if you think I'll let you blackmail me in my own home.'

Sophie stepped forward. 'Father, don't—'

'Good, you haven't lost your hubris.' Zaccheo's voice slashed across her sister's. 'I was counting on that. Here's what I'm going to do. In ten minutes I'm going to leave here with Eva, right in front of all your guests. You won't lift a finger to stop me. You'll tell them exactly who I am. Then you'll make a formal announcement that I'm the man your daughter will marry two weeks from today and that I have your blessing. I don't want to trust something so important to phone cameras and social media, although your guests will probably do a pretty good job. I noticed a few members of the press out there, so that part of your task should be easy. If the articles are written to my satisfaction, I'll be in touch on Monday to lay out how you can begin to make reparations to me. However, if by the time Eva and I wake up tomorrow morning the news of our engagement isn't in the press, then all bets are off.'

Oscar Pennington's breathing altered alarmingly. His

mouth opened but no words emerged. In the arctic silence that greeted Zaccheo's deadly words, Eva gaped at him.

'You're clearly not in touch with all of your faculties if you think those ridiculous demands are going to be met.' When silence greeted her response, she turned sharply to her father. 'Father? Why aren't you saying something?' she demanded, although the trepidation beating in her chest spelled its own doom.

'Because he can't, Eva. Because he's about to do exactly as I say.'

She rounded on him, and was once again rocked to the core by Zaccheo's visually powerful, utterly captivating transformation. So much so, she couldn't speak for several seconds. 'You're out of your mind!' she finally blurted.

Zaccheo's gaze didn't stray from its laser focus on her father. 'Believe me, *cara mia*, I haven't been saner than I am in this moment.'

CHAPTER THREE

ZACCHEO WATCHED EVA'S head swivel to her father, confusion warring with anger.

'Go on, Oscar. She's waiting for you to tell me to go to hell. Why don't you?'

Pennington staggered towards his desk, his face ashen and his breathing growing increasingly laboured.

'Father!' Eva rushed to his side—ignoring the poisonous look her sister sent her—as he collapsed into his leather armchair.

Zaccheo wanted to rip her away, let her watch her father suffer as his sins came home to roost. Instead he allowed the drama to play out. The outcome would be inevitable and would only go one way.

His way.

He wanted to look into Pennington's eyes and see the defeat and helplessness the other man had expected to see in his eyes the day Zaccheo had been sentenced.

Both sisters now fussed over their father and a swell of satisfaction rose at the fear in their eyes. Eva glanced his way and he experienced a different punch altogether. One he'd thought himself immune to, but had realised otherwise the moment he'd stepped off his helicopter and singled her out in the crowd.

That unsettling feeling, as if he were suffering from vertigo despite standing on terra firma, had intrigued and annoyed him in equal measures from the very first time he'd seen her, her voice silkily hypnotic as she crooned into a mic on a golden-lit stage, her fingers caressing the black microphone stand as if she were touching a lover.

Even knowing exactly who she was, what she represented,

he hadn't been able to walk away. In the weeks after their first meeting, he'd fooled himself into believing she was different, that she wasn't tainted with the same greed to further her pedigree by whatever means necessary; that she wasn't willing to do whatever it took to secure her family's standing, even while secretly scorning his upbringing.

Her very public denouncement of any association between them on the day of his sentencing had been the final blow. Not that Zaccheo hadn't had the scales viciously ripped from his eyes by then.

No, by that fateful day fourteen months ago, he'd known just how thoroughly he'd been suckered.

'What the hell do you think you're doing?' she muttered fiercely, her moss-green eyes firing lasers at him.

Zaccheo forced himself not to smile. The time for gloating would come later. 'Exacting the wages of sin, *dolcezza*. What else?'

'I don't know what you're talking about, but I don't think my father is in a position to have a discussion with you right now, Mr Giordano.'

Her prim and proper tones bit savagely into Zaccheo, wiping away any trace of twisted mirth. That tone said he ought to *know his place*, that he ought to stand there like a good little servant and wait to be addressed instead of upsetting the lord of the manor with his petty concerns.

Rage bubbled beneath his skin, threatening to erupt. Blunt nails bit into his wrist, but the pain wasn't enough to calm his fury. He clenched his jaw for a long moment before he trusted himself to speak.

'I gave you ten minutes, Pennington. You now have five. I suggest you practise whatever sly words you'll be using to address your guests.' Zaccheo shrugged. 'Or not. Either way, things *will* go my way.'

Eva rushed at him, her striking face and flawless skin flushed with a burst of angry colour as she stopped a few feet away.

Out on the terrace, he'd compelled himself not to stare too long at her in case he betrayed his feelings. In case his gaze devoured her as he'd wanted to do since her presence snaked like a live wire inside him.

Now, he took in that wild gypsy-like caramel-blonde hair so out of place in this polished stratosphere her family chose to inhabit. The striking contrast between her bright hair, black eyebrows and dark-rimmed eyes had always fascinated him. But no more than her cupid-bow lips, soft, dark red and sinfully sensual. Or the rest of her body.

'You assume I have no say in whatever despicable spectacle you're planning. That I intend to meekly stand by while you humiliate my family? Well, think again!'

'Eva…' her father started.

'No! I don't know what exactly is going on here, but I intend to play no part in it.'

'You'll play your part, and you'll play it well,' Zaccheo interjected, finally driving his gaze up from the mouth he wanted to feast on more than he wanted his next breath. *That'll come soon enough*, he promised himself.

'Or what? You'll carry through with your empty threats?'

His fury eased a touch and twisted amusement slid back into place. It never ceased to amaze him how the titled rich felt they were above the tenets that governed ordinary human beings. His own stepfather had been the same. He'd believed, foolishly, that his pedigree and connections would insulate him from his reckless business practices, that the Old Boys' Club would provide a safety net despite his poor judgement.

Zaccheo had taken great pleasure in watching his mother's husband squirm before him, cap in hand, when Zaccheo had bought his family business right from underneath his pompous nose. But even then, the older man had continued to treat him like a third-class citizen…

Just as Oscar Pennington had done. Just as Eva Pennington was doing now.

'You think my threats empty?' he enquired softly. 'Then do nothing. It's after all your privilege and your right.'

Something of the lethal edge that rode him must have transmitted itself to her. Apprehension chased across her face before she firmed those impossibly sumptuous lips.

'Do nothing, and watch me bury your family in the deepest, darkest, most demeaning pit you can dream of. Do nothing and watch me unleash a scandal the scale of which you can only imagine on your precious family name.' He bared his teeth in a mirthless smile and her eyes widened in stunned disbelief. 'It would be *my* privilege and pleasure to do so.'

Oscar Pennington inhaled sharply and Zaccheo's gaze zeroed in on his enemy. The older man rose from the chair. Though he looked frail, his eyes reflected icy disdain. But Zaccheo also glimpsed the fear of a cornered man weighing all the options to see how to escape the noose dangling ever closer.

Zaccheo smiled inwardly. He had no intention of letting Pennington escape. Not now, not ever.

The flames of retribution intensifying within him, he unclasped his hands. It was time to bring this meeting to an end.

'Your time's up, Pennington.'

Eva answered instead of her father. 'How do we know you're not bluffing? You say you have something over us, prove it,' she said defiantly.

He could've walked out and let them twist in the wind of uncertainty. Pennington would find out soon enough the length of Zaccheo's ruthless reach. But the thought of leaving Eva here when he departed was suddenly unthinkable. So far he'd allowed himself a brief glimpse of her body wrapped in that obscenely revealing red dress. But that one glimpse had been enough. Quite apart from the rage boiling his blood, the steady hammer of his pulse proved that he still wanted her with a fever that spiked higher with each passing second.

He would take what he'd foolishly and piously denied

himself two years ago. He would *take* and *use*, just as they'd done to him. Only when he'd achieved every goal he'd set himself would he feel avenged.

'You can't, can you?' Oscar taunted with a sly smile, bringing Zaccheo back to the room and the three aristocratic faces staring at him with varying degrees of disdain and fear.

He smiled, almost amused by the older man's growing confidence. 'Harry Fairfield is providing you with a bridging loan of fifteen million pounds because the combined running costs of the Pennington Hotels and The Spire have you stretched so thin the banks won't touch you. While you desperately drum up an adequate advertising budget to rent out all those overpriced but empty floors in The Spire, the interest owed to the Chinese consortium who own seventy-five per cent of the building is escalating. You have a meeting with them on Monday to request more time to pay the interest. In return for Fairfield's investment, you're handing him your daughter.'

Eva glared at him. 'So you've asked a few questions about Penningtons' business practices. That doesn't empower you to make demands of any of us.'

Zaccheo took a moment to admire her newfound grit. During their initial association, she'd been a little more timid, and in her father's shadow, but it looked as if the kitten had grown a few claws. He curbed the thrill at what was to come and answered.

'Yes, it does. Would you be interested to know the Chinese consortium sold their seventy-five per cent of The Spire to me three days ago? So by my calculation you're in excess of three months late on interest payments, correct?'

A rough sound, a cross between a cough and a wheeze, escaped Pennington's throat. There was no class or grace in the way he gaped at Zaccheo. He dropped back into his chair, his face a mask of hatred.

'I knew you were a worthless bet the moment I set eyes on you. I should've listened to my instincts.'

The red haze he'd been trying to hold back surged higher. 'No, what you wanted was a spineless scapegoat, a *capro espiatorio*, who would make you rich and fat and content and even give up his life without question!'

'Mr Giordano, surely we can discuss this like sensible business-minded individuals,' Sophie Pennington advanced, her hands outstretched in benign sensibility. Zaccheo looked from the hands she willed not to tremble to the veiled disdain in her eyes. Then he looked past her to Eva, who'd returned to her father's side, her face pale but her eyes shooting her displeasure at him.

Unexpectedly and very much unwelcome, a tiny hint of compassion tugged at him.

Basta!

He turned abruptly and reached for the door handle. 'You have until I ready my chopper for take-off to come to me, Eva.' He didn't need to expand on that edict. The *or else* hung in the air like the deadly poison he intended it to be.

He walked out and headed for the terrace, despite every nerve in his body straining to return to the room and forcibly drag Eva out.

True, he hadn't bargained for the visceral reaction to seeing her again. And yes, he hadn't quite been able to control his reaction to seeing another man's ring on her finger, that vulgar symbol of ownership hollowing out his stomach. The knowledge that she'd most likely shared that hapless drunk's bed, given the body he'd once believed to be his to another, ate through his blood like acid on metal. But he couldn't afford to let his emotions show.

Every strategic move in this game of deadly retribution hinged on him maintaining his control; on not letting them see how affected he was by all this.

He stepped onto the terrace and all conversation ceased. Curious faces gaped and one or two bolder guests even tried to intercept him. Zaccheo cut through the crowd, his gaze on the chopper a few dozen yards away.

She would come to him. As an outcome of his first salvo, nothing else would be acceptable.

His pulse thudded loud and insistent in his ears as he strolled down the steps towards the aircraft. The fireworks amid which he'd landed had long since gone quiet, but the scent of sulphur lingered in the air, reminding him of the volatility that lingered beneath his own skin, ready to erupt at the smallest trigger.

He wouldn't let it erupt. Not yet.

A murmur rose behind him, the fevered excitement that came with the anticipation of a spectacle. A *scandal*.

Zaccheo compelled himself to keep walking.

He ducked beneath the powerful rotors of his aircraft and reached for the door.

'Wait!'

He stopped. Turned.

Three hundred pairs of eyes watched with unabashed interest as Eva paused several feet from him.

Behind her, her father and sister stood on the steps, wearing similar expressions of dread. Zaccheo wanted them to stew for a while longer, but he found his attention drawn to the woman striding towards him. Her face reflected more defiance than dread. It also held pride and not a small measure of bruised disdain. Zaccheo vowed in that moment to make her regret that latter look, make her take back every single moment she'd thought herself above him.

Swallowing, he looked down at her body.

She held the flimsy wrap around her like armour. As if that would protect her from him. With one ruthless tug, he pulled it away. It fluttered to the ground, revealing her luscious, heart-stopping figure to his gaze. Unable to stem the frantic need crashing through him, he stepped forward and speared his fingers into the wild tumble of her hair.

Another step and she was in his arms.

Where she belonged.

* * *

The small pocket of air Eva had been able to retain in her lungs during her desperate flight after Zaccheo evaporated when he yanked her against him. Her body went from shivering in the crisp January air to furnace-hot within seconds. The fingers in her hair tightened, his other arm sliding around her waist.

Eva wanted to remain unaffected, slam her hands against his chest and remove herself from that dangerous wall of masculinity. But she couldn't move. So she fought with her words.

'You may think you've won, that you own me, but you don't,' she snapped. 'You never will!'

His eyes gleamed. 'Such fire. Such determination. You've changed, *cara mia*, I'll give you that. And yet here you are, barely one minute after I walked out of your father's study. Mere hours after you promised yourself to another man, here you are, Eva Pennington, ready to promise yourself to me. Ready to become whatever I want you to be.'

Her snigger made his eyes narrow, but she didn't care. 'Keep telling yourself that. I look forward to your shock when I prove you wrong.'

That deadly smile she'd first seen in her father's study reappeared, curling fear through her. It reeked with far too much gratification to kill that unshakeable sensation that she was standing on the edge of a precipice, and that, should she fall, there would be no saving her.

She realised the reason for the smile when he lifted her now bare fingers to his eye level. 'You've proved me right already.'

'Are you completely sure about that?' The question was a bold but empty taunt.

The lack of fuss with which Harry had taken back his ring a few minutes ago had been a relief.

She might not have an immediate solution to her family's

problems, but Eva was glad she no longer had to pretend she was half of a sham couple.

Zaccheo brought her fingers to his mouth and kissed her ring finger, stunning her back to reality. Flashes erupted as his actions were recorded, no doubt to be streamed across the fastest mediums available.

Recalling the conversation she'd just had with her father, she tried to pull away. 'This pound-of-flesh taking isn't going to last very long, so I suggest you enjoy it while it lasts. I intend to return to my life before midnight—'

Her words dried up when his face closed in a mask of icy fury, and his hands sealed her body even closer to his.

'Your first lesson is to stop speaking to me as if I'm the hired help. Refraining from doing so will put me in a much calmer frame of mind to deal with you than otherwise,' he said with unmistakeable warning.

Eva doubted that anyone had dared to speak to Zaccheo Giordano in the way he referred, but she wasn't about to debate that point with him with three hundred pairs of eyes watching. She was struggling enough to keep upright what with all the turbulent sensations firing through her at his touch. 'Why, Zaccheo, you sound as if you've a great many lessons you intend to dole out…' She tried to sound bored, but her voice emerged a little too breathless for her liking.

'Patience, *cara mia*. You'll be instructed as and when necessary.' His gaze dropped to her mouth and her breath lodged in her sternum. 'For now, I wish the talking to cease.'

He closed the final inch between them and slanted his mouth over hers. The world tilted and shook beneath her feet. Expertly sensual and demanding, he kissed her as if he owned her mouth, as if he owned her whole body. In all her adult years, Eva had never imagined the brush of a beard would infuse her with such spine-tingling sensations. Yet she shivered with fiery delight as Zaccheo's silky facial hair caressed the corners of her mouth.

She groaned at the forceful breach of his tongue. Her arms drifted over his taut biceps as she became lost in the potent magic of his kiss. At the first touch of his tongue against hers, she shuddered. He made a rough sound and his sharp inhalation vibrated against her. His fingers convulsed in her hair and his other hand drifted to her bottom, moulding her as he stepped back against the aircraft and widened his stance to bring her closer.

Eva wasn't sure how long she stood there, adrift in a swirl of sensation as he ravaged her mouth. It wasn't until her lungs screamed and her heart jackhammered against her ribs did she recall where she was…what was happening.

And still she wanted to continue.

So much so she almost moaned in protest when firm hands set her back and she found herself staring into molten eyes dark with savage hunger.

'I think we've given our audience enough to feed on. Get in.'

The calm words, spoken in direct counteraction to the frenzied look in his eyes, doused Eva with cold reality. That she'd made even more of a spectacle of herself hit home as wolf whistles ripped through the air.

'This was all for *show*?' she whispered numbly, shivering in the frigid air.

One sleek eyebrow lifted. 'Of course. Did you think I wanted to kiss you because I was so desperate for you I just couldn't help myself? You'll find that I have more self-restraint than that. Get in,' he repeated, holding the steel and glass door to the aircraft open.

Eva brushed cold hands over her arms, unable to move. She stared at him, perhaps hoping to find some humanity in the suddenly grim-faced block of stone in front of her. Or did she want a hint of the man who'd once framed her face in his hands and called her the most beautiful thing in his life?

Of course, that had been a lie. Everything about Zaccheo

had been a lie. Still she probed for some softness beneath that formidable exterior.

His implacable stare told her she was grasping at straws, as she had from the very beginning, when she'd woven stupid dreams around him.

A gust of icy wind blew across the grass, straight into her exposed back. A flash of red caught her eye and she blindly stumbled towards the terrace. She'd barely taken two steps when he seized her arm.

'What the hell do you think you're doing?' Zaccheo enquired frostily.

'I'm cold,' she replied through chattering teeth. 'My wrap…' She pointed to where the material had drifted.

'Leave it. This will keep you warm.' With one smooth move, he unbuttoned, shrugged off his tuxedo and draped it around her shoulders. The sudden infusion of warmth was overwhelming. Eva didn't want to drown in the distinctively heady scent of the man who was wrecking her world, didn't welcome her body's traitorous urge to burrow into the warm silk lining. And most of all, she didn't want to be beholden to him in any way, or accept any hint of kindness from him.

Zaccheo Giordano had demonstrated a ruthless thirst to annihilate those he deemed enemies in her father's study.

But she was no longer the naive and trusting girl she'd been a year and a half ago. Zaccheo's betrayal and her continued fraught relationship with her father and sister had hardened her heart. The pain was still there—would probably always be there—but so were the new fortifications against further hurt. She had no intention of laying her heart and soul bare to further damage from the people she'd once blithely believed would return the same love and devotion she offered freely.

She started to shrug off the jacket. 'No, thanks. I'd prefer not to be stamped as your possession.'

He stopped her by placing both hands on her arms.

Dark grey eyes pinned her to the spot, the sharper, icier

burst of wind whipping around them casting him in a deadlier, more dangerous light.

'You're already my possession. You became mine the moment you made the choice to follow me out here, Eva. You can kid yourself all you want, but this is your reality from here on in.'

CHAPTER FOUR

@Ladystclare OMG! Bragging rights=mine! Beheld fireworks w/in fireworks @P/Manor last night when LadyP eloped w/convict lover! #amazeballs

@Aristokitten Bet it was all a publicity stunt, but boy that kiss? Sign me up! #Ineedlatinlovelikethat

@Countrypile That wasn't love. That was an obscene and shameless money-grabbing gambit at its worst! #Donotencouragerancidbehaviour

EVA FLINCHED, her stomach churning at each new message that flooded her social-media stream.

The hours had passed in a haze after Zaccheo flew them from Pennington Manor. In solid command of the helicopter, he'd soared over the City of London and landed on the vertiginous rooftop of The Spire.

The stunning split-level penthouse's interior had barely registered in the early hours when Zaccheo's enigmatic aide, Romeo, had directed the butler to show her to her room.

Zaccheo had stalked away without a word, leaving her in the middle of his marble-tiled hallway, clutching his jacket.

Sleep had been non-existent in the bleak hours that had followed. At five a.m., she'd given up and taken a quick shower before putting on that skin-baring dress again.

Wishing she'd asked for a blanket to cover the acres of flesh on display, she cringed as another salacious offering popped into her inbox displayed on Zaccheo's tablet.

Like a spectator frozen on the fringes of an unfolding train wreck, she read the latest post.

@Uberwoman Hey ConvictLover, that flighty poor little rich girl is wasted on you. Real women exist. Let ME rock your world!

Eva curled her fist, refusing to entertain the image of any woman rocking Zaccheo's world. She didn't care one way or the other. If she had a choice, she would be ten thousand miles away from this place.

'If you're thinking of responding to any of that, consider yourself warned against doing so.'

She jumped at the deep voice a whisper from her ear. She'd thought she would be alone in the living room for at least another couple of hours before dealing with Zaccheo. Now she wished she'd stayed in her room.

She stood and faced him, the long black suede sofa between them no barrier to Zaccheo's towering presence.

'I've no intention of responding. And you really shouldn't sneak up on people like that,' she tagged on when the leisurely drift of those incisive eyes over her body made her feel like a specimen under a microscope.

'I don't sneak. Had you been less self-absorbed in your notoriety, you would've heard me enter the room.'

Anger welled up. 'You accuse *me* of being notorious? All this is happening because *you* insisted on gatecrashing a private event and turning it into a public spectacle.'

'And, of course, you were so eager to find out whether you're trending that you woke up at dawn to follow the news.'

She wanted to ask how he'd known what time she'd left her room, but Eva suspected she wouldn't like the answer. 'You assume I slept at all when sleep was the last thing on my mind, having been blackmailed into coming here. And, FYI, I don't read the gutter press. Not unless I want the worst kind of indigestion.'

He rounded the sofa and stopped within arm's length. She stood her ground, but she couldn't help herself ogling the breathtaking body filling her vision.

It was barely six o'clock and yet he looked as vitally masculine as if he'd been up and ready for hours. A film of sweat covered the hair-dusted arms beneath the pulled-up sleeves, and his damp white T-shirt moulded his chiselled torso. His black drawstring sweatpants did nothing to hide thick thighs and Eva struggled to avert her gaze from the virile outline of his manhood against the soft material. Dragging her gaze up, she stared in fascination at the hands and fingers wrapped in stained boxing gauze.

'Do you intend to spend the rest of the morning ogling me, Eva?' he asked mockingly.

She looked into his eyes and that potent, electric tug yanked hard at her. Reminding herself that she was immune from whatever spell he'd once cast on her, she raised her chin.

'I intend to attempt a reasonable conversation with you in the cold light of day regarding last night's events.'

'That suggests you believe our previous interactions have been unreasonable?'

'I did a quick search online. You were released yesterday morning. It stands to reason that you're still a little affected by your incarceration—'

His harsh, embittered laugh bounced like bullets around the room. Eva folded her arms, refusing to cower at the sound.

He stepped towards her, the tension in his body barely leashed. 'You think I'm a *"little affected"* by my incarceration? Tell me, *bella*,' he invited softly, 'do you know what it feels like to be locked in a six-by-ten, damp and rancid cage for over a year?'

A brief wave of torment overcame his features, and a different tug, one of sympathy, pulled at her. Then she reminded herself just who she was dealing with. 'Of course not. I just don't want you to do anything that you'll regret.'

'Your touching concern for my welfare is duly noted. But I suggest you save it for yourself. Last night was merely you and your family being herded into the eye of the storm. The real devastation is just getting started.'

As nightmarish promises went, Zaccheo's chilled her to the bone. Before she could reply, several pings blared from the tablet. She glanced down and saw more lurid posts about what *real women* wanted to do to Zaccheo.

She shut the tablet and straightened to find him slowly unwinding the gauze from his right hand, his gaze pinned on her. Silence stretched as he freed both hands and tossed the balled cloth onto the glass-topped coffee table.

'So, do I get any sort of itinerary for this impending apocalypse?' she asked when it became clear he was content to let the silence linger.

One corner of his mouth lifted. 'We'll have breakfast in half an hour. After that, we'll see whether your father has done what I demanded of him. If he has, we'll take it from there.'

Recalling her father's overly belligerent denial once Zaccheo had left the study last night, anxiety skewered her. 'And if he hasn't?'

'Then his annihilation will come sooner rather than later.'

Half an hour later, Eva struggled to swallow a mouthful of buttered toast and quickly chased it down with a sip of tea before she choked.

A few minutes ago, a brooding Romeo had entered with the butler who'd delivered a stack of broadsheets. The other man had conversed in Italian with a freshly showered and even more visually devastating Zaccheo.

Zaccheo's smile after the short exchange had incited her first panic-induced emotion. He'd said nothing after Romeo left. Instead he'd devoured a hearty plate of scrambled eggs, grilled mushrooms and smoked pancetta served on Italian bread with unsettling gusto.

But as the silence spread thick and cloying across the room she finally set her cup down and glanced to where he stood now at the end of the cherrywood dining table, his hands braced on his hips, an inscrutable expression on his face.

Again, Eva was struck by the change in him. Even now he was dressed more formally in dark grey trousers and a navy shirt with the sleeves rolled up, her eyes were drawn to the gladiator-like ruggedness of his physique.

'Eva.' Her name was a deep command. One she desperately wanted to ignore. It held a quiet triumph she didn't want to acknowledge. The implications were more than she could stomach. She wasn't one for burying her head in the sand, but if her father had done what Zaccheo had demanded, then—

'Eva,' he repeated. Sharper. Controlled but demanding.

Heart hammering, she glanced at him. 'What?'

He stared back without blinking, his body deathly still. 'Come here.'

Refusing to show how rattled she was, she stood, teetered on the heels she'd had no choice but to wear again, and strode towards him.

He tracked her with chilling precision, his eyes dropping to her hips for a charged second before he looked back up. Eva hated her body for reacting to that look, even as her breasts tingled and a blaze lit between her thighs.

Silently she cursed herself. She had no business reacting to that look, or to any man on any plane of emotion whatsoever. She had proof that path only ended in eviscerating heartache.

She stopped a few feet from him, made sure to place a dining chair between them. But the solid wood couldn't stop her senses from reacting to his scent, or her nipples from furling into tight, needy buds when her gaze fell on the golden gleam of his throat revealed by the gap in his shirt. Quickly crossing her arms, she looked down at the newspapers.

That they'd made headlines was unmistakable. Bold black letters and exclamation marks proclaimed Zaccheo's antics. And as for *that* picture of them locked together…

'I can't believe you landed a helicopter in the middle of a fireworks display,' she threw out, simply because it was easier than acknowledging the other words written on the page binding her to Zaccheo, insinuating they were something they would never be.

He looked from her face to the front-page picture showing him landing his helicopter during a particularly violent explosion. 'Were you concerned for me?' he mocked.

'Of course not. You obviously don't care about your own safety so why should I?'

A simmering silence followed, then he stalked closer. 'I hope you intend to act a little more concerned towards my well-being once we're married.'

Any intention of avoiding looking at him fled her mind. '*Married?* Don't you think you've taken this far enough?' she snapped.

'Excuse me?'

'You wanted to humiliate my father. Congratulations, you've made headlines in every single newspaper. Don't you think it's time to drop this?'

His eyes turned into pools of ice. 'You think this is some sort of game?' he enquired silkily.

'What else can it be? If you really had the evidence you claim to have, why haven't you handed it over to the police?'

'You believe I'm bluffing?' His voice was a sharp blade slicing through the air.

'I believe you feel aggrieved.'

'Really? And what else did you *believe*?'

Eva refused to quail beneath the look that threatened to cut her into pieces. 'It's clear you want to make some sort of statement about how you were treated by my father. You've done that now. Let it go.'

'So your father did all this—' he indicated the papers '—just to stop me throwing a childish tantrum? And what about you? Did you throw yourself at my feet to buy your family time to see how long my bluff would last?'

She flung her arms out in exasperation. 'Come on, Zaccheo—'

They both stilled at her use of his name. Eva had no time to recover from the unwitting slip. Merciless fingers speared into her hair, much as they had last night, holding her captive as his thumb tilted her chin.

'How far are you willing to go to get me to be *reasonable*? Or perhaps I should guess? After all, just last night you'd dropped to an all-time low of whoring yourself to a drunken boy in order to save your family.' The thick condemnation feathered across her skin.

Rage flared in her belly, gave her the strength to remain upright. He stood close. Far too close. She stepped back, but only managed to wedge herself between the table and Zaccheo's towering body. 'As opposed to what? Whoring myself to a middle-aged criminal?'

He leaned down, crowding her further against the polished wood. 'You know exactly how old I am. In fact, I recall precisely where we both were when the clock struck midnight on my thirtieth birthday. Or perhaps you need me to refresh your memory?' His smooth, faintly accented voice trailed amused contempt.

'Don't bother—'

'I'll do it anyway, it's no hardship,' he offered, as if her sharp denial hadn't been uttered. 'We were newly engaged, and you were on your knees in front of my penthouse window, uncaring that anyone with a pair of decent binoculars would see us. All you cared about was getting your busy, greedy little hands on my belt, eager to rid me of my trousers so you could wish me a happy birthday in a way most men fantasise about.'

Her skin flushed with a wave of heat so strong, she feared spontaneous combustion. 'That wasn't my idea.'

One brow quirked. 'Was it not?'

'No, you dared me to do it.'

His mouth twitched. 'Are you saying I forced you?'

Those clever fingers were drifting along her scalp, lazily caressing, lulling her into showing her vulnerability.

Eva sucked in a deep breath. 'I'm saying I don't want to talk about the past. I prefer to stick to the present.'

She didn't want to remember how gullible she'd been back then, how stupidly eager to please, how excited she'd been that this god of a man, who could have any woman he wanted with a lazy crook of his finger, had pursued *her*, chosen *her*.

Even after learning the hard way that men in positions of power would do anything to stay in that power, that her two previous relationships had only been a means to an end for the men involved, she'd still allowed herself to believe Zaccheo wanted her for herself. Finding out that he was no better, that he only wanted her to secure a *business deal*, had delivered a blow she'd spent the better part of a year burying in a deep hole.

At first his demands had been subtle: a business dinner here, a charity event there—occasions she'd been proud and honoured to accompany him on. Until that fateful night when she'd overheard a handful of words that had had the power to sting like nothing else.

She's the means to an end. Nothing more...

The conversation that had followed remained seared into her brain. Zaccheo, impatiently shutting her down, then brazenly admitting he'd said those words. That he'd used her.

Most especially, she recalled the savage pain in knowing she had got him so wrong, had almost given herself to a man who held such careless regard for her, and only cared about her pedigree.

And yet his shock when she'd returned his ring had made her wonder whether she'd done the right thing.

His arrest days later for criminal negligence had confirmed what sort of man she'd foolishly woven her dreams around.

She met his gaze now. 'You got what you wanted—your name next to mine on the front page. The whole world knows I left with you last night, that I'm no longer engaged to Harry.'

His hand slipped to her nape, worked over tense muscles. 'And how did Fairfield take being so unceremoniously dumped?' he asked.

'Harry cares about me, so he was a complete gentleman about it. Shame I can't say the same about you.'

Dark grey eyes gleamed dangerously. 'You mean he wasn't torn up at the thought of never having access to this body again?' he mocked.

She lifted a brow. 'Never say never.'

Tension coiled his body. 'If you think I'll tolerate any further interaction between you and Fairfield, you're severely mistaken,' he warned with a dark rumble.

'Why, Zaccheo, you sound almost jealous.'

Heat scoured his cheekbones and a tiny part of her quailed at her daring. 'You'd be wise to stop testing me, *dolcezza*.'

'If you want this to stop, tell me why you're doing this.'

'I'm only going to say it one more time, so let it sink in. I don't intend to stop until your father's reputation is in the gutter and everything he took from me is returned, plus interest.'

'Can I see the proof of what you accuse my father of?'

'Would you believe even if you saw it? Or will you cling to the belief that I'm the big, bad ogre who's just throwing his weight about?' he taunted.

Eva looked down at the papers on the table, every last one containing everything Zaccheo had demanded. Would her father have done it if Zaccheo's threats were empty?

'Last night, when you said you and I…' She stopped, unable to process the reality.

'Would be married in two weeks? *Sì*, I meant that, too. And to get that ball rolling, we're going shopping for an engagement ring in exactly ten minutes, after which we have a full day ahead, so if you require further sustenance I suggest you finish your breakfast.'

He dropped his fingers from her nape and stepped back. With a last look filled with steely determination, he picked up the closest paper and walked out of the room.

CHAPTER FIVE

THEIR FIRST STOP was an exclusive coat boutique in Bond Street. Zaccheo told himself it was because he didn't want to waste time. The truth mocked him in the form of needing to cover Eva Pennington's body before he lost any more brain cells to the lust blazing through his bloodstream.

In the dark cover of her family terrace and the subsequent helicopter journey home, he'd found relief from the blatant temptation of her body.

In the clear light of day, the red dress seemed to cling tighter, caress her body so much more intimately that he'd had to fight the urge to lunge for her each time she took a breath.

He watched her now, seated across from him in his limo as they drove the short twenty-minute distance to Thread-needle Street where his bankers had flown in the diamond collection he'd requested from Switzerland.

Her fingers plucked at the lapel of the new white cashmere coat, then dropped to cinch the belt tighter at her tiny waist.

'You didn't need to buy me a coat,' she grumbled. 'I have a perfectly good one back at my flat.'

He reined in his fascination with her fingers. 'Your flat is on the other side of town. I have more important things to do than waste an hour and a half sitting in traffic.'

Her plump lips pursed. 'Of course, extracting your pound of flesh is an all-consuming business, isn't it?'

'I don't intend to stop at a mere pound, Eva. I intend to take the whole body.'

One eyebrow spiked. 'You seem so confident I'm going to hand myself to you on a silver platter. Isn't that a tad foolish?'

There was that tone again, the one that said she didn't believe him.

'I guess we'll find out one way or the other when the sordid details are laid out for you on Monday. All you need to concern yourself about today is picking out an engagement ring that makes the right statement.'

Her striking green eyes clashed with his and that lightning bolt struck again. 'And what statement would that be?' she challenged.

He let loose a chilling half-smile that made his enemies quake. 'Why, that you belong to me, of course.'

'I told you, I've no intention of being your possession. A ring won't change that.'

'How glibly you lie to yourself.'

She gasped and he was once again drawn to her mouth. A mouth whose sweet taste he recalled vividly, much to his annoyance. 'Excuse me?'

'We both know you'll be exactly who and what I want you to be when I demand it. Your family has too much at stake for you to risk doing otherwise.'

'Don't mistake my inclination to go along with this farce to be anything but my need to get to the bottom of why you're doing this. It's what families *do* for each other. Of course, since you don't even speak about yours, I assume you don't know what I'm talking about.'

Zaccheo called himself ten kinds of fool for letting the taunt bite deep. He'd lost respect for his father long before he'd died in shame and humiliation. And watching his mother whore herself for prestige had left a bitter taste in his mouth. As families went, he'd been dealt a bad hand, but he'd learned long ago that to wish for anything you couldn't create with your own hard-working hands was utter folly. He'd stopped making wishes by the time he hit puberty. Recalling the very last wish he'd prayed night and day for as a child, he clenched his fists. Even then he'd known fate would laugh at his wish for a brother or sister. He'd known that wish, despite his mother being pregnant, would not come true. He'd *known*.

He'd programmed himself not to care after that harrowing time in his life.

So why the hell did it grate so much for him to be reminded that he was the last Giordano?

'I don't talk about my family because I have none. But that's a situation I intend to rectify soon.'

She glanced at him warily. 'What's that supposed to mean?'

'It means I had a lot of time in prison to re-examine my life, thanks to your family.' He heard the naked emotion in his voice and hardened his tone. 'I intend to make some changes.'

'What sort of changes?'

'The type that means you'll no longer have to whore out your integrity for the sake of the great Pennington legacy. You should thank me, since you seem to be the one doing most of the heavy lifting for your family.'

Zaccheo watched her face pale.

'I'm not a whore!'

He lunged forward before he could stop himself. 'Then what the hell were you doing dressed like a tart, agreeing to marry a drunken playboy, if not for cold, hard cash for your family?' The reminder of what she wore beneath the coat blazed across his mind. His temperature hiked, along with the increased throbbing in his groin.

'I didn't do it for money!' She flushed, and bit down on her lower lip again. 'Okay, yes, that was part of the reason, but I also did it because—'

'Please spare me any declarations of *true love*.' He wasn't sure why he abhorred the idea of her mentioning the word love. Or why the idea of her mentioning Fairfield's name filled him with rage.

Zaccheo knew about her friendship with Fairfield. And while he knew their engagement had been a farce, he hadn't missed the camaraderie between them, or the pathetic infatuation in the other man's eyes.

Si, he was jealous—Eva would be his and no one else's. But he also pitied Fairfield.

Because love, in all forms, was a false emotion. Nothing but a manipulative tool. Mothers declared their love for their children, then happily abandoned them the moment they ceased to be a convenient accessory. Fathers professed to have their children's interest at heart because of *love*, but when it came right down to it they put themselves above all else. And sometimes even forgot that their children *existed*.

As for Eva Pennington, she'd shown how faithless she was when she'd dropped him and distanced herself mere days before his arrest.

'I wasn't going to say that. Trust me, I've learned not to toss the word *love* about freely—'

'Did you know?' he sliced at her before he could stop himself.

Fine brows knitted together. 'Did I know what?'

'Did you know of your father's plans?' The question had been eating at him far more than he wanted to admit.

'His plans to do what?' she asked innocently. And yet he could see the caginess on her face. As if she didn't want him to probe deeper.

Acrid disappointment bit through him. He was a fool for thinking, perhaps *wishing*, despite all the signs saying otherwise, that she'd been oblivious to Oscar Pennington's plans to make him the ultimate scapegoat.

'We're here, sir.' His driver's voice came through the intercom.

Zaccheo watched her dive for the door. He would've laughed at her eagerness to get away from the conversation that brought back too many volatile memories, had he not felt disconcerting relief that his question had gone unanswered.

He'd been a fool to pursue it in the first place. He didn't need more lies. He had cold, hard facts proving the Penningtons' guilt. Dwelling on the whys and wherefores of Eva's actions was a fool's errand.

He stepped out into the winter sunshine and nodded at the bank director.

'Mr Giordano, welcome.' The older man's expression vacillated between obsequiousness and condescension.

'You received my further instructions?' Zaccheo took Eva's arm, ignoring her slight stiffening as he walked her through the doors of the bank.

'Yes, sir. We've adhered to your wishes.' Again he caught the man's assessing gaze.

'I'm pleased to hear it. Otherwise I'm sure there would be other banks who would welcome GWI's business.'

The banker paled. 'That won't be necessary, Mr Giordano. If you'll come with me, the jewellers have everything laid out for you.'

It should've given him great satisfaction that he'd breached the hallowed walls of the centuries-old establishment, that he'd finally succeeded where his own father had tried so hard and failed, giving his life in pursuit of recognition.

But all Zaccheo could hear, could *feel*, was Eva's presence, a reminder of why his satisfaction felt hollow. She was proof that, despite all he'd achieved, he was still regarded as the lowest of the low. A nobody. An expendable patsy who would take any treatment his betters doled out without protest.

We shall see.

They walked down several hallways. After a few minutes, Eva cleared her throat. 'What instructions did you give him?' she asked.

He stared down at her. 'I told him to remove all pink diamonds from the collection and instruct my jewellers that I do not wish to deal with diamonds of that colour in the future.'

'Really? I thought pink diamonds were all the rage these days?'

He shrugged. 'Not for me. Let's call it a personal preference.'

The penny dropped and she tried to pull away from his hold. He refused to let go. 'Are you really that petty?' she asked as they approached a heavy set of oak doors. 'Just because Harry gave me a pink diamond…' Her eyes widened when he caught her shoulders and pinned her against the wall. When she started to struggle, he stepped closer, caging her in with his body.

'You'll refrain from mentioning his name in my presence ever again. Is that understood?' Zaccheo felt his control slipping as her scent tangled with his senses and her curvy figure moved against him.

'Let me go and you'll need never hear his name again,' she snapped back.

'Not going to happen.' He released her. 'After you.'

She huffed a breath and entered the room. He followed and crossed to the window, struggling to get himself under control as the director walked in with three assistants bearing large velvet trays. They set them on the polished conference table and stepped back.

'We'll give you some privacy,' the director said before exiting with his minions.

Zaccheo walked to the first tray and pulled away the protective cloth. He stared at the display of diamonds in all cuts and sizes, wondering for a moment how his father would've reacted to this display of obscene wealth. Paolo Giordano had never managed to achieve even a fraction of his goals despite sacrificing everything, including the people he should've held dear. Would he have been proud, or would he have bowed and scraped as the bank director had a few moments ago, eager to be deemed worthy of merely touching them?

'Perhaps we should get on with choosing a stone. Or are we going to stare at them all day?' Eva asked.

Eva watched his face harden and bit her tongue. She wasn't sure why she couldn't stop goading him. Did part of her want to get under his skin as he so effortlessly got under hers?

Annoyed with herself for letting the whole absurd situation get to her, she stepped forward and stared down at the dazzling array of gems. Large. Sparkling. Flawless. Each worth more than she would earn in half her lifetime.

None of them appealed to her.

She didn't want to pick out another cold stone to replace the one she'd handed back to Harry before running after Zaccheo last night.

She didn't want to be trapped into yet another consequence of being a Pennington. She wanted to be free of the guilty resentment lurking in her heart at the thought that nothing she did would ever be enough for her family. Or the sadness that came with the insurmountable knowledge that her sister would continue to block any attempt to forge a relationship with her father.

She especially didn't want to be trapped in any way with Zaccheo Giordano. That display of his displeasure a few moments ago had reminded her she wanted nothing to do with him. And it was not about his temper but what she'd felt when her body had been thrust against his. She'd wanted to be held there…indefinitely.

Touching him.

Soothing his angry brow and those brief flashes of pain she saw in his eyes when he thought she wasn't looking.

God, even a part of her wanted to coax out that heart-stopping smile she'd glimpsed so very rarely when he was pursuing her!

What was wrong with her?

'Is that the one you wish for?'

She jumped and stared down at the stone that had somehow found its way into her palm. She blinked in shock.

The diamond was the largest on the tray and twice as obscene as the one that had graced her finger last night. No wonder Zaccheo sounded so disparaging.

'No!' She hastily dropped it back into its slot. 'I'd never wear anything so gratuitous.'

His coldly mocking gaze made her cringe. 'Really?'

Irritation skated over her skin. 'For your information, I didn't choose that ring.'

'But you accepted it in the spirit it was given—as the cost of buying your body in exchange for shares in Penningtons?'

Icy rage replaced her irritation. 'Your continuous insults make me wonder why you want to put up with my presence. Surely revenge can't be as sweet as you wish it if the object of your punishment enrages you this much?'

'Perhaps I enjoy tormenting you.'

'So I'm to be your punching bag for the foreseeable future?'

'Is this your way of trying to find out how long your sentence is to be?'

'A sentence implies I've done something wrong. I *know* I'm innocent in whatever you believe I've done.'

His smile could've turned a volcano into a polar ice cap. 'I've found that proclamations of innocence don't count for a thing, not when the right palm is greased.'

She inhaled at the fury and bitterness behind his words. 'Zaccheo…'

Whatever feeble reply she'd wanted to make died when his eyes hardened.

'Choose the diamond you prefer or I'll choose it for you.'

Eva turned blindly towards the table and pointed to the smallest stone. 'That one.'

'No.'

She gritted her teeth. 'Why not?'

'Because it's pink.'

'No, it's not…' She leaned closer, caught the faint pink glow, and frowned. 'Oh. I thought—'

A mirthless smile touched his lips. 'So did I. Perhaps I'll change bankers after all.' He lifted the cover of the second tray and Eva stared dispassionately at the endless rows of sparkling jewels. None of them spoke to her. Her heart hammered as it finally dawned on her why.

'Is there any reason why you want to buy me a new ring?'

He frowned. *'Scusi?'*

'When you proposed the first time, you gave me a different ring. I'm wondering why you're buying me a different one. Did you lose it?' Despite the circumstances surrounding his proposal and her subsequent rejection of him, she'd loved that simple but exquisite diamond and sapphire ring.

'No, I didn't lose it.' His tone was clipped to the point of brusqueness.

'Then why?'

'Because I do not wish you to have it.'

Her heart did an achy little dance as she waited for further elaboration. When she realised none would be forthcoming, she pulled her gaze from his merciless regard and back to the display.

He didn't want her to have it. Why? Because the ring held special meaning? Or because she was no longer worthy of it?

Berating herself for feeling hurt, she plucked a stone from the middle of the tray. According to the size chart it sat in mid-range, a flawless two carat, square-cut that felt light in her palm. 'This one.' She turned and found him staring at her, his gaze intense yet inscrutable.

Wordlessly, he held out his hand.

Her fingers brushed his palm as she dropped the stone and she bit back a gasp as that infernal electricity zinged up her arm.

His eyes held hers for a long moment before he turned and headed for the door. The next few minutes passed in a blur as Zaccheo issued clipped instructions about mountings, scrolls and settings to the jeweller.

Before she could catch her breath, Eva was back outside. Flashes went off as a group of paparazzi lunged towards them. Zaccheo handed her into the car before joining her. With a curt instruction to the driver, the car lurched into traffic.

'If I've achieved my publicity quota for the day, I'd like to be dropped at my flat, please.'

Zaccheo focused those incisive eyes on her. 'Why would I do that?'

'Aren't we done? I'd catch a bus home, but I left my handbag and phone at Pennington Manor—'

'Your belongings have been brought to my penthouse,' he replied.

'Okay, thanks. As soon as I collect them, I'll be out of your hair.' She needed to get out of this dress, shower and practise the six songs she would be performing at the club tonight. Saturday nights were the busiest of the week, and she couldn't be late. The music producer who'd been frequenting the club for the last few weeks might make another appearance tonight.

A little bubble of excitement built and she squashed it down as that half-smile that chilled her to the bone appeared on Zaccheo's face.

'You misunderstand. When I mentioned your belongings, I didn't mean your handbag and your phone. I meant everything you own in your bedsit has been removed. While we were picking your engagement ring, your belongings were relocated. Your rent has been paid off with interest and your landlady is busy renting the property to someone else.'

'What on earth are you talking about?' she finally asked when she'd picked up her jaw from the floor and sifted through his words. 'Of course I still live there. Mrs Hammond wouldn't just let you into my flat. And she certainly wouldn't arbitrarily end my lease without speaking to me first.'

Zaccheo just stared back at her.

'How dare you? Did you threaten her?'

'No, Eva. I used a much more effective tool.'

Her mouth twisted. 'You mean you threw so much money at her she buckled under your wishes?'

He shrugged rugged, broad shoulders. 'You of all people

should know how money sways even the most veracious hearts. Mrs Hammond was thrilled at the prospect of receiving her new hip replacement next week instead of at the end of the year. But it also helps that she's a hopeless romantic. The picture of us in the paper swayed any lingering doubts she had.'

Eva's breath shuddered out. Her landlady had lamented the long waiting list over shared cups of tea and Eva had offered a sympathetic ear. While she was happy that Mrs Hammond would receive her treatment earlier than anticipated and finally be out of pain, a huge part of her couldn't see beyond the fact that Zaccheo had ripped her safe harbour away without so much as a by your leave.

'You had absolutely no right to do that,' she blazed at him.

'Did I not?' he asked laconically.

'No, you didn't. This is nothing but a crude demonstration of your power. Well, guess what, I'm unimpressed. Go ahead and do your worst! Whatever crimes you think we've committed, maybe going to prison is a better option than this…this kidnapping!'

'Believe me, prison isn't an option you want to joke with.'

His lacerated tone made her heart lurch. She looked into his face and saw the agony. Her eyes widened, stunned that he was letting her witness that naked emotion.

'You think you know what it feels like to be robbed of your freedom for months on end? Pray you never get to find out, Eva. Because you may not survive it.'

'Zaccheo… I…' She stuttered to a halt, unsure of what to make of that raw statement.

His hand slashed through the air and his mask slid back into place. 'I wanted you relocated as swiftly as possible with a minimum of fuss,' he said.

A new wave of apprehension washed over her. 'Why? What's the rush?'

'I thought that would be obvious, Eva. I have deep-seated trust issues.'

Sadly, she'd reaped the rewards of betrayed trust, but the fierce loyalty to her family that continued to burn within her made her challenge him. 'How is that my family's fault?'

His nostrils flared. 'I trusted your father. He repaid that trust with a betrayal that sent me to prison! And you were right there next to him.'

Again she heard the ragged anguish in his voice. A hysterical part of her mind wondered whether this was the equivalent of a captor revealing his face to his prisoner. Was she doomed now that she'd caught a glimpse of what Zaccheo's imprisonment had done to him?

'So you keeping me against my will is meant to be part of *my* punishment?'

He smiled. 'You don't have to stay. You have many options available to you. You can call the police, tell them I'm holding you against your will, although that would be hard to prove since three hundred people saw you chase after me last night. Or you can insist I return your things and reinstate your lease. If you choose to walk away, no one will lift a finger to stop you.'

'But that's not quite true, is it? What real choice do I have when you're holding a threat over my father's head?'

'Leave him to flounder on his own if you truly believe you're guilt-free in all of this. You want to make a run for it? Here's your chance.'

His pointed gaze went to the door and Eva realised they'd completed the short journey from the bank to the iconic building that had brought Zaccheo into her life and turned it upside down.

She glanced up at the building *Architectural Digest* had called 'innovative beyond its years' and 'a heartbreakingly beautiful masterpiece'.

Where most modern buildings boasted elaborate glass edifices, The Spire was a study in polished, tensile steel. Thin sheets of steel had been twisted and manipulated around the towering spear-like structure, making the tallest building in

London a testament to its architect's skill and innovation. Its crowning glory was its diamond-shaped, vertiginous platform, within which was housed a Michelin-starred restaurant surrounded by a clear twenty-foot waterfall.

One floor beneath the restaurant was Zaccheo's penthouse. Her new home. Her prison.

The sound of him exiting the car drew her attention. When he held out his hand to her, she hesitated, unable to accept that this was her fate.

A muscle ticced in his jaw as he waited.

'You'd love that, wouldn't you? Me helping you bury my father?'

'He's going down either way. It's up to you whether he gets back up or not.'

Eva wanted to call his bluff. To shut the door and return everything to the way it was this time yesterday.

The memory of her father in that hospital bed, strung up to a beeping machine, stopped her. She'd already lost one parent. No matter how difficult things were between them, she couldn't bear to lose another. She would certainly have no hope of saving her relationship with her sister if she walked away.

Because one thing was certain. Zaccheo meant to have his way.

With or without her co-operation.

CHAPTER SIX

EVA BLEW HER fringe out of her eyes and glanced around her. The guest suite, a different one from the one she'd slept in last night, was almost three times the size of her former bedsit. And every surface was covered with designer gowns and accessories. Countless bottles of exclusive perfumes and luxury grooming products were spread on the dresser, and a team of six stylists each held an item of clothing, ready to pounce on her the moment she took off the dress she was currently trying on.

She tried hard to see the bright side of finally being out of the red dress. Unfortunately, any hint of brightness had vanished the moment she'd stepped out of the car and re-entered Zaccheo's penthouse.

'How many more before we're done?' She tried to keep her voice even, but she knew she'd missed amiability by a mile when two assistants exchanged wary glances.

'We've done your home and evening-wear package. We just need to do your vacation package and we'll be done with wardrobe. Then we can move on to hair and make-up,' Vivian, the chief stylist, said with a megawatt smile.

Eva tried not to groan. She needed to be done so she could find her phone and call her father. There was no way she was twiddling her thumbs until Monday to get a proper answer.

Being made into Zaccheo's revenge punchbag...his *married* revenge punchbag...wasn't a role she intended to be placed in. When she'd thought there was a glimmer of doubt as to Zaccheo's threat being real, she'd gone along with this farce. But with each hour that passed with silence from her father, Eva was forced to believe Zaccheo's threats weren't empty.

Would he go to such lengths to have her choose precious gems, remove her from her flat, and hire a team of stylists to turn her into the sort of woman he preferred to date, if this was just some sort of twisted game?

Her hand clenched as her thoughts took a different path. What exactly was Zaccheo trying to turn her into? Obviously he wasn't just satisfied with attaining her pedigree for whatever his nefarious purposes were. He wanted her to look like a well-dressed mannequin while he was at it.

'Careful with that, Mrs Giordano. That lace is delicate.'

She dropped the dress, her heart hammering far too fast for her liking. 'Don't call me that. I'm not Mrs Giordano—'

'Not yet, at least, right, *bellissima*?'

Eva heard the collective breaths of the women in the room catch. She turned as Zaccheo strode in. His eyes were fixed on her, flashing a warning that made her nape tingle. Before she could respond, he lifted her hands to kiss her knuckles, one after the other. Her breathing altered precariously as the silky hairs of his beard and the warm caress of his mouth threw her thoughts into chaos.

'It's only a few short days until we're husband and wife, *si*?' he murmured intimately, but loud enough so every ear in the room caught the unmistakeable statement of possession.

She struggled to think, to *speak*, as sharp grey eyes locked with hers.

'No…I mean, yes…but let's not tempt fate. Who knows what could happen in a *few short days*?' She fully intended to have placed this nightmare far behind her.

His thumbs caressed the backs of her hands in false intimacy. 'I've moved mountains to make you mine, *il mio prezioso*. Nothing will stand in my way.' His accent was slightly more pronounced, his tone deep and captivating.

Envious sighs echoed around the room, but Eva shivered at the icy intent behind his words. She snatched her hands from his. Or she attempted to.

'In that case, I think you ought to stop distracting me so I can get on with making myself beautiful for you.' She hoped her smile looked as brittle as it felt. That her intention to end this was clear for him to see. 'Or was there something in particular you wanted?'

His eyes held hers for another electrifying second before he released her. 'I came to inform you that your belongings have been unpacked.' He surveyed the room, his gaze taking in the organised chaos. 'And to enquire whether you wish to have lunch with me or whether you want lunch brought to you so you can push through?' He turned back to her, his gaze mockingly stating that he knew her choice before she responded.

She lifted her chin. 'Seeing as this makeover was a complete *surprise* that I'd have to *make* time for, we'll take lunch in here, please.'

He ignored her censorious tone and nodded. 'Your wish is my command, *dolcezza*. But I insist you be done by dinnertime. I detest eating alone.'

She bit her tongue against a sharp retort. The cheek of him, making demands on her time when *he'd* been the one to call in the stylists in the first place! She satisfied herself with glaring at his back as he walked out, his tall, imposing figure owning every square inch of space he prowled.

The women left three excruciating hours later. The weak sun was setting in grey skies by the time Eva dragged her weary body across the vast hallway towards the suite she'd occupied last night. Her newly washed and styled hair bounced in silky waves down her back and her face tingled pleasantly from the facial she'd received before the barely there makeup had been applied.

The cashmere-soft, scooped-neck grey dress caressed her hips and thighs as she approached her door. She'd worn it only because Vivian had insisted. Eva hadn't had the heart to tell her she intended to leave every single item untouched. But Eva couldn't deny that the off-shoulder, floor-length dress felt elegant and wonderful and exactly what she'd have chosen to wear for dinner. Even if it was a dinner she wasn't looking forward to.

Her new four-inch heels clicked on the marble floor as she opened the double doors and stopped. Her hands flew to cover her mouth as she surveyed the room. Surprise was followed a few seconds later by a tingle of awareness that told her she was no longer alone.

Even then, she couldn't look away from the sight before her.

'Is something wrong?' Zaccheo's enquiry made her finally turn.

He was leaning against the door frame, his hands tucked into the pockets of his black tailored trousers. The white V-necked sweater caressed his muscular arms and shoulders and made his grey eyes appear lighter, almost eerily silver. His slightly damp hair gleamed a polished black against his shoulders and his beard lent him a rakish look that was absolutely riveting.

His gaze caught and held hers for several seconds before conducting a detailed appraisal over her face, hair and down her body that made the tingling increase. When his eyes returned to hers, she glimpsed a dark hunger that made her insides quake.

Swallowing against the pulse of undeniable attraction, she turned back to survey the room.

'I can't believe everything's been arranged so precisely,' she murmured.

'You would've preferred that they fling your things around without thought or care?'

'That's not what I mean and you know it. You've reproduced my room almost exactly how it was before.'

He frowned. 'I fail to see how that causes you distress.'

She strolled to the white oak antique dresser that had belonged to her mother. It'd been her mother's favourite piece of furniture and one of the few things Eva had taken when she'd left Pennington Manor.

Her fingers drifted over the hairbrush she'd used only yesterday morning. It had been placed in the little stand just as she normally did. 'I'm not distressed. I'm a little disconcerted that my things are almost exactly as I left them at my flat yesterday morning.' When he continued to stare, she pursed her lips. 'To reproduce this the movers would've needed photographic memories.'

'Or a few cameras shots as per my instructions.'

She sucked in a startled breath. 'Why would you do that?'

His lashes swept down for a moment. Then he shrugged. 'It was the most efficient course of action.'

'Oh.' Eva wasn't sure why she experienced that bolt of disappointment. Was she stupid enough to believe he'd done that because he *cared*? That he'd wanted her to be comfortable?

She silently scoffed at herself.

Lending silly daydreams to Zaccheo's actions had led to bitter disappointment once before. She wasn't about to make the same mistake again.

She spotted her handbag on the bed and dug out her phone. The battery was almost depleted, but she could make a quick call to her father before it died. She started to press dial and realised Zaccheo hadn't moved.

'Did you need something?'

The corner of his mouth quirked, but the bleakness in his eyes didn't dissipate. 'I've been in jail for over a year, *dolcezza*. I have innumerable needs.' The soft words held a note of deadly intent as his gaze moved from her to the bed. Her heart jumped to her throat and the air seemed to evaporate from the room. 'But my most immediate need is sustenance. I've ordered dinner to be brought from upstairs. It'll be here in fifteen minutes.'

She managed to reply despite the light-headedness that assailed her. 'Okay. I'll be there.'

With a curt nod, he left.

Eva sagged sideways onto the bed, her grip on the phone tightening until her bones protested. In the brief weeks she'd dated Zaccheo a year and half ago, she'd seen the way women responded to his unmistakeable animal magnetism. He only needed to walk into the room for every female eye to zero in on him. She'd also witnessed his reaction. Sometimes he responded with charm, other times with arrogant aloofness. But always with an innate sexuality that spoke of a deep appreciation for women. She'd confirmed that appreciation by a quick internet search in a weak moment, which had unearthed the long list of gorgeous women he'd had shockingly brief liaisons with in the past. A young, virile, wealthy bachelor, he'd been at the top of every woman's 'want to bed' list. And he'd had no qualms about helping himself to their amorous attentions.

To be deprived of that for almost a year and a half...

Eva shivered despite the room's ambient temperature. No, she was the last woman Zaccheo would *choose* to bed.

But then, he'd kissed her last night as if he'd wanted to devour her. And the way he'd looked at her just now?

She shook her head.

She was here purely as an instrument of his vengeance. The quicker she got to the bottom of *that*, the better.

Her call went straight to voicemail. Gritting her teeth, she left a message for her father to call her back. Sophie's phone rang for almost a minute before Eva hung up. Whether her sister was deliberately avoiding her calls or not, Eva intended to get some answers before Monday.

Resolving to try again after dinner, Eva plugged in her phone to charge and left her room. She met two waiters wheeling out a trolley as she entered the dining room. A few seconds later, the front door shut and Eva fought the momentary panic at being alone with Zaccheo.

She avoided looking at his imposing body as he lifted the silver domes from several serving platters.

'You always were impeccably punctual,' he said without turning around.

'I suppose that's a plus in my favour.'

'Hmm…' came his non-committal reply.

She reached her seat and froze at the romantic setting of the table. Expensive silverware and crystal-cut glasses gleamed beneath soft lighting. And already set out in a bed of ice was a small silver tub of caviar. A bottle of champagne chilled in an ice stand next to Zaccheo's chair.

'Do you intend to eat standing up?'

She jumped when his warm breath brushed her ear. When had he moved so close?

'Of course not. I just wasn't expecting such an elaborate meal.' She urged her feet to move to where he held out her chair, and sat down. 'One would almost be forgiven for thinking you were celebrating something.'

'Being released from prison isn't reason enough to enjoy something better than grey slop?'

Mortified, she cursed her tactlessness. 'I…of course. I'm sorry, that was… I'd forgotten…' *Oh, God, just shut up, Eva.*

'Of course you had.'

She tensed. 'What's that supposed to mean?'

'You're very good at putting things behind you, aren't you? Or have you forgotten how quickly you walked away from me the last time, too?'

She glanced down at her plate, resolutely picked up her spoon and helped herself to a bite of caviar. The unique taste exploded on her tongue, but it wasn't enough to quell the anxiety churning her stomach. 'You know why I walked away last time.'

'Do I?'

'Yes, you do!' She struggled to keep her composure. 'Can we talk about something else, please?'

'Why, because your actions make you uncomfortable? Or does it make your skin crawl to be sharing a meal with an ex-convict?'

Telling herself not to rise to the bait, she took another bite of food. 'No, because you snarl and your voice turns arctic, and also because I think we have different definitions of what really happened.'

He helped himself to a portion of his caviar before he responded. 'Really? Enlighten me, *per favore.*'

She pressed her lips together. 'We've already been through this, remember? You admitted that you proposed to me simply to get yourself into the Old Boys' Club. Are you going to bother denying it now?'

He froze for several heartbeats. Then he ate another mouthful. 'Of course not. But I believed we had an agreement. That you knew the part you had to play.'

'I'm sorry, I must have misplaced my copy of the Zaccheo Giordano Relationship Guide.' She couldn't stem the sarcasm or the bitterness that laced her voice.

'You surprise me.'

'How so?' she snapped, her poise shredding by the second.

'You're determined to deny that you know exactly how this game is played. That you aristocrats haven't practised the *something-for-something-more* tenet for generations.'

'You seem to be morbidly fascinated with the inner workings of the peer class. If we disgust you so much, why do you insist on soiling your life with our presence? Isn't it a bit convenient to hold us all responsible for every ill in your life?'

A muscle ticced in his jaw and Eva was certain she'd struck a nerve. 'You think having my freedom taken away is a subject I should treat lightly?'

The trembling in her belly spread out to engulf her whole body. 'The *evidence* led to your imprisonment, Zaccheo. Now we can change the subject or we can continue to fight to see who gives whom indigestion first.'

He remained silent for several moments, his eyes boring into hers. Eva stared back boldly, because backing down would see her swallowed whole by the deadly volcanic fury lurking in his eyes. She breathed a tiny sigh of relief when that mocking half-smile made an appearance.

'As you wish.' He resumed eating and didn't speak again until their first course was done. 'Let's play a game. We'll call it *What If*,' he said into the silence.

Tension knotted her nape, the certainty that she was toying with danger rising higher. 'I thought you didn't like games?'

'I'll make an exception this time.'

She took a deep breath. 'Okay. If you insist.'

'What if I wasn't the man you think I am? What if I happened to be a stranger who was innocent of everything he's been accused of? What if that stranger told you that every day he'd spent in prison felt like a little bit of himself was being chipped away for ever? What would you say to him?' His voice held that pain-laced edge she'd first heard in the car.

She looked at his face but his eyes were downcast, his white-knuckled hand wrapped around his wine glass.

This was no game.

The tension that gripped her vibrated from him, engulfing them in a volatile little bubble.

'I'd tell you how sorry I was that justice wasn't served properly on your behalf.' Her voice shook but she held firm. 'Then I'd ask you if there was anything I could do to help you put the past behind you.'

Arctic grey eyes met hers. 'What if I didn't want to put it behind me? What if everything I believe in tells me the only way to achieve satisfaction is to make those responsible pay?'

'I'd tell you it may seem like a good course of action, but doing that won't get back what you've lost. I'd also ask why you thought that was the only way.'

His eyes darkened, partly in anger, partly with anguish. She half expected him to snarl at her for daring to dissuade him from his path of retribution.

Instead, he rose and went to dish out their second course. 'Perhaps I don't know another recourse besides crime and punishment?' he intoned, disturbingly calm.

Sorrow seared her chest. 'How can that be?'

He returned with their plates and set down her second course—a lobster thermidor—before taking his seat. His movements were jerky, lacking his usual innate grace.

'Let's say hypothetically that I've never been exposed to much else.'

'But you know better or you wouldn't be so devastated at the hand you've been dealt. You're angry, yes, but you're also wounded by your ordeal. Believe me, yours isn't a unique story, Zaccheo.'

He frowned at the naked bitterness that leaked through her voice. 'Isn't it? Enlighten me. How have *you* been wounded?'

She cursed herself for leaving the door open, but, while she couldn't backtrack, she didn't want to provide him with more ammunition against her. 'My family...we're united where it counts, but I've always had to earn whatever regard I receive, especially from my father. And it hasn't always been easy, especially when walls are thrown up and alliances built where there should be none.'

He saw through her vagueness immediately. 'Your father and your sister against your mother and you? There's no need to deny it. It's easy to see your sister is fashioning herself in the image of her father,' he said less than gently.

Eva affected an easy shrug. 'Father started grooming her when we were young, and I didn't mind. I just didn't understand why that meant being left out in the cold, especially...' She stopped, realising just how much she was divulging.

'Especially...?' he pressed.

She gripped her fork tighter. 'After my mother died. I thought things would be different. I was wrong.'

His mouth twisted. 'Death is supposed to be a profound leveller. But it rarely changes people.'

She looked at him. 'Your parents—'

'Were the individuals who brought me into the world. They weren't good for much else. Take from that what you will. We're also straying away from the subject. *What if* this stranger can't see his way to forgive and forget?' That ruthless edge was back in his voice.

Eva's hand shook as she picked up her glass of Chianti. 'Then he needs to ask himself if he's prepared to live with the consequences of his actions.'

His eyebrows locked together in a dark frown, before his lashes swept down and he gave a brisk nod. 'Asked and answered.'

'Then there's no further point to this game, is there?'

One corner of his mouth lifted. 'On the contrary, you've shown a soft-heartedness that some would see as a flaw.'

Eva released a slow, unsteady breath. Had he always been like this? She was ashamed to admit she'd been so dazzled with Zaccheo from the moment he'd walked into Siren two years ago, right until the day he'd shown her his true colours, that she hadn't bothered to look any deeper. He'd kissed her on their third date, after which, fearing she'd disappoint him, she'd stumblingly informed him she was a virgin.

His reaction had been something of a fairy tale for her. She'd made him out as her Prince Charming, had adored the way he'd treated her like a treasured princess, showering her with small, thoughtful gifts, but, most of all, his undivided time whenever they were together. He'd made her feel precious, adored. He'd proposed on their sixth date, which had coincided with his thirtieth birthday, and told her he wanted to spend the rest of his life with her.

And it had all been a lie. The man sitting in front of her had no softness, only that ruthless edge and deadly charm.

'Don't be so sure, Zaccheo. I've learnt a few lessons since our unfortunate association.'

'Like what?'

'I'm no longer gullible. And my family may not be perfect, but I'm still fiercely protective of those I care about. Don't forget that.'

He helped himself to his wine. 'Duly noted.' His almost

bored tone didn't fool her into thinking this subject had stopped being anything but volatile.

They finished their meal in tense silence.

Eva almost wilted in relief when the doorbell rang and Zaccheo walked away to answer it.

Catching sight of the time, she jumped up from the dining table and was crossing the living room when Zaccheo's hand closed over her wrist.

'Where do you think you're going?' he demanded.

'Dinner's over. Can you let me go, please? I need to get going or I'll be late.'

His brows furrowed, giving him a look of a dark predator. 'Late for what?'

'Late for work. I've already taken two days off without pay. I don't want to be late on top of everything else.'

'You still work at Siren?' His tone held a note of disbelief.

'I have to make a living, Zaccheo.'

'You still sing?' His voice had grown deeper, his eyes darkening to a molten grey as he stared down at her. Although Zaccheo's expression could be hard to decipher most of the time, the mercurial changes in his eyes often spelled his altered mood.

This molten grey was one she was familiar with. And even though she didn't want to be reminded of it, a pulse of decadent sensation licked through her belly as she recalled the first night she'd seen him.

He'd walked into Siren an hour before closing, when she'd been halfway through a sultry, soulful ballad—a song about forbidden love, stolen nights and throwing caution to the wind. He'd paused to order a drink at the bar, then made his way to the table directly in front of the stage. He'd sipped his whisky, not once taking his eyes off her. Every lyric in the three songs that had followed had felt as if it had been written for the man in front of her and the woman she'd wanted to be for him.

She'd been beyond mesmerised when he'd helped her off

the stage after her session. She'd said yes immediately when he'd asked her out the next night.

But she'd been wrong, so very wrong to believe fate had brought Zaccheo to the club. He'd hunted her down with single-minded intent for his own selfish ends.

God, how he must have laughed when she'd fallen so easily into his arms!

She yanked her arm free. 'Yes, I still sing. And I'd be careful before you start making any threats on my professional life, too. I've indulged you with the engagement-ring picking and the makeover and the homecoming dinner. Now I intend to get back to *my* reality.'

She hurried away, determined not to look over her shoulder to see whether he was following. She made it to her room and quickly changed into her going-to-work attire of jeans, sweater, coat and a thick scarf to ward off the winter chill. Scooping up her bag, she checked her phone.

No calls.

The unease in her belly ballooned as she left her suite.

Zaccheo was seated on the sofa in the living room, examining a small black velvet box. His eyes tracked her, inducing that feeling of being helpless prey before a ruthless marauder. She opened her mouth to say something to dispel the sensation, but no words emerged. She watched, almost paralysingly daunted as he shut the box and placed it on the coffee table next to him.

'Would it be too *indulgent* to demand a kiss before you leave for work, *dolcezza*?' he enquired mockingly.

'Indulgent, no. Completely out of the question, most definitely,' she retorted. Then silently cursed her mouth's sudden tingling.

He shook his head, his magnificent mane gleaming under the chandelier. 'You wound me, Eva, but I'm willing to wait until the time when you will kiss me freely without me needing to ask.'

'Then you'll be waiting an eternity.'

CHAPTER SEVEN

ZACCHEO PACED THE living room and contemplated leaving another voicemail message.

He'd already left five, none of which Eva had bothered to answer. It was nearly two a.m. and she hadn't returned. In his gloomy mood, he'd indulged in one too many nightcaps to consider driving to the club where she worked.

His temperament had been darkening steadily for the last four hours, once he'd found out what Eva's father was up to. Pennington was scrambling—futilely of course, because Zaccheo had closed every possible avenue—to find financial backing. That was enough to anger Zaccheo, but what fuelled his rage was that Pennington, getting more desperate by the hour, was offering more and more pieces of The Spire, the building that he would no longer own come Monday, as collateral. The blatant fraud Pennington was willing to perpetrate to fund his lifestyle made Zaccheo's fists clench as he stalked to the window.

The view from The Spire captured the string of bridges from east to west London. The moment he'd brought his vision of the building to life with the help of his experienced architects had been one of the proudest moments of his life. More than the properties he owned across the world and the empire he'd built from the first run-down warehouse he'd bought and converted to luxury accommodation at the age of twenty, this had been the one he'd treasured most. The building that should've been his crowning glory.

Instead it'd become the symbol of his downfall.

Ironically, the court where he'd been sentenced was right across the street. He looked down at the courthouse, jaw clenched.

He intended it to be the same place where his name was cleared. He would not be broken and humiliated as his father had been by the time he'd died. He would not be whispered about behind his back and mocked to his face and called a parasite. Earlier this evening, Eva had demanded to know why he'd been so fascinated with her kind.

For a moment, he'd wondered whether his burning desire to prove they were not better than him was a weakness. One he should *put behind him*, as Eva had suggested, before he lost a lot more of himself than he already had.

As much as he'd tried he hadn't been able to dismiss her words. Because he'd lied. He knew how to forgive. He'd forgiven his father each time he'd remembered that Zaccheo existed and bothered to take an interest in him. He'd forgiven his mother the first few times she'd let his stepfather treat him like a piece of garbage.

What Zaccheo hadn't told Eva was that he'd eventually learned that forgiveness wasn't effective when the recipient didn't have any use for it.

A weakening emotion like forgiveness would be wasted on Oscar Pennington.

A keycard clicked and he turned as the entry code released the front door.

Sensation very close to relief gut-punched him.

'Where the hell have you been?' He didn't bother to obviate his snarl. Nor could he stop checking her over from head to toe, to ascertain for himself that she wasn't hurt or hadn't been a victim of an accident or a mugging. When he was sure she was unharmed, he snapped his gaze to her face, to be confronted with a quizzical look.

Dio, was she *smirking* at him?

He watched her slide her fingers through her heavy, silky hair and ignored the weariness in the gesture.

'Is it Groundhog Day or something? Because I could've sworn we had a conversation about where I was going earlier this evening.'

He seethed. 'You finished work an hour and a half ago. Where have you been since then?'

She tossed a glare his way before she shrugged off her coat. The sight of the jeans and sweater she'd chosen to wear instead of the roomful of clothes he'd provided further stoked his dark mood.

'How do you know when I finished work?'

'Answer the question, Eva.'

She tugged her handbag from her shoulder and dropped it on the coffee table. Then she kicked off her shoes and pushed up on the balls of her feet in a smooth, practised stretch reminiscent of a ballet dancer.

'I took the night bus. It's cheaper than a cab, but it took forty-five minutes to arrive.'

'*Mi scusi?* You took the *night bus*?' His brain crawled with scenarios that made his blood curdle. He didn't need a spell in prison to be aware of what dangerous elements lurked at night. The thought that Eva had exposed herself, *willingly*, to—

'Careful there, Zaccheo, you almost sound like one of those snobs you detest so much.'

She pushed up again, her feet arching and flattening in a graceful rise and fall.

Despite his blood boiling, he stared, mesmerised, as she completed the stretches. Then he let his gaze drift up her body, knowing he shouldn't, yet unable to stop himself. The sweater, decorated with a D-minor scale motif, hugged her slim torso, emphasising her full, heavy breasts and tiny waist before ending a half-inch above her jeans.

That half-inch of flesh taunted him, calling to mind the smooth warmth of her skin. The simmering awareness that had always existed between them, like a fuse just waiting to be lit, throbbed deep inside. He'd tried to deny it earlier this evening in the hallway, when he'd discovered she still sang at Siren.

He'd tried to erase the sound of her sultry voice, the evocative way Eva Pennington performed on stage. He'd cursed himself when his body had reacted the way it had the very first time he'd heard her sing. That part of his black mood also stemmed from being viscerally opposed to any other man experiencing the same reaction he did from hearing her captivating voice, the way he had been two years ago, was a subject he wasn't willing to acknowledge, never mind tackle.

He pulled his gaze from the alluringly feminine curve of her hips and shapely legs and focused on the question that had been burning through him all night.

'Explain to me how you have two million pounds in your bank account, but take the bus to and from work.'

Her mouth gaped for several seconds before she regained herself. 'How the hell do you know how much money I have in my bank account?' she demanded.

'With the right people with the right skills, very easily. I'm waiting for an answer.'

'You're not going to get one. What I do with my money and how I choose to travel is *my* business.'

'You're wrong, *cara*. As of last night, your welfare is very much my business. And if you think I'm willing to allow you to risk your safety at times when drunken yobs and muggers crawl out of the woodwork, you're very much mistaken.'

'*Allow* me? Next you'll be telling me I need your permission to breathe!'

He spiked his fingers through his hair, wondering if she'd ever been this difficult and he'd somehow missed it. The Eva he remembered, before his eyes had been truly opened to her character, had possessed a quiet passion, not this defiant, wild child before him.

But no, there'd never been anything *child*like about Eva.

She was all woman. His libido had thrilled to it right from the first.

Understandably this acute reaction was because he'd been without a woman for over a year. Now was not the time to let it out of control. The time would arrive soon enough.

She tossed her head in irritation, and the hardening in his groin threatened to prove him wrong.

'Since I need you alive for the foreseeable future, no, you don't require my permission to breathe.'

She had the nerve to roll her eyes. 'Thank you very much!'

'From now on you'll be driven to and from work.'

'No, thanks.'

He gritted his teeth. 'You prefer to spend hours freezing at a bus stop than accept my offer?'

'Yes, because the *offer* comes at a price. I may not know what it is yet, but I've no intention of paying it.'

'Why do you insist on fighting me when we both know you don't have a choice? I'm willing to bet your father didn't return a single one of your phone calls last night.'

Wide, startled eyes met his for a second before she looked away. 'I'm sure he has his reasons.'

It spoke volumes that she didn't deny trying to reach Oscar. 'Reasons more important than answering the phone to his daughter? Do you want to know what he's been up to?'

'I'm sure you're about to apprise me whether I want to hear it or not.'

'He's been calling in every single favour he thinks he's owed. Unfortunately, a man as greedy as your father cashed in most of his favours a long time ago. He's also pleading and begging his way across the country in a bid to save himself from the hole he knows I'm about to bury him in. He didn't take your calls, but he took mine. I recorded it if you wish me to play it back to you?'

Her fists clenched. 'Go to hell, Zaccheo,' she threw at him, but he glimpsed the pain in her eyes.

He almost felt sorry for her. Then he remembered her part in all this.

'Come here, Eva,' he murmured.

She eyed him suspiciously. 'Why?'

'Because I have something for you.'

Her gaze dropped to his empty hands before snapping

back to his face. 'There's nothing you have that I could possibly want.'

'If you make me come over there, I'll take that kiss you owe me from last night.' *Dio*, why had he said that? Now it was all he could think about.

Heat flushed her cheeks. 'I don't owe you a thing. And I certainly don't owe you any kisses.'

The women he'd dated in the past would've fallen over themselves to receive any gift he chose to bestow on them, especially the one he'd tucked into his back pocket.

Slowly, he walked towards her. He made sure his intent was clear. The moment she realised, her hands shot out. 'Stop! Didn't your mother teach you about the honey versus vinegar technique?'

Bitterness drenched him. 'No. My mother was too busy climbing the social ladder after my father died to bother with me. When he was alive, she wasn't much use either.'

She sucked in a shocked breath and concern furrowed her brow. 'I'm sorry.'

Zaccheo rejected the concern and let the sound of her husky voice, scratchy from the vocal strain that came with singing, wash over him instead. He didn't want her concern. But the sex he could deal with.

The need he'd been trying to keep under tight control threatened to snap. He took another step.

'Okay! I'm coming.' She walked barefooted to him. 'I've done as you asked. Give me whatever it is you want to give me.'

'It's in my back pocket.'

She inhaled sharply. 'Is this another of your games, Zaccheo?'

'It'll only take a minute to find out. Are you brave enough, *dolcezza*?' he asked.

Her gaze dropped and he immediately tilted her chin up with one finger. 'Look at me. I want to see your face.'

She blinked, then gathered herself in that way he'd always found fascinating. Slowly, she reached an arm around him. Her fingers probed until she found the pocket opening.

They slipped inside and he suppressed a groan as her fingers caressed him through his trousers. His blood rushed faster south as she searched futilely.

'It's empty,' she stated with a suspicious glare.

'Try the other one.'

She muttered a dirty word that rumbled right through him. Her colour deepened when he lifted his eyebrow.

'Let's get this over with.' She searched his right pocket and stilled when she encountered the box.

'Take it out,' he commanded, then stifled another groan when her fingers dug into his flesh to remove the velvet box. It took all the control he could muster not to kiss her when her lips parted and he glimpsed the tip of her tongue.

During his endless months in prison, he'd wondered whether he'd overrated the chemistry that existed between Eva and him. The proof that it was as potent as ever triggered an incandescent hunger that flooded his loins.

Sì, this part of his revenge that involved Eva in his bed, being inside her and implanting her with his seed, would be easy enough and pleasurable enough to achieve.

'I cannot wait to take you on our wedding night. Despite you no longer being a virgin, I'll thoroughly enjoy making you mine in every imaginable way possible. By the time I'm done with you, you'll forget every other man that you dared to replace me with.'

Her eyelids fluttered and she shivered. But the new, assertive Eva came back with fire. 'A bold assertion. But one, sadly, we'll both see unproven since there'll be no wedding *or* wedding night. And in case I haven't mentioned it, you're the last man I'd ever welcome in my bed.'

Zaccheo chose not to point out that she still had her hand in his pocket, or that her fingers were digging more firmly into his buttock.

Instead, he slid his phone from his front pocket, activated the recording app and hit the replay button.

Despite her earlier assertion that she'd grown a thicker skin, shadows of disbelief and hurt criss-crossed her face as she listened to the short conversation summoning her father to a meeting first thing on Monday. Unlike the night before where Pennington had blustered his way through Zaccheo's accusations, he'd listened in tense silence as Zaccheo had told him he knew what he was up to.

Zaccheo had given him a taster of the contents of the documents proving his innocence and the older man had finally agreed to the meeting. Zaccheo had known he'd won when Pennington had declined to bring his lawyers to verify the documents.

Thick silence filled the room after the recording ended.

'Do you believe me now, Eva? Do you believe that your family has wronged me in the most heinous way and that I intend to exact equal retribution?'

Her nostrils flared and her mouth trembled before she wrenched back control. But despite her composure, a sheen of tears appeared in her eyes, announcing her tumultuous emotion. 'Yes.'

'Take the box out of my pocket.'

She withdrew it. His instructions on the mount and setting had been followed to the letter.

'I intended to give it to you after dinner last night. Not on bended knee, of course. I'm sure you'll agree that once was enough?'

Her eyes darkened, as if he'd hurt her somehow. But of course, that was nonsense. She'd returned his first ring and walked away from him after a brief argument he barely recalled, stating that she didn't wish to be married to *a man like him*.

At the time, Zaccheo had been reeling at his lawyers' news that he was about to be charged with criminal negligence. He hadn't been able to absorb the full impact of Eva's betrayal until weeks later, when he'd already been in prison. His trial had been swift, the result of a young, overeager judge desperate to make a name for himself.

But he'd had over a year to replay the last time he'd seen Eva. In court, sitting next to her father, her face devoid of emotion until Zaccheo's sentence had been read out.

In that moment, he'd fooled himself into thinking she'd experienced a moment of agony on his behalf. He'd murmured her name. She'd looked at him. It was then that he'd seen the contempt.

That single memory cleared his mind of any extraneous feelings. 'Open the box and put on the ring,' he said tersely.

His tone must have conveyed his capricious emotional state. She cracked open the small case and slid on the ring without complaint.

He caught her hand in his and raised it, much as he had on Friday night. But this time, the acute need to rip off the evidence of another man's ownership was replaced by a well of satisfaction. 'You're mine, Eva. Until I decide another fate for you, you'll remain mine. Be sure not to forget that.'

Turning on his heel, he walked away.

Eva woke on Monday morning with a heavy heart and a stone in her gut that announced that her life was about to change for ever. It had started to change the moment she'd heard Zaccheo's recorded conversation with her father, but she'd been too shocked afterwards to decipher what her father's guilt meant for her.

Tired and wrung out, she'd stumbled to bed and fallen into a dreamless sleep, then woken and stumbled her way back to work.

Reality had arrived when she'd exited Siren after her shift to find Zaccheo's driver waiting to bring her back to the penthouse. She'd felt it when Zaccheo had told her to be ready to attend his offices in the morning. She'd felt it when she'd walked into her suite and found every item of clothing she'd tried on Saturday neatly stacked in the floor-to-ceiling shelves in her dressing room.

She felt it now when she lifted her hand to adjust her collar and caught the flash of the diamond ring on her finger. The flawless gem she'd chosen so carelessly had been mounted on a bezel setting, with further diamonds in decreasing sizes set in a platinum ring that fitted her perfectly.

You're mine, Eva. Until I decide another fate for you, you'll remain mine.

She was marrying Zaccheo in less than a week. He'd brought forward the initial two-week deadline by a whole week. She would marry him or her father would be reported to the authorities. He'd delivered that little bombshell last night after dinner. No amount of tossing and turning had altered that reality.

When she'd agreed to marry Harry, she'd known it would be purely a business deal, with zero risk to her emotions.

The idea of attaching herself to Zaccheo, knowing the depth of his contempt for her and his hunger for revenge, was bad enough. That undeniably dangerous chemistry that hovered on the point of exploding in her face when she so much as looked at him…*that* terrified her on an unspeakable level. And not because she was afraid he'd use that against her.

What she'd spent the early hours agonising over was her own helplessness against that inescapable pull.

The only way round it was to keep reminding herself why Zaccheo was doing this. Ultimate retribution and humiliation was his goal. He didn't want anything more from her.

An hour later, she sat across from her father and sister and watched in growing horror as Zaccheo's lawyers listed her father's sins.

Oscar Pennington sat hunched over, his pallor grey and his forehead covered in light sweat. Despite having heard Zaccheo's recording last night, she couldn't believe her father would sink so low.

'How could you do this?' she finally blurted when it got

too much to bear. 'And how the hell did you think you'd get away with it?'

Her father glared at her. 'This isn't the time for histrionics, Eva.'

'And you, Sophie? Did you know about this?' Eva asked her sister.

Sophie glanced at the lawyers before she replied, 'Let's not lose focus on why we're here.'

Anger shot through Eva. 'You mean let's pretend that this isn't really happening? That we're not here because Father *bribed* the builders to take shortcuts and blamed someone else for it? And you accuse me of not living in the real world?'

Sophie's lips pursed, but not before a guilty flush rushed into her face. 'Can we not do this now, please?' Her agitated gaze darted to where Zaccheo sat in lethal silence.

Eva stared at her sister, a mixture of anger and sadness seething within her. She was beginning to think they would never get past whatever was broken between them. And maybe she needed to be more like Zaccheo, and divorce herself from her feelings.

Eva glanced at him and the oxygen leached from her lungs.

God!

On Friday night, his all-black attire had lent him an air of suave but icy deadliness reminiscent of a lead in a mafia movie. Since then his casual attires, although equally formidable in announcing his breathtaking physique, had lulled her into a lesser sense of danger.

This morning, in a dark grey pinstripe suit, teamed with a navy shirt, and precisely knotted silver and blue tie, and his hair and beard newly trimmed, Zaccheo was a magnificent vision to behold.

The bespoke clothes flowed over his sleekly honed muscles and olive skin, each movement drawing attention to his powerfully arresting figure.

It was why more than one female employee had stared in

blatant interest as they'd walked into GWI's headquarters in the City this morning. It was why she'd avoided looking at him since they'd sat down.

But she'd made the mistake of looking now. And as he started to turn his head she *knew* she wouldn't be able to look away.

His gaze locked on her and she read the ruthless, possessive statement of ownership in his eyes even before he opened his mouth to speak. 'Eva has already given me what I want—her word that she's willing to do whatever it takes to make reparations.' His gaze dropped to the ring on her finger before he faced her father. 'Now it's your turn.'

CHAPTER EIGHT

'HERE'S A LIST of businesses who withdrew their contracts because of my incarceration.' Zaccheo nodded to one of his lawyers, who passed a sheet across the desk to her father.

Eva caught a glimpse of the names on the list and flinched. While the list was only half a page, she noticed more than one global conglomerate on there.

'You'll contact the CEO of each of those companies and tell them your side of the story.'

Fear flashed across her father's face. 'What's to stop them from spilling the beans?'

Zaccheo gave that chilling half-smile. 'I have a team of lawyers who'll ensure their silence if they ever want to do business with me again.'

'You're sure they'll still want your business?' Her father's voice held a newly subdued note.

'I have it on good authority their withdrawal was merely a stance. Some to gain better leverage on certain transactions and others for appearances' sake. Once they know the truth, they'll be back on board. But even if they don't come back to GWI, the purpose of your phone call would've been achieved.'

'Is this really necessary? Your company has thrived, probably beyond your wildest dreams, even while you were locked up. And this morning's stock-market reports show your stock at an all-time high.' Eva could hear the panic in her father's voice. 'Do I really need to genuflect in front of these people to make you happy?' he added bitterly.

'Yes. You do.'

Her father's face reddened. 'Look here. Judging by that rock I see on Eva's finger, you're about to marry my daughter. We're about to be *family*. Is this really how you wish to start our familial relationship?'

Bitterness pushed aside her compassion when she realised her father was once again using her as leverage for his own ends.

'You don't think this is the least you can do, Father?' she asked.

'You're taking his side?' her father demanded.

Eva sighed. 'I'm taking the side of doing the right thing. Surely you can see that?'

Her father huffed, and Zaccheo's lips thinned into a formidable line. 'I have no interest in building a relationship with you personally. You can drop dead for all I care. Right after you carry out my instructions, of course.'

'Young man, be reasonable,' her father pleaded, realising that for once he'd come up against an immoveable object that neither his charm nor his blustering would shift.

Zaccheo stared back dispassionately. No one in the room could harbour the misguided idea that he would soften in any way.

'I don't think you have a choice in the matter, Father,' Sophie muttered into the tense silence.

Eva glanced at her sister, searching for that warmth they'd once shared. But Sophie kept her face firmly turned away.

Eva jumped as her father pushed back his chair. 'Fine, you win.'

Zaccheo brushed off imaginary lint from his sleeve. 'Excellent. And please be sure to give a convincing performance. My people will contact each CEO on that list by Friday. Make sure you get it done by then.'

Her father's barrel chest rose and fell as he tried to control his temper. 'It'll be done. Sophie, we're leaving.'

Eva started to rise, too, only to find a hand clamped on her hip. The electricity that shot through her body at the bold contact had her swaying on her feet.

'What are you doing?' she demanded.

Zaccheo ignored her, but his thumb moved lazily over her hip bone as he addressed her father. 'You and Sophie may leave. I still have things to discuss with my fiancée. My secretary will contact you with details of the wedding in the next day or two.'

Her father looked from her face to Zaccheo's. Then he stormed out of the door.

Eva turned to Zaccheo. 'What more could we possibly have to discuss? You've made everything crystal clear.'

'Not quite everything. Sit down.' He waited until she complied before he removed his hand.

Eva wasn't sure whether it was relief that burst through her chest or outrage. Relief, most definitely, she decided. Lacing her fingers, she waited as he dismissed all except one lawyer.

At Zaccheo's nod, the man produced a thick binder and placed it in front of Zaccheo, after which he also left.

She could feel Zaccheo's powerful gaze on her, but she'd already unsettled herself by looking at him once. And she was reeling from everything that had taken place here in the last hour.

When the minutes continued to tick by in silence, she raised her head. 'You want my father to help rebuild the damage he caused to your reputation, but what about your criminal record? I would've thought that would be more important to you.'

'You may marry a man with a criminal record come Saturday, but I won't remain that way for long. My lawyers are working on it.'

Her heart lurched at the reminder that in a few short days she would be his wife, but she forced herself to ask the question on her mind. 'How can they do that without implicating my father? Isn't withholding evidence a crime?'

'Nothing will be withheld. How the authorities choose to apply the rule of law is up to them.'

Recalling the state of her father's health, she tightened

her fists in anxiety. 'So you're saying Father can still go to prison? Despite letting him believe he won't?'

The kick in his stare struck deep in her soul. 'I'm the one who was wronged. I have some leeway in speaking on his behalf, should I choose to.'

The implied threat didn't escape her notice. They would either toe his line or suffer the consequences.

She swallowed. 'What did you want to discuss with me?'

He placed a single sheet of paper in front of her.

'These are the engagements we'll be attending this week. Make sure you put them in your diary.'

She pursed her lips, denying that the deep pang in her chest was hurt. 'At least you're laying your cards on the table this time round.'

'What cards would those be?'

She shrugged. 'The ones that state your desire to conquer the upper class, of course. Wasn't that your aim all along? To walk in the hallowed halls of the Old Boys' Club and show them all your contempt for them?'

His eyes narrowed, but she caught a shadow in the grey depths. 'How well you think you know me.'

She cautioned herself against probing the sleeping lion, but found herself asking anyway, 'Why, Zaccheo? Why is it so important that you bring us all down a peg or two?'

He shifted in his seat. If she hadn't known that he didn't possess an ounce of humility, she'd have thought he was uneasy. 'I don't detest the whole echelon. Just those who think they have a right to lord it over others simply because of their pedigree. And, of course, those who think they can get around the laws that ordinary people have to live by.'

'What about me? Surely you can't hate me simply because our relationship didn't work out?'

'Was that what we had—a *relationship*?' he sneered. 'I thought it was a means for you to facilitate your father's plans.'

'*What?* You think I had something to do with my father scapegoating you?'

'Perhaps you weren't privy to his whole plan like your sister was. But the timing of it all was a little too convenient, don't you think? You walked away *three days* before I was charged, with a flimsy excuse after an even flimsier row. What was it? Oh, yes, you didn't want to marry *a man like me?*'

She surged to her feet, her insides going cold. 'You think I staged the whole thing? Need I remind you that you were the one who initiated our first meeting? That you were the one to ask me out?'

'An event carefully orchestrated by your father, of course. Do you know why I was at Siren that night?'

'Will you believe me if I said no?'

'I was supposed to meet your father and two of his investors there. Except none of them showed.'

She frowned. 'That's not possible. My father hates that I sing. He hates it even more that I work in a nightclub. I don't think he even knows where Siren is.'

'And yet he suggested it. Highly recommended it, in fact.'

The idea that her father had engineered their first meeting coated her mouth with bitterness. He'd used her strong loyalty to their family to manipulate her long before she'd taken a stand and moved out of Pennington Manor. But this further evidence showed a meticulousness that made her blood run cold.

'Were you even a virgin back then?' Zaccheo sliced at her.

The question brought her back to earth. 'Excuse me?'

'Or was it a ploy to sweeten the deal?'

'I didn't know you existed until you parked yourself in front of the stage that night!'

'Maybe not. But you must've known who I was soon after. Isn't that what women do these days? A quick internet search while they're putting on their make-up to go on the first date?'

Eva couldn't stop her guilty flush because it was exactly what she'd done. But not with the reprehensible intentions he'd implied. Zaccheo's all-consuming interest in her had seemed too good to be true. She'd wanted to know more about the compelling man who'd zeroed in on her with such unnerving interest.

What she'd found was a long list of conquests ranging from supermodels to famous sports stars. She'd been so intimidated, she'd carefully kept her inexperience under wraps. It was that desperately embarrassing need to prove her sophistication that had led to her boldly accepting his dare to perform oral sex on him on his thirtieth birthday. She'd been so anxious, she'd bungled it even before she'd unfastened his belt. In the face of his wry amusement, she'd blurted her inexperience.

The inexperience he was now denouncing as a ploy.

'I don't care what you think. All I care about is that I know what I'm letting myself in for now. I know exactly the type of man you are.' One whose ruthless ambition was all he cared about.

He regarded her for several tense seconds. 'Then this won't surprise you too much.' He slid a thick burgundy folder across to her. 'It's a prenuptial agreement. On the first page you'll find a list of independent lawyers who can guide you through the legalese should you require it. The terms are non-negotiable. You have twenty-four hours to read and sign it.'

She glanced from him to the folder, her mouth dropping open in shock. 'Why would I need a prenup? I've agreed to your demands. Isn't this overkill?'

'My lawyers go spare if I don't get everything in writing. Besides, there are a few items in there we haven't discussed yet.'

Something in his voice made her skin prickle. Her belly quaked as she turned the first page of the thick document. The first few clauses were about general schedules and routines, making herself available for his engagements within

reason, how many homes he owned and her duty to oversee
the running of them, and his expectation of her availability
to travel with him on his business trips should he require it.

'If you think I'm going to turn myself into a pet you can
pick up and hop on a plane with whenever it suits you, you're
in for a shock.'

He merely quirked an eyebrow at her. She bristled but
carried on reading.

She paused at the sixth clause. 'We can't be apart for more
than five days in the first year of marriage?'

The half-smile twitched. 'We don't want tongues wagging too soon, do we?'

'You mean after the first year I can lock myself in a nunnery for a year if I choose to?'

For the first time since Zaccheo had exploded back into
her life, she glimpsed a genuine smile. It was gone before it
registered fully, but the effect was no less earth-shattering.
'No nunnery would accept you once you've spent a year in
my bed.'

Her face flamed and the look in his eyes made her hurriedly turn the page.

The ninth made her almost swallow her tongue. 'I don't
want your money! And I certainly don't need that much
money *every* month.' The sum stated was more than she
earned in a year.

He shrugged. 'Then donate it to your favourite charity.'

Since she wasn't going to win that one, she moved on to
the tenth and last clause.

Eva jerked to her feet, her heart pounding as she reread the
words, hoping against hope that she'd got it wrong the first
time. But the words remained clear and stark and *frightening*. 'You want…*children*?' she rasped through a throat gone
bone dry with dread.

'*Sì,*' he replied softly. 'Two. An heir and a spare, I believe
you disparagingly refer to that number in your circles. More
if we're lucky—stop shaking your head, Eva.'

Eva realised that was exactly what she was doing as he rose and stalked her. She took a step back, then another, until her backside bumped the sleek black cabinet running the length of the central wall.

He stopped in front of her, leaned his tall, imposing frame over hers. 'Of all the clauses in the agreement, this is non-negotiable.'

'You said they were all non-negotiable.'

'They are, but some are more non-negotiable than others.'

A silent scream built inside her. 'If this one is the most important why did you put it last?'

'Because you would be signing directly below it. I wanted you to feel its import so there would be no doubt in your mind what you were agreeing to.'

She started to shake her head again but froze when he angled himself even closer, until their lips were an inch apart. Their breaths mingling, he stared her down. Eva's heart climbed into her throat as she struggled to sift through the emotions those words on the page had evoked.

Zaccheo was asking the impossible.

Children were the reasons why her last two relationships before him had failed before they'd even begun.

Children were the reason she'd painfully resigned herself to remaining single. To spurning any interest that came her way because she hadn't been able to bear the thought of baring her soul again only to have her emotions trampled on.

She wouldn't cry. She wouldn't break down in front of Zaccheo. Not today. *Not ever.* He'd caused her enough turmoil to last a lifetime.

But he was asking the impossible. 'I can't.'

His face hardened but he didn't move a muscle. 'You can. You *will*. Three days ago you were agreeing to marry another man. You expect me to believe the possibility of children weren't on the cards with Fairfield?'

She shook her head. 'My agreement with Harry was different. Besides, he...' She stopped, unwilling to add to the flammable tension.

'He what?' Zaccheo enquired silkily.

'He didn't *hate* me!'

He seemed almost surprised at her accusation. Surprise slowly gave way to a frown. 'I don't hate you, Eva. In fact, given time and a little work, we might even find common ground.'

She cursed her heart for leaping at his words. 'I can't—'

'You have twenty-four hours. I suggest you take the time and review your answer before saying another word.'

Her stomach clenched. 'And if my answer remains the same?'

His expression was one of pure, insufferable arrogance. 'It won't. You make feeble attempts to kick at the demands of your ancestry and title, but inevitably you choose blood over freedom. You'll do anything to save your precious family name—'

'You really think so? After the meeting we just had? Are you really that blind, or did you not see the way my sister and my father treat me? We are not a close family, Zaccheo. No matter how much I wish it...' Her voice shook, but she firmed it. 'Have you stopped to think that you pushing me this way may be the catalyst I need to completely break away from a family that's already broken?'

Her terse words made his eyes narrow. But his expression cleared almost immediately. 'No, you're loyal. You'll give me what I want.'

'No—'

'Yes,' he breathed.

He closed the gap between them slowly, as if taunting her with the knowledge that she couldn't escape the inevitability of his possession.

His mouth claimed hers—hot, demanding, powerfully erotic. Eva moaned as her emotions went into free fall. He feasted on her as if he had all the time in the world, taking turns licking his way into her mouth before sliding his tongue against hers in an expert dance that had her desperately clutching his waist.

Wild, decadent heat swirled through her body as he lifted her onto the cabinet, tugged up the hem of her dress and planted himself between her thighs. Her shoulders met the wall and she gasped as one hand gripped her thigh.

Push him away. You need to push him away!

Her hands climbed from his waist to his chest, albeit far slower and in a far more exploratory fashion than her screeching brain was comfortable with. But she made an effort once she reached his broad shoulders.

She pushed.

And found her hands captured in a firm one-handed hold above her head. His other hand found her breast and palmed it, squeezing before flicking his thumb over her hardened nipple.

Sensation pounded through her blood. Her legs curled around his thickly muscled thighs and she found herself pulled closer to the edge of the cabinet, until the powerful evidence of his erection pushed at her core.

Zaccheo gave a deep groan and freed her hands to bury his in her hair. Angling her head for a deeper invasion, he devoured her until the need for air drove them apart.

Chests heaving, they stared at each other for several seconds before Eva scrambled to untangle her legs from around him. Every skin cell on fire, she struggled to stand up. He stopped her with a hand on her belly, his eyes compelling hers so effortlessly, she couldn't look away.

The other hand moved to her cheek, then his fingers drifted over her throbbing mouth.

'As much as I'd like to take you right here on my boardroom cabinet, I have a dozen meetings to chair. It seems everyone wants a powwow with the newly emancipated CEO. We'll pick this up again at dinner. I'll be home by seven.'

She diverted enough brainpower from the erotic images it was creating to reply. 'I won't be there. I'm working tonight.'

A tic throbbed at his temple as he straightened his tie. 'I see that I need to put aligning our schedules at the top of my agenda.'

She pushed him away and stood. 'Don't strain yourself too much on my account,' she responded waspishly. She was projecting her anger at her weakness onto him, but she couldn't help herself. She tugged her dress down, painfully aware of the sensitivity between her unsteady legs as she moved away from him and picked up her handbag and the folder containing the prenup. 'I'll see you when I see you.'

He took her hand and walked her to the door. 'I guarantee you it'll be much sooner than that.' He rode the lift down with her to the ground floor, barely acknowledging the keen interest his presence provoked.

Romeo was entering the building as they exited. The two men exchanged a short conversation in Italian before Zaccheo opened the door to the limo.

When she went to slide in, he stopped her. 'Wait.'

'What is it?' she demanded.

His lips firmed and he seemed in two minds as to his response. 'For a moment during the meeting, you took my side against your father. I'll factor that favourably into our dealings from now on.'

Eva's heart lifted for a moment, then plunged back to her toes. 'You don't get it, do you?'

He frowned. 'Get what?'

'Zaccheo, for as long as I can remember, all I've wished was for there to be *no sides*. For there not to be a *them* against *us*. Maybe that makes me a fool. Or maybe I'll need to give up that dream.'

His eyes turned a shade darker with puzzlement, then he shrugged. '*Sì, bellissima*, perhaps you might have to.'

And right in front of the early lunch crowd, Zaccheo announced his ownership of her with a long, deep kiss.

* * *

Eva could barely hear herself think above the excited buzz in Siren's VIP lounge as she cued the next song.

She was sure the unusually large Monday night crowd had nothing to with Ziggy Preston, the famous record producer who'd been coming to watch her perform on and off for the past month, and everything to do with the pictures that had appeared in the early-evening paper of her kissing Zaccheo outside his office this afternoon. Avoiding the news had been difficult, seeing as that kiss and a large-scale picture of her engagement ring had made front-page news.

One picture had held the caption *'Three Ring Circus'*—with photos of her three engagement rings and a pointed question as to her motives.

It'd been a relief to leave Zaccheo's penthouse, switch off her phone and immerse herself in work. Not least because blanking her mind stopped her from thinking about the last clause in the prenup, and the reawakened agony she'd kept buried since her doctor had delivered the harrowing news six years ago. News she'd only revealed twice, with devastating consequences.

She almost wished she could blurt it out to Zaccheo and let the revelation achieve what it had in the past—a swift about-face from keen interest to cold dismissal, with one recipient informing her, in the most callous terms, that he could never accept her as a full woman.

Pain flared wider, threatening the foundations she'd built to protect herself from that stark truth. Foundations Zaccheo threatened.

She clutched the mic and forced back the black chasm that swirled with desolation. Her accompanying pianist nodded and she cleared her throat, ready to sing the ballad that ironically exhorted her to be brave.

She was halfway through the song when he walked in. As usual, the sight of him sent a tidal wave of awareness through her body and she managed to stop herself from stumbling by the skin of her teeth. Heads turned and the buzz in the room grew louder.

Zaccheo's eyes raked her from head to toe before settling on her face. A table miraculously emptied in front of the stage. Someone took his overcoat and Eva watched him release the single button to his dinner jacket before pulling out a chair and seating himself at the roped-off table before her.

The sense of déjà vu was so overwhelming, she wanted to abandon the song and flee from the stage. She finished, she smiled and accepted the applause, then made her way to where he pointedly held out a chair for her.

'What are you doing here?' she whispered fiercely.

He took his time to answer, choosing instead to pull her close and place a kiss on each cheek before drawing back to stare at her.

'You couldn't make dinner, so I brought dinner to you.'

'You really shouldn't have,' she replied, fighting the urge to rub her cheeks where his lips had been. 'Besides, I can't. My break is only twenty minutes.'

'Tonight your break is an hour, as it will be every night I choose to dine with you here instead of at our home. Now sit down and smile, *mio piccolo uccello che canta*, and pretend to our avid audience that you're ecstatically happy to see your fiancé,' he said with a tone edged in steel.

CHAPTER NINE

ZACCHEO WATCHED MYRIAD expressions chase across her face. Rebellion. Irritation. Sexual awareness. A touch of embarrassment when someone shouted their appreciation of her singing from across the room. One glance from Zaccheo silenced that inebriated guest.

But it was the shadows that lurked in her eyes that made his jaw clench. All day, through the heady challenge of getting back into the swing of business life, that look in her eyes when she'd seen his last clause in the prenuptial agreement had played on his mind. Not enough to disrupt his day, but enough for him to keep replaying the scene. Her reaction had been extreme and almost…distressed.

Yes, it bothered him that she saw making a family with him abhorrent, even though he'd known going in that, had she been given a choice, Eva would've chosen someone else, someone more *worthy* to father her children. Nevertheless, her reaction had struck hard in a place he'd thought was no longer capable of feeling hurt.

The feeling had festered, like a burr under his skin, eating away at him as the day had progressed. Until he'd abruptly ended a videoconference and walked out of his office.

He'd intended to return home and help himself to fine whisky in a toast to striking the first blow in ending Oscar Pennington's existence. Instead he'd found himself swapping his business suit for a dinner jacket and striding back out of his penthouse.

The woman who'd occupied far too much of his thoughts today swayed to her seat and sat down. The pounding in his blood that had never quite subsided after that kiss in his boardroom, and increased the moment he'd entered the

VIP room and heard her singing, accelerated when his gaze dropped to her scarlet-painted lips.

Before he'd met Eva Pennington, Zaccheo had never labelled himself a possessive guy. Although he enjoyed the thrill of the chase and inevitable capture, he'd been equally thrilled to see the back of the women he'd dated, especially when the clinginess had begun.

With Eva, he'd experienced an unprecedented and very caveman-like urge to claim her, to make sure every man within striking distance knew she belonged to him. And only him. That feeling was as unsettling as it was hard to eradicate. It wasn't helped when she toyed with her champagne glass and avoided eye contact.

'I don't appreciate you messing with my schedule behind my back, Zaccheo,' she said.

He wasn't sure why the sound of his name on her lips further spiked his libido, but he wanted to hear it again. He wanted to hear it fall from her lips in the throes of passion, as he took her to the heights of ecstasy.

Dio, he was losing it. Losing sight of his objective. Which was to make sure she understood that he intended to give no quarter in making her his.

He took a bracing sip of champagne and nodded to the hovering waiters ready to serve the meal he'd ordered.

'It was dinner here or summoning you back to the penthouse. You should be thanking me for bending like this.'

She glared. 'You really are a great loss to the Dark Ages, you know that?'

'In time you'll learn that I always get my way, Eva. *Always.*'

Her eyes met his and that intense, inexplicable connection that had throbbed between them right from the very start pulled, tightened.

'Did it even occur to you that I may have said yes if you'd asked me to have dinner with you?'

Surprise flared through him, and he found himself asking, 'Would you?'

She shrugged. 'I guess you'll never know. We need to discuss the prenup,' she said.

He knew instinctively that she was about to refuse him again. A different sort of heat bloomed in his chest. 'This isn't the time or place.'

'I don't...' She paused when the waiters arrived at the table with their first course. As if recalling where they were, she glanced round, took a deep breath, and leaned forward. 'I won't sign it.'

Won't, not *can't*, as she'd said before.

Bitterness surged through his veins. 'Because the thought of my seed growing inside you fills you with horror?'

Her fingers convulsed around her knife, but, true to her breeding, she directed it to her plate with understated elegance to cut her steak.

'Why would you want me as the mother of your children, anyway? I would've thought you'd want to spare yourself such a vivid reminder of what you've been through.'

'Perhaps I'm the one to give the Pennington name the integrity it's been so sorely lacking thus far.'

She paled, and he cursed himself for pursuing a subject that was better off discussed in private. Although he'd made sure their table was roped off and their conversation couldn't be overheard, there was still more than enough interest in them for each expression flitting across Eva's face to be captured and assessed.

'So we're your personal crusade?' she asked, a brittle smile appearing on her face as she acknowledged someone over his shoulder.

'Let's call it more of an experiment.'

Her colour rose with the passionate fury that intrigued him. 'You'd father children based on an *experiment*? After what you've been through...what we've both been through, you think that's fair to the children you intend to have to be used solely as a means for you to prove a point?' Her voice was ragged and he tensed.

'Eva—'

'No, I won't be a part of it!' Her whisper was fierce. 'My mother may have loved me in her own way, but I was still the tool she used against my father when it suited her. If my grades happened to be better than Sophie's, she would imply my father was lacking in some way. And believe me, my father didn't pull his punches when the situation was reversed.' She swallowed and raised bruised eyes to his. 'Even if I cou—wanted to why would I knowingly subject another child to what I went through? Why would I give you a child simply to use to *prove a point*?'

'You mistake my meaning. I don't intend to fail my children or use them as pawns. I intend to be there for them through thick and thin, unlike my parents were for me.' He stopped when her eyes widened. 'Does that surprise you?'

'I... Yes.'

He shrugged, even though it occurred to him that he'd let his guard down more with her than he ever had with anyone. But she had no power to hurt him. She'd already rejected him once. This time he knew the lay of the land going in. So it didn't matter if she knew his parental ambitions for the children they'd have.

'My children will be my priority, although I'll be interested to see how your family fares with being shown that things can be done differently. The *right* way.'

He watched her digest his response, watched the shadows he was beginning to detest mount in her eyes. He decided against probing further. There'd been enough turbulent emotions today. He suspected there would be further fireworks when she found out the new business negotiations he'd commenced this afternoon.

That a part of him was looking forward to it made him shift in his seat.

Since when had he craved verbal conflict with a woman?

Never. And yet he couldn't seem to help himself when it came to Eva.

He was debating this turn of events as their plates were removed when a throat cleared next to them.

The man was around his age, with floppy brown hair and a cocky smile that immediately rubbed Zaccheo the wrong way.

'Can I join you for a few minutes?' he asked.

The *no* that growled up Zaccheo's chest never made it. Eva was smiling—her first genuine smile since he'd walked in—and nodding. 'Mr Preston, of course!'

'Thanks. And call me Ziggy, please. Mr Preston is my headmaster grandfather.'

'What can we do for you, *Ziggy*?' Zaccheo raised an eyebrow at the furious look Eva shot him.

The other man, who was staring at Eva with an avidness that made Zaccheo's fist clench, finally looked in his direction. 'I came to pay my compliments to your girlfriend. She has an amazing voice.'

Eva blushed at his words.

Zaccheo's eyes narrowed when he noticed she wasn't wearing her engagement ring. 'Eva's my fiancée, not my girlfriend. And I'm very much aware of her exceptional talent,' he said, the harsh edge to his voice getting through to the man, who looked from him to Eva before his smile dimmed.

'Ah, congratulations are in order, then?'

'*Grazie,*' Zaccheo replied. 'Was there something else you wanted?'

'Zaccheo!' Eva glared harder, and turned to Ziggy. 'Pardon my *fiancé*. He's feeling a little testy because—'

'I want her all to myself but find other *things* standing in my way. And because you're not wearing your engagement ring, *dolcezza*.'

She covered her bare fingers with her hand, as if that would remove the evidence of the absence of his ring. 'Oh,

I didn't want to risk losing it. I'm still getting used to it.' The glance she sent him held a mixture of defiance and entreaty.

Ziggy cleared his throat again. 'I don't want to play the *Do-you-know-who-I-am?* card, but—'

'Of course I know who you are,' Eva replied with a charming laugh.

Ziggy smiled and produced a business card. 'In that case, would you like to come to my studio next week? See if we can make music together?'

Eva's pleased gasp further darkened Zaccheo's mood. 'Of course I can—'

'Aren't you forgetting something, *luce mio*?' he asked in a quietly lethal tone.

'What?' she asked, so innocently he wanted to grab her from the chair, spread her across the table and make her see nothing, no one, but him. Make her recall that she had given her word to be his and only his.

'You won't be available next week.' He didn't care that he hadn't yet apprised her of the details. He cared that she was smiling at another man as if *he* didn't exist. 'We'll be on our honeymoon on my private island off the coast of Brazil where we'll be staying for the next two weeks.'

Her eyes rounded, but she recovered quickly and took the business card. 'I'll *make* time to see you before I go. Surely you don't want to deny me this opportunity, *darling*?' Her gaze swung to him, daring him to respond in the negative.

Despite his irritation, Zaccheo curbed a smile. 'Of course. Anything for you, *dolcezza*.'

Ziggy beamed. 'Great! I look forward to it.'

The moment he was out of earshot, she turned to Zaccheo. 'How dare you try and sabotage me like that?'

'Watching you smile at another man like that fills me with insane jealousy. It also brings out the jerk in me. My apologies,' he growled. Her mouth dropped open. 'Close your mouth, Eva.'

She shook her head as if reeling from a body blow.

Welcome to my world.

'Where's your ring?' He stared at her, his control on a knife-edge.

Perhaps sensing the dangerously shifting currents, she pulled up the gold chain that hung between her pert, full breasts. His ring dangled from it.

'Put it on. Now,' he said, struggling to keep his voice even.

Undoing the clasp, she took the ring off the chain and slid it back on her finger. 'There. Can I return to work now or are you going to harangue me about something else?'

He told himself he did it because he needed to put his rampaging emotions *somewhere*. That it was her fault for pushing him to his limit. But when he plucked her from her seat, placed her in his lap and kissed her insanely tempting mouth, Zaccheo knew it was because he couldn't help himself. She *got* to him in a way no one else did.

By the time he pulled away, they were both breathing hard. Her high colour filled him with immense satisfaction, helping him ignore his own hopeless loss of control.

'Don't take the ring off again, Eva. You underestimate the lengths I'm prepared to go to in making sure you stick to your word, but for your sake I hope you start taking me seriously.'

In contrast to the vividness of Zaccheo's presence, the rest of the night passed in a dull blur after he left. By the time Eva collapsed into bed in the early hours, her head throbbed with the need to do something severely uncharacteristic. Like scream. Beat her fists against the nearest wall. Shout her anger and confusion to the black skies above.

She did nothing of the sort. More than anything, she craved a little peace and quiet.

After that kiss in the club, even more eyes had followed her wherever she went. Hushed whispers had trailed her to the bathroom. By the time her shift had ended three hours later, she'd been ready to walk out and never return.

She wouldn't, of course. Working at Siren gave her the free time to write her songs while earning enough to live on. Despite Zaccheo's heavy-handedness, she could never see a time when she'd be dependent on anyone other than herself.

'You underestimate the lengths I'm prepared to go to...'

The forceful statement had lingered long after he'd left, anchored by the heavy presence of the prenuptial agreement in her handbag.

He'd said he wouldn't negotiate. Eva didn't see that he had a choice in this matter. Refusing to marry him might well spell the end for her father, but withholding the truth and marrying him knowing she could never fulfil her part of the bargain would be much worse.

Turning in bed, she punched her pillow, dreading the long, restless night ahead. Only to wake with sunshine streaming through the window and her clock announcing it was ten o'clock.

Rushing out of bed, she showered quickly and entered the dining room just as Romeo was exiting, having finished his own breakfast. The table was set for one and Eva cursed herself for the strange dip in her belly that felt very much like disappointment.

'Good morning. Shall I get the chef to make you a cooked breakfast?' The man whose role she was beginning to suspect went deeper than a simple second-in-command asked.

'Just some toast and tea, please, thank you.'

He nodded and started to leave.

'Is Zaccheo around or has he left for the office?'

'Neither. He left this morning for Oman. An unexpected hiccup in the construction of his building there.'

Eva was unprepared for the bereft feeling that swept through her. She should be celebrating her temporary reprieve. Finding a way to see if she could work around that impossible clause. 'When will he be back?'

'In a day or two. Latest by the end of the week to be ready in time for the wedding,' Romeo said in that deep, modulated voice of his. 'This is for you.' He handed her a folded note and left.

The bold scrawl was unmistakeably Zaccheo's.

Eva,
> *Treat my absence as you wish, but never as an excuse to be complacent.*
>
> *My PA will be in touch with details of your wedding dress fitting this morning and your amended schedule for the week.*
>
> *You have my permission to miss me.*

Z

Ugh! She grimaced at the arrogance oozing from the paper. Balling the note, she flung it across the table. Then quickly jumped up and retrieved it before Romeo returned. The last thing she wanted was for him to report her loss of temper to Zaccheo.

Her traitorous body had a hard enough time controlling itself when Zaccheo was around. She didn't want him to know he affected her just as badly when he was absent.

By the time breakfast was delivered, she'd regained her composure. Which was just as well, because close on the chef's heel was a tall, striking brunette dressed in a grey pencil skirt and matching jacket.

'Good morning, my name is Anyetta, Mr Giordano's PA. He said you were expecting me?'

'I was expecting a phone call, not a personal visit.'

Anyetta delivered a cool smile. 'Mr Giordano wanted his wishes attended to personally.'

Eva's appetite fled. 'I bet he did,' she muttered.

She poured herself a cup of tea as Anyetta proceeded to fill up her every spare hour between now and Saturday morning.

Eva listened until her temper began to flare, then tuned

out until she heard the word *makeover*. 'I've already had one makeover. I don't need another one.'

Anyetta's eyes drifted over Eva's hair, which she admitted was a little wild since she hadn't brushed it properly before she'd rushed out to speak to Zaccheo. 'Not even for your wedding day?'

Since there wasn't likely to be a wedding day once she told Zaccheo she had no intention of signing the agreement, she replied, 'It'll be taken care of.'

Anyetta ticked off a few more items, verified that Eva's passport was up to date, then stood as the doorbell rang. 'That'll be Margaret with your wedding dress.'

The feeling of being on a runaway train intensified as Eva trailed Anyetta out of the dining room. She drew to a stunned halt when she saw the middle-aged woman coming towards her with a single garment bag and a round veil and shoebox.

'Please tell me you don't have a team of assistants lurking outside ready to jump on me?' she asked after Anyetta left.

Margaret laughed. 'It's just me, Lady Pennington. Your fiancé was very specific about his wishes, and, meeting you now, I see why he chose this dress. He did say I was to work with you, of course. So if you don't like it, we can explore other options.'

Eva reminded herself that this situation hadn't arisen out of a normal courtship, that Zaccheo choosing her wedding dress for her shouldn't upset her so much. Besides, the likelihood of this farce ever seeing the light of day was very low so she was better off just going along with it.

But despite telling herself not to care, Eva couldn't suppress her anxiety and excitement.

She gasped as the dress was revealed.

The design itself was simple and clean, but utterly breathtaking. Eva stared at the fitted white satin gown overlaid with lace and beaded with countless tiny crystals. Delicate capped sleeves extended from the sweetheart neckline and the tiniest train flared out in a beautiful arc. At the back, more crystals had been embedded in mother-of-pearl buttons that went from nape to waist. Unable to resist, Eva reached out to touch the dress, then pulled herself back.

There was no point falling in love with a dress she'd never wear. No point getting butterflies about a marriage that would never happen once she confessed her flaw to Zaccheo. Her hands fisted and she fought the desolation threatening to break free inside her.

For six years, she'd successfully not dwelt on what she could never have—a husband who cared for her and a family of her own. She'd made music her life and had found fulfilment in it. She wasn't about to let a heartbreakingly gorgeous dress dredge up agonies she'd sealed in a box marked *strictly out of bounds.*

'Are you ready to try it on?' Margaret asked.

Eva swallowed. 'Might as well.'

If the other woman found her response curious, she didn't let on. Eva avoided her gaze in the mirror as the dress was slipped over her shoulders and the delicate chiffon and lace veil was fitted into place. She mumbled her thanks as Margaret helped her into matching-coloured heels.

'Oh, I'm pleased to see we don't need to alter it in any way, Lady Pennington. It fits perfectly. Looks like your fiancé was very accurate with your measurements. You'd be surprised how many men get it wrong…'

She kept her gaze down, frightened to look at herself, as Margaret tweaked and tugged until she was happy.

Eva dared not look up in case she began to *hope* and *wish.* She murmured appropriate responses and turned this way and that when asked and breathed a sigh of relief when the ordeal was over. The moment Margaret zipped up the bag and left, Eva escaped to her suite. Putting her headphones on, she activated the music app on her tablet and proceeded to drown out her thoughts the best way she knew how.

But this time no amount of doing what she loved best could obliterate the thoughts tumbling through her head.

At seventeen when her periods had got heavier and more painful with each passing month, she'd attributed it to life's natural cycle. But when stronger painkillers had barely alleviated the pain, she'd begun to suspect something major was wrong.

Collapsing during a university lecture had finally prompted her to seek medical intervention.

The doctor's diagnosis had left her reeling.

Even then, she'd convinced herself it wasn't the end of the world, that compared to her mother's fight against cancer, a fight she'd eventually lost a year later, Eva's problem was inconsequential. Women dealt with challenging problems like hers every day. When the time came, the man she chose to spend the rest of her life with would understand and support her.

Eva scoffed at her naiveté. Scott, the first man she'd dated in the last year of university, had visibly recoiled from her when she'd mentioned her condition. She'd been so shocked by his reaction, she'd avoided him for the rest of her time at uni.

Burnt, she'd sworn off dating until she'd met George Tremayne, her fellow business intern during her brief stint at Penningtons. Flattered by his attentiveness, she'd let down her guard and gone on a few dates before he'd begun to pressure her to take things further. Her gentle rejection and confession of her condition had resulted in a scathing volley of insults, during which she'd found out exactly why her father had been pressing her to work at Penningtons after graduation.

Oscar Pennington, already secure in his conscript of Sophie as his heir, was eager to offload his remaining daughter and had lined up a list of suitable men, George Tremayne, the son of a viscount, being on the top of that list. George's near-identical reaction to Scott's had hurt twice as much, and convinced Eva once and for all that her secret was best kept to herself.

Finding out she was yet another means to an end for Zaccheo had rocked her to the core, but she'd taken consolation in the fact the secret she'd planned on revealing to him shortly after their engagement was safe.

That secret was about to be ripped open.

As she turned up the volume of her music Eva knew disclosing it to Zaccheo would be the most difficult thing she would ever do.

CHAPTER TEN

ZACCHEO SCROLLED THROUGH the missed calls from Eva on his phone as he was driven away from the private hangar. Romeo had relayed her increasingly frantic requests to reach him. Zaccheo had deliberately forbidden his number from being given to her until this morning, once he'd confirmed his return to London.

His jaw flexed as he rolled tight shoulders. The number of fires he'd put out in Oman would've wiped out a lesser man. But Zaccheo's name and ruthless nature weren't renowned for nothing, and although it'd taken three days to get the construction schedule back on track, his business partners were in no doubt that he would bring them to their knees if they strayed so much as one millimetre from the outcome he desired.

It was the same warning he'd given Oscar Pennington when he'd called yesterday and attempted an ego-stroking exercise to get Zaccheo to relent on his threats. Zaccheo had coldly reminded him of the days he'd spent in prison and invited Pennington to ask for clemency when hell froze over.

No doubt Eva's eagerness to contact him was born of the same desire as her father's. But unlike her father, the thought of speaking to Eva sent a pleasurable kick of anticipation through his blood, despite the fact that with time and distance he'd looked back on their conversations since his release with something close to dismay.

Had he really revealed all those things about his time in prison and his childhood to her?

What was even more puzzling was her reaction. She hadn't looked down her nose at him in those moments. Had in fact exhibited nothing but empathy and compassion. Pushing the bewildering thought away, he dialled her number, gratified when she picked up on the first ring.

'*Ciao*, Eva. I understand you're experiencing pre-wedding jitters.'

'You understand wrong. This wedding isn't going to happen. Not once you hear what I have to say.'

His tension increased until the knots in his shoulders felt like immoveable rocks. He breathed through the red haze blurring his vision. 'I take it you didn't miss me, then?' he taunted.

She made a sound, a cross between a huff and a sigh. 'We really need to talk, Zaccheo.'

'Nothing you say will alter my intention to make you mine tomorrow,' he warned.

She hesitated. Then, 'Zaccheo, it's important. I won't take up too much of your time. But I need to speak to you.'

He rested his head against the seat. 'You have less than twenty-four hours left as a single woman. I won't permit anything like male strippers anywhere near you, of course, but I won't be a total bore and deny you a hen party if you wish—'

'I don't want a damn hen party! What I want is five minutes of your time.'

'Are you dying of some life-threatening disease?'

'*What?* Of course not!'

'Are you afraid I won't be a good husband?' he asked, noting the raw edge to his voice, but realising how much her answer meant to him.

'Zaccheo, this is about me, not you.'

He let her non-answer slide. 'You'll be a good wife. And despite your less than auspicious upbringing, you'll be a good mother.'

He heard her soft gasp. 'How do you know that?'

'Because you're passionate when you care. You just need to channel that passion from your undeserving family to the one we will create.'

'I can't just switch my feelings towards my family off.

Everyone deserves someone who cares about them, no matter what.'

His heart kicked hard and his grip tightened around the phone as bitterness washed through him. 'Not everyone gets it, though.'

Silence thrummed. 'I'm sorry about your parents. Is... your mother still alive?' Her voice bled the compassion he'd begun to associate with her.

It warmed a place inside him even as he answered. 'That depends on who you ask. Since she relocated to the other side of the world to get away from me, I presume she won't mind if I think her dead to me.'

'But she's alive, Zaccheo. Which means there's hope. Do you really want to waste that?' Her pain-filled voice drew him up short, reminding him that she'd lost her mother.

When had this conversation turned messy and emotional?

'You were close to your mother?' he asked.

'When she wasn't busy playing up to being a Pennington, or using me to get back at my father, she was a brilliant mother. I wish... I wish she'd been a mother to both Sophie *and* me.' She laughed without humour. 'Hell, I used to wish I'd been born into another family, that my last name wasn't Pennington—' She stopped and a tense silence reigned.

Zaccheo frowned. Things weren't adding up with Eva. He'd believed her surname was one she would do just about anything for, including help cover up fraud. But in his boardroom on Monday, she'd seemed genuinely shocked and hurt by the extent of her father's duplicity. And there was also the matter of her chosen profession and the untouched money in her bank account.

A less cynical man would believe she was the exception to the abhorrent aristocratic rule...

'At least you had one parent who cared for you. You were lucky,' he said, his mind whirling with the possibility that he could be wrong.

'But that parent is gone, and I feel as if I have no one now,' she replied quietly.

The need to tell her she had him flared through his mind. He barely managed to stay silent. After a few seconds, she cleared her throat. Her next words made him wish he'd hung up.

'I haven't signed the prenup,' she blurted out. 'I'm not going to.'

Because of the last clause.

For a brief moment, Zaccheo wanted to tell her why he wanted children. That the bleak loneliness that had dogged him through his childhood and almost drowned him in prison had nearly broken him. That he'd fallen into a pit of despair when he'd realised no one would miss him should the worst happen.

His mother had emigrated to Australia with her husband rather than stay in the same city as him once Zaccheo had fully established himself in London. That had cut deeper than any rejection he'd suffered from her in the past. And although the news of his trial and sentencing had been world-wide news, Zaccheo had never once heard from the woman who'd given him life.

He could've died in prison for all his mother cared. That thought had haunted him day and night until he'd decided to do something about it.

Until he'd vowed to alter his reality, ensure he had some-one who would be proud to bear his name. Someone to whom he could pass on his legacy.

He hadn't planned for that person to be Eva Pennington until he'd read about her engagement in the file. But once he had, the decision had become iron cast.

Although this course was very much a sweeter, more last-ing experience, Zaccheo couldn't help but wonder if it was all worth the ground shifting so much beneath his feet.

Eva was getting beneath his skin. And badly.

Dio mio. Why were the feelings he'd bottled up for over two decades choosing *now* to bubble up? He exhaled harshly.

Rough and ruthless was his motto. It was what had made him the man he was today. 'You'll be in your wedding dress at noon tomorrow, ready to walk down the aisle where our six hundred guests will be—'

'*Six hundred?* You've invited six *hundred* people to the wedding?' Her husky disbelief made his teeth grind.

'You thought I intended to have a hole-in-the-wall ceremony?' A fresh wave of bitterness rolled over him. 'Or did you think my PA was spouting gibberish when she informed you of all this on Tuesday?'

'Sorry, I must've tuned out because, contrary to what you think, I don't like my life arranged for me,' she retorted. 'That doesn't change anything. I *can't* do this…'

Zaccheo frowned at the naked distress in her voice.

Eva was genuinely torn up about the prospect of giving herself to him, a common man only worthy of a few kisses but nothing as substantial as the permanent state of matrimony.

Something very much like pain gripped his chest. 'Is that your final decision? Are you backing out of our agreement?'

She remained silent for so long, he thought the line was dead. 'Unless you're willing to change the last clause, yes.'

Zaccheo detested the sudden clenching of his stomach, as if the blow he'd convinced himself would never come had been landed. The voice taunting him for feeling more than a little stunned was ruthlessly smashed away.

He assured himself he had another way to claim the justice he sought. 'Very well. *Ciao.*'

He ended the phone call. And fought the urge to hurl his phone out of the window.

Eva dropped the phone onto the coffee-shop table. She'd arrived at work only to discover she'd been taken off the roster due to her impending wedding. Since she had holiday due to her anyway, Eva hadn't fought too hard at suddenly finding herself with free time.

Her session with Ziggy yesterday had gone well, despite her head being all over the place. If nothing else came of it, she could add that to her CV.

Curbing a hysterical snort, she stared at her phone.

She'd done the right thing and ended this farce before it went too far. Before the longings she'd harboured in the last three days got any more out of control.

Deep in her heart, she knew Zaccheo would react the same way to her secret as Scott and George had. He wouldn't want to marry half a woman, especially when he'd stated his expectations in black and white in a formal agreement drafted by a team of lawyers, and then confounded her with his genuine desire to become a father.

So why hadn't she just told him over the phone?

Because she was a glutton for punishment?

Because some part of her had hoped telling him face-to-face would help her gauge whether there was a chance he would accept her the way she was?

Fat chance.

It was better this way. Clean. Painless.

She jumped as her phone pinged. Heart lurching, she accessed the message, but it was only the manageress from Siren, wishing her a lovely wedding and sinfully blissful honeymoon.

Eva curled her hand around her fast-cooling mug. Once the news got out that she'd broken her third engagement in two years, her chances of marrying anyone, let alone a man who would accept her just as she was, would shrink from nil to no chance in hell.

Pain spiked again at the reminder of her condition. Exhaling, she wrenched her mind to more tangible things.

Like finding a place to live.

She weighed her options, despair clutching her insides

when, two hours later, she faced the only avenue open to her. Going back home to Pennington Manor.

Reluctantly, she picked up her phone, then nearly dropped it when it blared to life. The name of the caller made her frown.

'Sophie?'

'Eva, what's going on?' The fear in her voice shredded Eva's heart.

'What do you mean?'

'I've just had to call the doctor because Father's had another episode!'

Eva jerked to her feet, sending her coffee cup bouncing across the table. 'What?'

'We got a call from Zaccheo Giordano an hour ago to say the wedding was off. Father's been frantic. He was about to call you when he collapsed. The doctor says if he's subjected to any more stress he could have a heart attack or a stroke. Is it true? Did you call off the wedding?' The strain in her sister's voice was unmistakeable.

'Yes,' Eva replied. She grabbed her bag and hurried out of the coffee shop when she began to attract peculiar looks. Outside, she shrugged into her coat and pulled up her hoodie to avoid the light drizzle.

'Oh, God. Why?' her sister demanded.

'Zaccheo wanted me to sign a prenuptial agreement.'

'So? Everyone does that these days.'

'One of the terms…he wants *children*.'

Her sister sighed. 'So he backed out when you told him?'

'No, he doesn't know.'

'But… I'm confused,' Sophie replied.

'I tried to tell him but he wouldn't listen.'

'You tried. Isn't that enough?'

Eva ducked into a quiet alley and leaned against a wall. 'No, it's *not* enough. We've caused enough harm where he's concerned. I won't go into this based on a lie.'

'Father's terrified, Eva.'

'Can I talk to him?'

'He's sleeping now. I'll let him know you called when he wakes up.' Sophie paused. 'Eva, I've been thinking…what you said on Saturday, about you not being out to replace me… I shouldn't have bitten your head off. It's just… Father isn't an easy man to please. He was relying on me to see us through this rough patch…'

'I didn't mean to step on your toes, Sophie.'

Her sister inhaled deeply. 'I know. But everything seems so effortless for you, Eva. It always has. I envied you because Mother chose you—'

'Parents shouldn't choose which child to love and which to keep at arm's length!'

'But that was our reality. He wanted a son. And I was determined to be that son. After Mother died, I was scared Father would think I wasn't worth his attention.'

'You were. You still are.'

'Only because I've gone along with whatever he's asked of me without complaint, even when I knew I shouldn't. This thing with Zaccheo… Father's not proud of it. Nor am I. I don't know where we go from here, but once we're through this, can we get together?' Sophie asked, her voice husky with the plea.

Eva didn't realise her legs had given way until her bottom touched the cold, hard ground.

'Yes, if you want,' she murmured. Her hands shook as she hung up.

The last time she'd seen Sophie's rigid composure crumble had been in the few weeks after they'd buried their mother. For a while she'd had her sister back. They'd been united in their grief, supporting each other when their loss overwhelmed them.

As much as Eva missed *that* Sophie, she couldn't stomach having her back under similar circumstances. Nor could she bear the danger that her father faced.

She wasn't sure how long she sat there.

Cold seeped into her clothes. Into her bones. Into her heart.

Feeling numb, she dug into her bag and extracted the pre-nup and read through it one more time.

She couldn't honour Zaccheo's last clause, but that didn't mean she couldn't use it to buy herself, and her father, time until they met and she explained. Despite his own past, he wanted a family. Maybe he would understand why she was trying to salvage hers.

Slowly, she dialled. After endless rings, the line clicked through.

'Eva.' His voice was pure cold steel.

'I...' She attempted to say the words but her teeth still chattered. Squeezing her eyes shut, she tried again. 'I'll sign the agreement. I'll marry you tomorrow.'

Silence.

'Zaccheo? Are you there?'

'Where are you?'

She shivered at his impersonal tone. 'I'm...' She looked up at the street sign in the alley and told him.

'Romeo will be there in fifteen minutes. He'll witness the agreement and bring it to me. You'll return to the penthouse and resume preparations for the wedding.' He paused, as if waiting for her to disagree.

'Will I see you today?' She hated how weak her voice sounded.

'No.'

Eva exhaled. 'Okay, I'll wait for Romeo.'

'Bene.' The line went dead.

The grey mizzle outside aptly reflected Eva's mood as she sat, hands clasped in her lap, as the hairdresser finished putting up her hair. Behind her, Sophie smiled nervously.

Eva smiled back, knowing her sister's nervousness stemmed from the fear that Eva would change her mind again.

But this time there was no going back. She meant to come clean to Zaccheo at the first opportunity and open herself up to whatever consequences he sought.

Just how she would manage that was a puzzle she hadn't untangled yet, but since Zaccheo was hell-bent on this marriage, and she was giving him what he wanted, technically she was fulfilling her side of the bargain.

God, when had she resorted to seeing things in shades of grey instead of black and white, truth and lie? Was Zaccheo right? Did her Pennington blood mean she was destined to do whatever it took, even if it meant compromising her integrity, for the sake of her family and pedigree?

No. She wouldn't care if she woke up tomorrow as ordinary Eva Penn instead of Lady Pennington. And she *would* come clean to Zaccheo, no matter what.

Except that was looking less likely to happen *before* the wedding. Zaccheo hadn't returned to the penthouse last night. She hadn't deluded herself that he was observing the quaint marriage custom. If anything, he was probably making another billion, or actively sowing his last wild oats. She jerked at the jagged pain that shot through her.

Sophie stood up. 'What's wrong?'

'Nothing. How's Father?'

Sophie's face clouded. 'He insists he's well enough to walk you down the aisle.' Her sister's eyes darted to the hairdresser who had finished and was walking out to get Margaret. 'He's desperate that everything goes according to plan today.'

Eva managed to stop her smile from slipping. 'It will.'

Sophie met her gaze in the mirror. 'Do you think I should talk to Zaccheo…explain?'

Eva thought about the conversation she'd had with Zaccheo yesterday, the merciless tone, the ruthless man on a mission who'd been released from prison a mere week ago. 'Maybe not just yet.'

Sophie nodded, then flashed a smile that didn't quite make it before she left Eva alone as Margaret entered.

Any hopes of talking to Zaccheo evaporated when she found herself at the doors of the chapel an hour later.

Catching sight of him for the first time since Monday, she felt her heart slam around her chest.

Romeo stood in the best-man position and Eva wondered again at the connection between the two men. Did Zaccheo have any friends? Or had he lost all of them when her family's actions had altered his fate?

The thought flitted out of her head as her gaze returned almost magnetically to Zaccheo.

He'd eschewed a morning coat in favour of a bespoke three-piece suit in the softest dove-grey silk. Against the snowy white shirt and white tie completing the ensemble, his long hair was at once dangerously primitive and yet so utterly captivating, her mouth dried as her pulse danced with a dark, decadent delight. His beard had been trimmed considerably and a part of her mourned its loss. Perhaps it was that altered look that made his eyes so overwhelmingly electrifying, or it was the fact that his face was set in almost brutal lines, but the effect was like lightning to her system the moment her eyes connected with his.

The music in the great hall of the cathedral he'd astonishingly managed to secure on such short notice disappeared, along with the chatter of the goggle-eyed guests who did nothing to hide their avid curiosity.

All she could see was him, the man who would be her husband in less than fifteen minutes.

She stumbled, then stopped. A murmur rose in the crowd. Eva felt her father's concerned stare, but she couldn't look away from Zaccheo.

His nostrils flared, his eyes narrowing in warning as fear clutched her, freezing her feet.

'Eva?' Her father's ragged whisper caught her consciousness.

'Why did you insist on walking me down the aisle?' she asked him, wanting in some way to know that she wasn't

doing all of this to save a man who had very little regard
for her.

'What? Because you're my daughter,' her father replied
with a puzzled frown.

'So you're not doing it just to keep up appearances?'

His face creased with a trace of the vulnerability she'd
glimpsed only once before, when her mother died, and her
heart lurched. 'Eva, I haven't handled things well. I know
that. I was brought up to put the family name above all else,
and I took that responsibility a little too far. Despite our less
than perfect marriage, your mother was the one who would
pull me back to my senses when I went a little too far. Without her…' His voice roughened and his hand gripped hers.
'We might lose Penningtons, but I don't want to lose you
and Sophie.'

Eva's throat clogged. 'Maybe you should tell her that? She
needs to know you're proud of her, Father.'

Her father looked to where her sister stood, and he nodded. 'I will. And I'm proud of you, too. You're as beautiful
as your mother was on our wedding day.'

Eva blinked back her tears as murmurs rose in the crowd.

She turned to find Zaccheo staring at her. Something
dark, sinister, curled through his eyes and she swallowed as
his mouth flattened.

*I can't marry him without him knowing! He deserves to
know that I can't give him the family he wants.*

'My dear, you need to move now. It's time,' her father
pleaded.

Torn by the need for Zaccheo to know the truth and the
need to protect her father, she shook her head, her insides
churning.

Churning turned into full-blown liquefying as Zaccheo
stepped from the dais, his imposing body threatening to
block out the light as he headed down the aisle.

She desperately sucked in a breath, the knowledge that
Zaccheo would march her up the aisle himself if need be fi-

nally scraping her feet from the floor. He stopped halfway, his gaze unswerving, until she reached him.

He grasped her hand, his hold unbreakable as he turned and walked her to the altar.

Trembling at the hard, pitiless look in his eyes, she swallowed and tried to speak. 'Zaccheo—'

'No, Eva. No more excuses,' he growled.

The priest glanced between them, his expression benign but enquiring.

Zaccheo nodded.

The organ swelled. And sealed her fate.

CHAPTER ELEVEN

'GLARING AT IT won't make it disappear, unless you have superhero laser vision.'

Eva jumped at the mocking voice and curled her fingers into her lap, hiding the exquisite diamond-studded platinum ring that had joined her engagement ring three hours ago.

'I wasn't willing it away.' On the contrary, she'd been wondering how long it would stay on her finger once Zaccheo knew the truth.

The reception following the ceremony had been brief but intense. Six hundred people clamouring for attention and the chance to gawp at the intriguing couple could take a lot out of a girl. With Zaccheo's fingers laced through hers the whole time, tightening commandingly each time she so much as moved an inch away from him, Eva had been near-blubbering-wreck status by the time their limo had left the hall.

Once she'd stopped reeling from the shock of being married to Zaccheo Giordano, she'd taken a moment to take in her surroundings. The Great Hall in the Guildhall was usually booked for years in advance. That Zaccheo had managed to secure it in a week and thrown together a stunning reception was again testament that she'd married a man with enough power and clout to smash through any resistance.

Zaccheo, despite his spell in prison, remained a formidable man, one, she suspected, who didn't need her father's intervention to restore his damaged reputation. So why was he pursuing it so relentlessly? Throughout the reception, she'd watched him charm their guests with the sheer force of his charisma. By the time her father had got round to giving the edifying toast welcoming Zaccheo to the Pennington family, the effort had seemed redundant.

She watched Zaccheo now as the car raced them to the airport, and wondered if it was a good time to broach the subject burning a hole in her chest.

'Something on your mind?' he queried without raising his gaze from his tablet.

Her heart leapt into her throat. She started to speak but noticed the partition between them and Romeo, who sat in the front passenger seat, was open. Although she was sure Romeo knew the ins and outs of the document he'd been asked to witness yesterday, Eva wasn't prepared to discuss her devastating shortcomings in his presence.

So she opted for something else plaguing her. She smoothed her hands on her wedding dress. 'Do I have your assurance that you'll speak on my father's behalf once you hand over the documents to the authorities?'

He speared her with incisive grey eyes. 'You're so eager to see him let off the hook, aren't you?'

'Wouldn't you be, if it was your father?' she asked.

Eva was unprepared for the strange look that crossed his face. The mixture of anger, sadness, and bitterness hollowed out her stomach.

'My father wasn't interested in being let off the hook for his sins. He was happy to keep himself indebted to his betters because he thought that was his destiny.'

Her breath caught. 'What? That doesn't make sense.'

'Very little of my father's actions made sense to me, not when I was a child, and not as an adult.'

The unexpected insight into his life made her probe deeper. 'When did he die?'

'When I was thirteen years old.'

'I'm sorry.' When he inclined his head and continued to stare at her, she pressed her luck. 'How did he—?'

'Zaccheo,' Romeo's deep voice interrupted them. 'Perhaps this is not a subject for your wedding day?'

A look passed between the friends.

When Zaccheo looked at her again, that cool impassivity he'd worn since they'd left the reception to thunderous applause had returned.

'Your father has done his part adequately for now. Our lawyers will meet in a few days to discuss the best way forward. When my input is needed, I'll provide it. *Your* role, on the other hand, is just beginning.'

Before she could reply, the door opened. Eva gaped at the large private jet standing mere feet away. Beside the steps, two pilots and two stewardesses waited.

Zaccheo exited and took her hand. The shocking electricity of his touch and the awareness in his eyes had her scrambling to release her fingers, but he held on, and walked her to his crew, who extended their congratulations.

Eva was grappling with their conversation when she stepped into the unspeakable luxury of the plane. To the right, a sunken entertainment area held a semicircular cream sofa and a separate set of club chairs with enough gadgets to keep even the most attention-deficient passenger happy. In a separate area a short flight of stairs away, there was a conference table with four chairs and a bar area off a top-line galley.

Zaccheo stepped behind her and her body zapped to life, thrilling to his proximity. She suppressed a shiver when he let go of her fingers and cupped her shoulders in his warm hands.

'I have several conference calls to make once we take off. And you...' He paused, traced a thumb across her cheek. The contact stunned her, as did the gentle look in his eyes. 'You look worn out.'

'Is that a kind way of saying I look like hell?' She strove for a light tone and got a husky one instead.

That half-smile appeared, and Eva experienced something close to elation that the icy look had melted from his face. 'You could never look like hell, *cara*. A prickly and challenging puzzle that I look forward to unravelling, most definitely. But never like hell.'

The unexpected response startled her into gaping for several seconds before she recovered. 'Should I be wary that you're being nice to me?'

'I can be less…monstrous when I get my way.'

The reminder that he wouldn't be getting his way and the thought of his reaction once he found out brought a spike of anxiety, rendering her silent as he led her to a seat and handed her a flute of champagne from the stewardess's tray.

'Zaccheo…' She stopped when his thumb moved over her lips. Sensation sizzled along her nerve endings, setting her pulse racing as he brushed it back and forth. The heat erupting between her thighs had her pressing her legs together to soothe the desperate ache.

She hardly felt the plane take off. All she was aware of was the mesmerising look in Zaccheo's eyes.

'I haven't told you how stunning you look.' He leaned closer and replaced his thumb with his lips at the corner of her mouth.

Delicious flames warmed her blood. 'Thank you.' Her voice shook with the desire moving through her. More than anything, she was filled with the blind need to turn her head and meet his mouth with hers.

When his lips trailed to her jaw, then to the curve between her shoulder and neck, Eva let out a helpless moan, her heart racing with sudden, debilitating hunger.

His fingers linked hers and she found herself being led to the back of the plane. Eva couldn't summon a protest. Nor could she remind herself that she needed to come clean, sooner rather than later.

The master bedroom was equally stunning. Gold leaf threaded a thick cream coverlet on a king-sized bed and plush carpeting absorbed their footsteps as he shut the door.

'I intend us to have two uninterrupted weeks on the island. In order for that to happen, I need to work with Romeo to clear my plate work-wise. Rest now. Whatever's on your mind can wait for a few more hours.' Again there was no bite to his words, leaving her lost as to this new side of the man she'd married.

She stood, almost overpowered by the strength of her emotions, as he positioned himself behind her and slowly undid her buttons. The heavy dress pooled at her feet and she stood in only her white strapless bra, panties, and the garter and sheer stocking set that had accompanied her dress.

A rough, tortured sound echoed around the room. '*Stai mozzafiato,*' Zaccheo muttered thickly. 'You're breathtaking,' he translated when she glanced at him.

A fierce blush flared up. Eyes darkening, he circled her, tracing her high colour with a barest tip of his forefinger. Her gaze dropped to the sensual line of his mouth and she bit her own lip as need drowned her.

She gasped, completely enthralled, as he dropped to his knees and reached for her garter belt, eyes locked on hers. He pulled it off and tucked it deep in his inner pocket. When he stood, the hunger on his face stopped her breath, anticipation sparking like fireworks through her veins.

He lightly brushed her lips with his.

'Our first time won't be on a plane within listening distance of my staff.' He walked to the bed and pulled back the covers. He waited until she got in and tucked her in. About to walk away, he suddenly stopped. 'We will make this marriage work, Eva.'

Her mouth parted but, with no words to counter that unexpected vow, she slowly pressed her lips together as pain ripped through her.

'Sleep well, *dolcezza,*' he murmured, then left.

Despite her turmoil, she slept through the whole flight, rousing refreshed if unsettled as to what the future held.

Dressing in a light cotton sundress and open sandals, she left her hair loose, applied a touch of lip gloss and sunscreen and exited the plane.

They transferred from jet to high-speed boat with Romeo at the wheel. The noise from the engine made conversation impossible but, for the first time, the silence between Zaccheo and Eva felt less fraught. The strange but intense feeling that had engulfed them both as he'd undressed her on the plane continued to grip them as they raced towards their final destination. When she caught her hair for the umpteenth time to keep it from flying in the wind, he captured the strands in a tight grip at the base of her neck, then used the hold to pull her closer until she curved into his side. With his other arm sprawled along the back of their seat, he appeared the most at ease Eva had ever seen him.

Perhaps being forced to wait for a while to tell him hadn't been a bad thing.

She let the tension ooze out of her.

Despite the shades covering his eyes, he must have sensed her scrutiny, because he turned and stared down at her for endless minutes. She felt the power of that look to the tips of her toes and almost fell into him when he took her mouth in a voracious kiss.

He let her up for air when her lungs threatened to burst. Burying his face in her throat, he rasped for her ears only, 'I cannot wait to make you mine.'

By the time the boat slowed and pulled into a quiet inlet, Eva was a nervous wreck.

'Welcome to Casa do Paraíso,' he said once the engine died.

Enthralled, Eva looked around. Tropical trees and lush vegetation surrounded a spectacular hacienda made of timber and glass, the mid-morning sun casting vibrant shades of green, orange and blue on the breathtaking surroundings. Wide glass windows dominated the structure and, through them, Eva saw white walls and white furniture with splashes of colourful paintings on the walls perpetuated in an endless flow of rooms.

'It's huge,' she blurted.

Zaccheo jumped onto the sugary sand and grabbed her hand.

'The previous owner built it for his first wife and their eight children. She got it in the divorce, but hated the tropical heat so never visited. It was run-down by the time I bought the island from her, so I made substantial alterations.'

The mention of children ramped up the tension crawling through her belly and, despite her trying to shrug the feeling away, it lingered as she followed him up the wide front porch into the stunning living room.

A staff of four greeted them, then hurried out to where Romeo was securing the vessel. She gazed around in stunned awe, accepting that Zaccheo commanded the best when it came to the structures he put his stamp on, whether commercial or private.

'Come here, Eva.' The order was impatient.

She turned from admiring the structure to admire the man who'd created it. Tall, proud and intensely captivating, he stood at the base of a suspended staircase, his white-hot gaze gleaming dangerously, promising complete sexual oblivion.

Desire pulsed between them, a living thing that writhed, consumed with a hunger that demanded to be met, fulfilled.

Eva knew she should make time now they were here to tell him. Lay down the truth ticking away inside her like a bomb.

After years of struggling to forge a relationship with her father and sister, she'd finally laid the foundations of one today.

How could she live with herself if she continued to keep Zaccheo in the dark about the family he hoped for himself?

Her feet slapped against the large square tiles as she hurried across the room. His mouth lifted in a half-smile of satisfaction. She'd barely reached him when he swung her into his arms and stormed up the stairs.

And then the need to disclose her secret was suddenly no longer urgent. It'd been superseded by another, more pressing demand. One that every atom in her body urged her to assuage. *Now.* Before the opportunity was taken from her. Before her confession once again found her in the brutal wasteland of rejection.

His heat singed where they touched. Unable to resist, she sank her fingers into his hair and buried her face in his neck, eager to be closer to his rough primitiveness.

Feeling bold, she nipped at his skin.

His responding growl was intoxicating. As was the feeling of being pressed against the hard, masculine planes of his body when he slowly lowered her to her feet.

'I've waited so long to be inside you. I won't wait any longer,' he vowed, the words fierce, stamped with decadent intent.

Arms clamped around her waist, he walked her backwards to the vast white-sheeted bed. In one clean move, he pulled her dress over her head and dropped it. Her bra and panties swiftly followed.

Zaccheo stopped breathing as he stared down at her exposed curves.

As he'd done on the plane, he circled her body, this time trailing more fingers over her heated skin, creating a fiery path that arrowed straight between her thighs. She was swaying under the dizzying force of her arousal by the time he faced her again.

'Beautiful. So beautiful,' he murmured against her skin, then pulled her nipple into his mouth, surrounding the aching bud with heat and want.

Eva cried out and clutched his shoulders, her whole body gripped with a fever that shook her from head to toe. He moved his attention to her twin breast while his fingers teased the other, doubling the pleasure, doubling her agony.

'Zaccheo,' she groaned.

He straightened abruptly and reefed his black T-shirt over his head, exposing hard, smooth pecs and a muscle-ridged stomach. But as intensely delectable as his torso was, it wasn't what made her belly quiver. It was the intriguing tattooed band of Celtic knots linked by three slim lines that circled his upper arm. The artwork was flawless and beautiful, flowing gracefully when he moved. Reaching out, she touched the first knot. He paused and stared down at her.

It struck her hard in that moment just how much she didn't know about the man she'd married.

'You seem almost nervous, *dolcezza*.'

Eva struggled to think of a response that wouldn't make her sound gauche. 'Don't you feel nervous, even a little, your first time with a new lover?' she replied.

He froze and his lips compressed for a fraction of a second, as if she'd said something to displease him. Then his fingers went to his belt. 'Nerves, no. Anticipation that a long-held desire is about to be fulfilled? Most definitely.' He removed his remaining clothes in one swift move.

Perfection. It was the only word she could think of.

'Even when you've experienced it more than a few dozen times?'

She gasped when his fingers gripped hers in a tight hold. When he spoke, his voice held a bite that jarred. 'Perhaps we should refrain from the subject of past lovers.'

Hard, demanding lips slanted over hers, his tongue sliding into her mouth, fracturing the last of her senses. She clung to him, her body once again aflame from the ferocious power of his.

Cool sheets met her back and Zaccheo sprawled beside her. After an eternity of kissing, he raised his head.

'There are so many ways I wish to take you I don't know where to begin.'

Heat burst beneath her skin and he laughed softly.

'You blush with the ease of an innocent.' He trailed his hand down her throat, lingering at her racing pulse, before it curved around one breast. 'It's almost enough to make me forget that you're not.' Again that bite, but less ferocious this time, his accent growing thicker as he bent his head and tongued her pulse.

She jerked against him, her fingers gliding over his warm skin of their own accord. 'On what basis do you form the opinion that I'm not?' she blurted before she lost her nerve.

He stilled, grey eyes turning that rare gunmetal shade that announced a dangerously heightened emotional state. His hand abandoned her breast and curled around her nape in an iron grip. 'What are you saying, Eva?' His voice was a hoarse rumble.

She licked nervous lips. 'That I don't want to be treated like I'm fragile…but I don't wish my first time to be without mercy either.'

He sucked in a stunned breath. 'Your *first*… *Madre di Dio*.' His gaze searched hers, his breathing growing increasingly erratic.

Slowly, he drew back from her, scouring her body from head to toe as if seeing her for the first time. He parted her thighs and she moved restlessly, helplessly, as his eyes lingered at her centre. Stilling her with one hand, he lowered his head and kissed her eyes, her mouth, her throat. Then lower until he reached her belly. He licked at her navel, then rained kisses on her quivering skin. Firm hands held her open, then his shoulders took over the job. Reading his intention, she raised her head from the pillow.

'Zaccheo.' She wasn't sure whether she was pleading for or rejecting what was coming.

He reared up for a second, his hands going to his hair to twist the long strands into an expert knot at the back of his head. The act was so unbelievably hot, her body threatened to melt into a useless puddle. Then he was back, broad shoulders easily holding her legs apart as he kissed his way down her inner thighs.

'I know what I crave most,' he muttered thickly. 'A taste of you.'

The first touch of his mouth at her core elicited a long, helpless groan from her. Her spine arched off the bed, her thighs shaking as fire roared through her body. He held her down and feasted on her, the varying friction from his mouth and beard adding an almost unholy pleasure that sent her soaring until a scream ripped from her throat and she fell off the edge of the universe.

She surfaced to feel his mouth on her belly, his hands trailing up her sides. That gunmetal shade of grey reflected deep possession as he rose above her and kissed her long and deep.

'Now, *il mio angelo*. Now I make you mine.'

He captured her hands above her head with one hand. The other reached between her thighs, gently massaging her core before he slid one finger inside her tight sheath. His groan echoed hers. Removing his finger, he probed her sex with his thick shaft, murmuring soft, soothing words as he pushed himself inside her.

'Easy, *dolcezza*.'

Another inch increased the burn, but the hunger rushing through her wouldn't be denied. Her fingers dug into his back, making him growl. 'Zaccheo, please.'

'*Sì*, let me please you.' He uttered a word that sounded like an apology, a plea.

Then he pushed inside her. The dart of pain engulfed her, lingered for a moment. Tears filled her eyes. Zaccheo cursed, then kissed them away, murmuring softly in Italian.

He thrust deeper, slowly filling her. Eva saw the strain etched on his face.

'Zaccheo?'

'I want this to be perfect for you.'

'It won't be unless you move, I suspect.'

That half-smile twitched, then stretched into a full, heart-stopping smile. Eva's eyes widened at the giddy dance her heart performed on seeing the wave of pleasure transform his face. Her own mouth curved in response and a feeling unfurled inside her, stealing her breath with its awesome power. Shakily, she raised her hand and touched his face, slid her fingers over his sensual mouth.

He moved. Withdrew and thrust again.

She gasped, her body caught in a maelstrom of sensation so turbulent, she feared she wouldn't emerge whole.

Slowly his smile disappeared, replaced by a wild, predatory hunger. He quickened the pace and her hands moved to his hair, slipping the knot free and burying her fingers in the thick, luxurious tresses. When her hips moved of their own accord, meeting him in an instinctive dance, he groaned deep and sucked one nipple into his mouth. Drowning in sensation, she felt her world begin to crumble. The moment he captured her twin nipple, a deep tremor started inside her. It built and built, then exploded in a shower of lights.

'Perfetto.'

Zaccheo sank his fingers into Eva's wild, silky hair, curbing the desire to let loose the primitive roar bubbling within him.

Mine. Finally, completely mine.

Instead he held her close until her breathing started to return to normal, then he flipped their positions and arranged her on top of him.

He was hard to the point of bursting, but he was determined to make this experience unforgettable for her. Seeing his ring on her finger, that primitive response rose again, stunning him with the strength of his desire to claim her.

His words on the plane slashed through his mind.

Sì, he *did* want this to work. Perhaps Eva had been right. Perhaps there was still time to salvage a piece of his soul...

Her eyes met his and a sensual smile curled her luscious mouth. Before he could instruct her, she moved, taking him deeper inside her before she rose. Knowing he was fast losing the ability to think, he met her second thrust. Her eyes widened, her skin flushing that alluring shade of pink as she chased the heady sensation. Within minutes, they were both panting.

Reaching down, he teased her with his thumb and watched

her erupt in bliss. Zaccheo followed her, his shout announcing the most ferocious release he'd experienced in his life.

Long after Eva had collapsed on top of him, and slipped into an exhausted sleep, he lay awake.

Wondering why his world hadn't righted itself.

Wondering what the hell this meant for him.

CHAPTER TWELVE

EVA CAME AWAKE to find herself splayed on top of Zaccheo's body.

The sun remained high in the sky so she knew she hadn't slept for more than an hour or two. Nevertheless, the thought that she'd dropped into a coma straight after sex made her cringe.

She risked a glance and found grey eyes examining her with that half-smile she was growing to like a little more than she deemed wise.

He brushed a curl from her cheek and tucked it behind her ear. The gentleness in the act fractured her breathing.

'Ciao, dolcezza.'

'I didn't mean to fall asleep on you,' she said, then immediately felt gauche for not knowing the right after-sex etiquette.

He quirked a brow. 'Oh? Who did you mean to fall asleep on?' he asked.

She jerked up. 'No, that's not what I meant...' she started to protest, then stopped when she saw the teasing light in his eyes.

She started to settle back down, caught a glimpse of his chiselled pecs and immediately heat built inside her. A little wary of how quickly she was growing addicted to his body, she attempted to slide off him.

He stopped her with one hand at her nape, the other on her hip. The action flexed his arm and Eva's gaze was drawn to the tattoo banding his upper arm.

'Does this have a special meaning?'

His smile grew a little stiffer. 'It's a reminder not to accept less than I'm worth or compromise on what's important to me. And a reminder that, contrary to what the privileged would have us believe, all men are born equal. It's power that is wielded unequally.'

Eva thought of the circumstances that had brought her to this place, of the failings of her own family and the sadness she'd carried for so long, but now hoped to let go of.

'You wield more than enough share of power. Men cower before you.'

A frown twitched his forehead. 'If they do, it is their weakness, not mine.'

She gave an incredulous laugh. 'Are you saying you don't know you intimidate people with just a glance?'

His frown cleared. 'You're immune to this intimidation you speak of. To my memory, you've been disagreeable more often than not.'

She traced the outline of the tattoo, revelling in the smooth warmth of his skin. 'I've never been good at heeding bellowed commands.'

The hand on her hip tightened. 'I do not bellow.'

'Maybe not. But sometimes the effect is the same.'

She found herself flipped over onto her back, Zaccheo crouched over her like a lethal bird of prey. 'Is that why you hesitated as you walked down the aisle?' he asked in a harsh whisper. The look in his eyes was one of almost…hurt.

Quickly she shook her head. 'No, it wasn't.'

'Then what was it? You thought that I wasn't good enough, perhaps?' he pressed. And again she glimpsed a hint of vulnerability in his eyes that caught at a weak place in her heart.

She opened her mouth to *finally* tell him. To lay herself bare to the scathing rejection that would surely follow her confession.

The words stuck in her throat.

What she'd experienced in Zaccheo's bed had given her a taste that was unlike anything she'd ever felt before. The need to hold on to that for just a little while longer slammed into her, knocking aside her good intentions.

Eva knew she was playing with volcanic fire, that the eventual eruption would be devastating. But for once in her life, she wanted to be selfish, to experience a few moments of unfettered abandon. She could have that.

She'd sacrificed herself for this marriage, but in doing so she'd also been handed a say in when it ended.

And it would be sooner rather than later, because she couldn't stand in the way of what he wanted...what he'd been deprived of his whole life...a proper family of his own.

She also knew Zaccheo would want nothing to do with her once he knew the truth. Sure, he wasn't as monstrous as he would have others believe, but that didn't mean he would shackle himself to a wife who couldn't give him what he wanted.

She squashed the voice that cautioned she was naively burying her head in the sand.

Was it really so wrong if she chose to do it just for a little while?

Could she not live in bliss for a few days? Gather whatever memories she could and hang on to them for when the going got tough?

'Eva?'

'I had a father-daughter moment, plus bridal nerves,' she blurted. He raised a sceptical eyebrow and she smiled. 'Every woman is entitled to have a moment. Mine was thirty seconds of hesitation.'

'You remained frozen for five *minutes*,' he countered.

'Just time enough for anyone who'd been dozing off to wake up,' she responded, wide-eyed.

The tension slowly eased out of his body and his crooked smile returned. Relief poured through her and she fell into the punishing kiss he delivered to assert his displeasure at her hesitation.

She was clinging to him by the time he pulled away, and Eva was ready to protest when he swung out of bed. Her protest died when she got her first glimpse of his impressive manhood, and the full effect of the man attached to it.

Dry-mouthed and heart racing, she stared. And curled her fingers into the sheets to keep from reaching for him.

'If you keep looking at me like that, our shower will have to be postponed. And our lunch will go cold.'

A blush stormed up her face.

He laughed and scooped her up. 'But I'm glad that my body is not displeasing to you.'

She rolled her eyes. *As if.* 'False humility isn't an attractive trait, Zaccheo,' she chided as he walked them through a wide door and onto an outdoor bamboo-floored shower. Despite the rustic effects, the amenities were of the highest quality, an extra-wide marble bath sitting opposite a multi-jet shower, with a shelf holding rows upon rows of luxury bath oils and gels.

Above their heads, a group of macaws warbled throatily, then flew from one tree to the next, their stunning colours streaking through the branches.

As tropical paradises went, Eva was already sure this couldn't be topped, and she had yet to see the rest of it.

Zaccheo set her down and grabbed a soft washcloth. 'Complete compatibility in bed isn't a common thing, despite what magazines would have you believe,' he said.

'I wouldn't know.' There was no point pretending otherwise. He had first-hand knowledge of her innocence.

His eyes flared with possession as he turned on the jets and pulled her close.

'No, you wouldn't. And if that knowledge pleases me to the point of being labelled a caveman, then so be it.'

They ate a sumptuous lunch of locally caught fish served with pine-nut sauce and avocado salad followed by a serving of fruit and cheeses.

After lunch, Zaccheo showed her the rest of the house and the three-square-kilometre island. They finished the trek on the white sandy beach where a picnic had been laid out with champagne chilling in a silver bucket.

Eva popped a piece of papaya in her mouth and sighed at the beauty of the setting sun casting orange and purple streaks across the aquamarine water. 'I don't know how you can ever bear to leave this place.'

'I learned not to grow attached to things at an early age.'

The crisp reply had her glancing over at him. His shades were back in place so she couldn't read his eyes, but his body showed no signs of the usual forbidding *do not disturb* signs so she braved the question. 'Why?'

'Because it was better that way.'

She toyed with the stem of her champagne flute. 'But it's also a lonely existence.'

Broad shoulders lifted in an easy shrug. 'I had a choice of being lonely or just…solitary. I chose the latter.'

Her heart lurched at the deliberate absence of emotion from his voice. 'Zaccheo—'

He reared up from where he'd been lounging on his elbows, his mouth set in a grim line. 'Don't waste your time feeling sorry for me, *dolcezza*,' he said, his voice a hard snap that would've intimidated her, had she allowed it.

'I wasn't,' she replied. 'I'm not naive enough to imagine everyone has a rosy childhood. I know I didn't.'

'You mean the exclusive country-club memberships, the top boarding schools, the winters in Verbier weren't enough?' Despite the lack of contempt in his voice this time round, Eva felt sad that they were back in this place again.

'Don't twist my words. Those were just *things*, Zaccheo. And before you accuse me of being privileged, yes, I was. My childhood was hard, too, but I couldn't help the family I was born into any more than you could.'

'Was that why you moved out of Pennington Manor?'

'After my mother died, yes. Two against one became unbearable.'

'And the father-daughter moment you spoke of? Did that help?' he asked, watching her with a probing look.

A tiny bit of hope blossomed. 'Time will tell, I guess. Will you try the same with your mother and stepfather?'

'No. My mother didn't think I was worth anything. My stepfather agreed.'

Her heart twisted. 'Yet you've achieved success beyond most people's wildest dreams. Surely the lessons of your childhood should make you proud of who you are now, despite hating some aspects of your upbringing?'

'I detested all of mine,' he said with harsh finality. 'I wouldn't wish it on my worst enemy.'

The savage edge of pain in his voice made her shiver. She opened her mouth to ask him, but he surged to his feet.

'I don't wish to dwell in the past.' That half-smile flashed on and off. 'Not when I have a sunset as stunning as this and a wife to rival its beauty.' He plucked the glass from her hand and pulled her up.

Tucking her head beneath his chin, he enfolded her in his arms, one around her waist and the other across her shoulders. Eva knew it was a signal to drop the subject, but she couldn't let it go. Not just yet.

She removed his shades and stared into his slate-coloured eyes. 'For what it's worth, I gave away my country-club membership to my best friend, I hated boarding school, and I couldn't ski to save my life so I didn't even try after I turned ten. I didn't care about my pedigree, or who I was seen with. Singing and a family who cared for me were the only things that mattered. One helped me get through the other. So, you see, sometimes the grass *may* look greener on the other side, but most of the time it's just a trick of the light.'

Several emotions shifted within his eyes. Surprise. Shock. A hint of confusion. Then the deep arrogance of Zaccheo Giordano slid back into place.

'The sunset, *dolcezza*,' he said gruffly. 'You're missing it.'

* * *

The feeling of his world tilting out of control was escalating. And it spun harder out of sync the more he fought it.

Zaccheo had been certain he knew what drove Eva and her family. He'd been sure it was the same greed for power and prestige that had sent his father to a vicious and premature death. It was what had made his mother abandon her homeland to seek a rich husband, turn herself inside out for a man who looked down his nose at her son and ultimately made Clara Giordano pack her bags and move to the other side of the world.

But right from the start Eva had challenged him, forced him to confront his long-held beliefs. He hadn't needed to, of course. Oscar Pennington's actions had proven him right. Eva's own willingness to marry Fairfield for the sake of her family had cemented Zaccheo's belief.

And didn't you do the same thing?

He stared unseeing at the vivid orange horizon, his thoughts in turmoil.

He couldn't deny that the discovery of her innocence in bed had thrown him for a loop. Unsettled him in a way he hadn't been for a long time.

For as long as he could remember, his goal had been a fixed, tangible certainty. To place himself in a position where he erased any hint of neediness from his life, while delivering an abject lesson to those who thought themselves entitled and therefore could treat him as if he were common. A spineless fool who would prostrate himself for scraps from the high table.

He'd proven conclusively yesterday at his wedding reception that he'd succeeded beyond his wildest dreams. He'd watched blue-blooded aristocrats fall over themselves to win his favour.

And yet he'd found himself unsatisfied. Left with a hollow, bewildering feeling inside, as if he'd finally grasped the brass ring, only to find it was made of plastic.

It had left Zaccheo with the bitter introspection of whether a different, deeper goal lay behind the burning need to prove himself above the petty grasp for power and prestige.

The loneliness he'd so offhandedly dismissed had in fact eaten away at him far more effectively than his mother's rejection and the callous disregard his father had afforded him when he was alive.

Impatiently, he dismissed his jumbled feelings. He didn't do *feelings*. He *achieved*. He *bested*. And he *triumphed*.

One miscalculation didn't mean a setback. Finding out Eva had had no previous lovers had granted him an almost primitive satisfaction he wasn't going to bother to deny.

And if something came of this union sooner rather than later... His heart kicked hard.

Sliding a hand through her silky hair, he angled her face to his. Her beauty was undeniable. But he wouldn't be risking any more heart-to-hearts. She was getting too close, sliding under his skin to a place he preferred to keep out of bounds. A place he'd only examined when the cold damp of his prison cell had eroded his guard.

He was free, both physically and in guilt. He wouldn't return to that place. And he wouldn't allow her to probe further. Satisfied with his resolution, he kissed her sexy, tempting mouth until the need to breathe forced him to stop.

The sun had disappeared. Lights strung through the trees flickered on and he nodded to the member of staff who hovered nearby, ready to pack up their picnic.

He caught the glazed, flushed look on his wife's face and came to a sudden, extremely pleasing decision.

'Tonight, *il mio angelo*, we'll have an early night.'

The first week flew by in a dizzy haze of sun, sea, exquisite food, and making love. Lots and lots of making love.

Zaccheo was a fierce and demanding lover, but he gave so much more in return. And Eva was so greedy for everything he had to give, she wondered whether she was turning into a sex addict. She'd certainly acted like one this morning, when she'd initiated sex while Zaccheo had been barely awake. That her initiative had seemed to please him had been beside the point.

She'd examined her behaviour afterwards when Zaccheo had been summoned to an urgent phone call by Romeo.

This was supposed to be a moment out of time, a brief dalliance, which would end the moment she spilled her secret to him. And yet with each surrender of her body, she slid down a steeper slope, one she suspected would be difficult to climb back up. Because it turned out that, for her, sex wasn't a simple exchange of physical pleasure. With each act, she handed over a piece of herself to him that she feared she'd never reclaim.

And that more than anything made her fear for herself when this was over.

A breeze blew through an open window and Eva clutched the thin sarong she'd thrown over her bikini. Dark clouds were forming ominously over the island. Shivering, she watched the storm gather, wondering if it was a premonition for her own situation.

Lightning flashed, and she jumped.

'Don't worry, Mrs Eva.' Zaccheo's housekeeper smiled as she entered and turned on table lamps around the living room. 'The storm passes very quickly. The sun will be back out in no time.'

Eva smiled and nodded, but she couldn't shake the feeling that *her* storm wouldn't pass so quickly.

As intense rain pounded the roof she went in search of Zaccheo. Not finding him in his study, she climbed the stairs, her pulse already racing in anticipation as she went down the hallway.

She entered their dressing room and froze.

'What are you doing?' she blurted.

'I would've thought it was obvious, *dolcezza*.' He held clippers inches from his face.

'I can see what you're doing but...*why*?' she snapped. 'You already got rid of most of it for the wedding.' Her voice was clipped, a feeling she couldn't decipher moving through her.

Zaccheo raised an eyebrow, amusement mingled with something else as he watched her. 'I take it this look works for you?'

She swallowed twice before she could speak. When she finally deciphered the feeling coursing through her, she was so shocked and so afraid he would read her feelings, she glanced over his head.

'Yes. I prefer it,' she replied.

For several seconds he didn't speak. Her skin burned at his compelling stare. Schooling her features, she glanced into his eyes.

'Then it will remain untouched.' He set the clippers down and faced her.

Neither of them moved for several minutes. The storm raged outside, beating against the windows and causing the timber to creak.

'Come here, Eva.' Softly spoken, but a command nonetheless.

'I'm beginning to think those are your three favourite words.'

'They are only when you comply.'

She rolled her eyes, but moved towards him. He swivelled in his chair and pulled her closer, parting his thighs to situate her between them.

'Was that very hard to admit?' he rasped.

Her skin grew tight, awareness that she stood on a precipice whose depths she couldn't quite fathom shivering over her. 'No.'

He laughed. 'You're a pathetic liar. But I appreciate you finding the courage to ask for what you want.'

'An insult and a compliment?' she said lightly.

'I wouldn't want you to think me soft.' He caught her hands and placed them on his shoulders. 'You realise that

I'll require a reward for keeping myself this way for your pleasure?'

The way he mouthed *pleasure* made hot need sting between her thighs. Several weeks ago, she would've fought it. But Eva was fast learning it was no use. Her body was his slave to command as and when he wished. 'You got your stylists to prod and primp me into the image you wanted. I've earned the right to do the same to you.' Her fingers curled into the hair she would've wept to see shorn.

He smiled and relaxed in the chair. 'I thought being primped and plucked to perfection was every woman's wish?'

'You thought wrong. I was happy with the way I looked before.'

That wasn't exactly true. Although she'd loved her thick and wild hair, she had to admit it was much easier to tend now the wildness had been tamed a little. And she loved that she could brush the tresses without giving herself a headache. As for the luxurious body creams she'd been provided with, she marvelled at how soft and silky her skin felt now compared to before.

But she kept all of it to herself as he untied the knot in her sarong and let it fall away. 'You were perfect before. You're perfect now. And mine,' he breathed.

Within seconds, Eva was naked and craving what only he could give her, her eventual screams as loud as the storm raging outside.

CHAPTER THIRTEEN

'COME ON, we're taking the boat out today. As much as I'd like to keep you to myself, I think we need to see something of Rio before we leave tomorrow.'

Eva stopped tweaking the chorus of the melody she'd been composing and looked up as Zaccheo entered the living room.

The perverse hope that he would grow less breathtaking with each day was hopelessly thwarted. Dressed in khaki linen trousers and a tight white T-shirt with his hair loose around his shoulders, Zaccheo was so visually captivating, she felt the punch to her system each time she stared at him.

He noticed her staring and raised an eyebrow. Blushing, she averted her gaze to her tablet.

'Where are we going?' She tried for a light tone and breathed an inward sigh of relief when she succeeded.

'To Ilha São Gabriel, three islands away. It's a tourist hotspot, but there are some interesting sights to see there.' He crouched before her, his gaze going to the tablet. Reaching out, he scrolled through her compositions, his eyes widening at the three dozen songs contained in the file.

'You wrote all these?' he asked.

She nodded, feeling self-conscious as he paused at a particularly soul-baring ballad about unrequited love and rejection. She'd written that one a week after Zaccheo had gone to prison. 'I've been composing since I was sixteen.'

His eyes narrowed on her face. 'You've had two million pounds in your bank account for over a year and a half, which I'm guessing is your shareholder dividend from your father's deal on my building?'

Warily, she nodded.

'That would've been more than enough money to pursue your music career without needing to work. So why didn't you use it?' he queried.

She tried to shrug the question away, but he caught her chin in his hand. 'Tell me,' he said.

'I suspected deep down that the deal was tainted. I hated doubting my father's integrity, but I could never bring myself to use the money. It didn't feel right.' Being proved right had brought nothing but hurt.

He watched her for a long time, a puzzled look on his face before he finally nodded. 'How was your session with Ziggy Preston?' he asked.

She saw nothing of the sour expression he'd sported that night in the club. 'Surprisingly good, considering I'd thought he'd have me on the blacklist of every music producer after your behaviour.'

An arrogant smile stretched his lips. 'They'd have had to answer to me had they chosen that unfortunate path. You're seeing him again?'

She nodded. 'When we get back.'

'Bene.' He rose and held out his hand.

She slipped her feet into one of the many stylish sandals now gracing her wardrobe and he led her outside to the jetty.

Climbing on board, he placed her in front of the wheel and stood behind her. She looked around, expecting Zaccheo's right-hand man to be travelling with them. 'Isn't Romeo coming?'

'He had business to take care of in Rio. He'll meet us there.'

The trip took twenty-five minutes, and Eva understood why the Ilha São Gabriel was so popular when she saw it. The island held a mountain, on top of which a smaller version of the Cristo Redentor in Rio had been erected. Beneath the statue, bars, restaurants, parks and churches flowed right down to the edge of a mile-long beach.

Zaccheo directed her to motor past the busy beach and round the island to a quieter quay where they moored the boat. 'We're starting our tour up there.' He pointed to a quaint little building set into the side of a hill about a quarter of a mile up a steep path.

She nodded and started to walk up when she noticed Romeo a short distance away. He nodded a greeting but didn't join them as they headed up. The other man's watchfulness made Eva frown.

'Something on your mind?' Zaccheo asked.

'I was just wondering…what's the deal with Romeo?'

'He's many things.'

'That's not really an answer.'

Zaccheo shrugged. 'We work together, but I guess he's a confidant.'

'How long have you known him?'

When Zaccheo pulled his shades from the V of his T-shirt and placed them on, she wondered whether she'd strayed into forbidden territory. But he answered, 'We met when I was thirteen years old.'

Her eyes rounded in surprise. 'In London?'

'In Palermo.'

'So he's your oldest friend?'

Zaccheo hesitated for a second. 'Our relationship is complicated. Romeo sees himself as my protector. A role I've tried to dissuade him from to no avail.'

Her heart caught. 'Protector from what?'

His mouth twitched. 'He seems to think you're a handful that he needs to keep an eye on.'

She looked over her shoulder at the quiet, brooding man.

'My father worked for his father,' he finally answered.

'In what capacity?'

'As whatever he wanted him to be. My father didn't discriminate as long as he was recognised for doing the job. He would do anything from carrying out the trash to kneecapping a rival gang's members to claiming another man's bastard child so his boss didn't have to. No job was too small or large,' he said with dry bitterness.

The blood drained from her face. 'Your father worked for the *Mafia*?'

His jaw clenched before he jerked out a nod. 'Romeo's father was a *don* and my father one of his minions. His role was little more than drudge work, but he acted as if he was serving the Pope himself.'

She glanced over her shoulder at Romeo, her stomach dredging with intense emotions she recognised as anguish—even without knowing what Zaccheo was about to divulge.

'That bastard child you mentioned…'

He nodded. 'Romeo. His father had an affair with one of his many mistresses. His mother kept him until he became too much of a burden. When he was thirteen, she dumped him on his father. He didn't want the child, so he asked my father to *dispose* of him. My father, eager to attain recognition at all costs, brought the child home to my mother. She refused but my father wouldn't budge. They fought every day for a month until she ended up in hospital. It turned out she was pregnant. After that she became even more adamant about having another woman's child under her roof. When she lost her baby, she blamed my father and threatened to leave. My father, probably for the only time in his life, decided to place someone else's needs above his ambition. He tried to return Romeo to his father, who took grave offence. He had my father beaten to death. And I…' his face tightened '…I went from having a friend, a mother and father, and a brother or sister on the way, to having nothing.'

Eva frowned. 'But your mother—'

'Had hated being the wife of a mere gofer. My father's death bought her the fresh start she craved, but she had to contend with a child who reminded her of a past she detested. She moved to England a month after he died and married a man who hated the sight of me, who judged me because of who my father was and believed my common blood was an affront to his distinguished name.' The words were snapped out in a staccato narrative, but she felt the anguished intensity behind them.

Eva swallowed hard. Stepping close, she laid her head on his chest. 'I'm so sorry, Zaccheo.'

His arms tightened around her for a heartbeat before he pulled away and carried on up the steps. 'I thought Romeo had died that night, too, until he found me six years ago.'

She glanced at Romeo and her heart twisted for the pain the unfortunate friends had gone through.

They continued up the hill in silence until they reached the building.

They entered the cool but dim interior and as her eyes adjusted to the dark she was confronted by a stunning collection of statues. Most were made of marble, but one or two were sculpted in white stone.

'Wow, these are magnificent.'

'A local artist sculpted all the patron saints and donated them to the island over fifty years ago.'

They drifted from statue to statue, each work more striking than the last. When they walked through an arch, he laced his fingers with hers. 'Come, I'll show you the most impressive one. According to the history, the artist sculpted them in one day.'

Smiling, she let him tug her forward. She gasped at the double-figured display of St Anne and St Gerard. 'Patron saints of motherhood and fertility…' She stopped reading as her heart dropped to her stomach.

Zaccheo traced a forefinger down her cheek. 'I can't wait to feel our child kick in your belly,' he murmured.

A vice gripped her heart, squeezed until it threatened to stop beating. 'Zaccheo—'

His finger stopped her. 'I meant what I said, Eva. We can make this work. And we may not have had the best of role models in parents, but we know which mistakes to avoid. That's a good basis for our children, *si*?' he asked, his tone gentle, almost hopeful.

She opened her mouth, but no words formed. Because the truth she'd been hiding from suddenly reared up and slapped her in the face.

Zaccheo wanted children, not as a tool for revenge, but for himself. The man who'd known no love growing up wanted a family of his own.

And she'd led him on, letting him believe he could have it with her. The enormity of her actions rocked her to the core, robbing her of breath.

'Eva? What's wrong?' he asked with a frown.

She shook her head, her eyes darting frantically around the room.

'You're as pale as a ghost, *dolcezza*. Talk to me!'

Eva struggled to speak around the misery clogging her throat. 'I…I'm okay.'

His frown intensified. 'You don't look okay. Do you want to leave?'

She grasped the lifeline. 'Yes.'

'Okay, let's go.'

They emerged into bright sunlight. Eva took a deep breath, which did absolutely nothing to restore the chaos fracturing her mind.

The urge to confess *now*, spill her secret right then and there, powered through her. But it was neither the time nor the place. A group of tourist students had entered the room and the place was getting busier by the second.

Zaccheo led her down the steps. He didn't speak, but his concerned gaze probed her.

The island seemed twice as crowded by the time they descended the hill. The midday sun blazed high and sweat trickled down her neck as they navigated human traffic on the main promenade. When Zaccheo steered her to a restaurant advertising fresh seafood, Eva didn't complain.

Samba music blared from the speakers, thankfully negating the need for conversation. Sadly it didn't free her from her thoughts, not even when, after ordering their food, Zaccheo moved his chair closer, tugged her into his side and trailed his hand soothingly through her hair.

It was their last day in Rio. Possibly their last as husband and wife. Her soul mourned what she shouldn't have craved.

Unbearable agony ripped through her. She'd been living in a fool's paradise. Especially since she'd told herself it wouldn't matter how much time passed without her telling Zaccheo.

It mattered very much. She'd heard his pain when he'd recounted his bleak childhood. With each day that had passed without her telling him she couldn't help him realise his dream, she'd eroded any hope that he would understand why she'd kept her secret from him.

A moan ripped from her throat and she swayed in her seat. Zaccheo tilted her face to his and she read the worry in his eyes.

'Do you feel better?'

'Yes, much better.'

'*Bene*, then perhaps you'd like to tell me what's going on?' he asked.

She jerked away, her heart hammering. 'I got a little lightheaded, that's all.'

His frown returned and Eva held her breath. She was saved when Romeo entered. 'Everything all right?' he asked.

Romeo's glance darted to her. The knowledge in his eyes froze her insides, but he said nothing, directing his gaze back to his friend.

Zaccheo nodded. '*Sì*. We'll see you back at Paraíso.'

The moment he left, Zaccheo lowered his head and kissed her, not the hungry devouring that tended to overtake them whenever they were this close, but a gentle, reverent kiss.

In that moment, Eva knew she'd fallen in love with him.

And that she would lose the will to live the moment she walked away from him.

Their food arrived and they ate. She refused coffee and the slice of *chocotorta* the waiter temptingly offered. Zaccheo ordered an espresso, shooting her another concerned glance. Praying he wouldn't press her to reveal what was wrong just yet, she laid her head on his shoulder and buried her face in his throat, selfishly relishing the moment. She would never get a moment like this once they returned to Casa do Paraíso. He placed a gentle kiss on her forehead and agony moved through her like a living entity.

You brought this on yourself. No use crying now.

She started as the group they'd met on their exit from the museum entered the restaurant. Within minutes, someone had started the karaoke machine. The first attempt, sung atrociously to loud jeers, finished as the waiter returned with Zaccheo's espresso.

Eva straightened in her seat, watching the group absently as each member refused to take the mic. The leader cast his eyes around the room, met Eva's gaze and made a beeline for her.

'No.' She shook her head when he reached her and offered the mic.

He clasped his hands together. *'Por favor,'* he pleaded.

She opened her mouth to refuse, then found herself swallowing her rebuttal. She glanced at Zaccheo. He regarded her steadily, his face impassive. And yet she sensed something behind his eyes, as if he didn't know what to make of her mood.

She searched his face harder, wanting him to say something, *anything*, that would give her even the tiniest hope that what she had to tell him wouldn't break the magic they'd found on his island. Wouldn't break *her*.

In a way it was worse when he offered her that half-smile. Recently his half-smiles had grown genuine, were often a precursor to the blinding smiles that stole her breath…made her heart swell to bursting.

The thought that they would soon become a thing of the past had her surging to her feet, blindly striding for the stage to a round of applause she didn't want.

All Eva wanted in that moment was to drown in the oblivion of music.

She searched through the selection until she found a song she knew by heart, one that had spoken to her the moment she'd heard it on the radio.

She sang the first verse with her eyes shut, yearning for the impossible. She opened her eyes for the second verse. She could never tell Zaccheo how she felt about him, but she could sing it to him. Her eyes found his as she sang the last line.

His gaze grew hot. Intense. Her pulse hammered as she sang the third verse, offering her heart, her life to him, all the while knowing he would reject it once he knew.

She stifled a sob as the machine clicked to an end. She started to step off the stage, but the group begged for another song.

Zaccheo rose and moved towards her. They stared at each other as the clamouring grew louder. Her breath caught when the emotion in his eyes altered, morphing into that darker hue that held a deeper meaning.

He wasn't angry. Or ruthlessly commanding her to bend to his will. Or even bitter and hurt, as he'd been on the hill.

There was none of that in his expression. This ferocity was different, one that made her world stop.

Until she shook herself back to reality. She was grasping at straws, stalling with excuses and foolish, reckless hope. She might have fallen in love with Zaccheo, but nothing he'd said or done had indicated he returned even an iota of what she felt. Their relationship had changed from what it'd been in the beginning, but she couldn't lose sight of *why* it'd begun in the first place. Or why she couldn't let it continue.

Heavy-hearted, she turned back to the machine. She'd seen the song earlier and bypassed it, because she hadn't been ready to say goodbye.

But it was time to end this. Time to accept that there was no hope.

Something was wrong. It'd been since they'd walked down the hill.

But for once in his life, he was afraid to confront a problem head-on because he was terrified the results would be unwelcome. So he played worst-case scenarios in his head.

Had he said or done something to incite this troubled look on Eva's face? Had his confession on the hill reminded her that he wasn't the man she would've chosen for herself? A wave of something close to desolation rushed over him. He clenched his jaw against the feeling. Would it really be the end of the world if Eva decided she didn't want him? The affirmative answer echoing through him made him swallow hard.

He discarded that line of thought and chose another, dissecting each moment he'd spent with her this afternoon.

He'd laid himself bare, something he'd never done until recently. She hadn't shown pity or disgust for the debasing crimes his father had committed, or for the desperately lonely child he'd been. Yet again she'd only showed compassion. Pain for the toll his jagged upbringing had taken on him.

And the songs…what had they meant, especially the second one, the one about saying *goodbye*? He'd witnessed the agony in her eyes while she'd sung that one. As if her heart was broken—

A knock came at his study door, where he'd retreated to pace after they'd returned and Eva had expressed the need for a shower. Alone.

'Zaccheo?'

He steeled himself to turn around, hoping against hope that the look on her face would be different. That she would smile and everything would return to how it was before they'd gone on that blasted trip.

But it wasn't. And her next words ripped through him with the lethal effect of a vicious blade.

'Zaccheo, we need to talk.'

CHAPTER FOURTEEN

EVERY WORD SHE'D practised in the shower fled her head as Eva faced him. Of course, her muffled sobs had taken up a greater part of the shower so maybe she hadn't got as much practice in as she'd thought.

'I…' Her heart sank into her stomach when a forbidding look tightened his face. 'I can't stay married to you.'

For a moment he looked as if she'd punched him hard in the solar plexus, then ripped his heart out while he struggled to breathe. Gradually his face lost every trace of pain and distress. Hands shoved deep in his pockets, he strolled to where she stood, frozen inside the doorway.

'Was this your plan all along?' he bit out, his eyes arctic. 'To wait until I'd spoken on your father's behalf and he was safe from prosecution before you asked for a divorce?'

She gasped. 'You did that? When?' she asked, but his eyes poured scorn on her question.

'Is being married to me that abhorrent to you, Eva? So much so you couldn't even wait until we were back in London?'

'No! Believe me, Zaccheo, that's not it.'

'*Believe* you? Why should I? When you're not even prepared to give us a chance?' He veered sharply away from her and strode across the room, his fingers spiking through his hair before he reversed course and stopped in front of her once more. 'What I don't understand is why. Did I do something? Say something to make you think I wouldn't want this relationship to work?'

The confirmation that this marriage meant more to him was almost too hard to bear.

'Zaccheo, please listen to me. It's not you, it's—'

His harsh laughter echoed around the room. 'Are you *seriously* giving me that line?'

Her fists balled. 'For once in your life, just shut up and listen! I can't have children,' she blurted.

'You've already used that one, *dolcezza*, but you signed along the dotted line agreeing to my clause, remember? So try again.'

Misery quivered through her stomach. 'It's true I signed the agreement, but I lied to you. I *can't* have children, Zaccheo. I'm infertile.'

He sucked in a hoarse breath and reeled backwards on his heels. 'Excuse me?'

'I tried to tell you when I first saw the clause, but you wouldn't listen. You'd made up your mind that I'd use any excuse not to marry you because I didn't want you.'

The stunned look morphed into censure. 'Then you should've put me straight.'

'How? Would you have believed me if I'd told you about my condition? Without evidence to back it up? Or perhaps I should've told Romeo or your PA since they had more access to you than I did in the week before the wedding?'

He looked at her coldly. 'If your conscience stung you so deeply the first time round, why did you change your mind?'

Her emotions were raw enough for her to instinctively want to protect herself. But what did she have to lose? Zaccheo would condemn her actions regardless of whether she kept her innermost feelings to herself or not. And really, how much worse could this situation get? Her heart was already in shreds.

She met his gaze head on. 'You know I lost my mother to cancer when I was eighteen. She was diagnosed when I was sixteen. For two years we waited, hoping for the best, fearing the worst through each round of chemo. With each treatment that didn't work we knew her time was growing shorter. Knowing it was coming didn't make it any easier. Her death ripped me apart.' She stopped and gathered her courage. 'My father has been suffering stress attacks in the last couple of months.' She risked a glance and saw his brows clamped in a forbidding frown. 'He collapsed on Friday after you called to tell him the wedding was off.'

Zaccheo's mouth compressed, but a trace of compassion flashed through his eyes. 'And you blame me? Is that what this is all about?'

'No, I don't. We both know that the blame for our current circumstances lies firmly with my father.' She stopped and licked her lips. 'He may have brought this on himself, but the stress was killing him, Zaccheo. I've watched one parent die, helpless to do anything but watch them fade away. Condemn me all you want, but I wasn't going to stand by and let my father worry himself to death over what he'd done. And I didn't do it for my family name or my blasted *pedigree*. I did it because that's what you do for the people you love.'

'Even when they don't love you back?' he sneered, his voice indicating hers was a foolish feeling. 'Even when they treat you like an afterthought for most of your life?'

Sadness engulfed her. 'You can't help who you love. Or choose who will love you back.'

His eyes met hers for a charged second, before his nostrils flared. 'But you can choose to tell the truth no matter how tough the telling of it is. You can choose *not* to start a marriage based on lies.'

Regret crawled across her skin. 'Yes. And I'm sorry—'

His hand slashed through air, killing off her apology. Walking around her, he slammed the door shut and jerked his chin towards the sofa. He waited until she'd sat down, then prowled in front of her.

'Tell me of this condition you have.'

Eva stared at her clasped hands because watching his face had grown unbearable. 'It's called endometriosis.' She gave him the bare facts, unwilling to linger on the subject and prolong her heartache. 'It started just before I went to university, but, with everything going on with my mother, I didn't pay enough attention to it. I thought it was just something that would right itself eventually. But the pain got worse. One day I collapsed and was rushed to hospital. The diagnosis was made.' She stopped, then made herself go on. 'The doctor said the…scarring was too extensive…that I would never conceive naturally.'

She raised her head and saw that he'd stopped prowling and taken a seat opposite her with his elbows on his knees. 'Go on,' he bit out.

Eva shrugged. 'What else is there to add?' She gave a hollow laugh. 'I never thought I'd be in a position where the one thing I couldn't give would be the difference between having the future I want and the one I'd have to settle for. You accused me of starting this marriage based on lies, but I didn't know you wanted a real marriage. You did all this to get back at my father, remember?'

'So you never sought a second opinion?' he asked stonily, as if she hadn't mentioned the shifted parameters of their marriage.

'Why would I? I'd known something was wrong. Having the doctor confirm it merely affirmed what I already suspected. What was the point of putting myself through further grief?'

Zaccheo jerked to his feet and began prowling again. The set of his shoulders told her he was holding himself on a tight leash.

Minutes ticked by and he said nothing. The tension increased until she couldn't stand it any more. 'You can do whatever you want with me, but I want your word that you won't go after my family because of what I've done.'

He froze, his eyes narrowing to thin shards of ice. 'You think I want you to martyr yourself on some noble pyre for my sick satisfaction?'

She jumped to her feet. 'I don't know! You're normally so quick to lay down your demands. Or throw out orders and expect them to be followed. So tell me what you want.'

That chilling half-smile returned with a vengeance. 'What I want is to leave this place. There's really no point staying, is there, since the honeymoon is well and truly over?'

The flight back was markedly different from the outbound journey. The moment Zaccheo immersed himself in his work, she grabbed her tablet and locked herself in the bedroom.

She threw herself on the bed and sobbed long and hard into the pillow. By the time the plane landed in London, she was completely wrung out. Exhaustion seeped into her very bones and all she wanted was to curl into a foetal position and wish the world away.

She sank further into grey gloom when she descended the steps of the aircraft to find Zaccheo's limo waiting on the tarmac, along with a black SUV.

Zaccheo, wearing a black and navy pinstriped suit, stopped next to her, his expression remote and unfriendly.

'I'm heading to the office. Romeo will drive you to the penthouse.'

He strode to the SUV and drove off.

Eva realised then that throughout their conversation on the island, she'd made the same mistake as when she'd foolishly disclosed her condition before. She'd allowed herself to *hope* that the condition fate had bestowed on her wouldn't matter to that one *special person*. That somehow *love* would find a way.

A sob bubbled up her chest and she angrily swallowed it down.

Grow up, Eva. You're letting the lyrics of your songs cloud your judgement.

'Eva?' Romeo waited with the car door open.

She hastily averted her gaze from the censure in his eyes and slid in.

The penthouse hadn't changed, and yet Eva felt as if she'd lived a lifetime since she was last here.

After unpacking and showering, she trailed from room to room, feeling as if some tether she hadn't known she was tied to had been severed. When she rushed to the door for the third time, imagining she'd heard the keycard activate, she grabbed her tablet and forced herself to work on her compositions.

But her heart wasn't in it. Her mood grew bleaker when Romeo found her curled on the sofa and announced that Zaccheo wouldn't be home for dinner either tonight or the next two weeks, because he'd returned to Oman.

The days bled together in a dull grey jumble. Determined not to mope—because after all she'd been here before—Eva returned to work.

She took every spare shift available and offered herself for overtime without pay.

But she refused to sing.

Music had ceased to be the balm she'd come to rely on. Her heart only yearned for one thing. Or *one man*. And he'd made it abundantly clear that he didn't want her.

Because two weeks stretched to four, then six with no word from Zaccheo, and no answer to her phone calls.

At her lowest times, Eva hated herself for her lethargy, for not moving out of the penthouse. For sitting around, wishing for a miracle that would never materialise.

But the thought of flat-hunting, or, worse, moving back to Pennington Manor, filled her with a desperate heartache that nothing seemed to ease.

Romeo had brought her coffee this morning at the breakfast table. The pitying look he'd cast her had been the final straw.

'If you have something to say, just say it, Romeo.'

'You're not a weak woman. One of you has to take the situation in hand sooner or later,' he'd replied.

'Fine, but he won't return my calls so give him a message from me, will you?'

He'd nodded in that solemn way of his. 'Of course.'

'Tell him I'm fast reaching my tolerance level for his stupid silence. He can stay in Oman for the rest of his life for all I care. But he shouldn't expect to find me here when he deigns to return.'

That outburst had been strangely cathartic. She'd called her ex-landlady and discovered her flat was still unlet. After receiving a hefty payday from Zaccheo, the old woman hadn't been in a hurry to interview new tenants. She'd invited Eva to move back whenever she wanted.

Curiously, that announcement hadn't made her feel better—

'You've been cleaning that same spot for the last five minutes.'

Eva started and glanced down. 'Oh.'

Sybil, Siren's unflappable manageress, eyed her. 'Time for a break.'

'I don't need a—'

'Sorry, love,' Sybil said firmly. 'Orders from above. The new owner was very insistent. You take a break now or I get docked a week's wages.'

Eva frowned. 'Are you serious? Do we know who this new owner is?'

Sybil's eyes widened. 'You don't know?' When she shook her head, the manageress shrugged. 'Well, I'm not one to spread gossip. Shoo! Go put your feet up for a bit. I'll finish up here.'

Eva reluctantly handed over the cleaning supplies. She turned and stopped as the doors swung open and Ziggy Preston walked in.

The smile she tried for failed miserably. 'Ziggy, hello.'

He smiled. 'I heard you were back in town.'

She couldn't summon the curiosity to ask how he knew. 'Oh?'

'You were supposed to call when you got back. I hope that doesn't mean you've signed up with someone else? Because that'd devastate me,' he joked.

Eva tried for another smile. Failed again. 'I didn't sign with anyone, and I don't think I will.'

His face fell. 'Why not?'

She had a thousand and one reasons. But only one that mattered. And she wasn't about to divulge it to another soul. 'I've decided to give the music thing a break for a while.' Or for ever, depending on whether she felt anything but numb again.

Ziggy shoved his hands into his coat pocket, his features pensive.

'Listen, I was supposed to do a session with one of my artists tomorrow afternoon, but they cancelled. Come to the studio, hang out for a while. You don't have to sing if you don't want to. But come anyway.'

She started to shake her head, then stopped. It was her day off tomorrow. The extra shift she'd hoped to cover had suddenly been filled. She could either occupy herself at Ziggy's studio or wander Zaccheo's penthouse like a lost wraith, pining for what she could never have. 'Okay.'

'Great!' He handed her another business card, this one with his private number scribbled on the back, and left.

A couple of months ago, being pursued by a top music producer would've been a dream come true. And yet, Eva could barely summon the enthusiasm to dress the next day, especially when Romeo confirmed he'd given Zaccheo her message but had no reply for her.

Jaw clenched, she pulled on her jeans and sweater, determined not to succumb to the unending bouts of anguish that had made her throw up this morning after her conversation with Romeo.

She wasn't a pearl-clutching Victorian maiden, for heaven's sake!

Her life might *feel* as if it were over, but she'd been through the wringer more than once in her life. She'd survived her diagnosis. She'd survived her mother's death. Despite the odds, she'd mended fences with her father and sister.

Surely she could survive decimating her heart on a love that had been doomed from the start?

Deliberately putting a spring in her step, she arrived at Ziggy's studio in a different frame of mind. Looking around, she repeated to herself that *this* was a tangible dream. Something she could hang on to once Zaccheo returned and she permanently severed the ties that had so very briefly bound them.

Eva was sure she was failing in her pep talk to herself when Ziggy gave up after a third attempt to get her to sample an upbeat pop tune.

'Okay, shall we try one of yours?' he suggested with a wry smile.

Half-heartedly, she sifted through her list, then paused, her heart picking up its sluggish beat as she stared at the lyrics to the song she'd composed that last morning on the island.

'This one,' she murmured.

At Ziggy's nod, she sang the first line.

His eyes widened. 'Wow.' Nodding to the sound booth, he said, 'I'd love to hear the whole thing if you're up to it?'

Eva thought of the raw lyrics, how they offered love, pleaded for for ever and accepted any risks necessary, and breathed deeply.

If this was what it took to start healing herself, then so be it. 'Sure.'

She was singing the final notes when an electrifying wave of awareness swept over her. Her gaze snapped up to the viewing gallery above the booth, where she knew music moguls sometimes listened in on artists. Although the mirrored glass prevented her from seeing who occupied it, she swore she could smell Zaccheo's unique scent.

'Are you okay?' Ziggy asked.

She nodded absently, her gaze still on the gallery window. 'Can you sing the last two lines again?'

'Umm...yes,' she mumbled.

She really was losing it. If she couldn't sing a song she'd written with Zaccheo in mind without imagining she could feel him, smell him, she was in deep trouble. Because as she worked through the other songs Ziggy encouraged her to record, Eva realised all her songs were somehow to do with the man who'd taken her heart prisoner.

She left the studio in a daze and got into the waiting limo. Physically and emotionally drained, she couldn't connect two thoughts together. When she finally accepted what she needed to do, she turned to Romeo.

'Can you take me to Zaccheo's office, please?'

He looked up from the laptop he'd been working on. After a few probing seconds, he nodded.

A wave of dizziness hit her as they waited for the lift at GWI. She ignored the curious glances, and concentrated on staying upright, putting one foot in front of the other as she made her way down the plushly decorated corridor to Zaccheo's office.

Anyetta's coolly professional demeanour visibly altered when she saw Eva, then turned to shock as her gaze travelled from her head to her toes.

Eva wanted to laugh, but she couldn't be sure she wouldn't dissolve into hysteria. When Anyetta stood, Eva waved her away.

'I know he's not in. I was hoping *you* would email him for me.'

'But—'

'It won't take long, I promise.'

The tall brunette looked briefly bewildered, but her features settled back into serene composure and she sat down.

'Mark it *urgent*. Presumably, you can tell when he opens emails from you?' Eva asked.

Warily, Zaccheo's PA nodded.

'Good.' Eva approached, pushing back the errant curls obscuring her vision. She folded her arms around her middle and prayed for just a few more minutes of strength.

Anyetta's elegant fingers settled on the keyboard.

Eva cleared her throat.

Zaccheo.

Since you refuse to engage with me, I can only conclude that I'm free of my obligations to you. To that end, I'd be grateful if you would take the appropriate steps to end this marriage forthwith. My family lawyers will be on standby when you're ready, but I'd be obliged if you didn't leave it too late. I refuse to put my life on hold for you, so take action or I will.

For the record, I won't be accepting any of the monetary compensation offered, nor will I be seeking anything from you, except my freedom. If you choose to pursue my family, then you'll do so without my involvement, because I've done my duty to my family and I'm moving on. I won't let you use me as a pawn in your vendetta against my father. You're aware of the state of my father's health, so I hope you'll choose mercy over retribution.

Regardless of your decision, I'll be moving out of the penthouse tomorrow.

Please don't contact me.

Eva.

'Send it, please,' she said.

Anyetta clicked the button, then looked up. 'He just opened it.'

Eva nodded jerkily. 'Thank you.'

She walked out with scalding tears filling her eyes. A solid presence registered beside her and when Romeo took her arm, Eva didn't protest.

At the penthouse, she dropped her bag in the hallway, tugged off her boots and coat as her vision greyed. She made it into bed as her legs gave way and she curled, fully clothed, into a tight ball. Her last thought before blessed oblivion claimed her was that she'd done it.

She'd survived her first hour with a heart broken into a million tiny pieces. If there was any justice, she might just make it through the rest of her life with a shredded heart.

CHAPTER FIFTEEN

IN THE SPLIT SECOND before wakefulness hit, Eva buried her nose in the pillow that smelled so much like Zaccheo she groaned with pure, incandescent happiness.

Reality arrived with searing pain so acute, she cried out.

'Eva.'

She jolted upright at the sound of her name. Jagged thoughts pierced her foggy brain like shards of bright light through glass.

She was no longer in her own suite, but in Zaccheo's.

Her clothes were gone, and she was stripped down to her bra and panties.

Zaccheo was sitting in an armchair next to the bed, his eyes trained on her.

And he was clean-shaven.

His thick stubble was gone, his hair trimmed into a short, neat style that left his nape bare.

Despite his altered appearance, his living, breathing presence was far too much to bear. She jerked her head away, stared down at the covers she clutched like a lifeline.

'What are you doing here?' she asked.

'You summoned me. So here I am,' he stated.

She shook her head. 'Please. Don't make it sound as if I have any power over your actions. If I did you would've answered my numerous phone calls like a normal person. And that email wasn't a summons. It was a statement of intent, hardly demanding your presence.'

'Nevertheless, since you went to so much trouble to make sure it reached me, I thought it only polite to answer it in person.'

'Well, you needn't have bothered,' she threw back hotly,

'especially since we both know you don't have a polite bone in your body. Things like *consideration* and *courtesy* are alien concepts to you.'

He looked perturbed by her outburst. Which made her want to laugh. And cry. And scream. 'Are you going to sit there with that insulting look that implies I'm out of my mind?'

'You must forgive me if that's what my expression implies. I meant to wear a look that says I was hoping for a civilised conversation.'

She threw out her hands. 'You have a damned nerve, do you know that? I...' She stopped, her eyes widening in alarm as an unpleasant scent hit her nostrils. Swivelling, she saw the breakfast tray containing scrambled eggs, smoked pancetta, coffee, and the buttered brioche she loved.

Correction. She'd *once* loved.

Shoving the covers aside, she lunged for the bathroom, uncaring that she was half-naked and looked like a bedraggled freak. All she cared about was making it to the porcelain bowl in time.

She vomited until she collapsed against the shower stall, desperately catching her breath. When Zaccheo crouched at her side, she shut her eyes. 'Please, Zaccheo. Go away.'

He pressed a cool towel to her forehead, her eyelids, her cheeks. 'A lesser man might be decimated at the thought that his presence makes you physically ill,' he murmured gravely.

Her snort grated her throat. 'But you're not a lesser man, of course.'

He shrugged. 'I'm saved by Romeo's report that you've been feeling under the weather recently.'

Eva opened her eyes, looked at him, then immediately wished she hadn't. She'd thought his beard and long mane made him gloriously beautiful, but the sight of his chiselled jaw, the cut of his cheekbones, and the fully displayed sensual lips was almost blinding.

'I can't do this.' She tried to stand and collapsed back against the stall.

With a muttered oath, he scooped her up in his arms and strode to the vanity. Setting her down, he handed her a toothbrush and watched as she cleaned her teeth.

Eva told herself the peculiar look turning his eyes that gunmetal shade meant nothing. Zaccheo had probably come to ensure she vacated his penthouse before succumbing to whatever was ailing her.

Steeling her spine, she rinsed her mouth. He reached for her as she moved away from the vanity, but she sidestepped him, her heart banging against her ribs. 'I can walk on my own two feet.'

Zaccheo watched her go, her hips swaying in that impertinent, yet utterly sexy way that struck pure fire to his libido.

He slowly followed, paused in the doorway and watched her pace the bedroom.

Although he'd primed himself for her appearance, he hadn't been quite prepared for when he'd finally returned to the penthouse last night and found her asleep in her suite. All the excuses he'd given himself for staying away had crumbled to dust.

As he'd stood over her, his racing heart had only been able to acknowledge one thing—that he'd missed her more than his brain could accurately fathom. He'd thought the daily reports on her movements would be enough. He'd thought buying Siren and ensuring she didn't overwork herself, or silently watching her from the gallery at Preston's studio yesterday, listening to her incredible voice, would be enough.

It wasn't until he'd received her email that his world had stopped, and he'd forced himself to face the truth.

He was nothing without her.

For the last six weeks he'd woken to a tormenting existence each morning. Each time, something had broken inside him. Something that would probably slot neatly under the banner of heartache. It had nothing to do with the lone-liness that had plagued his childhood and led him to believe he needed a family to soothe the ache. It had nothing to do with the retribution he was no longer interested in exacting from Oscar Pennington.

It had everything to do with Eva. Flashes of her had struck him at the most inappropriate times—like the brightness of her smile when he was involved in tense negotiation. The feeling of being deep inside her when he was teetering on the edge of a platform three hundred metres above ground, with no net to catch him should he fall. And everywhere he'd gone, he'd imagined the faintest trace of her perfume in the air.

Nothing had stopped him from reaching out for her in the dead of the night, when his guard was at its lowest and all he could feel was *need*. Ferocious, all-consuming need.

Even the air of sadness that hung around her now wasn't enough to make him *not* yearn for her.

His heart kicked into his stomach, knowing it was his fault she wore that look.

Her throat worked to find the words she needed. He forced himself to remain still, to erect a force field against anything she might say.

'Let's end this now, Zaccheo. Divorce me. Surely you'd prefer that to this mockery of a marriage?'

He'd expected it. Hell, her email had left him in no doubt as to her state of mind.

Yet the words punched him in the gut…*hard*. Zaccheo uttered an imprecation that wasn't fit for polite company.

Give her what she wants. Stop this endless misery and be done with it.

It was the selfless thing to do. And if he needed to have learned anything from the stunning, brave woman in front of him, it was selflessness. She'd sacrificed herself for her family and turned over her innermost secrets when she could've just kept quiet and reaped untold wealth. She'd continued to stay under his roof, continued to seek him out, when fear had sent *him* running.

He *needed* to be selfless for her.

But he couldn't. He walked stiffly to the side table and poured a coffee he didn't want.

'There will be no divorce.'

She glared at him. 'You do realise that I don't need your permission?'

He knew that. He'd lived with that fear ever since she'd announced back in Rio that she didn't want to be married to him any more.

'*Sì,*' he replied gruffly. 'You can do whatever you want. The same way I can choose to tie you up in endless red tape for the next twenty years.'

Her mouth dropped open, then she shut her beautiful, pain-filled eyes. 'Why would you do that, Zaccheo?'

'Why indeed?'

She shook her head, and her hair fluttered over her shoulders. 'Surely you can't want this? You deserve a family.'

There it was again. That selflessness that cut him to the core, that forced him to let go, to be a better man. *Dio mio*, but he wanted her to be selfish for once. To claim what she wanted. To claim him!

'How very noble of you to think of me. But I don't need a family.'

Shock widened her eyes. 'What did you say?'

'I don't need a family, *il mio cuore*. I don't need anything, or anyone, if I have you.' *She* was all he wanted. He'd prostrate himself at her feet if that was what it took.

She stared at him for so long, Zaccheo felt as if he'd turned to stone. He knew that any movement would see him shatter into useless pieces.

But he had to take the leap. The same leap she'd taken on the island, when she'd shared something deeply private and heartbreaking with him.

'If you have *me*?'

He risked taking a breath. 'Yes. I love you, Eva. I've been racking my brain for weeks, trying to find a way to make you stay, convince you to stay my wife—'

'You didn't think to just *ask* me?'

'After walking away from you like a coward?' He shook his head. 'You've no idea how many times I picked up the phone, how many times I summoned my pilot to bring me back to you. But I couldn't face the possibility of you saying no.' He gave a hollow laugh. 'Believe it or not, I convinced myself I'd rather spend the rest of my life living in another country but still married to you, than face the prospect of never having even the tiniest piece of you.'

Her face crumbled and he nearly roared in pain. 'That's no life at all, Zaccheo.'

'It was a reason for me to *breathe*. A selfish but *necessary* reason for me to keep functioning, knowing I had a piece of you even if it was your name next to mine on a marriage certificate.'

'Oh, God!' Tears filled her eyes and he cursed. He wanted to take her in his arms. But he had no right. He'd lost all rights when he'd forced her into marriage and then condemned her for trying to protect herself from his monstrous actions.

He clenched his fists against the agony ripping through him. 'But that's no life for you. If you wish for a divorce, then I'll grant you one.'

'What?' Her face lost all colour. She started to reach for him, but faltered. 'Zaccheo…'

A different sort of fear scythed through him as she started to crumple.

'Eva!'

By the time he caught her she was unconscious.

Muted voices pulled her back to consciousness. The blinds in the strange room were drawn but there was enough light to work out that she was no longer in Zaccheo's penthouse. The drip in her right arm confirmed her worst fears.

'What...happened?' she croaked.

Shadowy figures turned, and Sophie rushed to her side.

'You fainted. Zaccheo brought you to the hospital,' Sophie said.

'Zaccheo...' Memory rushed back. Zaccheo telling her he loved her. Then telling her he would divorce her...

No!

She tried to sit up.

The nurse stopped her. 'The doctors are running tests. We should have the results back shortly. In the meantime, you're on a rehydrating drip.'

Eva touched her throbbing head, wishing she'd stop talking for a moment so she could—

She stared at her bare fingers in horror. 'Where are my rings?' she cried.

The nurse frowned. 'I don't know.'

'No...please. I need...' She couldn't catch her breath. Or take her eyes off her bare fingers. Had Zaccheo done it so quickly? While she'd been unconscious?

But he'd said he loved her. Did he not love her enough? Tears brimmed her eyes and fell down her cheeks.

'It's okay, I'll go and find out.' The nurse hurried out.

Sophie approached. Eva forced her pain back and looked at her.

'I hope you don't mind me being here? You didn't call when you got back so I assume you don't want to speak to me, but when Zaccheo called—'

Eva shook her head, her thoughts racing, her insides shredding all over again. 'You're my family, Sophie. It may take a while to get back to where we were before, but I don't hate you. I've just been a little...preoccupied.' Her gaze went to the empty doorway. 'Is...Zaccheo still here?'

Sophie smiled wryly. 'He was enraged that you didn't have a team of doctors monitoring your every breath. He went to find the head of the trauma unit.'

Zaccheo walked into the room at that moment, and Sophie

hastily excused herself. The gunmetal shade of his eyes and the self-loathing on his face made Eva's heart thud slowly as she waited for the death blow.

He walked forward like a man facing his worst nightmare.

Just before she'd fainted, she'd told herself she would fight for him, as she'd fought for her sister and father. Seeing the look on his face, she accepted that nothing she did would change things. Her bare fingers spoke their own truth.

'Zaccheo, I know you said…you loved me, but if it's not enough for you—'

Astonishment transformed his face. 'Not enough for *me*?'

'You agreed to divorce me…'

Anguish twisted his face. 'Only because it was what *you* wanted.'

She sucked in a breath when he perched on the edge of the bed. His fingers lightly brushed the back of her hand, over and over, as if he couldn't help himself.

'You know what I did last night before I came home?'

She shook her head.

'I went to see your father. I had no idea where I was headed until I landed on the lawn at Pennington Manor. Somewhere along the line, I entertained the idea that I would sway your feelings if I smoothed my relationship with your father. Instead I asked him for your hand in marriage.'

'You did what?'

He grimaced. 'Our wedding was a pompous exhibition from start to finish. I wanted to show everyone who'd dared to look down on me how high I'd risen.'

Her heart lurched. 'Because of what your mother and stepfather did?'

He sighed. 'I hated my mother for choosing her aristocrat husband over me. Like you, I didn't understand why it had to be an either-or choice. Why couldn't she love me *and* her husband? Then I began to hate everything he stood for. The need to understand why consumed me. My stepfather was easy to break. Your father was a little more cunning.

He used you. From the moment we met, I couldn't see beyond you. He saw that. I don't know if I'll ever be able to forgive that, but he brought us together.' He breathed deep and shoved a hand through his short hair. 'Possessing you blinded me to what he was doing. And I blamed you for it, right along with him when the blame lay with me and my obsession to get back at you when I should've directed my anger elsewhere.'

'You were trying to understand why you'd been rejected. I tried for years to understand why my father couldn't be satisfied with what he had. Why he pushed his family obsession onto his children. He fought with my mother over it, and it ripped us apart. Everything stopped when she got sick. Perversely, I hoped her illness would change things for the better. For a while it did. But after she died, he reverted to type, and I couldn't take it any more.' She glanced at him. 'Hearing you tell that newspaper tycoon that I was merely a means to an end brought everything back to me.'

Zaccheo shut his eyes in regret. He lifted her hand and pressed it against his cheek. 'He was drunk, prying into my feelings towards you. I was grappling with them myself and said the first idiotic thing that popped into my head. I don't deny that it was probably what I'd been telling myself.'

'But afterwards, when I asked you…'

'I'd just found out about the charges. I knew your father was behind it. You were right there, his flesh and blood, a target for my wrath. I regretted it the moment I said it, but you were gone before I got the chance to take it back.' He brought her hand to his mouth and kissed it, then her palm before laying it over his heart. *'Mi dispiace molto, il mio cuore.'*

His heart beat steady beneath her hand. But her fingers were bare.

'Zaccheo, what you said before I fainted…'

Pain ravaged his face before he nodded solemnly. 'I meant it. I'll let you go if that's what you want. Your happiness means everything to me. Even if it's without me.'

She shook her head. 'No, not that. What you said before.'

He looked deep into her eyes, his gaze steady and true. 'I love you, Eva. More than my life, more than everything I've ever dared to dream of. You helped me redeem my soul when I thought it was lost.'

'You touched mine, made me love deeper, purer. You taught me to take a risk again instead of living in fear of rejection.'

He took a sharp breath. 'Eva, what are you saying?'

'That I love you too. And it tears me apart that I won't be able to give you children—'

His kiss stopped her words. 'Prison was hell, I won't deny it. In my lowest times, I thought having children would be the answer. But you're the only family I need, *amore mio*.'

Zaccheo was rocking her, crooning softly to comfort her when the doctor walked in.

'Right, Mrs Giordano. You'll be happy to hear we've got to the bottom of your fainting spell. There's nothing to worry about besides—'

'Dehydration and the need to eat better?' she asked with a sniff.

'Well, yes, there's that.'

'Okay, I promise I will.'

'I'll make sure she keeps to it,' Zaccheo added with a mock frown. He settled her back in the bed and stood. 'I'll go get the car.'

The doctor shook his head. 'No, I'm afraid you can't leave yet. You need to rest for at least twenty-four hours while we monitor you and make sure everything's fine.'

Zaccheo tensed and caught her hand in his. 'What do you mean? Didn't you say you'd got to the bottom of what ails her?' His eyes met hers, and Eva read the anxiety there.

'Zaccheo…'

'Mr Giordano, no need to panic. The only thing that should ail your wife is a short bout of morning sickness and perhaps a little bed rest towards the end.'

Zaccheo paled and visibly trembled. 'The *end*?'

Eva's heart stopped. 'Doctor, what are you saying?' she whispered.

'I'm saying you're pregnant. With twins.'

EPILOGUE

ZACCHEO EMERGED FROM the bedroom where he'd gone to change his shirt—the second of the day due to his eldest son throwing up on him—to find Eva cross-legged on the floor before the coffee table, their children cradled in her arms as she crooned Italian nursery rhymes she'd insisted he teach her.

On the screen via a video channel, Romeo leaned in closer to get a better look at the babies.

Zaccheo skirted the sofa and sat behind his wife, cradling her and their children in his arms.

'Do you think you'll make it for Christmas?' she asked Romeo. Zaccheo didn't need to lean over to see that his wife was giving his friend her best puppy-dog look.

'*Sì*, I'll do my best to be there tomorrow.'

Eva shook her head. 'That's not good enough, Romeo. I know Brunetti International is a huge company, and you're a super busy tycoon, but it's your godsons' first Christmas. They picked out your present all by themselves. The least you can do is turn up and open it.'

Zaccheo laughed silently and watched his friend squirm until he realised denying his wife anything her heart desired was a futile exercise.

'If that's what you wish, *principessa*, then I'll be there.'

Eva beamed. Zaccheo spread his fingers through her hair, resisting the urge to smother her cheek and mouth in kisses because she thought it made Romeo uncomfortable.

The moment Romeo signed off, Zaccheo claimed his kiss, not lifting his head until he was marginally satisfied.

'What was that for?' she murmured in that dazed voice that was like a drug to his blood.

'Because you're my heart, *dolcezza*. I cannot go long without it. Without you.'

Eva's heart melted as Zaccheo relieved her of their youngest son, Rafa, and tucked his tiny body against his shoulder. Then he held out his hand and helped her up with Carlo, their eldest by four minutes.

Zaccheo pulled them close until they stood in a loose circle, his arms around her. Then, as he'd taken to doing, he started swaying to the soft Christmas carols playing in the background.

Eva closed her eyes to stem the happy tears forming. She'd said a prayer every day of her pregnancy as they'd faced hurdles because of her endometriosis. When the doctors had prescribed bed rest at five months, Zaccheo had immediately stepped back from GWI and handed over the day-to-day running of the company to his new second-in-command.

Their sons had still arrived two weeks early but had both been completely healthy, much to the joy and relief of their parents. Relations were still a little strained with her father and sister, but Oscar doted on his grandsons, and Sophie had fallen in love with her nephews at first sight. But no one loved their gorgeous boys more than Zaccheo. The love and adoration in his eyes when he cradled his sons often made her cry.

And knowing that love ran just as deep for her filled her heart with so much happiness, she feared she would burst from it.

'You've stopped dancing,' he murmured.

She began to sway again, her free hand rising to his chest. She caught sight of her new rings—the engagement ring belonging to his grandmother, which he'd kept but not given her because the circumstances hadn't been right, and the new wedding band he'd let her pick out for their second, family-only wedding—and her thoughts turned pensive. 'I was thinking about your mother.'

Zaccheo tensed slightly. She caressed her hand over his heart until the tension eased out of him. 'What were you thinking?' he asked grudgingly.

'I sent her pictures of the boys yesterday.'

A noise rumbled from Zaccheo's chest. 'She's been asking for one since the day they were born.'

She leaned back and looked into her husband's eyes. 'I know. I also know you've agreed to see her at Easter after my first album comes out.'

Tension remained between mother and son, but when his mother had reached out, Zaccheo hadn't turned her away.

Standing on tiptoe, Eva caressed the stubble she insisted he grow again, and kissed him. 'I'm very proud of you.'

'No, Eva. Everything good in my life is because of *you*.' He sealed her lips with another kiss. A deeper, more demanding kiss.

By mutual agreement, they pulled away and headed for the nursery. After bestowing kisses on their sleeping sons, Zaccheo took her hand and led her to the bedroom.

Their lovemaking was slow, worshipful, with loving words blanketing them as they reached fulfilment and fell asleep in each other's arms.

When midnight and Christmas rolled around, Zaccheo woke her and made love to her all over again. Afterwards, sated and happy, he spread his fingers through her hair and brought her face to his.

'Buon Natale, amore mio,' he said. 'You're the only thing I want under my Christmas tree, from now until eternity.'

'Merry Christmas, Zaccheo. You make my heart sing every day and my soul soar every night. You're everything I ever wished for.'

He touched his forehead to hers and breathed deep. *'Ti amero per sempre, dolcezza mia.'*

* * * * *

Don't miss Romeo's story in
BRUNETTI'S SECRET SON
available December 2015.

MILLS & BOON®

MODERN™

POWER, PASSION AND IRRESISTIBLE TEMPTATION

A sneak peek at next month's titles...

In stores from 20th November 2015:

- **The Price of His Redemption** – Carol Marinelli
- **The Innocent's Sinful Craving** – Sara Craven
- **Talos Claims His Virgin** – Michelle Smart
- **Ravensdale's Defiant Captive** – Melanie Milburne

In stores from 4th December 2015:

- **Back in the Brazilian's Bed** – Susan Stephens
- **Brunetti's Secret Son** – Maya Blake
- **Destined for the Desert King** – Kate Walker
- **Caught in His Gilded World** – Lucy Ellis

Available at WHSmith, Tesco, Asda, Eason, Amazon and Apple

Just can't wait?
Buy our books online a month before they hit the shops!
visit www.millsandboon.co.uk

These books are also available in eBook format!